Erin Connor lives in the Pacific Northwest with her spouse, two giant dogs, two lazy cats, and more houseplants than she can count. When not daydreaming about meet-cutes, she enjoys hiking, cooking, and relaxing to the soothing sounds of heavy metal. *Unromance* is her debut novel, and it is her love letter to rom-coms, a genre that is unapologetically joyful and cliché in the best possible way.

You can find out more at:
    erin-connor.com
    Instagram: @ErinConnorBooks

T0318123

'The chemistry between Sawyer and Mason is electric, and this book is properly funny and deeply charming. A real love letter to romance fans'
Laura Wood, author of *Under Your Spell*

'Deliciously deadpan, ridiculously charming, and features the funniest, hottest couple that ever did meet. It's like Erin Connor took all the best vibes from all the best rom-coms and weaved them together'
Catherine Walsh, author of *Snowed In*

'Filled with sparkling banter, clever nods to the genre, and scorching hot scenes, *Unromance* made me want to sing and dance across the bleachers declaring my love, made me want to hold a boom box over my head, made me want to run to catch the plane to tell it to never end'
Alicia Thompson, author of *With Love, from Cold World*

'Filled with razor-sharp banter and a happily-ever-after that will make every reader swoon in the most epic way, *Unromance* is written for those of us utterly obsessed with rom-coms'
Chip Pons, author of *You & I, Rewritten*

'A love letter to romance and its readers, *Unromance* is an impossibly charming love story . . . a sexy, delightful read'
Anita Kelly, author of *Love & Other Disasters*

'Delivers sharp wit, deliciously steamy moments, and so much charm that I was kicking my feet from the first page to the very last'
Jessica Joyce, author of *The Ex Vows*

UNROMANCE

ERIN CONNOR

ONE PLACE. MANY STORIES

HQ
An imprint of HarperCollins*Publishers* Ltd
1 London Bridge Street
London SE1 9GF

www.harpercollins.co.uk

HarperCollins*Publishers*
Macken House, 39/40 Mayor Street Upper,
Dublin 1, D01 C9W8, Ireland
This edition 2025

1

First published in Great Britain by HQ,
an imprint of HarperCollins*Publishers* Ltd 2025

ISBN: 9780008621032

This book contains FSC™ certified paper and other controlled sources to ensure responsible forest management.

For more information visit: www.harpercollins.co.uk/green

Succulent art by Taylor Navis

Printed and bound in the UK using 100%
Renewable Electricity by CPI Group (UK) Ltd

For Abby,
No one else can play your part.

CHAPTER ONE

<u>THE MEET-CUTE</u> – The love interests meet.
It's cute. It upends their entire lives.

H old the door!"

Sawyer shot her arm out automatically, shoving her hand between the nearly closed elevator doors. She was going to lose a limb one day, but she believed all these little acts of kindness would pay off for her eventually.

Hell, maybe today was that day.

The elevator doors parted to reveal one of the most beautiful men she'd ever seen. Black curls peeked out beneath a navy beanie, his dark brown eyes bright from his mad dash for the elevator. Snow still clung to the broad shoulders of his peacoat and the tops of his boots, like he hadn't had time to shake it off.

"Thank you," the guy panted, slipping through the doors. He reached out to push the button for his floor only to find it already lit. "I'm so late," he confessed.

"I'll let you get off first, then." She cleared her throat. "Get *out* first," she corrected herself, repressing a laugh.

She could feel his eyes boring into the side of her face. She caved, her gaze drifting back to his, his eyes crinkled at the corners in amusement. His lips pressed together, rolling inward, as if to rein in the quick quip on the tip of his tongue. While Sawyer didn't normally enjoy innuendo from strangers, she found herself holding her breath, the promise of a good banter in the quirk of his mouth. Then, as if remembering himself, his face slid into a demure mask. "Thank you."

Ducking her head, she smirked at her reflection in the mirrored walls. He might not have taken the bait, but she was already looking forward to watching him walk away, to see if his back was as swoon-worthy as his front. Sawyer fell in love about twenty times a day. She didn't *actually*—for years she had made a point of avoiding falling in love—but it was a by-product of being a romance author. She could make a meet-cute out of anything. Well, she used to be able to.

She shoved the thought—and everything that came with it— from her mind. She came out tonight to *not* think about that.

"That is a lot of books," he commented, eyeing the lumpy tote cradled in her arms. For how heavy it was, it was a feat she'd forgotten about it, but her arm had gone numb long ago. Shifting the sack around to her front, she cradled the bottom of the eco-friendly bag to relieve the ache in her shoulder.

Back at her tiny apartment, Sawyer's bookshelves were immaculately arranged in bookstagram-ready rainbow order. Out of frame of her carefully curated Zoom background, however, were *the piles*—"to be read," "to be blurbed," and "to be donated." She was no Marie Kondo, but the attempt to purge was an honest one, at least. So, every month, Sawyer schlepped her donations here, and every month, she forgot to find a less backaching way to transport the books.

"The bartender and I have an agreement," she said mysteriously, the alluring effect she was going for no doubt neutralized by her Gollum-esque posture.

He raised an eyebrow at her. One eyebrow. How dare he be able to do that when she could not?

"He's a nurse. I have way too many books. I funnel him books for the nursing home library, and he lets me drink for free."

Whatever he had been about to say was cut short as the elevator shook violently, an earsplitting screech filling the air. The lights flickered, and the elevator stopped, the orchestral holiday music cutting off with an ominous diminuendo.

"You have got to be kidding me," he muttered. He pushed a few buttons, but nothing lit up.

Sawyer laughed.

"You think this is funny?" he asked, as if concerned for her sanity.

"No," she said, the giggle bubbling past her lips contradicting her. She cleared her throat. "No," she managed more seriously. "It's just—I read a lot of romance—" She gestured to her bag of books. "Two people getting stuck in an elevator? It's a classic meet-cute, but I didn't think it actually *happened*."

His brows knit together, definitely questioning her sanity. "I don't get it. What about this is cute?" He wrapped his arms around his chest, as if trying to hold himself together.

Sawyer sobered up. "You don't like elevators, do you?"

"No," he said around a strained inhale, running a hand over his ridiculously attractive face. "Keep talking, please. Tell me more about this meet-cute."

She shrugged. Telling escapist stories was her livelihood, but she was suddenly coming up blank. An apt metaphor for the current state of her career, unfortunately. Panic began to rise in her throat, but she shoved it down. "Uh, I don't know. Two people get stuck in an elevator—usually two people unlikely to fall in love, but y'know, trapped together—"

His fist was now covering his mouth in the universal signal of someone trying not to be sick. "More on the cute part, please, less on the 'trapped' and 'stuck'—".

"Right, sorry," she mumbled. "Uh, so, in my favorite one, after getting"—she mouthed the word *stuck* to spare him—"in an elevator together and sharing her purse cheese, the two strangers agree to start fake dating to make the guy's ex jealous—"

"I don't want to make my ex jealous," he said matter-of-factly.

She fixed him with a look. "I wasn't offering."

A strangled laugh escaped him as her words sank in.

He had a good laugh, husky and deep. She wanted to make him laugh again so she could hear it one more time. But, like, some other time, when he wasn't simultaneously trying to curb a panic attack. Didn't elevators have a connection to the fire department or something? Why hadn't anyone come over the speaker to console them? Why *hadn't* she packed purse cheese?

The elevator shuddered, whirring back to life.

"Oh, thank God," he groaned. He turned to her, tugging off his beanie and ruffling his hair. It was unfair how soft it looked. "Sorry, I have a thing about enclosed spaces."

"Really? I love being trapped."

"Funny," he deadpanned.

The elevator dinged as they reached the fourteenth floor, the doors sliding open. She gestured for him to go first, given his lateness.

"Thank you. I owe you one," he said sincerely. He doubled back. "Hey—if you have an ex you need to make jealous—"

"Absolutely not!"

He grinned mischievously before jogging backward, only turning when he rounded the corner, robbing her of a view of what she suspected to be a deliciously V-shaped back.

Sawyer laughed under her breath. If the romance gods wanted to dupe her into believing in happily ever afters again, they would have to try a lot harder than a pretty face and an elevator meet-cute.

She dawdled in the lobby to avoid that awkward moment when you say goodbye and then head in the exact same direction. Once she was certain Elevator Guy would be out of sight, she followed in his wake toward the restaurant that occupied most of the fourteenth floor. The first time she'd shown up with a tote full of books, the posh hostesses had side-eyed her. Now they waved her on, past the small queue of patrons waiting to be seated. When she reached the bar, she heaved her bag onto it with a relieved sigh.

The restaurant was far more swanky than Sawyer could afford, but when it was free, she could. Shoving all depressing thoughts of the budget she'd made to calculate how long she had until her advance ran out, she slid onto a barstool, her heart heavier than the sack of books.

"You're an angel," Alex crooned as he placed a napkin in front of her. "The ladies were harassing me for more books just last night."

Sawyer beamed. "Happy to help. Plus, you're saving me from ending up on *Hoarders*, so thank you."

Alex moved the bag onto the back bar before pouring her a double shot of her favorite bourbon. "Hungry?" he asked.

"Always," she replied. "Surprise me."

She'd met Alex last year when her best friend, Lily, dragged her here in an attempt to "casually" run into the cast of *Diagnostics*, the Chicago medical drama that filmed at the hospital down the street. Lily didn't rub elbows with any B-list actors that night, but Sawyer left with an unorthodox solution to her buried-alive-by-books problem. Sure, she could deliver the books to the nursing home herself, but at best, she'd leave with a pocketful of stale Werther's. This way, she left with a full stomach and the buzz only free top-shelf whiskey could provide. She preferred this way.

As Alex rang in food for her, she shrugged out of her coat and tugged her current read from her backpack—a romance, one of the smutty ones she always double- and triple-checked didn't end up in her donation piles.

"Another bodice ripper?" Alex said with a click of his tongue. "Who are you, and what have you done with the Sawyer Greene who lectured me for not reading more diversely?"

"Yeah, you exclusively read nonfiction. It's unnatural," she said with a crinkle of her nose. "Besides, this counts as research, thank you very much. And even if I wasn't desperate for inspiration, happy endings are my favorite brand of fantasy."

"Same," Alex agreed with an impish tilt of his head. "But I don't think we're talking about the same thing."

"Alex!" She smacked the back of his arm with her book.

He tugged on the corners of his mouth to conceal his grin. "How's it going? The book?"

"Good," she lied. "Had a call with my agent this morning." That part was true, but the call was about how she most definitely wasn't going to have her book done on time and was going to need another extension.

"That's great," Alex said genuinely. "I knew you could do it."

That made one of them. Guilt twisted her insides at Alex's misplaced faith in her. He laid a roll of silverware in front of her before excusing himself to check in on the couple at the other end of the bar.

She couldn't see his face, but she recognized the guy as Elevator Guy. Next to him sat a very pretty brunette. His date did not look happy. He must have been *very* late.

"Sucks to suck," she muttered. She thumbed her book back open and took a sip of whiskey, relishing the warmth as it spread through her body. Chicago winters were a bitch—but that's what whiskey was for.

She ate her dinner without further fanfare, getting so lost in her book that she forgot all about the depressing call with her agent and her dwindling bank balance. She didn't even notice when Alex refilled her whiskey, surprised to find it full again when she picked it up. She blinked away the story playing out in her mind's eye to take in her surroundings. While she'd been reading, the restaurant had emptied, affording her an uninterrupted view of the grid of Chicago, lit up beyond the wall of windows.

She dog-eared a page in her book as it reached a steamy scene. She could never read those in public, too paranoid an innocent bystander would glance over, the word *cock* or *climax* jumping off the page to alert everyone she was single and horny.

Not that there was anything wrong with being single. In fact, she preferred it. The second part, however—well, she could handle that most days, but sometimes it was nice not to have to do everything yourself. The hard part was finding someone who wouldn't expect more from her than she was willing to give, and it had been, well, *a while* since she'd found someone.

She tucked her book back into her bag, sipping as she took in the view. From fourteen floors up, the city looked like a winter wonderland with its fresh blanket of snow. Holiday lights twinkled in every storefront window, the city already fully decorated for Christmas despite Thanksgiving being a full week away.

"So," a low voice asked.

She turned to find Elevator Guy leaning next to her, his forearms propped on the bar.

"What do two people stuck in an elevator with no exes they wish to make jealous do?"

She studied him over the rim of her glass. "Get on with their lives?"

He choked out a laugh. "Damn."

She raised her brows—both brows, because unlike him, she couldn't do just one. "You literally just left a date—" She jerked her head toward the now-empty corner of the bar where he had been sitting. "To come hit on me with that half-baked line. What were you expecting me to say?"

He studied her curiously. "It wasn't a date."

She surveyed him with a disbelieving look.

"If you must know . . . it was a breakup."

Sawyer sat up straighter. "Oh. Shit." She clinked her glass against his beer. "Sorry."

He shrugged. "It's alright. We were on a break for the past six months while she was in LA for work, so—let's just say it was a long time coming."

"Ah," she said as if she got it, which she most certainly did not. She didn't think people actually did "breaks," just like people didn't actually get stuck in elevators and end up falling in love.

Sawyer loved romance—devoured it—but she didn't actually believe in it. At least, not in the head-over-heels, swept-away kind of way. She had once, and been proven very, very wrong. Now it was a fun fantasy, like the books she wrote—used to write. She hadn't been able to finish one in two years. Her last book had hit shelves earlier this year, and right now, she should be promoting her next release. Except, she hadn't written it yet. Didn't even have an idea for one, much to her publisher's dismay.

"Anyway," he said with a heavy sigh, mercifully cutting through her thoughts. "I'm gonna take a dating hiatus for a bit. But I wanted to be forewarned, y'know, if there was anything else I should be wary of to avoid any more accidental meet-cutes. And you're clearly an expert, so—"

Sawyer couldn't help but smile. She hadn't felt like much of an expert lately, so his offhand comment felt like the height of flattery. "You could say that." She braced her arms on the back of her barstool thoughtfully. "Well, elevators are clearly out to get you, so you should probably avoid them for a bit."

He nodded seriously. "Easy. Stairs only. Got it."

"And definitely no coffee shops," she warned.

He pouted charmingly. "Really? Damn."

"You gotta commit," she said gravely.

"You're right," he agreed, taking a long pull of his beer. "Okay, tell me more."

"If you go to an inn—"

"An *inn*?!"

"Yes, an inn," she said curtly, the ends of her words clipped. "Make absolutely sure there is more than one bed."

He bit on his lip to keep from smiling, and Sawyer couldn't help but notice he had a very nice mouth. Very kissable. Very bitable. Fuck, she needed to get laid. She pushed the thought away. "And God forbid we inexplicably bump into each other again: Run. Just run or we're both doomed."

He laughed, his cheeks dimpling. He was unfairly handsome. "Noted. I'll keep gym shoes handy just in case."

"I appreciate that." Sawyer downed the last of her whiskey, laying a cash tip on the bar for Alex before pushing back. "Well, it was nice *not* meet-cute-ing you."

She stood, but wasn't much taller standing than sitting. In fact, she may have lost an inch. He straightened, and she had to tilt her head to maintain eye contact.

"Sorry, I didn't catch your name," he asked, his eyes intent on her.

"It's probably best if we don't know," she said ominously, enjoying this bit they had going far too much.

"Right," he said seriously. "So we don't fall in love with each other."

"Correct."

"Because two attractive people stuck in an elevator couldn't help themselves otherwise."

She ignored the swoop of her stomach at the word *attractive*, just like she ignored the way he hadn't denied that he'd come over with the intention of hitting on her. "Clearly."

"So we're going to do the opposite of that."

"Yeah?" Why had that come out like a question?

It didn't go unnoticed, the corner of his mouth quirking up. "You wanna go somewhere? Get a drink?"

She laughed, shaking her head. "We're literally at a bar right now."

"I was thinking somewhere else—"

"If you say your place, I swear to God—"

He waited for her to finish her threat, dark eyes piercing hers.

She knew what the romance gods were up to. Most people would take one look at that pretty face and start planning their wedding, but all Sawyer wanted to do with that pretty face was sit on it.

She knew what she *should* do. She should go home, put on a face mask, and finish her smutty book. Or…for the first time in far too long, she could actually get laid instead of just reading about it.

And why shouldn't she? People on the rebound were the perfect no-strings-attached hookup. They didn't know each other—didn't even know each other's names. He was clearly only looking for a one-night stand. For all Sawyer's commitment to keeping things casual, she'd never had one. Maybe the new experience would be the inspiration she needed to shake her out of her writer's block.

Before she could talk herself out of it, she shrugged nonchalantly, though she felt the exact opposite of nonchalant, the thrill of doing something out of character waking her up faster than plunging into Lake Michigan. "Alright, fuck it. But only because a one-night stand is the opposite of a meet-cute, and I really think we should nip this in the bud—for both our sakes."

The romance gods worked hard, but Sawyer Greene worked harder.

"It's the responsible thing to do," he agreed solemnly.

She smiled, gesturing for him to lead the way. Falling into step behind him, she grinned. His back *was* as attractive as his front.

CHAPTER TWO

SECRETLY FAMOUS – Person privileged with
fame pretends to be a commoner. Ninety percent of the
time, it comes back to bite them in the ass, every time.

I s it safe for us to be in here?" Mason eyed the elevator doors distrustfully.

Book Girl smiled up at him, tightening the belt on her coat in preparation for the impending cold. "We're handling it."

He laughed under his breath. This was not how he expected tonight to go.

In fact, he'd written off the night before it even started. He knew the whole purpose of meeting up with Kara was to officially end things so she could go public with her costar whom she didn't know he knew she was seeing. When she first went to LA six months ago, he honestly thought their "break" was a formality and that they'd get back together once she returned to Chicago. Nothing changed—at first. A month into it, when the frequency of her calls and texts and FaceTimes tapered, he knew.

He knew exactly what the tabloids would say.

Mason West Can't Keep a Girl

Mason West Back on the Market. Again!

Which Costar Will Mason West Date Next?

Glancing sidelong at the woman next to him, he bit down on his lip to keep from grinning. He wasn't sure why he'd gone to talk to her after Kara left, other than not wanting to be alone with his own thoughts while he finished his drink.

That, and he felt indebted to her. She'd attempted to distract him while the elevator was stuck, and though her efforts were questionably effective, they had been amusing once he'd calmed down enough to appreciate them.

He thought he'd buy her a drink to thank her—somewhere other than the bar he'd just been dumped in, but when she misinterpreted that as him trying to get her back to his place and *agreed*—well, he wasn't going to say no. It wasn't that he'd been holding out for Kara to return, he just hadn't had time to date anyone during the off-season. At least, that's what he told himself and anyone who asked, a story that would be a lot more convincing if he could tell literally anyone what he *had* been doing these past few months. And yeah, he was more than a little intrigued by the romance aficionado who seemed to want nothing to do with romance.

"Is your place close?" she asked, glancing up at him as she shoved a maroon beanie onto her head.

She was the most colorful person he'd ever seen. She wore army-green pants tucked into brown leather boots, and he knew under her mustard-yellow coat she wore a conservative cream-colored turtleneck that clung to her curves in a way that had Mason questioning his previous aversion to turtlenecks. In contrast to her clothes, everything about her was understated. Her hair was so blond it was practically white, fringe framing her face like a 1970s rock groupie. Her brows were heavy and dark by comparison, arching over startling light green eyes.

"What?" she asked uncertainly, wiping the corners of her bow mouth. "Do I have food on my face?"

Whoops. He'd been staring far too long. He worked with beautiful actresses every day, and yet, there was something about this tiny, sour woman that struck him.

"Eyelash," he improvised, wiping the imaginary lash from her cheek. "And yeah, my place is close," he answered, her words finally registering.

"Is it covered in plastic tarps?" she asked, her eyes trained forward. "Like *Dexter*?"

She nodded.

He pressed his lips together to keep from laughing. "No tarps. Not a serial killer."

"Sounds like something a serial killer would say," she said dubiously as the elevator dinged, the doors sliding open.

He couldn't hold back the laugh this time, his shoulders relaxing as they exited the elevator. "My name is Mason, by the way," he told her as he opened the lobby door for her. Biting Chicago wind wrapped around him as they stepped outside, stealing all his warmth.

"Hey!" she cried incredulously.

He cringed internally, anticipating the uncomfortable conversation to come.

"We said no names."

He glanced at her sidelong. "You said that, not me."

She frowned, sighing in resignation. "Sawyer Greene."

"That's definitely fake," he teased.

"All real, baby. I'm just blessed like that." As she spoke, she did an adorable little dance. She nudged him with her elbow as they waited for the crosswalk light to change. "What's yours, then?"

Mason chewed on the inside of his cheek before making a split-second decision. "Mason Álvarez."

Sawyer snorted, rolling her eyes. "Okay, that's *definitely* fake. Sounds like a soap opera star."

He blinked down at her in surprise. So she really didn't know who he was—didn't know how close her guess actually was. Well, fuck if he was going to tell her. Being anonymous for a night sounded amazing.

Somehow, telling the truth *felt* like a lie. His last name was Álvarez, but he could count on one hand the number of people who knew him as such. He'd tried to stay out of the family business, but he'd been sucked in all the same, and his soap star mother's name held more clout there, so most people knew him as Mason West. Mason West couldn't have casual hookups. Mason Álvarez, however... Smiling to himself, he gestured for her to follow him.

Her eyes darted to his mouth, and he had goddamn butterflies. It had been so long since he'd done this—flirted. The "break" with Kara was probably the longest he'd been single since he was prepubescent.

His building came into view, and his steps slowed. Sawyer glanced back the way they'd come. Barely two blocks.

The tabloids often accused him of being a simp for his partners—though Mason was pretty sure that said more about them than him—but he did have *some* pride. Kara had let him pick the location for their meeting, and he'd be damned if he went out of his way to get dumped. Re-dumped? On-a-break breakup?

Luther, his building's doorman, held open the lobby door, and Mason watched as Sawyer stepped inside wordlessly, eyes wide as she took in the space. He spent more time on set than here, and he forgot how nice it was. Sawyer stomped the snow out of her boots, Mason doing the same before leading her over to the elevators. He'd bought this place before the nightmarish day on set that left him with an aversion to elevators. In a few months, when he moved to LA, he would make sure his new place was a walk-up.

Mason tolerated elevators on a good day—they were unavoidable in a city full of skyscrapers, but after the near incident earlier, it took a concerted effort to step into yet another one. Though he supposed the odds of being stuck in an elevator twice in one day were rather astronomical. He tried to take comfort in that and not focus on the shiny, immovable metal walls, tried not to picture them closing in on him…

"Hey," Sawyer called quietly.

He tore his eyes away from the elevator doors, anxiously awaiting them to open, meeting her curious gaze.

"You and elevators have old beef, huh? Did an elevator steal your girl?"

"My lunch money, actually," he said heavily. "For years…"

She clicked her tongue. "It's always the ones you never suspect."

He huffed a laugh as the doors opened on his floor. He stepped out quickly, inhaling fully for the first time since entering.

He glanced back at her, and she stopped chewing on her cheek to flash him a smile. He paused with his key in his hand. He didn't normally do this—*casual*. The media followed his dating life like a religion. At first, he'd been uncomfortable with it, but growing up in the spotlight, he'd gotten used to it. But doing this, being anonymous for a night and losing himself in another person, telling no one, thrilled him. It hadn't been his intention when he'd suggested leaving the bar, but she'd been so confident, he wanted to say yes, to get a taste of the way everyone else lived, able to be casual with their feelings and their bodies, with no TMZ to say a damn thing about it.

Except…he wasn't everyone else. Was this a mistake—a mistake he was dragging her into unwittingly?

"We can go somewhere else," he began.

Her brows shot up. "And make you get in *another* elevator?" she asked incredulously.

The corners of his mouth quirked up. "I'm just saying—"

The words died on his tongue as she sidled up in front of him, her fingers curling under the lapels of his peacoat. "Just open the door, Code Name: Álvarez."

At her proximity, all thoughts of not doing this flew from his mind. He leaned forward, pressing her up against the doorframe, delighting in the slight hitch of her breath, the way her lips parted slightly. He slid his key into the lock and twisted, pushing the door open. "After you, Totally Fake Name Greene."

She flashed him a grin before slipping under his arm and entering his apartment.

He watched her shrug out of her coat, revealing what he was fairly certain was the only sexy turtleneck in existence. Something warm and molten pooled in his stomach, something more than heady lust. This might be a one-time thing, but he had a feeling this night, this woman—Sawyer Greene—was going to stick with him for a while.

CHAPTER THREE

THE ONE-NIGHT STAND – Romance math
dictates that the less likely a character is to have a
one-night stand, the more likely they are to
run into said one-night stand again.

Holy shit, his place was nice. If Sawyer was going to get murdered, at least she would go out knowing she died somewhere clean, as her mother would have wanted. Mason took her coat from her, hanging it in the closet by the front door. If he was a serial killer, he was a polite one. She missed the warmth of her coat, though she was fairly certain the chill clinging to her was more from nerves than actual cold.

She didn't do this. She didn't let guys—or gals—pick her up at bars, and she didn't do the picking up. Yet here she was, in this stranger's very nice apartment that she basically invited herself back to. He hadn't batted an eye. Strangers must hit on him all the time. She'd gone out tonight in need of distraction, and as far as distractions went, he was a great one.

As he hung up his coat next to hers, she realized she'd been giving the coat too much credit. Yes, there was some undeniable magic about peacoats and how they made anyone wearing them instantly 27 percent hotter. But the broad shoulders and the V-shaped back? He came by that naturally.

She wondered what else he came by naturally, her fingers fumbling with the frozen laces of her boots as she tried her best not to fling snow sludge all over his tiled entryway.

"Is bourbon okay?" he called.

Following the sound of his voice down the short foyer, she nearly tripped as she passed through the kitchen, the black cabinets and countertops falling away to reveal floor-to-ceiling windows, the view of Lake Michigan reflecting the skyline back to them.

"Bourbon is preferred," she said once she picked her jaw up off the floor.

It was obscene how nice his place was. What the fuck did he do for a living? Probably something incredibly boring with stocks or numbers, utilizing a very expensive Ivy League degree his parents bought him in between snatching up yachts and summer homes.

Either that, or this was the place of the last girl he went home with, and she was stuffed in the walls somewhere.

She should probably listen to fewer true-crime podcasts.

Or more.

It was up in the air at this point.

He pulled two glasses and a bottle of bourbon out of a hutch, and she sighed in relief. If he had one of those bar carts with crystal decanters or ice in an ice bucket, that would have been too far. She wasn't sure why *that* was where she drew the line on acceptably rich and unacceptably rich, but it was.

"Ice?" he asked.

"Are they those big, fancy spheres?" she teased.

He grimaced. "Only the regular kind from the freezer, I'm afraid."

"Perfect," she said genuinely. "I'll take two regular-ass ice cubes, please."

One corner of his mouth curved upward in bemusement as he brushed past her to grab the ice. She leaned a hip against the corner of his sofa, straightening when the leather groaned, as if offended by the touch of her thrifted pants. Thankfully, Mason returned before she could slight the ottoman, too, handing her a tumbler with a healthy pour of bourbon, and she clinked her glass against his.

"Cheers." Notes of cinnamon, vanilla, and caramel danced across her tongue, and she hated that drinking good whiskey always made her think of her ex.

She wanted to send a picture of the drink with the skyline lit up in the background to her, knowing it would make Sadie froth at the mouth that she wasn't drinking out of the "ideal glassware for optimal nose and palate." As if they hadn't met while drinking warm beer out of red Solo cups at a frat party, two queer redneck girls from southern Indiana bonding over living in "the city" for the first time. It was no surprise Sadie now worked at a distillery.

"You don't like it?" he asked, misreading the scowl on her face.

Sawyer hastily slapped a smile on her face. "No—it's delicious. My ex was just really into booze, and I hate that I acquired my love of fancy whiskey from her."

"And an aversion to spherical ice cubes, I take it," he deduced correctly.

She angled her drink toward him in confirmation before taking another sip. The bourbon burned less than memories of Sadie. It wasn't fair how, years later, no matter how over her she was, her past resurfaced to haunt her in new and unexpected ways, like strong opinions about ice cube shapes. "She would probably keel over, roll onto her back, legs twitching in the air like a dying cockroach if she saw the bargain box of rosé currently in my fridge."

Mason barked out a laugh as he leaned against the kitchen counter opposite her. "You have a way with words, you know that?"

She smirked. "Y'know, I've been told that before." She wasn't surprised he hadn't recognized her name when she told him. Names on the *New York Times* bestsellers list weren't given the same amount of reverence as the ones on movie posters or sportsball jerseys.

"How long ago did you two break up?" he hedged.

"You can just ask me if I'm also on the rebound. It's fine."

He smiled down at his drink, swirling the contents contemplatively. "I wouldn't say I'm on the rebound..."

She raised her brows with a quirk of the head as if to say, *Sure, bud*.

He shook his head at the ceiling. "As far as I'm concerned, we broke up six months ago."

"And did you see anyone else during your 'break'?"

Sucking on his teeth, he visibly deflated. "No. But I was busy, okay?"

"Uh-huh," she said skeptically.

He crossed his arms, giving her an assessing look that flooded through her, melting the chill in her bones. "And you've been living it up since your ex... How long ago?"

Tugging her beanie off her head, she fluffed out her hair and arranged her bangs before answering. "Three years. Haven't dated anyone since, haven't wanted to, best decision of my life."

He tried to keep his face impassive, but his brows knit together slightly, creasing in the middle.

She knew people expected her answer to be something shorter, like six months or a year ago. But no, she lived this way on purpose, actually.

"So, let me get this straight: you read romance...but you hate romance?"

She aimed finger guns at him. "Nailed it."

Mason ran a hand through his hair, ruffling it before throwing his hand in the air in defeat. "I don't get it."

Sawyer shrugged. "It's a fantasy," she said simply. "Like warlocks and elves and fairies. It's nice to think about, but it's not real. There is no happily ever after, fade to black, ride off into the sunset. The fact that we're told to aspire to that—it sends us chasing our tails, looking for signs where there aren't any, making us stay with the wrong person because we're so scared of being alone that we tell ourselves we're happy when we're miserable. We willingly misinterpret things in the hope that it all means something, when really they're not being secretive because they're planning a surprise party or proposing but because they're sleeping with someone else and somehow that's *your* fault because you're too focused on your work because it makes you happy and how dare you? *They're* supposed to be what makes you happy. Your cup should runneth over simply because you belong to someone, right? It's fucking bullshit." She exhaled heavily, not having meant to ramble-rant. But this was her third whiskey tonight, so, oops.

Mason regarded her through narrowed eyes. "I don't know if I want to clap or cry or...*both*?"

"Both." She laughed. "Definitely both."

He grinned, pushing off the counter to stand before her. Her heart rate picked up automatically as she lifted her gaze to meet his. "Well, then—" He held his nearly empty glass up between them. "Cheers to being single."

She matched his grin, clinking her glass against his before draining it. Every time she stated her credo on the Lies Hollywood Has Fed Us, people brushed it off like she was a philosophizing teenager. For once, she didn't feel like she was being mocked.

As he set his empty glass on the counter behind her, she rested her hands on his hips, guiding him closer. Fuck, he was attractive. Why had she wasted so much time being broken up over Sadie, then casually dating or insisting on friends with benefits, when she could have been having one-night stands instead? No-fuss sex. No coy beating around the bush. They both knew why they were here, and no one was going to get in too deep and get their feelings hurt.

He brushed her hair back from her face, tucking it behind her ear, only for her bangs to slide right back into place, tickling the tops of her cheeks. As his fingers came to rest at the hinge of her jaw, goose bumps of nerves and excitement erupted on her skin.

"I should probably tell you something." She couldn't meet his gaze, her hands traveling slowly from his hips to his chest. Her mouth went dry at the muscles she felt beneath his shirt. No way he was in finance, not with a body like that.

He pinched her chin between his thumb and forefinger, guiding her to look at him. "Is it that your vagina has teeth? Because if so—" Mason sucked in a sharp breath. "That's gonna be a deal-breaker for me, sorry."

Sawyer laughed. "Nah, Coochie Mane doesn't have teeth."

A surprised laugh bubbled past his lips that turned into a full-body shake. With effort, he calmed himself, tugging on the corners of his mouth to keep from smiling. She slid her finger between the buttons of his shirt absentmindedly. "This is my first one-night stand." She wasn't sure why she told him. She blamed the whiskey for making her tongue loose. That, and the knowledge she'd never see him again, emboldened her. "Not that, like, it's a big deal, or anything, I just—I dunno, thought you should know."

He placed his hand over hers, flattening her palm over his heart. "I'm honored."

"You should be," she quipped.

"I will do my best to make it worth your time."

His voice had dropped to a low timbre, and Sawyer sagged against the counter, her brain taking slightly longer than usual to produce a response. "Well, I expected that regardless."

His laugh coasted across her cheek, his chin dipping down to rest against his chest. As he regarded her through heavy lidded eyes, her stomach fluttered with the realization that they were done talking. Which was a shame, really. Sawyer couldn't remember the last time she'd laughed so much with someone, and she would never see him again after tonight.

The thought flew from her mind as his fingers grazed her jaw. Her eyes locked onto his, the air between them taut with expectation as both of them waited for the other to make the first move.

And then they were both moving. She tilted her face back in invitation, and he took it, brushing his lips against hers once, her lips parting as her mind went blank, his mouth coming back to hers in a kiss that was much too sweet for what they were here to do.

She buried her hands in his hair, cursing against his mouth when she found it was as soft as it looked, twining her fingers through his dark curls enviously. She made a mental note to scope out his shampoo brand before she left. His hands slid into her back pockets, squeezing softly and eliciting a smile from her.

"You don't have to be so gentle," she murmured against his mouth.

A low growl escaped him, his fingers flexing more forcefully.

She crushed her mouth against his, every fiber of her attuned to his wandering hands. She didn't normally like to talk during sex, found it embarrassing, but she didn't really care about impressing him. So she told him when he did something she liked—which was pretty much everything he did—and she didn't bother stifling her moans or gasps.

"Why do we still have clothes on?"

He palmed her breast through her shirt. "I have no idea, but," he panted, "the inventor of turtlenecks should send you a thank-you note."

Sawyer laughed. "I mean, I can leave it on."

Mason gave her an assessing once-over, shaking his head infinitesimally. "No," he said gutturally.

"I can take it off?" she suggested with a lazy grin.

"In a minute."

Before she could respond, he unfastened the button of her pants, yanking them down to her knees in one fluid motion. Clearly, he had other priorities, which was fine by her. He gave her ass another none-too-gentle squeeze before hoisting her up on the counter and pulling her pants all the way off. He kissed her roughly before making his way down her body, lowering himself onto his knees.

They were going to do this here. In his kitchen. She supposed it *was* an appropriate place to get eaten out.

Shoving their empty drink glasses out of the way, she lay back atop the kitchen island, hands tangled in his hair as his tongue and teeth and fingers gently teased her, taking cues from her moans and gasps and whimpers of "*Yes.*"

At one point, she may have even whimpered, "Thank you," to the romance gods for delivering her a man who treated cunnilingus like a job and his rent was due. She didn't care if she was about to come too quickly. She didn't care if Mason Álvarez was a fake name or if he thought Sawyer Greene was fake, too, because right now, as he coaxed her over the edge atop his kitchen counter in his obscenely nice apartment, she didn't remember what her name was, what his name was, or if it even mattered.

She sucked in a shaky breath as Mason kissed his way up her body, pushing her shirt up under her breasts. "Bedroom. Now," she rasped.

He guided her legs around his waist before picking her up. She was still limp-noodle-limbed, so it was a feat that he managed to move her at all, but she supposed he didn't have all those muscles for nothing. Speaking of...

As he carried her down the hallway to the primary bedroom—how big was this fucking condo, honestly?—she pressed kisses along his jawline, keeping one arm around his neck while the other began slowly undoing the buttons of his shirt. He lowered her onto the bed, and she tucked her legs beneath her, rising up on her knees to finish unbuttoning his shirt. She needed to see what her fingers had felt earlier, before she got too distracted again. The last button undone, she pressed her palms against his chest, pushing the shirt back over his shoulders, sending it cascading to the ground.

"Are you kidding?" she blurted.

"What?" he asked in alarm, glancing down at himself.

"Who actually has abs like that? Who has the time?" she bleated.

He glanced at her, a ghost of a smile playing across his lips, cheeks dimpling. Fucking unreal. This man was not real. This was some highly vivid sex dream she was having, which was why she allowed herself to stare unabashedly, her hands roving over his chest, her fingers dipping between the muscles of his abdomen. Absurd. *Ab*-surd. Sawyer laughed under her breath.

"Could you *not* laugh while touching my body?" Mason chastised lightly.

She tore her eyes off his stupidly perfect body to look him in the eye while her hand continued roaming south, palming his erection through his pants. His eyes fluttered shut, his Adam's apple bobbing as he swallowed thickly. She grinned to herself, making quick work of unbuttoning his pants and undoing his fly, his pants pooling on the ground next to his shirt. She snaked a hand around his waist, slipping beneath his boxers to squeeze his ass.

His teeth clamped down on his bottom lip to keep from grinning. He did that a lot, and now that she knew how those teeth felt when scraping across her skin, nipping at it—she forgot what she was doing for a moment, needing to feel his mouth on hers again. He moaned, pulling her against him brusquely before pushing her back on the bed and crawling on top of her.

She always thought she wouldn't enjoy a one-night stand, too self-conscious to get out of her own head, but Mason was like a fantasy plucked straight from her daydreams. He groaned every time she ground her hips against his, sighed when she took his bottom lip between her teeth, touched her where she wanted and also where he wanted.

He worked her shirt over her head, sighing contentedly, though she wore her most boring nude bra—she was wearing a white shirt, what else was she supposed to wear underneath? But the way his eyes lit up, she glanced down expecting to see that she'd worn one of the lacy-cutout bralettes that barely kept her boobs from spilling out. As he reached around to unhook her bra, she reached down, running her hand over the length of him. His teeth sank into her shoulder and she moaned, stroking him again.

"Fuck," he swore into her neck, breathing heavily.

She tugged on the waistband of his boxers, his erection springing free. He bit down on her shoulder once more as she wrapped her hand around him, pumping once, twice, before pushing him onto his back. She made a show of shrugging out of her bra, his pupils blown wide. He wanted to play with her breasts—badly. She wanted it, too, but first, she had a favor to repay. She kissed her way down his body before taking him into her mouth. When he'd gone down on her, she'd forgotten her name, his name—how to make words in general, really—but Mason did not. He moaned and swore and cursed her name incessantly. He wasn't one of those men who bit back his noises, and the way he made his pleasure known with his guttural groans and gasped swears—was really fucking hot.

"Fuck, Sawyer, please," he moaned, guiding her face back up to his.

"Yes?" was all she managed before he crushed his mouth against hers, rolling her under him and pressing her into the mattress.

Just as suddenly, his warmth was gone. Disappointed, she propped up on her elbows to see him sitting on his feet at the edge of the bed, rifling through his nightstand. The dim lighting caught on the foil packet, and she sighed in relief. This foreplay was amazing, but she was fairly certain she was at risk of becoming dehydrated from how goddamn wet she was.

As he came to hover over her, she held up a hand, rolling onto her stomach. "I'm not doing fucking missionary for my first one-night stand."

He gently guided her hips up before pressing his chest against her back. Brushing her hair off to the side, his lips grazed the shell of her ear. "Just because it's a one-night stand doesn't mean we only get to go one round."

Her witty retort died on her tongue as he eased slowly into her. Oh, fuck yes. They were definitely going multiple rounds. Sawyer was fairly certain she entered some sort of sex-induced fugue state, only coming to when he had her on her back in some new position she'd never done before and wasn't sure why not. Sure, it wasn't the most flattering angle for her, but it was a *great* angle for the only part of her body she cared about right now. Fanfuckingtastic actually.

Was this what she'd been missing out on all this time? Were all one-night stands this mind-blowingly good? Why had she wasted so many years of her prime doing anything but this? Or was it just Mason? It was unfortunate that this could only be a one-time thing. She could use a few more nights of this. As she hurtled over the edge for the nth time, she vowed to rename all her vibrators Mason.

CHAPTER FOUR

<u>SWORN OFF RELATIONSHIPS</u> – The hero
says, "I'm giving up on love to focus on my career," and
the universe says, "Lol, hold my beer."

Mason knew this was coming, but *not like this*. He'd been staring down at his phone the past few minutes, unable to read further than the headline and photo, glaring daggers at Diedre Browne's byline underneath.

Two weeks ago, Browne had written "*People*'s Favorite On- and Off-Screen Romances." She'd included Dr. Santiago and Nurse Lia, Mason and Kara's characters on *Diagnostics*. Innocuous enough, except he and Kara weren't together anymore—on- or off-screen, the writers leaving the show's central romance up in the air after the midseason finale. Mason was sympathetic to the fans' outrage, considering his real-life relationship with Kara had been "up in the air" for six months. But now, every article about the two of them, recycling some months-old picture, was like being on a roller coaster, inching higher and higher, knowing the terrifying drop was moments away.

Last week, Browne penned another article: "Sleigh Bells or Wedding Bells for Zest?" He was numb to the media's corny Zhao-West portmanteau, but the photo that accompanied the article had sparked a media frenzy the likes of which Mason had never had to deal with before. Sure, he played a hot doctor on TV and had a history of dating costars, which the media loved, but the great thing about living in Chicago was he didn't get recognized nearly as much as he had in LA. However, he might have gotten a little too used to it.

Two weeks ago, when his mom asked him to pick up the necklace she'd had re-clasped from the jeweler, he hadn't thought twice about it. And yeah, maybe he'd wandered over to the ring case while he waited, daydreaming about what it might be like to one day pick one out for someone, but he didn't think the security camera footage would be sold to *People*. For the past week, the tabloids had been up in arms about a pending Christmastime Zest proposal.

Until today. Mason had to hand it to Diedre Browne. She'd clearly been planning this all along, hyping up Zest before announcing their split. The photo of Kara cozied up to her new costar wouldn't have sold nearly as many copies without the accompanying photo of Mason looking heartbroken and sporting a Grizzly Adams beard. He wasn't heartbroken or bearded. The photo was many years old, from a role in his friend Alissa's breakout project.

Speaking of, his phone buzzed with an incoming text from Alissa. They'd been best friends since they were teenagers, when they'd played siblings in the blockbuster Disney movie *The Heir Apparent(ly)*. Alissa left acting shortly after that role, but they'd worked on a number of indie films together, Alissa directing, Mason acting or producing or both—and occasionally growing a Grizzly Adams beard. Not that anyone remembered anything on his résumé beyond Disney and Hot Doctor.

Mason braced himself as he clicked the link Alissa had sent to a well-known tabloid.

Mason West's Long List of Ex-Lovers

Jesus Christ. How did other actors deal with this shit? His fame had always been mediocre at best. A small article here or there, never a cover story. Nothing like this. Now, he couldn't go to the grocery store without seeing his face plastered across the tabloids.

Worse yet, it wasn't even his fault this was so sensational. He was collateral damage in the publicity parade surrounding Kara since she landed the Marvel role alongside her new beau, Peter Levine, the disgustingly handsome son of a former Bond girl. The media *loved* them together, and were having a field day making a circus out of Mason's literal life.

He'd had six months to get over Kara—plus the three weeks since she officially ended it, so it wasn't that. It was the feeling of helplessness, like he was a spectator while others wrote his life story. Sure, he played a reformed rake on TV, and yes, he'd dated his fair share of women, but he wasn't the "toot-it-and-boot-it" type like this article was suggesting. But according to his agent and PR team, all he could do was weather the storm, wait for something else to become the story of the week.

He was no stranger to the media documenting his love life. Before, it had all been complimentary, cooing over whatever costar he was dating. He didn't mind when they called him "whipped" for chartering a private yacht and a personal chef for his fifth date with Kara. There were worse things to be known as than romantic. Now, the articles questioned why their favorite romantic couldn't keep a steady relationship postproduction, questioned whether *he* was the problem. Worse, he was beginning to wonder the same. He did everything the movies said you should do, and yet—

His phone buzzed with an incoming call. "Hey," he said dejectedly as soon as the line connected. He sank further into his pillows. It was nearly ten a.m., and he had yet to get out of bed, opting to doomscroll instead.

"Heyyy," Alissa hedged carefully. "How are you hanging in there?"

He grunted in response.

"Yeah," she agreed sadly. "I—I'm sorry. This sucks. If it's any consolation, everyone who matters knows you're not that guy."

It did little to cheer him up. Alissa knew better than anyone that once your name is ruined, it's hard to come back from that. She advocated for herself on set for years, earning a reputation as "difficult to work with" that led to her being shut out of roles she would have been perfect for. She didn't let that stop her, pivoting to directing and now starting her own production company with the sole focus of creating a safe space to tell women's stories. A production company Mason was helping her start. Guiding Light was set to announce its first project next week.

Mason's head hit the headboard with a thud. "Alissa," he sighed. "About Guiding Light…"

On the other end of the line, Alissa inhaled sharply. "Yeah, I was calling to talk to you about that."

"I haven't given *Diagnostics* an answer yet about my contract, so—" Bile rose in the back of his throat. The stability of a six-year contract had been half the allure of making the jump to television. But the past few seasons had felt like a trap he couldn't escape, and he'd been fantasizing about the day he could turn down the option for a seventh season, but now… "I'll just do another season and see where we're at a year from now. I don't want my mess affecting Guiding Light's launch."

"What? Mason, no," Alissa said emphatically. "That's not what I want at all. The tabloids will *move on*. Yeah, optics aren't great for us to announce a production company focused on female empowerment while the media's painting you as a manwhore—"

"*Ouch.*"

"Well…" Alissa trailed off. Mason could picture her grimacing semi-regretfully. "Anyway, I sent you that article because I think you need to pull a TSwift."

"Let the media reduce my entire career to my dating life?" he asked in disbelief. "I think we're already there."

"No! God, no. You need to fucking disappear, like post-*Reputation*-era TSwift. The media is doing you dirty, and you need to go lick your wounds in private. We'll push the Guiding Light announcement back until after the holidays, when all of this has blown over. You just need to not date anyone for a few months and stay out of the tabloids. Think you can do that?"

Easier said than done. Yes, he wanted to fall in love, settle down, have that secret language where you could communicate whole paragraphs with a single look, but he didn't seek it out. Like the elevator meet-cute with Sawyer, he didn't do that on *purpose*. And while he'd thoroughly enjoyed "ruining" their meet-cute, it couldn't be more different from what he'd usually do. Normally, he'd do exactly what she'd ranted about: read too far into it, catch feelings, and before he knew it, they'd have drawers at each other's apartments. He was an incurable romantic.

Plus, being single over the holidays sounded horrible. Not that he'd ever brought anyone home for the holidays, but having someone to text when his mom got too meddlesome in his career, someone to call and decompress with when family time felt less like "family time" and more like they had agreed to do that *Meet the Wests* reality show after all—and his mom was the only one with the script. It was a comfort, having someone. And yeah, he was a little insecure about not having anyone to kiss on New Year's for the first time in—he couldn't count how many years.

Maybe Alissa had a point, but the point still stung.

"I don't date all the time *on purpose*," he grumbled.

"Just like Taylor. She's so awesome, men are drawn to her. And notice how no one judges *them*. Just like you. But, maybe a little break wouldn't hurt, yeah? You not doing Guiding Light is out of the question. I need you and your charming self to convince people to give us their money."

Mason sighed, scratching at the stubble on his chin—oh God, *was* he going full Grizzly Adams? A quick glance in the mirror over his dresser confirmed it was only a few days of growth.

He hated that Alissa was pushing back the announcement— they'd worked for years to get to this point, but she was making the smart call. Despite his offer to bow out, he didn't want to. He loved acting, but with every season of his six-year *Diagnostics* contract, their showrunner grew more toxic. Mason needed out, wanted to be a part of the change this industry so desperately needed. Even if it meant uprooting his entire life all over again.

"Yeah, I can do that. No point in dating when I'll be in LA soon anyway." He knew firsthand that long distance didn't last. Starting something new was inviting disaster—and his reputation couldn't afford any more disasters right now. If he was coming on as head of production at Guiding Light, he needed people to respect him, not be the guy they read tabloids about while waiting in line at the grocery store. You don't give that guy money to make films.

Alissa cleared her throat pointedly. "Speaking of LA: Where are we at with telling the family? I haven't heard the banshees wail yet, so I assume your mother doesn't know and hasn't yet begun planning my murder for stealing her son from her."

Mason groaned. "I'll tell them—soon," he lied. He would avoid that particular conversation for as long as possible. If Alissa was pushing back the announcement, then it wouldn't hurt to wait until after the holidays, right?

Rolling out of bed, he headed over to the floor-to-ceiling windows and parted the blackout curtains. He flinched back at the wall of white that greeted him.

He left LA for Chicago five years ago, when he landed the role on *Diagnostics*. It was the kind of role he'd always sworn he wouldn't take, not wanting to follow in his mom's footsteps. Her hearty approval of him taking a TV role had nearly made him turn it down. He loved the indie films he'd been doing, but he was tired of uprooting his life multiple times a year and leaving behind more than just apartments. *Diagnostics* provided stability, and it put him in the same city as his sister and his nephews. So Mason signed his life away, packed up his laughably small amount of personal belongings, and moved to Chicago.

Chicago, the land of wind and snow and rarely ever sunshine.

In the five years he'd been there, he'd never seen so much snow, and never so early. Usually they made it through the New Year before it really started coming down. Not this year, apparently. He would kill for a bit of sunshine, even if it was single-digit temperatures. The closest thing he'd come to sunshine in weeks was Sawyer Greene.

He spent a lot more time thinking about her than he should, especially first thing in the morning when his dick was hard and his bed was empty.

And yeah, he'd googled her. He had to know if her name really was Sawyer Greene. Shockingly enough, it was. He was both surprised and unsurprised to learn she was a well-known romance author. One of her books had been adapted into a movie Mason auditioned for. He hadn't gotten the part, much to his chagrin, as it turned out to be an instant classic—even if it came under fire from loyal book fans for barely resembling the source material.

There was hardly anything on her Instagram about the movie, and what was there screamed, *I was contractually obligated to post this*. She hadn't posted much at all, really, since her third book came out at the beginning of the year. Mason didn't know much about publishing except, like Hollywood, everything moved slowly. She seemed to release one book a year, but there was absolutely nothing on her Instagram or website about a fourth book. He liked to think it was because she was writing, too busy to update. He thought about that a lot more than he should, too, because the alternative, the idea of a creator not creating . . . He knew the feeling a little too well, even if his situation was a little different.

"I lost you, didn't I?" Alissa's voice came from his speaker, and he almost dropped his phone. He'd forgotten she was on the line.

"Yeah, sorry," Mason said sheepishly. "Just thinking. I'll tell them after the holidays, I promise." He would have to, but he was dreading it. At times, Alissa felt more like his family than, well, his actual family. He and his sister got along, but they never talked this openly with each other. That's why he'd moved home, to get closer with them after his younger self had pushed them all away to figure out who he was without their influence—namely, his mom's influence—but he'd been young and thought he had to do it all on his own back then. Things were better now, but no amount of family dinners could undo the volatility of those early years of his career, his mom circling like a helicopter, his father and sister wordlessly watching it happen . . .

"Oh! Hey, did you send me a book?"

Mason scratched absently at the coarse hair below his navel. "Yeah, I did. I forgot to tell you." Hell, he'd forgotten he'd done it, shipping a copy to her with two clicks at one in the morning after he'd finished reading. "Might be something for Guiding Light."

Alissa hummed in interest. "I did want to add something lighter to the docket. But since when do you read romance? No shame, just...surprised?"

He grinned. "Read it. Thank me later. It's a bisexual, gender-bent *High Fidelity*."

"You had me at bi. There's a role for you in it, yeah?"

"If you want," he said offhand.

Alissa scoffed. "It's your pitch. Of course I want you involved—either in front of or behind the camera. Or both."

"You haven't even read it yet," he pointed out.

"I trust you."

He smiled to himself as he heard her thumbing through the book. If Alissa adapted it, his role wouldn't be huge, supporting at best, but maybe after leaving *Diagnostics*—once he told them he was leaving—it could be what he needed to shed the "hot doctor" stereotype once and for all. He'd inherited his father's roguish looks, which meant he often got sent scripts for Lothario types. The recent media fanfare was definitely piggybacking off that, and he was ready to shake off that typecast. He missed the thrill of developing a character, the secret backstory only he knew and translating it on-screen. He hadn't felt that way about acting in years, and it was like an itch he couldn't scratch, one he wouldn't be able to, if he stayed.

His phone buzzed in his hand, and he tore his attention away from the blinding wall of white outside his windows.

Running a few minutes late, sorry!

Mason swore. Between doomscrolling the tabloids and Alissa's call, he'd completely lost track of time. He was supposed to meet his sister at the Christkindlmarket in five minutes, and he lived ten minutes away.

"Hey—Alissa, I gotta run. I'm late to meet someone."

She groaned loudly. "*Puh-lease* tell me it's not a date."

His laugh was muffled as he tugged on the first pair of pants and shirt he could find—it didn't matter, it would all be hidden beneath his winter coat. "It's ten a.m. on a Tuesday, Alissa. I'm meeting up with the family," he said distractedly as he attempted to smooth back his hair. God, he really needed to cut it. Not having to have it trimmed Dr. Santiago short was his offseason rebellion, but in the six months since shooting wrapped, it had grown unwieldy. "Taking a break from dating, actually."

"Oh, really?" Alissa cooed, faking surprise. "But seriously," she said more softly. "This will all blow over, and once we're in LA, doing our thing at Guiding Light, everyone will see the Mason West I know and love."

"Thanks," he said thickly. "I love you, too."

"Tell the fam I said hello and remember: What Would Taylor Do?"

"Will do," he laughed, shoving on his boots as they said their goodbyes.

He hurtled out of his apartment and into the elevator, jamming the button for the lobby with more force than necessary. Propping his boots on the wall, he tied his laces as the elevator slid slowly down to the lobby.

He still hated elevators, but he was grateful that it had brought him a little bit of sunshine in the midst of an otherwise bleak winter.

CHAPTER FIVE

WE'VE GOT TO STOP MEETING LIKE THIS –
No matter how big the city, rom-com geography
dictates you will run into the one person you're
trying to avoid. *Especially* if you had a
one-night stand with them.

In the three weeks following her all-nighter with Mason, Sawyer spent a lot of time daydreaming about it. Even though she'd bolted when things got a bit too sweet the following morning, she'd hoped the new experience would unlock something in her brain, presenting her with a new angle to write her next book from. At least, that was the excuse she told herself for thinking about him so much. The words never came, but Sawyer did. She masturbated thinking about that night far more than she should ever admit. She wasn't sure if it was that she hadn't had sex in a long time or if it had simply been That Good.

Okay, yes, she totally knew it was the latter.

The blank Word document stared back at her, the cursor blinking ominously. She just needed to type something, get the words flowing, and then more words would come. It didn't matter if it sucked. She could make it not suck later. Except . . . she didn't know what she wanted to write. She smashed the keys in frustration. She always had a million ideas percolating in her brain, but none of them felt right, felt *ready*.

There was some saying about doing the same thing over and over again and expecting different results. Besides her one-night stand with Mason, Sawyer had been doing the same thing over and over again for months. She woke up, masturbated, showered, made a pot of tea, sat down at her laptop to write, and *didn't write*.

She could practically feel Emily, her editor, looming over her shoulder, breathing down her neck. Their call this morning hadn't gone well. She was off the hook for a *Why We're Not Together* sequel, but she still owed them another book—any book. While Emily had agreed to push her deadline from February to March, the implication was there that this was the last extension Sawyer would get. Come March, the book would be a year late. She was already in breach of contract by being so embarrassingly late. If they dropped her, if she had to pay back her advance . . . she couldn't afford to pay it back. The royalties from her previous books and the movie weren't enough to pay her bills. The check from the streaming service would have set her up nicely—except she used it to pay off her mountain of student loans in one fell swoop. It had seemed like a smart use of the money at the time. Now, however . . . if she didn't finish this draft and get her next installment payment . . . she was fucked.

She needed to do something different. Literally anything. She would clean, but she'd been cleaning so much lately to avoid writing that there wasn't anything to tidy up except the solitary spoon in her sink from her morning yogurt.

Resting her forehead on the edge of her desk—aka her kitchen table—she took a series of controlled breaths. Writing had always been the one thing she'd been good at. She'd risked everything for her career, and now…she could feel the walls closing in on her. She needed to get out of her apartment.

With a few taps of her phone screen, she had her best friend's number pulled up, her thumb hesitating over the dial button when she remembered Lily was out of town visiting her new in-laws. Sawyer knew she needed to acclimate to doing things by herself again. It was no longer Sawyer and Lily. It was Lily and Beau. And while Sawyer was lonely, she wasn't bitter. She was fine. She hadn't let herself need anyone else in a long time, not since Sadie. Not since all her friends had chosen Sadie in the breakup. She was used to doing most things alone.

She closed out of her phone's Favorites list and opened Google. It was the dead of winter in Chicago. But it *was* Chicago. There was always something going on, right?

Feeling like a damn tourist, she googled "things to do in Chicago."

Half an hour later, she was out the door and on her way to the Christkindlmarket, the German Christmas market she'd seen countless times on Instagram. Sawyer was a travesty at social media. With no new books to announce, there were only so many "writing is hard" stories she could post. She needed some content and some inspiration. And hell, she really liked Christmas decorations. Maybe, for the first time in years, she'd get a real tree. She could do it this weekend, spend the next few days decorating and sipping boozy hot chocolate and blasting Ariana Grande's Christmas album like the basic Christmas bitch she was.

As she hopped off the L, a smile spread across her face, the smell of cider and mulled wine reaching her. Fat globs of snow floated lazily to the ground, and Sawyer pretended she was the protagonist in a Hallmark Christmas movie.

The air was painfully cold, but it made her feel alive for the first time in weeks, slicing through the cloying monotony of her failures and tamping down the panic that lived in the back of her throat like a barely suppressed scream.

The market stalls and their heat lamps beckoned her closer, all the vendors decked out in German garb. One of them boasted some sort of Christmas angel, a beautiful woman in a gold dress with a matching tiara reading Christmas stories to a gaggle of children.

Sawyer bought a cider and a pretzel, the spiced mustard waking up her taste buds as she tucked herself into an alcove to people watch. She didn't consider herself a people person, but she loved watching them. The little gestures they made while telling a story. The innocuous touches they gave their companions, the need for contact an unconscious choice.

She loved creating little stories for them. The couple debating which Santa ornament to buy. The little boy begging his father for the reindeer toy. Sawyer watched a little blond girl dancing to the music completely off beat, leaping through the air and landing with a twirl, beaming from ear to ear like she'd done something grandiose. That had been Sawyer at that age. Always in her own world, convinced what she was doing there was real and magic.

Sawyer still felt like she was in her own world most of the time. Maybe that was why she'd never been a people person. She didn't spend enough time inhabiting this plane of existence to really get to know them, always too in her head, lost in a daydream or riddling out her latest plot problem.

She'd wanted to be an author for as long as she could remember. Getting published right out of college was a fool's hope, but it had happened for her. Then it all went sideways.

Everything had happened so quickly, and she thought she had to say yes to every opportunity when she really shouldn't have. She had told herself to be grateful, that others would kill for these opportunities, but she had been juggling so many new things so fast that she dropped the ball. She had dropped a lot of things. She lost Sadie to being a workaholic, and while Sawyer wished she'd done some things differently, the thing she hated most was how when her book finally debuted, when she hit the *New York Times* bestsellers list, the goal she'd sacrificed everything for, she had no one to celebrate with.

She hated that she felt that way, decided then and there she was done with romantic notions. Her career would be her One True Love. Every relationship since Sadie only hardened her resolve.

Dating a writer was a novelty. Sawyer's midnight writing sprints or five a.m. alarms were endearing at first, but when she had to miss parties or shut off her phone for days at a time to hit a deadline, her exes found her selfish, though she'd never dream of punishing them for doing their jobs. So, she kept her flings brief, light, no strings. She expected nothing from her partners but orgasms. Maybe she got lonely sometimes, but it worked for her. She didn't want to apologize for loving her job.

Even if she was currently failing at it.

Her success was a fluke. She was twenty-six years old and out of stories to tell. She'd written rough drafts of her second and third books before her first book hit shelves, before everything fell apart with Sadie. She'd managed to edit those two books into something she was proud of, but starting over from scratch had thus far proven impossible. She defined herself by her writing, and if she couldn't finish this next book, what had she sacrificed it all for?

Suppressing that thought before panic could claw its way up her throat, she took in the market. She could feel the familiar prickle of a story idea taking root. She always started with the characters, never the setting, but something about this little market was speaking to her. Why not start with the setting? Clearly, her usual methods weren't working.

Tossing her empty pretzel paper into the recycling, she wandered over to the nearest vendor, one of the ones so colorful it was nearly offensive to the eyes. Though that was probably what most people thought when they saw her apartment. ROY G BIV had practically vomited all over her place. Well, Roy and Lily. Not that Lily had *literally* vomited all over her place.

They'd met two years ago at an art gallery and had immediately bonded, skulking in a corner and giggling over a piece of phallic modern art. While Sawyer later abandoned her artist character research, she latched on to her new artist best friend—and roommate. At least, until Lily's high school ex moved to Chicago and they rekindled their romance with such sincere sweetness even Sawyer was tempted to believe in love again—even if it meant her person now had a new person. When Lily moved out, they split custody of Lily's art. Sawyer adorned her new one-bedroom's walls with it so it still felt like her friend lived there, like Sawyer wasn't alone. Again.

Wandering into one of the vendor stalls, Sawyer eyed an owl ornament made out of burlap with a bundle of twigs clutched in its feet and a tuft of fuzz on its head. She loved colorful things, but when it came to Christmas decorations, she loved the stillness of a more muted color palette, letting the green of the Christmas tree take center stage. There was something so calming about twinkling white lights, the smell of an evergreen, and delicate ornaments set against a windowsill covered in snow.

She had to get a real tree this year. Inspiration demanded it. She had no idea how she'd get one up to her third-story apartment, but she *would*. And if she was getting a tree, it deserved a new ornament.

Ignoring the way her bank balance screamed at her from her budgeting app—she could already see her accountant's skeptical look when she submitted this as a write-off for research and development—she took the burlap owl off the rack, her thumb gently stroking the soft fuzz atop its head.

She paid the vendor, clutching her small paper bag like a treasure as she set out to explore the rest of the market. As she passed a stall full of toy trains, she froze.

A man in a gray peacoat and navy beanie stood with his back to her, but she knew that back. She'd run her fingernails down it just before Thanksgiving—and she was *very* thankful for what he gave.

As if sensing her gaze, Mason turned, the corners of his mouth twitching up. He thanked the woman working the booth as she handed him his package before crossing over to her.

"Actually Real Name Greene," he said by way of greeting.

She laughed through her nose. So he'd looked her up. She tried not to be flattered. She'd scoured Instagram for Mason Álvarez, too, but only found a Spanish soccer player who, while also hot as sin, was not him. Which was probably for the best. What if he had one of those douche-bro online personas? It would ruin all her fantasies and she desperately needed her emotional support daydreams. "Álvarez," she countered, still unsure whether that was his last name or not.

He glanced around uncertainly. "Listen, I know I promised if we saw each other again that I would run, but I'm kind of in the middle of shopping with my nephews, so is it cool if I finish?"

Sawyer's stomach did a weird flip, pushing all thoughts of how adorable that was from her mind. "Of course. You know I'm a big fan of finishing."

Mason's cheeks dimpled as he grinned. "Do not keep making sex jokes, or I will fall in love with you."

Sawyer fixed him with a hard look. "Don't you dare."

He winked at her. They were standing in the middle of the thoroughfare, the sea of shoppers parting around them. People stared at them for the inconvenience, their gazes softening as they lingered on Mason.

"How are you?" he asked. Sensation shot up her spine when he placed a hand at her back, guiding them off the main path and into a sweetshop booth.

Sawyer shrugged, studying the confections disinterestedly. "Trying to write my next book. Failing. Came here to shake things up, maybe get inspired."

"And are you—inspired?" he asked, taking a box of fudge off the shelf.

"Starting to be," she said hopefully.

He glanced up at her, his expression seeming to mirror her own cautious hope and relief. "I'm happy to hear that."

Sawyer pressed her lips together to keep from smiling, trailing behind him as he picked up more overpriced sweets. "How are you?" She asked to be polite, but also…she wanted to know. "Have any more meet-cutes? Get stuck in any more elevators with pretty girls?"

He flashed her a grin. "Just the one, thank God."

She rolled her eyes, grateful she could blame the flush in her cheeks on the cold.

Mason counted the boxes in his arms, adding two more before queuing up to pay. He must have noticed Sawyer eyeing his massive stack, his grin turning conspiratorial. "What?" he said innocently. "I have a big family! I'm not above bribery to maintain favorite uncle status." As if to accentuate his point, he grabbed a bag of chocolate coins from the display by the register, adding it to his pile with a flourish.

As they left the sweetshop, Mason turned suddenly, Sawyer nearly running bodily into him. Taking a step back, she put an acceptable amount of space between them. It shouldn't matter. They'd slept together, for fuck's sake. It wasn't like she didn't know exactly what was beneath that peacoat. But she'd never had a one-night stand before, and she wasn't really sure what the protocol was if you ran into them again. Going Christmas shopping with them in the cutest market you'd ever seen probably *wasn't* it. Especially not when the twinkling white lights overhead reflected in their eyes and—

Jesus, Sawyer, get it together, she chastised herself.

"Hey," he said quietly. "What are you doing after this?"

Sawyer's jaw went slack, her lips parting in surprise. Absolutely not. They'd agreed it was a one-time thing. She could not start hanging out with *Elevator Guy*. Especially not when she was on the most precarious of deadlines.

"Uncle Mason!" a high-pitched voice screeched.

The crowd around them parted, spitting out a small boy that immediately began trying to drag him in the opposite direction.

"Uncle Mason! You gotta come see!"

Mason gave her a bemused look before scooping the boy into his arms and hauling him over his shoulder like a firefighter.

"You hungry?" Mason asked, as if there weren't a squirming child on his shoulder.

"Um," Sawyer mumbled, glancing around for some sort of magical excuse.

A pretty brunette appeared beside Mason, the boy in her arms the spitting image of the boy Mason had over his shoulder. She could only be his sister, her exhausted-looking husband half a step behind her. How was she supposed to politely refuse him in front of his family?

"Kuma's? In an hour?" he pressed.

The woman next to him studied her curiously, her manicured brows raising slightly as her gaze bounced between the two of them. Sawyer was now feeling very hot beneath her many winter layers, and wanted nothing more than to be out of this uncomfortable conversation before introductions could be made. And that was the only reason why she mumbled, "Yeah, sure," before making a beeline for the exit.

CHAPTER SIX

THE CONTRACT – When two characters make a pact, replete with rules, which they are *totally* going to follow.

Surely, running into Sawyer again was a sign.

So why, of all the restaurants in Chicago, had he suggested to meet up at Kuma's, one of the least romantic places? Normally, he'd pick something like The Purple Pig, where they could cuddle in one of the tiny booths, sharing tapas—not a heavy metal bar that served burgers the size of his face.

Despite the decidedly unromantic choice, his sister had still given him the third degree about the woman in the "hideously yellow coat." Margot might not have followed in their mother's footsteps by going into acting, but she'd definitely inherited her primal need to meddle. He sometimes thought the universe giving her two hellions for sons was its way of humbling her—humbling all of them. Mason loved his nephews—how could he not? They were half his sister and half his best friend, but they were going to be absolute nightmares as teenagers. And while he loved spending time with them, he was always grateful that he got to leave them with Margot and Luis and go back to his apartment childless.

Or go to a heavy metal bar that served burgers the size of his face.

He liked that freedom a lot. He also liked the sight of Sawyer wait-ing for him at the bar, glass of whiskey in front of her. She lifted her hand half-heartedly in greeting as she spotted him working his way through the crowd toward her. Kuma's was always busy, which he hadn't thought about when he'd picked it. Her yellow coat—which he found not at all hideous—was slung over the barstool next to her, saving his seat.

"Have you been waiting long?" he asked apologetically, even though he was ten minutes early.

She shrugged. "I can entertain myself," she said with a prim sip of her drink. "Prime people-watching spot," she added with a subtle nod across the bar.

He diverted his attention to the middle-aged couple across from them, hunched over their burgers as Metallica blared from the ste-reo. Sawyer leaned closer, and he caught the cloying spiced scent of the Christkindlmarket still clinging to her. It actually smelled nice when not so concentrated. Underneath it all, the smell he didn't real-ize until now he associated with her: coconut. It was everywhere on her that night. On her skin and in her hair and he was pretty sure even in her lip balm.

"My guess is tourists who heard this was the burger spot but didn't research what kind of place it was."

Mason settled onto the barstool, assessing the couple for clues. "Locals from the suburbs," he countered. "Downtown to holiday shop. He's here to relive his glory days when his ZZ Top beard was trendy. She has tinnitus from the rock shows they went to in said glory days, so it's hard for her to hear, but coming here reminds her of that first spark—their meet-cute at the Led Zeppelin barricade."

Sawyer's red lips pursed as if sucking on a lemon. "That is

disgustingly romantic, but—" She half sighed, half groaned. "Also really good character building," she admitted begrudgingly. "Could I borrow your brain to write my book?"

Mason laughed, the smile freezing on his face as an idea came to him. *Could* she borrow his brain—and he could he borrow hers?

A tattooed bartender surveyed them over the beer taps, jerking his head in Mason's direction. He ordered the first IPA he saw, still mulling over her throwaway comment.

The bartender slid Mason his beer without looking, his eyes on Sawyer. "You good, hon?"

She smiled, red lips parting to reveal white teeth. "Yes, thank you."

As the bartender tossed their tab into a cup in front of them with yet another glance at Sawyer, Mason realized she was completely oblivious to his attempts at catching her eye. If a hot bartender was making eyes at Mason like that, he would already be halfway done planning their perfect first date. By the time entrees arrived, he would've been three pages deep in a Zillow search, hunting for their dream apartment.

Maybe he was wrong. Maybe running into Sawyer again wasn't a sign that they were destined to be together. Maybe they were meant to help each other.

The words were out of his mouth before he could stop himself. "I think us running into each other again is a sign."

"Oh my God," she grumbled before tossing back the last of her drink. "Mason," she began gravely, leaning forward as if proximity would make letting him down hurt less.

"Not because we're fated or soulmates or whatever the fuck," he rushed out. She tensed, as if deciding whether or not to bolt. "I think we're meant to cure each other."

Her dark brows disappeared beneath her bangs. "I didn't realize we were sick."

He shifted sideways in his seat to look at her fully, mentally grasping at the hazy beginnings of an idea that was either genius or folly, only pausing long enough to figure out how to phrase it without having to get into the Mason West of it all. To her, he was still just Mason Álvarez. He hadn't realized how heavy being Mason West had become until, suddenly, he didn't have to be.

He knew he needed to tell her who he was—he was keeping enough secrets from enough people already—but given the current media coverage, being Mason West wasn't exactly a point in his favor. But that was why fate had brought Sawyer back to him. Because he *wasn't* the person the tabloids depicted.

He couldn't control what the tabloids wrote, but he could control what he did—or didn't do. And he needed help from an expert. He needed Sawyer.

"What if we *could* borrow each other's brains?"

Sawyer laughed in disbelief. "What?"

"What you said the other night—" It had been weeks since they slept together, but the memory felt like yesterday. "We're taught that all these inane things are signs from the universe. That this person is our person because we got stuck in an elevator together or locked eyes across the coffee shop, when really, it's a faulty elevator or accidental eye contact with a stranger. Yet, I always fall for it. I'm so worried about missing my own epic love story that I spend all this energy chasing down women in Christmas markets because *what if* she's the one? But she never is, and...I'm exhausted." Mason sighed heavily. "I need to stay single for a bit. So, I need to stop—I need to *learn* how to stop. Enter you, a romance expert with no interest in dating me. I want you to ruin me."

Sawyer tilted her head to the side curiously. "What, exactly, are you suggesting, Álvarez?"

He smiled at her switch to his surname. "Exposure therapy: Let's do it all—all the cheesy shit no one does outside of a rom-com. Let's do it and feel nothing for each other. Then, the next time I think, 'This is a sign,' I won't fall for it because I've already been there, done that, and it didn't mean anything."

"You want me to ruin romance for you?" Sawyer said slowly.

"Yes. And in return, maybe you'll get some more inspiration. That's what you were looking for today, right? You keep me too busy—and too jaded—to date, and I'll let you borrow my heart-shaped, rose-colored glasses."

She chewed thoughtfully on her bottom lip.

He really needed her to stop doing that, or he was going to have a hard time not kissing her—a harder time than he was already having. Which, he realized, was an unexpected bonus of doing this with Sawyer. There was no future for them, and he would have to learn how to squash an attraction rather than pursue it.

"What're you so worried about, Greene?" he asked in challenge, smirking over the rim of his pint glass. "That you'll fall for me?"

Sawyer batted her eyelashes. "Not in the slightest."

"Good," he said, leaning closer. "I'm gonna woo you so fucking hard, you'll be writing a trilogy before you know what hit you."

Sawyer snorted loudly. "So, you wanna show up outside my window with a boom box and play a crap eighties song I hate?"

"Sure." He shrugged, holding up a finger. "But only if you'll ruin the Spider-Man kiss for me."

"Which Spider-Man?" she asked seriously.

Mason scoffed. "Upside down, in the rain, Tobey Maguire and Kirsten Dunst, obviously."

She hummed thoughtfully. "Do I have to wear the fake nipples?"

Mason was fairly certain his heart skipped a beat, his brain short-circuiting as his jeans suddenly felt too tight. He swallowed thickly. "Your real ones will do," he mumbled before hastily taking a sip of his beer. He needed a cold shower but a cold drink would have to suffice.

Sawyer laughed under her breath but it didn't reach her eyes. "I like where your head is at," she began slowly. He had a feeling she didn't mean the nipples. "I'll do anything to jog my inspiration at this point. I'm in." Definitely not the nipples.

He took another sip of his beer, unable to stifle a daydream of them reenacting that cinematic rain kiss.

"First trope—"

"Right now?" he asked in alarm, glancing around the packed bar. He was trying to keep a low profile—not that she knew that. If she burst out into a musical number now—

"A contract. Some ground rules."

He exhaled slowly, relieved she was not about to attract the attention of every person in the room. Only the bartender paid them any mind, having given up all pretense of not checking Sawyer out.

Oblivious, Sawyer continued, "Rule number one: no falling in love or catching feelings of any kind," she said as if it were obvious, staring at him expectantly.

"Naturally," he agreed, a beat too late. This was why he was here, after all. Falling in love with Sawyer Greene had disaster written all over it on a normal day, much less when he was caught in the middle of a tabloid-fabricated love triangle and an impending cross-country move.

"And no sex."

He choked on the sip of beer he'd just taken. It didn't go unnoticed by her.

"It'll only muddy the waters," she said matter-of-factly.

Maybe the other night hadn't been as good for her as it had been for him, but he was pretty sure it was. At least, he hoped it was. But fair enough. They'd agreed up front it was a one-time-only thing. Probably best if they stuck with that.

"No feelings and no orgasms. Got it," he repeated back to her.

Her gaze snagged on his at the word *orgasm*, a ringing starting in his ears that had nothing to do with the Iron Maiden blaring from the speakers.

"We doing alright?" the bartender asked, tapping the counter in front of them with a tattooed hand.

This time, Mason was grateful for the interruption, exhaling heavily as Sawyer turned her attention to the bartender instead. She ordered another round and a burger. Mason drained the last of his drink before doing the same. Luis was going to kill him tomorrow for drinking beer and eating a burger twice the size any person had a right to eat. The downside of your best friend being your trainer was Mason couldn't lie to Luis. The upside was Luis always forgave him—in fact, Luis was usually sitting right next to him, with a burger as big as Mason's.

"Oh!" Tucking one leg underneath her and leaning over the bar top, Sawyer beckoned their bartender back over. He was in front of her in an instant. "Can I borrow a pen? And some paper?"

He had a feeling the bartender would give her literally anything she asked for. He could empathize. Mason smiled smugly to himself, imagining the bartender's disappointment when the pen and paper weren't so she could leave him her number.

"Okay." Sawyer clicked the pen pensively. She wrote the number one and circled it, writing "no feelings," then the number two and "no sex." She pushed her platinum hair back over her shoulder. "What other safeguards should we have?"

"Can we see other people while we do this?" he asked.

Her brows disappeared beneath her bangs. "I thought the whole point was for you to stay single."

Mason smiled. "I wasn't asking for me. I was asking for that guy." He jerked his head in the direction of their bartender, who was covertly watching Sawyer as he dried pint glasses.

The corner of Sawyer's red mouth quirked up. She scrawled a phone number at the bottom of the paper before tearing it off. He expected her to surreptitiously slip it into the glass that held their bill, but instead, she tucked it into the front pocket of Mason's jeans.

"You should probably have that so we can coordinate logistics." She clicked the pen twice. "Now...what should we ruin first?"

CHAPTER SEVEN

<u>LUMBERJACK/LUMBERJANE</u> – Romance science
decrees that all persons wearing a red plaid flannel
become 42 percent more attractive. If the sleeves are
rolled up and the forearms are out, add an additional
17 percent and gird your loins.

Sawyer smiled to herself as she stepped into the elevator, heavy
bag of books in hand. Her hand was cramping, but she was too
excited to be mad at herself for—yet again—forgetting to come up
with a better way of transporting her book haul. The one upside of
not writing was it left her even more time to read, and she was burning through books faster than ever.

The trip to the Christkindlmarket had lit a spark in her. She still
wasn't writing, but her fingers twitched, the seed of an idea growing
in the back of her mind so long as she didn't look at it too closely.
Instead, she decided to feed it. If she was going to write a holiday
rom-com, she was going all out.

She'd always loved Christmas, but she hadn't properly decorated
in years. Not since Sadie. They'd decorated to the nines when they
were together, taking in all their other friends whose only family
were of the found variety. While she'd lost her friends in the breakup,
she hadn't lost her love of Christmas. It had always seemed like a lot

of effort to decorate just for herself, but maybe if she decorated hard enough, the first draft of her book would write itself.

In addition to tearing through books all week, she'd watched an inhumane amount of rom-coms to brainstorm things to ruin with Mason. While she was studying tropes and clichés, she suspected Mason had simply contributed actual dates and grand gestures he'd done. She was beginning to think he truly was a walking, talking, bodice-ripping romance hero, replete with abs.

They'd been texting back and forth all week, trying to combine multiple clichés into one outing to get as much bang for their buck as possible. In the spirit of Christmas, she'd made a list and checked it twice:

Mission: (un)Romance:

1. Christmas Tree Farm

This would accomplish two things: getting her tree and ruining the setting for half of Hallmark's Christmas movies. Mason wearing a red flannel was nonnegotiable.

2. Ice-Skating in Millennium Park

Sawyer was horrible at ice-skating but Mason said that only made it more on brand for a rom-com—and easier for her to make Not Fun. She relented only when he promised to bring a thermos of spiked cider.

3. New Year's Eve Midnight Kiss

Sawyer wasn't a big fan of New Year's in general, but Mason was practically written by Nora Ephron, and thus she couldn't ethically leave him unchaperoned for one of the most impossible-to-be-single moments of the year, or else he was sure to relapse into hopeless romanticism.

4. IKEA Shopping

They agreed *500 Days of Summer* wasn't a romance, but still worth crossing off the list, just to be safe. Plus, Mason needed a new end table or something.

5. Musical Number???

This one was still up in the air as neither of them liked grand public displays, receiving or performing. They agreed to draw straws on it later.

6. Notecard Scene from *Love, Actually*

Sawyer was adamant that this scene was creepy and weird, but Mason insisted it was too iconic to leave unruined.

That was as far as she'd gotten. It turned out to be a lot harder than Sawyer anticipated, and she wasn't sure how they were going to pull half of them off. There were no fairs or carnivals this time of year, so Mason couldn't win her a giant stuffed bear. The closest thing was the Christkindlmarket, and they'd already done that. They couldn't dance and kiss in the rain, because they'd agreed their "no sex" rule should include all intimacy—with one exception.

The New Year's Eve kiss felt like too big a cliché to *not* include it. Mason already had plans for the night—some work party—and had updated his RSVP to include her. Thank God, too, because Sawyer's only New Year's invite was from Lily, but it was also Lily's first wedding anniversary, and if Sawyer exposed Mason to Lily and Beau's marital bliss, all their work to ruin romance would be undone with one sappy look. She'd suggested being Mason's fake girlfriend at the NYE party to knock out another classic cliché, but he'd gotten weirdly cagey about it, so she dropped it.

Stepping out of the elevator, she hauled her sack of books to the bar, heaving it on top and waiting for Alex to finish up with a guest.

Taking the list out of her pocket, she read over it once more. She wasn't sure if it was enough, too much, or not enough. Grabbing a discarded pen, she wrote "end date???" at the bottom of her scrap of paper. Was this over when they finished the list or when they got sick of each other? Or was getting sick of each other when they needed to keep going, to put the final nails in the Coffin of Love?

"Book Angel," Alex purred as he moved the sack of books to the back bar. He reached for a roll of silverware, but she held up her hand.

"Rain check," she promised. "I needed to clear out my space so I could move a Christmas tree into my apartment this afternoon."

Alex grinned. "Aren't you adorable and Christmassy."

Sawyer struck a pose. "Trying new things. I'll tell you about it next time. It's good." Alex would appreciate her and Mason's mission.

"Does it have anything to do with you leaving with Mason West last time you were in?" he asked conspiratorially.

She froze. Mason *West*? Why did that name sound familiar? Trying to keep her tone casual, she feigned disinterest by inspecting her nails. "You know Mason?"

Alex's brows rose. "Yeah, the *Diagnostics* cast comes in here a lot.

They film at the hospital down the street. Why—why are you looking at me like that?"

Sawyer didn't have cable, so she'd never seen the show, but she definitely knew *of* it. Lily was going to have a cow when she found out Sawyer had accidentally succeeded in meeting a member of the cast that had eluded them at this very same bar a year ago. And she'd done a lot more than *meet* one of them. Something was suddenly lodged in her throat. Perhaps a scream. Clearing her throat, she tucked her hair behind her ear as she regained her composure. "I, uh, I have to get going," she managed. "Same time next month?"

Alex nodded slowly. "You alright?"

"Yeah," she insisted. "I'm fine." Totally fine, save for she apparently slept with someone very famous from a very popular show she didn't watch because she hated procedurals and now she had to go see Mason and pretend she didn't know who he was or that she hated his show. Okay, *hate* was a strong word. She'd never actually seen his show. Maybe it was good.

She gave Alex a half-hearted wave as she backed away from the bar, hoping her mental spiral wasn't written all over her face. She pushed the elevator button with more force than necessary, tugging her phone from her pocket with her other hand. As she waited, she pulled up Google and typed "Mason West Diagnostics." Maybe there were two Mason Wests in Chicago.

There weren't.

"Oh, fuck me," she mumbled as she scrolled past a picture of him with Dakota Johnson. It was a goddamn bisexual thirst trap of a photo.

Her brain was melting.

Mason Álvarez, known professionally as Mason West . . .

He hadn't lied about his name, but he hadn't exactly told the truth either.

It didn't matter.

It *shouldn't* matter.

She was successful in her field—or had been—and he knew who she was. What difference did it make if the reason his place was so goddamn nice was due to him being an actor and not a trust fund baby? Though Google told her he was *also* likely a trust fund baby. His mother, Moira West, was some famous soap opera actress. As the elevator doors dinged open, she closed out of Mason's Wikipedia page and toggled over to Google Images as she walked blindly into the elevator and pushed the button for the lobby.

Mason West Fills Costar Kara Zhao's Trailer with 1,000 Roses

A Sneak Peek at Mason West's Romantic Valentine's Day Plans

10 Things All Men Could Learn from Mason West: The Blueprint

Good gravy. He really was a walking, talking romance hero. The more recent articles sang a different tune, however.

Her attention snagged on a photo of him with the pretty girl she'd seen him with at the bar the night they met. Someone had photoshopped it to appear torn down the middle. The image had been recycled for multiple articles. At the top was "Mason West's Long List of Ex-Lovers," which was clever but cruel. The next headline was worse: "Kara Zhao Leaves *Diagnostics* and Costar Mason West: Coincidence? TMZ Has the Inside Scoop…"

TMZ needed to mind its business. And so did Sawyer.

She forced herself to close out of Google before she could learn more than she should know. That didn't stop all the pieces from falling into place in the back of her mind, however. His ex had been in LA for "work," which Sawyer now surmised meant "filming." She resisted the urge to reopen Google and read the first article. Her exes weren't spelled out online, so it wasn't fair that she should have access to that information when he did not. Besides, why did she care who he'd dated?

Shoving her phone into her pocket, she exhaled slowly. It didn't matter that he was famous. It changed nothing—except that they might have to do a little sneaking around, which, frankly, sounded kinda fun. No wonder he hadn't wanted to fake date her at a work party. *Holy shit.* Maybe after this, she could write a "secretly famous" book. She made a mental note to add it to her romance tropes encyclopedia later. It had started as research for the list, but the multipage Google Doc now had a permanent tab on her browser, each addition kindling to the near-dormant embers of her love of writing. She hoped it would catch fire soon, her fingers flying over the keyboard like they used to.

The elevator doors dinged open, and she spied a familiar gray coat by the revolving door.

Mason grinned warmly at her. "Figured it was easier if I just met you here," he said brightly. Studying her face as she approached, his expression switched to one of concern. "You alright, Greene?"

"I'm fine, West," she said coolly, coming to a halt in front of him.

He didn't react at first, then—he blinked multiple times in succession, his hand coming up to rub the back of his neck nervously. He cleared his throat. "I was going to talk to you about that today. I understand if you're mad. I—" He sighed heavily. "I wanted to be anonymous for a night, and then when I saw you again…There's not really a way to say, 'Hey, by the way, I'm mildly famous,' without sounding like a complete dick. I didn't want to make it weird or for you to treat me differently, but I may have done that anyway, huh?" He shrugged helplessly.

Something inside her melted at his tone. She was no stranger to people treating her differently when they thought they could get something from her.

"I'm not mad," she said sincerely. "I get why you didn't say anything. It's nice being anonymous. Only, now my bartender thinks I slept with some actor guy because he saw me leave with you."

Mason smiled down at her. "You *did* sleep with me."

Sawyer waved away his comment. "*Yeah*, but I don't want him to know that."

Mason shoved his hands in his coat pockets, shoulders ratcheting up to his ears. "So, where do we go from here?" he asked nervously. "I promise full transparency moving forward—"

"No," Sawyer interjected, holding up her hand. "I think this is good, actually. We agreed no names that night—"

"Which I ruined—"

"Yeah, but I think we should reapply that rule now." Mason raised his brows skeptically at the glaring flaw. "It's too late for our names, obviously, but everything else—we don't need each other's life story to do this. In fact, if we're doing a bunch of romantic shit, probably best if we *don't* know each other too well."

"Surface level," Mason mused, dimples appearing as he pursed his lips. "Smart. Add it to the rules."

Sawyer grinned, banging an imaginary gavel. "Motion passed." Surface level was where she lived, paid rent and property taxes, the whole shebang. Why hadn't she thought of this safeguard before?

"But as it pertains to our list, I think I should know: Are you gonna be recognized everywhere we go?"

Mason shook his head. "We should be fine. The only paparazzi in Chicago are fans with smartphones, but we'll keep public stuff to a minimum. And when we do go out, best thing about winter is that a coat and a hat do wonders to make you anonymous. Most people won't recognize me if I'm not in scrubs."

Sawyer chewed on the inside of her cheek. She had no desire to get dragged into his publicity mess, but googling him had only fortified her belief that if anyone could go toe-to-toe with her staunch attitude toward love, it would be the hopeless romantic standing before her now. She'd accepted Mason's offer to cure each other on a whim, but she was quickly beginning to view it as a lifeline. Researching things to ruin with him was the most creative inspiration she'd felt in months. She needed this to work.

"We're already here," Mason said reasonably. "Give me today, one list item. I promise I won't be recognized, and if you're not inspired—at least a little bit—by the end of the day, I won't waste your time with the rest of the list."

Narrowing her eyes, Sawyer met his gaze. "Is that a challenge?"

Mason grinned, opening his arms in invitation. "Do your worst, Greene. Ruin me."

Sawyer couldn't help but return his grin. "Alright. But, full disclosure: I don't have cable, so I've never seen your show." Though the visual of Mason in scrubs did tempt her nether regions. She might have to *start* watching, but that might make not sleeping with him again impossible, and she did not have time for that kind of distraction right now. A one-night stand was one thing, but a relationship while she was on deadline? She knew all too well how that went.

He smiled. "I figured. If you do ever watch it, don't tell me."

Sawyer laughed. "Fair enough. I'm the same way about my books."

"Oh," he said mischievously. "I already read your books."

She blinked at him, eyes widening in surprise. "Books? Plural?"

"Oh yeah. *Almost Lovers*"—he counted each one on his fingers—"*Friends & Other F Words*, and *Why We're Not Together*."

"Oh my God," she mumbled, hiding her face. "Why?!"

He laughed. "I didn't think I was going to see you again and I was curious! I auditioned for the *Almost Lovers* movie, but I didn't get the part—obviously."

Sawyer peered out from between her fingers. "Are you serious?"

"One hundred percent. Also, I get it now: the book *is* way better than the movie."

Sawyer placed her hand over her heart. "Thank you."

Shoving his hands deep into his coat, he grinned shyly down at her. "So, are we good? We still on?"

Pursing her lips in mock contemplation, she tugged open the collar of his coat, spying the agreed-upon red flannel underneath. A smile spread slowly across her face. "Oh hell yeah. C'mon, Álvarez-West, daylight's wasting."

His face lit up as he hurried to get in front of her so he could open the door for her. "Where's your car?"

She gestured proudly to her car out front, a premium parking spot.

Mason burst out laughing. "You've got to be kidding me."

CHAPTER EIGHT

<u>CRASH LANDING</u> – Falling for them—literally.
Bonus points for landing on top of them,
faces millimeters apart.

It was the tiniest car she could possibly own. It was adorable and suited her perfectly.

"What?" Sawyer said defensively. "It has great tires, and the roads are clear."

Mason bit down on his lip to keep from grinning. That was *not* what he was worried about, but if she hadn't realized the flaw in her master plan, then he wasn't going to point it out. Not yet. He held up his hands innocently, cutting in front of her to beat her to her door, opening it with a flourish.

She gave him an unbelieving shake of her head as she sank into the driver's seat. Mason grinned to himself as he crossed around to the passenger side of the old Volkswagen Beetle. Inspiring romance? He was born for this.

The Christmas tree farm was forty-five minutes outside the city, but the drive went by in a blink—partially because Sawyer drove like a madwoman on the highway and partially because Mason may have shut his eyes in preservation instinct more than once. Her car was so old it didn't have "Oh Shit" handles, otherwise he would have been grabbing them as she slipped between lanes of traffic with barely a glance.

It was best if he didn't watch the road, so he watched her instead. She talked animatedly as she described all her favorite Christmas traditions, often getting sidetracked mid-story and starting another tale, only to seamlessly slip back into her original point. Her mind was chaotic and fascinating.

"So, besides the tree, what else do you have planned for the holidays?" he asked.

Her face fell, and he swore even her blinker blinked half-heartedly. "We're here!" Her voice was strained, and he knew her enthusiasm was for show, to avoid answering the question. He couldn't figure out why. The Queermas traditions she'd spent the past half hour describing sounded better than any holiday party he'd ever attended.

She pulled into the lot, her car comically small next to the SUVs and pickup trucks in the makeshift muddy parking area. He hazarded a glance, waiting for her to realize the flaw in her plan, but the smile on her face that had been taut before was now soft.

"What?" she asked defensively.

"You really like Christmas, don't you?"

She shrugged. "You don't?"

Mason frowned. "Not since Santa stopped being real. The only tradition we had was my mom designing the perfect tree for us to pose in front of for her Christmas card with a letter highlighting all the most glamorous things we'd done over the past year—which were all things she'd signed us up for."

Sawyer made a face that said, *Yikes*.

He tensed. They'd *just* agreed to keep things superficial. He hadn't meant to share so much, never talked openly about his mom with anyone outside of Luis or Alissa. His relationship with his mother was complicated, but he knew the front she put up—while exhausting—had always been to sate the curiosity of the media so she could have as normal a life as possible behind the scenes. He trusted Sawyer wasn't the type to run off to the tabloids, but his mother's media training was second nature to him at this point, and he couldn't resist the urge to smooth it over.

"I love my family. I do. It's just—sometimes, I can't tell if I really did luck into having the perfect family or if it's just a role we were all coached into playing." So much for smoothing it over. They were well past surface level at this point. It was more honest than he'd ever been, even inside his own head. The night they met, he thought it was just the anonymous one-night-stand effect that had put him so at ease around her, but at Kuma's and now, his usual filter continued to malfunction. "Anyway..." He rubbed the back of his neck uncomfortably. He really didn't want to get into his complicated family dynamics and ruin their day.

Thankfully, it seemed Sawyer was also pointedly avoiding... *something*, and glossed over it without missing a beat.

"That's showbiz, baby," Sawyer said in what Mason assumed was her best showman voice.

He fixed her with a look before flinging open the car door and unfolding himself. The crisp air filled his lungs, and he smiled. Half the time, the city made him hate the snow and long for sunny LA winters. But outside the city, where evergreen branches were dusted with fluffy white powder, happy little trees befitting a Bob Ross painting, it wasn't so bad.

A violent shudder rattled Sawyer's petite frame as they shuffled forward in the queue to buy their tree. "The thing Hallmark doesn't prepare you for is freezing your fucking tits off."

Mason choked on a laugh, shrugging out of his coat and draping it over her shoulders.

She frowned, reluctantly burrowing into its warmth. The way she inhaled his scent from the fabric awoke something in him he was having a hard time stifling.

"For the record, I'm only allowing this cliché gesture because, one: I'm cold," she said. "And two: you're an idiot for giving up your coat when wind chill is in the single digits, and I'm hoping this will break you of your romantic tendencies."

He was about to point out that it wasn't that cold today, but then a gust of wind stole all his body heat. But fuck if he was going to admit she was right. Gritting his teeth to keep them from chattering, he forced a grin. "Why be pragmatic when you can be romantic?"

She stared up at him like he had three heads.

"C'mon," he goaded her, nudging her with his elbow. "You added this to the list. Surely you must find something romantic about it?"

Sawyer hummed thoughtfully, but whatever she was about to say, he never found out. As they shuffled forward in line, the pine needles on the ground shifted underfoot to reveal a patch of ice. He careened backward, windmilling his arms in a futile attempt to regain his balance. Gravity won out, and he went down, his ass meeting the ground with a *smack*.

Sawyer covered her mouth, but it did little to conceal her throaty laugh. "Are you okay?"

"I'm fine," Mason grumbled, embarrassment stinging his cheeks as sharply as his ass cheeks smarted from hitting the semi-frozen ground.

"You know what?" she said around a laugh. "Call me a convert. I'm finding this all to be *very* romantic. Aren't you?"

She extended a hand to help him up—the idea that five-foot-nothing

Sawyer Greene could pick him up was laughable—but he took it anyway. Everything went sideways from there. As he pushed off the ground, the muddy slush beneath Sawyer's boots shifted, and she lost her footing. He caught her mid-fall, but he couldn't stop their foreheads from colliding with a resounding smack. Rearing back, he stared up at the gray sky, laid out on the muddy ground for a second time.

Sawyer collapsed on top of his chest with an *oof*, their faces a millimeter apart. Her bangs tickled the tops of his cheeks. Her narrowed eyes flicked down to his mouth, a hairbreadth from hers. "You did that on purpose," she accused with a frown.

"I didn't," he laughed. "Romance must be in the air."

"Gross," Sawyer grumbled. Disentangling their legs, she pushed off his chest and clumsily got to her feet.

Mason ensured she was steady—and not standing on another ice patch—before picking himself up off the ground with as much dignity as he could muster. Wiping off the seat of his pants, he groaned when his hands came away muddy.

"Don't worry," Sawyer reassured him through relentless giggles as she inspected his backside. "It only *kinda* looks like you shit yourself."

"Fantastic," he deadpanned.

Taking pity, she fussed over him, brushing pine needles off his shirt. She pinched a spot below the breast pocket, tugging at it. To his mortification, she pulled a sticker off his newly purchased flannel.

"When I asked you if you had a plaid flannel to wear, and you said yes—?" She let the rest of the question hang in the air.

"I went and bought one," he confessed.

"Mason, I asked you that *this morning*. You could've said no!"

"I aim to please, and if the lumberjack look does it for you, then…" He flashed his trademark sultry smirk that fans of *Diagnostics* went wild for.

Sawyer tucked her fingers into his belt loops, tugging him closer. Tilting her head back, she looked up at him through heavy-lidded eyes. "It really, really does," she purred. His attention drifted over her cheeks, rosy from the cold, down to her red-painted mouth. "But how did you know," she continued in her low, raspy bedroom voice, "that my real weakness is men who shit themselves?"

Mason's eyes fluttered shut as the realization washed over him. She was fucking with him. He'd fallen for it without a second thought.

She shoved him away playfully before stepping up to the little red ticket booth to pay for her tree. When he reached for his wallet, she bent over the counter, sticking out her ass to put space between him and the card reader. "Be a dear and grab us a saw, Mr. Lumberjack."

It was a good thing their mission didn't require them to keep score, because if it did, well, he'd definitely be losing. If this were a first date, if he really were trying to woo Sawyer, then this was the worst show he'd ever put on.

Hardening his resolve, Mason wandered over to the shelter that housed the handsaws, picking through them. He wasn't the most handy, something his dad loved to rib him about. His parents were an odd match, yet the perfect cliché. The ex-army stuntman and the leading lady. His dad tinkered with muscle cars and wouldn't pay for anyone to fix anything around their grand house until his mother insisted—or scheduled it without his knowledge. He'd tried to teach Mason how to do all of that, but Mason never had a knack for it. Margot had gotten the How Things Work gene, but she preferred numbers and dollar signs to carburetors and spark plugs.

Still, Mason didn't spend as much time as he did with a trainer to *not* be able to cut down a tree.

In a flannel.

Yeah, he'd lied when Sawyer asked him if he had a red lumberjack flannel. He owned no such thing and had run out to buy one. But the way her eyes had lit up when she spied it under his coat? Worth it.

The same light was currently brightening her green eyes, her irises now the viridescent green of a new leaf. She came to halt in front of him, brandishing her tree receipt like a golden ticket.

"Let's go, lumberjack," she said, beaming. Looping her arm through his, she practically dragged him behind her on her quest to find the perfect tree. With Christmas only two weeks away, the pickings were slim.

Sawyer was cooing over a shapely fir when a little girl in a pink reindeer hat ran up to it, hugging it and proclaiming it the best tree ever. Sawyer agreed, and they waited until the girl's family caught up before beginning their tree hunt anew.

Mason smiled. He was beginning to suspect Sawyer wasn't as sour as she pretended. Somewhere beneath the jaded layers, there was a cinnamon roll soul. He just needed her to teach him her secret, how he could guard his heart more effectively, stop handing it out so readily.

Sawyer turned right suddenly, letting go of his arm as she circled a tree as tall as her—aka not very tall.

"Alright," Sawyer proclaimed, hands on her hips. "This is it."

Mason screwed up his face. "It has a giant hole."

Sawyer frowned, ruffling the gap in the branches affectionately. "Don't we all," she said sagely. "I'll tuck it away where no one can see it, and cover it in cute ornaments. You'll never know the difference."

Somewhere, a therapist shuddered.

Kneeling down, he shoved the bottom branches aside to find a good spot to start cutting. "I guess if you don't take it home, who will, right?"

Sawyer hummed in agreement. "My good deed for the year."

Mason glanced up at her through the branches as he made the first cut. "It's not the New Year yet."

"I know," she said brightly. "I meant for this year. Was really worried I wasn't gonna be able to squeeze it in."

Mason shook his head, focusing on sawing. "Because you're such a horrible person."

"A true Grinch."

"Except you love Christmas," he pointed out. He was nearly halfway through the base of the tree now, so he couldn't see her expression when she took a beat longer than usual to reply.

"It's everything else that my heart is three sizes too small for."

She said it so quietly it was a miracle he heard it at all, and he had a hunch she hadn't meant for him to hear, so he didn't comment on it. He especially wasn't going to comment on the fact that her being so against romance and feelings was evidence that her heart was not too small at all, but she, like him, had given it to the wrong person. He was definitely not pointing that out. He wasn't here to change or "fix" her. He was here to learn from her.

With the rumors that Kara was leaving *Diagnostics* confirmed, investors had already started blowing up Alissa's phone, concerned that Mason's tendency to date coworkers would destabilize production. As if every set wasn't incestuous. You spent all day, every day with the same crew. Who else were you supposed to date? Nonetheless, he'd already gotten a call from his manager, echoing Alissa's idea to stay single and let it all blow over.

Mason channeled all his frustration with the tabloids into each stroke of the saw, making quick progress. Each time the saw's teeth snagged, he pushed harder, the sensation cathartic. Maybe he should work with his hands more often. Once he was over halfway, he paused, sinking back onto his knees.

"Alright." Grabbing hold of the trunk, he gestured for Sawyer to join him on the ground.

Coming to stand before him, she picked debris out of his hair before smoothing it back, the sensation of her hands in his hair shooting straight to his dick. His gaze flicked unwittingly up to hers, her red mouth smirking. "You look good on your knees." She punctuated her sentence with a wink.

He ignored her comment—he couldn't acknowledge it so long as "Rule #2: No sex" was still on the table. "Just get down here," he growled with a jerk of his head.

She sank to her knees obediently, making a show of wiggling her ass as she situated herself beneath the boughs.

Two could play that game. He draped himself over her, his front pressed to her back as he helped her position the saw, like he was a pool shark teaching his date billiards. "A few more strokes should do it."

Sawyer laughed throatily at the word *strokes*, and Mason extricated himself from the tree before she could become aware of what the sound did to him.

As Sawyer went to work on the tree, he watched the kids running around with reckless abandon, so bundled up in coats and scarves that they looked like padded poufs with legs as they wove between trees, laughing gleefully. His nephews had convinced Margot to put up their pre-decorated fake tree the day after Thanksgiving, so it was too late for this year, but he made a mental note to convince Margot to get a real tree next year. He knew she'd gripe about the mess— Margot *hated* mess—but the boys would love it.

All thoughts of his nephews flew from his mind as Sawyer began sawing, the vibrations of the blade cutting through the trunk shooting up his arm and to his already misbehaving dick. Good God. Was every outing with her going to be like this? He wasn't going to survive. Gritting his teeth, he attempted to wrangle his hormones under control.

Flirting with Sawyer was effortless. Inspiring romance seemed an easy task when he agreed to it, but just like when he had to act out an emotional scene on set, the real trick was convincing his body that all of the emotions weren't real. He wasn't actually an ER doctor saving lives, and Sawyer wasn't actually his.

This was his problem. Sawyer Greene was the last woman in the world he should be lusting after. She had no interest in dating him and he had no business dating anyone right now. Tabloids notwithstanding, he was moving to LA in a few months. Yet, here he was, mooning over her like she'd been his first one-night stand. She wasn't. Though, come to think of it, most of his attempts at casual flings *had* escalated into relationships. Not on purpose—but regardless, he needed to break the cycle. The falling was fun, yes, but the problem with falling was you eventually hit the ground. Mason had yet to stick the landing, and his partners always hit the ground running—running off to the next exciting thing while Mason was left bruised and wondering where the hell he'd gone wrong.

With a shudder, the tree came loose, and Sawyer whooped.

When she reappeared from the boughs of the tree, she was beaming. "I did it!" she exclaimed, flexing her arms and kissing her biceps.

"All by yourself," Mason drawled. "Very impressive."

She poked him in the side as she straightened. "With the help of my handsome lumberjack, of course. My Hallmark heart is all aflutter," she gushed. She wrapped a leg around him, placing a hand on her forehead and swooning like a heroine on the cover of a bodice-ripping romance novel. Did that make him Fabio?

"The flannel's really doing it for you, huh?"

"Oh yeah," she said sarcastically. "You're gonna have to throw me in the back of your pickup truck and yee my haw."

Mason laughed, shaking his head. Before he could let that visual play out in his mind, he jerked his head toward the tree. "Alright. I got the base. Grab the tip."

She wasn't the only one capable of innuendo. See how she liked it.

Sawyer snorted, waggling her eyebrows suggestively before grabbing hold of the top of the tree. Together, they carried it all the way back to her car. As her steps slowed, he wished he was standing in front of her to watch the realization dawn on her.

"Oh dear," she said fussily, eyeing the massive tree and the tiny car in turn.

Mason grinned, lowering the tree to rest against the side of her car. "I'll grab some twine."

"Maybe a lot of twine," she said around a laugh, falling into step beside him.

As they waited for the family in front of them to finish unspooling twine for themselves, Mason's attention drifted to the other holiday decorations for sale. Wreaths made from tree scraps, reindeer yard ornaments made from logs, ribbon-wrapped mistletoe. A young couple picked up a piece, nuzzling the tips of their noses together before collapsing in a fit of laughter.

Mason couldn't help but smile, their love infectious.

Beside him, Sawyer cleared her throat.

"What?" he said defensively. "They're cute."

She rolled her eyes. "You're hopeless."

Mason swiped a bundle of mistletoe off the table, dangling it above them.

Sawyer glared at him. "Against the rules, bud."

He pressed a finger to her lips. "Close your eyes," he murmured.

Sawyer shot daggers at him before complying.

"You're at a party," he began quietly so no one else could hear. "The person you've been secretly into for quite some time is there. They look fucking fantastic. You've been making eyes across the room all night. You can feel the way they'd touch you if only one of you would make the first move." He tucked her bangs behind her ear, and they stubbornly sprang back into place as he trailed his finger along her jaw. A smirk tugged at his lips when her breath hitched, her lashes fluttering with the effort of keeping her eyes closed. "But making the first move is risky, until, you find yourselves under the mistletoe, the perfect icebreaker for the tension between you—"

Mason ran his thumb across her bottom lip, her mouth parting slightly. Her eyes flew open, a series of emotions playing out in rapid succession—lust, confusion, surprise, and then: fear.

Sawyer screamed, spiking the mistletoe out of his hand, the bundle of green and red landing in a patch of snow slush at their feet. Sawyer doubled over, dry heaving.

Mason rolled his eyes. "Don't be dramatic, Greene. Kissing me isn't so abhorrent. If I remember correctly, you liked it—"

Still clutching her side, Sawyer grabbed hold of his lapel, pulling him down with her and pointing to the mistletoe.

"What—" The question died on his tongue when he saw the massive brown spider scuttle out of it.

Mason brought his fist to his mouth, swallowing down the rising tide of bile. He shivered like he could feel the spider crawling all over him. "Oh God. Okay, mistletoe kisses are officially ruined for me forever. Thank you. Cross that off the list."

Sawyer shuddered. Regaining her composure, she mimed keeping score in the air, adding a tally mark for herself.

Mason pursed his lips. "I don't think you can reasonably take credit for that. I was definitely winning before the spider so rudely interrupted."

Sawyer grinned smugly up at him as she stepped up to grab their share of twine. "I can, and I will. Besides," she added with a jerk of her head in the direction of the young couple purchasing a bundle of (hopefully) spider-free mistletoe. "They're cute, but they won't survive spending the holidays with each other's families."

The corners of Mason's mouth turned down of their own volition. Even his romanticism didn't stretch that far. He didn't bring his partners home to meet his mother for a reason.

When he didn't object, Sawyer fixed him with a knowing look before drawing another imaginary tally mark in the air.

Looping her arm through his, she guided him back to the car, where they studied the roof and the tree in turn before a fit of giggles overtook them at their quandary.

They managed to tie the tree to the top of her car by looping the twine through the windows and around the bumper, Sawyer laughing as she darted around the car while Mason held the tree steady— a true feat, as Sawyer was determined to spank him with the twine every time she lobbed it from one side of the car to the other. He rested his head against his muddy, sap-covered forearm, unable to stop laughing as Sawyer tied off the tree. He hadn't laughed this much in a long time.

He hoped she was feeling inspired, because they weren't ruining this trope for him at all.

CHAPTER NINE

"JUST FRIENDS" – The ancient romance myth
that you—a mere mortal—can be platonic
acquaintances with the sex god who blew your
back out a fortnight ago.

Even with the help of the tiny wine corkscrew knife Sawyer kept
in her bag for emergencies—Mason gracefully not questioning
the validity of a wine emergency—Sawyer's fingers were frozen by
the time they managed to free the tree from the top of her car. She'd
managed to find parking around the block from her apartment, and
was immensely grateful Mason's ridiculous physique was good for
more than just ogling as he hefted the tree overhead and followed
behind her on the gray, slush-covered sidewalk.

Regardless, she couldn't help but ask, "Is it really necessary for a
doctor to be that in shape?" Glancing back, she caught the cocksure
smile he flashed her.

"Oh yes, Dr. Santiago does all his surgeries shirtless."

"As one does," she quipped, opening the door to her building for
him. When they reached the tight corner of the stairs and Mason
paused to reposition the tree, she unbuttoned his peacoat to reveal the
red plaid flannel straining at the buttons. "Better?"

Mason shook his head down at her. "You're shameless."

She winked at him before flouncing up the stairs and gesturing for him to follow her down the hall. As she unlocked her door, she panicked. Her place wasn't nearly as nice as Mason's. Her only view was of the gore special effects artists across the street, dismembered body parts casually resting on their windowsills. Well, that's the story she'd made up for them. She had stories for all her neighbors.

At least all of her time spent Not Writing meant her apartment was clean. Swinging the door wide, she followed him inside. Unlacing her boots, she watched him take in her space while kicking off his own shoes. His eyes scanned over her cerulean velvet couch, the emerald, leaf-shaped pillows that were the closest Sawyer would ever get to keeping a plant alive, the gallery wall overhead of framed stick figure drawings and watercolors from Lily.

Her TV stand was still sans television, all the cubbies bursting at the seams with books. Even with her monthly donations to Alex, there were some she could never part with. She kept them close by so she could thumb back through them, reliving highlights of her favorite characters' lives or revisiting perfect turns of phrase that had left her breathless.

Mason's gaze lingered on the mustard-yellow hutch where she stored her extensive mug collection. His mouth quirked up as he spotted her favorite, a white mug with a pattern of tits of all shapes and sizes.

"In the corner?" he asked, gesturing to the tree stand she'd dragged out of her storage locker earlier that morning.

She nodded, following him over and holding the tree steady as he tightened the screws into the base. As he worked, she was hit with how strange this was. This was *Elevator Guy*. He was the one-night stand she was never supposed to see ever again. Yet, here he was, in her apartment that was a quarter the size of his, on his knees, screwing in her tree.

Glancing down, she could see Mason's red flannel had ridden up, revealing two dimples on his lower back that she wanted to dip her fingers into. Before her mind could wander further, she cleared her throat.

"What did you do before?"

"Before what?" he asked distractedly. He gave the tree a jostle to assess his handiwork, grinning softly when it stayed upright.

Backing up to check that the tree was straight, she smiled to herself. It was slightly crooked, but Mason seemed so proud of himself that she couldn't bring herself to have him fix it.

"Before resuscitating coma patients with your hotness on *Diagnostics*."

He straightened, nearly too tall for her low ceilings. "A bunch of indie movies with my friend Alissa. We met on the set of *The Heir Apparent(ly)*, but after Disney we both wanted to prove ourselves as 'serious artists.'" Mason made a mock gagging noise. "So we moved into the indie space and ended up falling in love with it—her with directing, me with acting. There was more freedom there, and everyone I worked with was invested and passionate. The creative process was so different and collaborative—sorry, I'm rambling," he mumbled.

Sawyer shook her head. "No, I—that sounds amazing, but YOU WERE IN *THE HEIR APPARENT(LY)*?"

Mason's eyes fluttered shut as he nodded in resignation. "Yes."

"Who?!" Sawyer exclaimed. Preteen Sawyer had *loved* that movie, yet she couldn't place Mason anywhere in the cast. His friend Alissa, on the other hand, she knew immediately. She'd only been Sawyer's bi awakening, after all.

"I was the quirky older brother. I had green hair."

She gasped. "Oh my God! That *was* you!" She resisted the urge to ask more about his Disney days. "So, why the switch to TV?"

"I was tired. When you live on location, you form these intense relationships with the cast and crew—" She had a hunch Mason was skirting around mentioning a specific type of relationship. "These people become your family, and when it's done, you all just move on to the next thing. And then Margot had Max, and even though my family exhausts me, all I wanted was to be closer to them." He blinked, as if not meaning to say so much. "And the pay's not bad either."

Sawyer couldn't understand wanting to be close to family, but money, she understood. It's why she sold her first book's film rights. Yeah, she'd wanted to see her characters brought to life, but she was also a broke college student. A blindly trusting college student that hadn't asked enough questions, too blindsided by the zeros on the check they cut her for handing over her debut characters.

Had it allowed her to write full-time? Yes.

Would she do it again? No.

She couldn't think about that book, the characters she'd spent years crafting, pouring the parts of herself she couldn't talk about into them, only to see them mangled by Hollywood. She couldn't change it now, but she had learned from it. Her characters belonged to her and her readers, and she would happily stay in her book lane with no more detours to La-La Land.

There was something in the set of Mason's mouth that made her heart pang with familiarity. The way he lit up when talking about working with Alissa, and how quickly that light fizzled out when talking about his present. "But you don't love it?"

"I did—I do," he corrected himself hastily. He shrugged, rubbing the back of his neck subconsciously. "It's complicated."

She met his gaze. He was bullshitting her, and they both knew it. She let it drop. He didn't owe her an explanation. They'd agreed to keep things surface level, but Sawyer couldn't help but read between the lines of Mason's tiny admissions and careful omissions. Their situations were wildly different, yet she felt like she got him—or was beginning to, at least.

Silence fell between them, and she wondered if he, too, was trying to figure out how to backpedal out of the conversational deep waters they'd waded into.

"So," Mason said brusquely, clearing his throat. "How did I do? Are you feeling inspired?"

Sawyer scoffed, but she couldn't quite shake the image of the couple nuzzling noses by the mistletoe. "Did I ruin romance for you yet?"

He fixed her with a look, confirming what she knew: neither of them had really succeeded in their mission. "Maybe," he hedged. "We should do a few more items from the list. For science."

To be fair, if today was a test run, it wasn't a complete loss. She had a lot of ideas she was itching to write down. She wanted to see this through.

"For science," she agreed. Wandering over to her hutch, she grabbed a bottle of whiskey and put a healthy pour into two mugs. The mug she handed Mason read "BDE" in bold letters, and in a smaller font underneath, "(bisexual disaster energy)."

Mason laughed under his breath as he read the mug, raising it to clink against her titty mug before taking a sip.

"For the record," she said quietly, not sure how to tactfully broach this subject. She considered herself to be a master of many things, but tact had never been one of them. "I know this—" She gestured between the two of them. "Is an unusual venture that we're on, but anything you say to me is in confidence. I don't really have anyone to tell." Fuck, that was an embarrassingly honest thing to admit. She cleared her throat and avoided Mason's overly soft expression. "I just meant, I don't have TMZ on speed dial."

The corner of Mason's mouth quirked up. "Thank you. I didn't mean to change the subject—well, yes I did. But not because I don't trust you. It's just…" He stared down into his mug as if it were alphabet soup, praying it would spell out the perfect nonanswer. When it didn't, he shrugged. "I love the cast, the crew, my character, but—" He scrunched up his nose. "Let's just say, if it were my show, I'd run things *very* differently. But…" He shrugged in defeat. "It feels really fucking shitty to complain when I have something most people would kill for."

Even without saying much, he'd still managed to speak volumes.

Sawyer nodded in understanding. "I get that. My editor is begging me for my next book, and I can't even write one. Meanwhile, there are tons of brilliant writers waiting for that shot, and here I am, squandering mine." She took a large gulp of whiskey, wincing at the burn. She'd drafted multiple messages to her writer friends to talk about this very thing and deleted every single one, not wanting to seem ungrateful, and here she was word vomiting it all out to Elevator Guy.

The nickname stung worse than the whiskey. Mason wasn't just One-Night Stand Elevator Guy. Not anymore. What did you call your friends with benefits when "benefits" were against the rules?

A…friend?

Sawyer didn't want to think too hard about how long it took for that word to bubble to the surface. A new friend. Clearly, Mason was already rubbing off on her, because the mere concept of friendship had her heart racing.

They were supposed to be keeping things superficial, but she supposed they could still be friends, in a way. Like the classmates you did a group project with and then never spoke to again once the semester was over.

It was nice, having someone to talk to about these things. Outside of Lily, she hadn't made many new friends since losing her college friends in the breakup with Sadie. She had writer friends, but she'd been beating the same, sad writer's block drum for so long now that where they'd once been supportive, their condolences and words of affirmation had now gone stale, a refrain repeated too many times.

But she *was* trying. What she was doing with Mason would sound ridiculous if she tried to explain it, but the fact was, she was feeling more inspired in the past few weeks than she had in years.

At this point, her editor, Emily, would take anything, but every time they agreed on a new pitch for her next book, the harder she pushed herself, the more "The End" eluded her. She needed to create, the outlet it provided, but it remained out of reach. And it was slowly suffocating her. Writing had always been her safe space, something that was wholly hers, and in her yearslong writer's block, it was like the very foundation of her life was crumbling beneath her feet. She'd already sacrificed so much for her career, and there was nothing she wouldn't sacrifice to get it back.

"So," Mason said softly, cutting through her downward spiral. "Are we going to decorate this tree or what?"

Sawyer's eyes widened. "Oh, I wasn't going to force you to sit through all my decorating traditions. I already took up enough of your time, but thank you. Seriously. I wouldn't have been able to get a real tree without you."

Mason's face fell, but he hastily replaced it with a practiced smile.

"What?" she asked suspiciously.

He shrugged, boyishly bashful and adorable in a way that had Sawyer's insides melting. "I was kinda hoping to help. We never

really did the whole decorating thing as a kid. Ours was always professionally decorated and picture perfect. Besides," he said with a
roguish grin that made a very specific part of her melt. "I'm dead
curious to see if your ornament collection is half as interesting as
your mugs." He raised the BDE mug in demonstration.

She laughed. She'd planned to ask Lily to come over and decorate
with her, but she didn't want to wait for her to get back from snow-
birding with the in-laws.

Her Bluetooth speakers beeped loudly as she flipped them on, and
she queued up Ariana Grande. The tree farm excursion had fanned
the embers of inspiration that the Christkindlmarket had sparked,
and she wanted to keep this feeling going. "Well, if you're going to be
here for a while, take off your pants."

"Miss Greene," he admonished, placing a scandalized hand over
his heart. "Rule number two."

"You're covered in mud, sweetheart," she reminded him smarmily.

Mason grunted, tossing back his whiskey with one hand and
unbuttoning his jeans with the other. He hesitated before lowering
his fly, brows raising in question.

"What?" Sawyer laughed.

"Turn around," he requested.

Sawyer choked on her own spit. "I've already seen you naked!"

"Seeing me in my boxers is not a surface-level privilege."

Sawyer pressed her lips together, shaking her head as she turned
around. "There's a robe on the back of my bathroom door that *might*
cover—" She gestured vaguely in the air. "Something."

"My modesty thanks you," Mason sniffed, pressing his muddy
jeans into her waiting palm.

She started the laundry and had begun decorating before he reappeared. But when he did—

Sawyer nearly swallowed her tongue.

"Shirt was dirty, too," he called from the kitchen, adding the flannel to the wash.

Sawyer tittered softly. She opted not to point out that the brightly patterned chiffon robe was barely long enough to cover his ass, his modesty still in dire straits. Still, she was grateful he'd done it. Mason in a red flannel and boxers would be hard to resist, and it would be all too easy to throw Rule #2 out the window and fill the void with him. Hanging out with him like this, as friends, was already pushing the limits of their "surface level" rule. The robe added a much-needed air of silliness.

This wasn't on their list, but the boyish joy on Mason's face when he asked to help decorate, the same joy now on his face as he inspected each ornament curiously, carefully selecting the ideal branch to hang it from—she couldn't deny him this. She'd allow this deviation from their mission, but it was better, safer, if they kept to the list—and their rules—from now on.

They decorated in silence for a bit, dancing around each other in the cramped corner of her apartment, their limbs occasionally brushing as they sought the perfect spot for each ornament. When Sawyer unwrapped the Polaroid ornament of her and Sadie hosting their first Queermas dinner, she surreptitiously hid it between two books on the nearby shelf, a hollow feeling in her gut. She hadn't decorated with anyone since Sadie, the traditions they'd crafted together now the Ghost of Christmas Past.

Mason placed a hand on her shoulder to keep her still as he reached around to hang a particularly heavy reindeer ornament on a top bough. The heat of him as he pressed up against her . . . She coughed to conceal an involuntary *hnng*.

"So what's wrong with you?" she blurted.

Mason laughed. "What?"

Spinning around, she tilted her head back to take him in. "You're attractive, employed, tolerable to be around, and want to settle down. You're, like, the ideal partner, for people who are into that sort of thing."

His mouth quirked up at the corner. "So why can't I keep a girl?"

Sawyer shrugged. "I mean, I'm all for ruining romance for you. I'm grateful for the opportunity, truly. But eventually, once all this tabloid nonsense blows over, you're going to date again, right?"

He nodded slowly. "And even if you successfully shatter my rose-colored glasses and I pick the right person, will I still fuck it up?"

She tried to look sympathetic, but she was fairly certain it looked more like a grimace. "I mean..." She frowned. "Have you ever thought about it? Or asked?"

"Like, track down my exes *High Fidelity*–style?" He did that sexy one-eyebrow-quirked thing before leaning down and whispering in her ear, "Like *Why We're Not Together*?"

Sawyer shivered. Her books were so incredibly personal—and so incredibly steamy—that she normally wanted to crawl into a hole and die when people she knew read her books. But there was something endearing about Mason reading hers after they met, with no expectation they'd ever see each other again. "Yes, like that." She cleared her throat to rid her voice of the odd strain it'd taken on. "It's a solid cliché–plot device–trope thing. We could add it to the list and then cross it off?"

Mason leaned back, twisting his mouth off to the side, thinking. Tugging his phone from his pocket, he tapped through a series of screens.

"I—oh, I didn't mean *now*," she stammered. Why was she nervous? This had nothing to do with her, but the mere idea of reaching out to any of her exes made her want to break out in hives. She hovered her hand over his screen to stop him from hitting dial. "Maybe you should tackle this one on your own? I'm supposed to be spoiling your hopeless romanticism, not—" She gestured to the phone. "Whatever that's going to be."

He nodded, sliding his phone back into his pocket.

Sawyer exhaled slowly, heart hammering in her ears. Taking a sip of her whiskey, she banished the vision of calling up Sadie and hearing all the reasons why they hadn't worked. She already knew the answer to that question.

Mason grabbed her phone from the hutch, holding it out to her so she could enter her passcode. Once unlocked, she watched as he interrupted Ariana's rendition of "Last Christmas" in favor of "Thank U, Next."

Humming along with Ariana's gratefulness for her exes, they shoved the ugliest of her ornament collection into the hole in the tree's boughs, and hid it from view.

CHAPTER TEN

<u>HOLIDAY HALLMARK MOVIE</u> – Equal parts
twinkling lights and patterned scarves, three dashes of
hot-as-cocoa lingering looks, sprinkle in a tree-lighting
ceremony, and serve up, at an ice skating rink
in the town square.

All publicity is good publicity, Mason."

Mason bit his tongue. Sometimes he wished he could vent to his mom and not have it become a TED talk on Moira West's Five Steps to Making It as a Working Actor. He knew she thought she was helping. She made her career working on soaps, had faked relationships and frenemy feuds for publicity because viewers ate it up. But his relationship with Kara had been real—not media fodder. And this "good publicity" was having real repercussions on his career trajectory. Not that she knew that, because he still hadn't told her he was leaving *Diagnostics*, because that would require him to tell her about Guiding Light and the impending LA move.

Mason groaned. Fuck. If he announced leaving the show now, it would look like he also left because of the breakup.

"Honey, you sound like a very sad cow. What's wrong? I thought you and Kara were a PR stunt. I didn't think it was serious. At least not serious enough that you bothered introducing us."

That had been intentional. His mother's meddling in his professional life had nearly destroyed their relationship ten years ago, and while she was better-*ish* about it now, he wasn't eager to find out how those plotting powers could be diverted to his personal life, if given the chance.

Family was everything to Moira West. She fed the media machine what they wanted to see and then retreated to her perfectly crafted private life. When she'd been his manager, she'd done the same for him, too. It was fine when he thought they were in it together. Then, when he was sixteen, he found out the real reason his crush had changed her tune about not dating costars. His mother had advised her to give him a shot, that it would be good buzz for the film. Everyone knew it was a PR relationship—except him. It wasn't until she dumped him at the premiere after-party that he learned the truth. He and his mother didn't speak for a long time after that.

"Mom," he sighed placatingly. "I'm not like you. I never wanted to play the game the way you did."

Moira sniffed fussily. "Well, that's all well and good, Mason, but we're *family*. I really wish I didn't have to find out about these things from the tabloids, honey."

He'd told his mom about the breakup weeks ago, and she hadn't been nearly as passionate about it then, so why was she so upset now? He snatched his phone off the dresser, hastily typing in Kara's name.

He stumbled backward until his feet hit the bed frame, sinking onto the edge of the mattress.

People. E! *Elle.* TMZ. All had posted the same picture. She was wearing a beanie and sunglasses, but there was no mistaking that it was Kara snuggled into her new costar's side. In her parents' small-town Starbucks. The week before Christmas. With a ring on her left hand.

Kara Zhao and Peter Levine's Whirlwind Romance

Peter and Kara Take the Heat Off-Screen

Everything You Need to Know About Peter and Kara, Our New Favorite It Couple

Mason didn't "need to know" anything—in fact, he wished he knew less. But maybe this was a good thing. Maybe they'd finally leave him out of it. Oh, *greaaat*. TMZ had been kind enough to include that damn photo of bearded, disgruntled Mason, dredging back up the narrative that he wasn't handling the breakup very well.

His mother seemed to be looking at the same article, tutting. "I really wish they'd used a better picture," his mother's voice trilled from his speaker.

"That's kinda the point, Mom."

She sighed in exasperation. "Well, I don't like it. If you'd just let me leak something to course correct their coverage. Something tasteful about our holiday plans as a family—perhaps how excited I am to host your new lady friend for Christmas—"

"I'm not seeing anyone."

"So? I could set you up, Brenda's daughter is trying to break into modeling and—"

"Mom. *No*."

Moira heaved a beleaguered sigh. "Fine. Well— I'm just sorry you still have to work with her. Speaking of," she transitioned none too subtly. He should have started a timer to see how long it took her to pivot to prying into his work life, the only thing that trumped her love of prying into his romantic life. He'd worked hard to establish boundaries between work and family, but Moira West worked harder, drilling holes in the careful walls he'd built. They probably resembled Swiss cheese at this point. "Have you signed your renewal contract yet? You should use this buzz to get more money."

He tuned her out as she told him a story about the time she'd taken the network for all they were worth to pay her as much as her male costar, a story he'd heard a hundred times.

His phone buzzed, and he opened the new text automatically, desperate for a reprieve.

running late! gimme five!! sorry!!!!! <3

Mason could've kissed Sawyer for her perfectly timed interruption. "Hey, Mom, I've gotta go."

She cut off mid-story. "Meeting someone?" she asked hopefully. "A date? You *should* be seen out with someone new, dear."

His derisive laugh was muffled as he tugged a soft Henley over his head. "The exact opposite of a date, actually."

"Okay. I don't know what that means and, as your mother, I don't think I want to, especially if it has anything to do with those apps."

Call the press. Mark your calendars. Moira West *not* prying. Monumental. Historic.

He said none of this, hurrying his mom off the phone and promising to call her again tomorrow to discuss the Christmas plans she'd called to talk about today before she had launched into an immediate dissection of his life.

He was dressed and out the door in two minutes, glad to be away from the conversation that seemed to linger in the air of his apartment. As the ruthless Chicago wind chafed his face, he found himself wishing he still had the beard from the TMZ photo.

The Millennium Park skating rink was only a few blocks away, but Sawyer still beat him there, immediately recognizable in her mustard-yellow coat. A smile spread across his face when he spotted her, and the knot in his gut loosened a fraction.

He tried not to think too hard about what that meant.

"You ready to do this?" he asked with a forced cheeriness.

She shook her head side to side, green eyes wide.

"Shit," he said, tugging off his beanie in frustration. "I forgot the cider."

"It's fine," she insisted. "Probably best if I'm sober while knives are strapped to my feet. I have a feeling I won't need any extra help ruining today's cliché," she added with a furtive glance toward the rink.

Mason caught the eye of a gaggle of shoppers, one of them narrowing her eyes as if trying to place his face. He shoved his beanie back on his head. "C'mon," he said gruffly.

Sawyer glanced up at him, attempting to follow his gaze as he took her hand and guided her toward the rental booth. "Everything alright?"

He glanced back, but the group had moved on. He exhaled slowly. "It's fine. Crisis averted."

Her brows rose at the word *crisis*. She squeezed his hand, which he was still grasping like a lifeline. He immediately dropped it, not consciously having meant to grab it in the first place. If someone had seen, snapped a photo…He could see the headline now: "Rebound Wars: Who Did It Better?" His mother would be elated.

He blinked, and Sawyer was still smiling softly up at him, dark brows arched in concern. "If you're worried this is too public, we can go another time, some tiny rink—or better yet, *not* do this."

He shoved all thoughts of the tabloids from his mind. "Oh, we're doing this. It's on the list."

"Damn it," Sawyer swore. "Sevens, please," she said in resignation when they reached the front of the queue for skates.

The rink was packed with tourists and holiday shoppers taking a break, which was better than a smaller rink. The crowd would be easier for them to lose themselves in. Besides, he'd always wanted to come on a date here. They needed to ruin this fantasy.

They settled onto a nearby bench to lace up their skates, Sawyer chewing on the inside of her cheek as she watched the groups skating around the rink.

Mason nudged her with his shoulder, gesturing toward a father cheering on his daughter as she skated clumsily with the assistance of a plastic penguin-shaped skate trainer. "I can get you one of those, if you like," he teased.

"Is that a short joke?" she clapped back.

He grinned, unable to stop his gaze from roving over her tiny frame. His attention snagged on her hastily tied laces. "Oh no. You want them tight." Crouching down, he propped her skate against his thigh and undid her laces. Once the first had been sufficiently tightened, he guided her other foot into his lap. He could feel her eyes on him, meeting her gaze as he retied the second skate. Her mouth curved up ever so slightly at the corners. "If you make a joke about me on my knees again, I swear—"

She leaned forward, so close that the white clouds of their breath intermingled. "You'll what?"

Tearing his attention from her insufferable mouth and the coconut lip balm that he could now smell, he shook his head. He hadn't forgotten about Rule #2. She was only teasing him to test him. He wouldn't fall for it so easily this time.

Rising to his feet, he held out his hand. "Ready?"

She flashed him a nervous grin, eyes on the skaters as she allowed him to pull her to her feet. Her shoulders ratcheted up toward her ears, and he realized how truly nervous she was. "You know I got you, right?" he murmured.

She met his gaze, the pucker between her brows smoothing as she nodded. "Yeah. I trust you," she said equally as soft. His chest suddenly felt tight. "It's those fuckers I don't trust." She pointed behind him, to a pair of experienced skaters zipping between the slower-moving groups.

A young girl let out a startled yelp as one of them whizzed by her, and Mason frowned. "Well, I don't know if you know this," he began conspiratorially, guiding her toward the rink's opening. "But when not performing shirtless surgeries, I make an excellent bodyguard."

"Ooooh," Sawyer cooed. "Bodyguard romance. *Classic.*"

"So, I'm winning this one," Mason said with a smirk.

"Hardly," she scoffed. "I find nothing romantic about this. Why did you put it on the list? What about this does it for you?"

Mason laughed, placing a hand at her elbow to steady her as they queued up to get onto the rink. Glancing around, the smile on his face took up permanent residence as he watched the numerous couples holding hands, their gliding steps in sync as they skated beneath the canopy of twinkling lights, the instrumental Christmas music soft enough for whispered, intimate conversation. "Everything?" he breathed.

Sawyer rolled her eyes. "But it's so crowded."

He nodded toward a couple on the other side of the plexiglass, the way they grinned, eyes only for each other. "They have no idea there's anyone here but them."

Sawyer stumbled slightly as the toe of her skate snagged on the padded walkway. She heaved a heavy sigh. "You paid way too much for these rental skates."

Mason shrugged. "Experiences are worth it."

Sawyer pointed out a woman hitting the ice bum-first. "You're so right," she drawled sarcastically. "Nothing screams 'romantic experience' like a broken tailbone."

As soon as the words left her lips, a man circled back to help the fallen woman up. The woman got back on her feet—albeit a little clumsily, like a colt using its legs for the first time—but there was no mistaking the mirth in her eyes as the man encircled her in his arms, the two of them laughing it off together.

"C'mon, that's pretty cute," Mason insisted.

Sawyer pursed her lips up at him obstinately, and he mimed adding a tally mark under his name midair.

They'd reached the edge of rink, and Mason stepped onto the ice, holding out a hand for her. She took it, and he could practically hear her teeth grinding together as she stepped onto the ice and... froze. Her other hand shot out, grasping his arm in a death grip.

At the sheer look of panic on Sawyer's face, all plans of proving to her that this was romantic flew from Mason's mind. A crowd was forming behind her, glaring at her to move so they could get onto the ice. He glared back before refocusing his attention on getting Sawyer through this list item safely.

"Sawyer," he said quietly, her eyes snapping to his. "Walk toward me."

She stared down at her feet like she was wearing cement blocks instead of skates. Tucking his hand under her chin, he guided her to look at him. He offered her a reassuring smile, turning so he was facing her fully and extending his other hand for her to hold. "Walk toward me."

She took one wobbly step forward, careening into his chest. "Well, I think this cliché is sufficiently ruined," she joked half-heartedly. "Let's go."

"We can leave whenever you want. Exit's right there." He gestured across the rink. He could see by her thousand-yard stare that it was taking everything in her not to go against the stream of skaters and walk backward out of the entrance they'd just come through.

"One lap," she bargained, straightening, pride tingeing her cheeks pink. "I can do one."

"You can totally do one," he agreed heartily.

She took another hesitant step, and he mirrored her, keeping his hand at her elbow. She flinched as the speedy skaters zipped by, and he positioned himself in front of her again. "Don't worry about them. Just look at me and I'll look out for them."

She nodded, taking another step, both her hands grasping his forearms for balance. Her steps grew more certain, Mason skating backward and glancing over his shoulder occasionally to make sure he didn't plow over a toddler. Speaking of, the girl with the skate trainer glided past on slightly less wobbly legs.

"Oh God," Sawyer murmured. "Did we just get lapped by a five-year-old?"

Mason couldn't help but laugh.

"How did you learn, anyway?" she huffed, her breath clouding in front of her.

"My sister, Margot, was really into it when we were younger, though I think she was mostly into it for the costumes."

Sawyer gasped. "Why didn't we get costumes?"

"Next time," he promised.

"Yeah?" She gave him a shit-eating grin. "I'd love to see you in head-to-toe bedazzled Lycra."

"Whatever does it for you, I guess." He wasn't even sure what he was saying anymore, but she was skating now, paying more attention to their conversation than on moving her legs. Confident that she wouldn't face-plant, he shifted so he could skate beside her. Sawyer swallowed thickly, her eyes trained on the exit. "It wouldn't be very inconspicuous."

"Are you worried about that—being recognized—here?" she asked disjointedly.

He shook his head. "We should be fine." He hoped that wasn't a lie.

"Are you sure? You seemed distracted when you got here."

"It's not that," he dodged.

"Then what is it?"

The exit drew near, and Mason raised a brow in question.

"One more," she said with quiet defiance. "Besides, you can't avoid my question if you're trapped on here with me."

"Trickster," he teased. They skated in silence for a moment, Mason waiting until they were past the group of teenage girls taking selfies before relaying the latest tabloid headlines to her.

"She couldn't have kept it under wraps until after the New Year?" Sawyer said vehemently when he was done. "She broke up with you, like, a few weeks ago!"

Her protectiveness made him smile, the knot in his stomach from reliving the story loosening. Not that it meant anything. With Sawyer, it could never mean anything. "I already knew there was someone else. It's not that. It's—"

He probably shouldn't talk about this here, in public, but he *wanted* to tell her. He hadn't told anyone because his family was too invested and would find a way to make this about them. Talking about it with Alissa was fine, but she was also his business partner and thus also very invested. He just wanted to *talk* and have someone listen without an agenda.

"I'm leaving," he said quietly. He waited, half expecting every person on the rink to stop and stare, to start taking photos and clamor for the exclusive. But no one paid them any mind. No one had any idea that in his two-word admission, Mason felt a million times lighter.

"I'm leaving the show." He couldn't resist saying it again. He'd been keeping so many secrets to protect the feelings of everyone around him, he hadn't realized how suffocating it was until confessing one to Sawyer made breathing feel a thousand times easier. This was definitely breaking their surface-level rule, but he needed to talk about this. More than that, he wanted to talk about this with *her*. "I'm moving to LA to start a production company with Alissa. We were supposed to announce it earlier this month, but with the tabloids making me out like a womanizer one day and a heartbroken fool the next, it's—"

He sighed. It was a mess, is what it was. He finally felt like he was doing something in his career that wasn't chosen by his mother or in spite of his mother. This change was 100 percent for him, a way to reclaim the joy of acting and creating. He hated keeping it to himself like a dirty little secret, not being able to celebrate this giant leap forward.

"Hence our mission," Sawyer said wisely. "To keep you single and out of the tabloids, so the focus is on your new company and not your love life."

Mason nodded. "No one wants to trust a guy with their money if they think he's just chasing skirts. I need to show them that *this* is my priority."

Sawyer frowned. "Breakups suck. I can't imagine going through one publicly."

He could tell she meant it. For all her talk of a Grinch heart, she felt more than she let on. "Can I ask you something?" As soon as the words left his mouth, he wanted to shove them back in.

"Sure," she said guardedly.

He could feel his cheeks burning, fully aware he was breaking their rules by asking, but they'd spent three laps discussing Kara, so... "Breakups do suck, but do you ever think that maybe your breakup was just a bad experience—the exception, not the rule?"

Silence fell between them, an apology for pushing too far on the tip of his tongue, when she spoke first.

"Of course I've thought that," she answered quietly, her meek words like a blow to his gut. "But it's more than that." She chewed on the inside of her cheek, eyes fixed straight ahead as she and Mason continued to skate. "My entire life imploded when Sadie and I broke up. I lost my girlfriend, my apartment, my entire friend group. And you—you should be shouting your news from the rooftops. Instead, your breakup is holding your joy prisoner. As if getting your heart broken isn't bad enough, they get to hold the things we love hostage, too? It's bullshit, and it's not fair." Quietly, under her breath she admitted, "I can't risk that again."

She rolled her lips inward, and he waited. If she wanted to keep talking, he wanted to hear it.

She glanced at him sidelong. "This is where you try to change my mind by extolling your grand philosophies on—" She lowered her voice like even saying the word would risk summoning it. "*Romance*."

Mason barked out a laugh. "Why do you say that like it's dangerous?"

"Isn't it?" she asked, voice pitched high. "It's not that I had one bad breakup and gave up," she said slowly, her voice faraway. "It's like this: I was on this writing panel once, and someone asked a fellow author how she juggled being a mom and a writer. And she explained that it really is juggling, and you have to know which balls are glass and which are plastic. If you drop a plastic ball, it bounces. If you drop a glass ball, it shatters.

"Over the past few years, I've dropped a lot of glass balls thinking they were plastic, sacrificing them for plastic balls that I thought were glass. And even though I'm juggling a lot less now, I'm struggling. I can't juggle any more balls—do not laugh at that," she said, despite laughing herself. "I knew I was dropping the ball with Sadie, but I thought our relationship was plastic, and would bounce back. I don't know if my career is glass or plastic. My life is this incredibly sad circus of me trying to keep this one ball up in the air because if I drop it—I don't know if it will bounce back, if *I* will bounce back." She swallowed thickly. "So, yeah, romance is dangerous. One more ball to juggle when I'm already barely coping? That's not fair to the person trusting me to keep them up in the air."

Her eyes were glassy, an edge of panic to her voice that always appeared when she talked about writing. He didn't press for more, tucking the information away to mull over later. For now, he said, "Could you say 'balls' one more time?"

Sawyer laughed—though that wasn't exactly the right word for it. More like a honk. Once she composed herself, she glanced sidelong at him. "Balls," she whispered.

"Balls," he said, marginally louder.

"Balls."

"Balls."

"BALLS!" she screamed, dragging him out of the rink.

Mason surreptitiously tucked his face deeper into his scarf, though Sawyer had perfectly timed her outburst. Everyone on the rink that had heard was glancing around at neighboring skaters for the source, not along the sidelines, where Sawyer was hobbling unsteadily on her skates, bent at the waist she was laughing so hard.

What a strange person. He liked her so much.

As a friend.

He liked her as a friend so much.

CHAPTER ELEVEN

THE QUIRKY BEST FRIEND – They're weird,
know how to push all your buttons, and
you love them for it. No notes.

Mason's hands slid between Sawyer's legs, his long fingers teasing her. He was close—*so close*—to where she needed him. When he finally relented, giving her what she wanted, Sawyer gasped.

With a shudder, Sawyer sat up in bed, rubbing sleep from her eyes. She covered herself with the comforter, though there was no need. She was alone. She blinked away the dream as her dimly lit, Mason-less bedroom came into focus in front of her. With a sigh, she sank back against her pillow, rolling over and screaming into it.

She'd made a pact with herself to stop thinking about Mason when she touched herself, but the memories of their night together had a habit of sneaking in anyway, which meant she'd given up masturbating altogether. And that was a shame, because if getting yourself off was an Olympic sport, she'd have more medals than Michael Phelps.

Squeezing her legs together to ease the ache, she counted backward from ten. Fantasizing about Mason had been one thing when she thought she'd never see him again, but now, she couldn't, or she'd want to act on her fantasies. And she couldn't do that, obviously. Not only was it against their rules, but the more she got to know Mason, the more convinced she was that she would be the exact wrong person for him. He wanted the romance, the all-consuming rush of a new relationship. Sawyer simply didn't have time for that. She had a book to write, and if she was struggling to even fantasize about love, she was in no position to plan and execute romantic overtures in the real world.

Mason was off-limits. She knew that. Hell, she'd been the one to draw that line. But the memory of his hands on her, the feeling of him inside her…It was haunting her—a very specific, very *needy* part of her.

Just as one of her hands began to drift south, her alarm blared, and she jolted out of bed. Staring back at the rumpled sheets traitorously, she toggled off her alarm and trudged away to start a cold shower and get ready to brave the mall.

Normally, the mall was Sawyer's favorite place to people watch. The mall the day before Christmas, however, was a madhouse.

"When I agreed to do last-minute Christmas shopping with you," she grumbled to Lily as they queued up for coffee, "I thought you meant antique stores and thrifting, not throwing 'bows in the Apple Store."

In retrospect, she should have known. Lily's husband Beau was a techie. The two could not be more different, and yet, even Sawyer's Grinch heart could admit they were rom-com-worthy. Childhood sweethearts turned second-chance romance. They were the exception, not the rule. And the rule was, when the glass ball drops, it shatters, and no amount of grand, romantic gestures will put it back together the way it was before, and you'll only drop more things in the process of trying to save something that's already broken. Sawyer wouldn't make that mistake again.

"I can't believe you're going to IKEA after this," Lily mumbled.

Sawyer had anticipated some form of sarcastic response from Lily when Sawyer caught her up to speed on how One-Night Stand Elevator Guy was now Mission: (un)Romance Guy, but thus far, Lily's only hang-up was the IKEA of it all. "That place is going to be way worse than this."

"Is it?" she questioned, her voice unnaturally high. "When I'm making my Christmas list, I'm not thinking, 'Ah, yes, there's nothing I want more than to spend my Christmas morning rage-quitting furniture assembly.'"

Though the Christmas Eve chaos was an added bonus. There was no way Mason could make IKEA romantic on a normal day, much less on one of the busiest days of the year. She was definitely going to win this list item—not that they were keeping score. But if they were, well, this one was primed for ruining.

The barista called out their names, and Lily passed Sawyer her coconut milk latte before grabbing her own drink—Sawyer had already forgotten the sentence-length order Lily had placed. Lily propped her cane against the coffee bar before further modifying her order with a few shakes of this and that. Lily treated coffee like she did her canvases—the more layers and mixed media, the better.

"Besides, we gotta ruin *500 Days of Summer*," Sawyer said with a shrug.

"That movie is *not* a romance," Lily insisted.

"I know, but that's kinda the point right?" Sawyer mused. "Everyone thinks it is when, really, the villain is Tom—not Summer. She's very clear she doesn't want a relationship, and Tom goes falling anyway."

Lily stirred her coffee contemplatively. "So, Mason is Tom?"

Sawyer's head bounced from side to side as she considered. "Mason is kinda Tom, but I don't think he's a villain. It's more that we've got to stop reading into everything and assigning some cosmic significance to it. Two people can go to a tree farm or Christkindlmarket or IKEA and have fun, and they don't have to fall in love."

Scooping up her coffee in one hand and her cane in the other, Lily leaned in close as she swept past Sawyer out of the packed coffee shop. "But they could, say, sleep together again."

Sawyer had to double her pace to keep up. Even on the days when Lily's osteonecrosis necessitated the use of her cane, her long legs still outpaced Sawyer's. "Oh my God, Lily."

"Whaaat?" Lily said innocently. "Multiple. Orgasms," she said, smacking her cane on the ground after each word. "Don't waste that, Sawyer!"

She sniffed primly. "My vibrators give me that." Never mind that she'd followed through on her resolution to rename all her vibrators Mason.

Lily loosed a long-suffering sigh. "Fine. I'll get you and your vibrator a twenty-four-pack of batteries for Christmas." Without so much as taking a breath, she plowed on. "Wait, if Mason is Tom, are you Zooey Deschanel? If so, seems like you're doomed to have him fall in love with you."

Sawyer had definitely considered that. They were having fun and she liked spending time with Mason, but he wanted the epic romance. She was fairly confident he was self-aware enough to realize she was not the person to give him that. Though how he was planning on finding that in LA, while managing a new production company, she didn't know. RIP to his next partner. He was going to be married to his work.

Sawyer's heart twisted uncomfortably, knowing all too well what it was like to be left for pursuing a dream. She knew their mission was logically a little flimsy, but *fuck*. If she could help Mason even a little, spare him from going through what she did with Sadie...it was worth it.

She grasped tight to that resolve, blinking as she came back to the present, in a mall packed with people and a Lily who was staring at her a little too knowingly. Time to shut that down. Lily and her imagination could not be left to their own devices. "He's moving to LA so there's not really any future there, even if either of us wanted it. Which we do not."

"Okay, so there's no future, but in the present, there could be orgasms."

Sawyer groaned. Lily wasn't going to drop this, and she was so desperate to get her to drop it that she slipped.

"I've thought about it," she admitted. "The sex was great, but I don't think he knows how to keep it casual. When we slept together—" Sawyer shook her head in disbelief as the memory came back to her. "He prepared this whole breakfast-in-bed spread. Like, not just a post–booty call bagel and a coffee and get on your way. Like, fruit, homemade pancakes, French press, yogurt and granola...I never understood those sitcom kids who woke up to that and took, like, *one* strawberry and ran out the door but—" Sawyer shuddered. "It was too much. I couldn't get out of there fast enough. I didn't even grab a single strawberry."

Lily's mouth hung open. "I'm sorry," she said breathlessly. "Did you say breakfast, as in Little Miss Never Spends the Night *spent the night?*"

Fuck.

Sawyer held up her finger in warning. "It was late, and I accidentally fell asleep." Under her breath, she confessed in a rush, "Andthemorningsexwassogoodlfellbackasleep."

Lily nodded in faux seriousness. "Of course. You poor thing, getting your back blown out and then he has *the audacity* to bring you breakfast in bed? The horror! You definitely shouldn't sleep with him again. Sounds…terrible," she said wistfully. "Unbearable, to be so attentively taken care of. It's a feat you survived, really."

Sawyer clenched her jaw so hard she was in danger of cracking a tooth.

Lily mimicked Sawyer's stony expression back at her. "All I'm saying is, would it be so bad to sleep with someone you actually like for once?"

Sawyer nearly swallowed her tongue. "What does that mean?"

Lily snorted. "Please. We both know you purposefully pick partners you know you won't get attached to."

Craning her neck, she feigned concentrating on finding an unoccupied table, but the food court was as crowded as the coffee shop. "I don't have time for that right now, I'm—"

"Focusing on my career," they said in unison, Lily with a mocking undertone.

Sawyer scoffed. "Why do you say that like it's a bad thing?"

"Because you can do more than one thing at once, Sawyer." She wasn't sure if the growl Lily let out was frustration at her or the tweens who stole the empty table they were angling toward.

"The last time I tried to do both," Sawyer mumbled. "I fucked up both. I just…I need to get my shit together, and falling head over heels is the antithesis of feeling *together*."

"You're the one who keeps talking about feelings," Lily pointed out smugly. "Not me."

Sawyer sighed through her nose. "*My point* is he doesn't know how to be casual. So no, we can't keep sleeping together."

Lily hummed thoughtfully. "Fair. It would be torture if the sex god caught feelings for you."

"He's moving to LA!" Sawyer bleated.

Lily raised her eyebrows. "The perfect out," she said reasonably. "Unless it's not him catching feelings you're worried about. I mean, you drove here and paid way too much for parking all so you could drive forty-five minutes to Schaumburg after this and brave IKEA with him. That's—" She began singing Meatloaf's "I'd Do Anything for Love (but I Won't Do That)" under her breath.

At Sawyer's scathing look, Lily held up her hands innocently. "Fine, fine, I'm done. So what's in LA that he can't find here?"

"Besides sunshine?" She loved Chicago, but she wouldn't mind a bit more sunshine in her life to balance out the never-ending winter. "He's going for work," she hedged carefully.

"Oh, what does he do?"

She hadn't told Lily about that particular revelation. She stalled for time as they pushed their way through the crowd in pursuit of a table that wasn't occupied. "He's an actor."

Lily perked up immediately. "What theater?" Lily loved Chicago's theater scene, and was a regular at more than one collective. Sawyer had sat front row at more avant-garde Shakespeare reimaginings than she could count.

"TV, not theater," Sawyer clarified.

Lily's cane impeded her path, stopping her in her tracks so she had to face her friend. "Mason *who*?"

Sawyer sighed, stalling. "Mason West," she mumbled.

Lily's wide eyes grew even wider. "Elevator Guy is Mason West? You had—and I quote—a 'mind-blowing' one-night stand with Mason fucking West?"

"I don't think I said 'mind-blowing,'" Sawyer deflected. Even though, yes, it had been. The man knew his way around a woman's body, and she wasn't mad about it. But when she'd told her best friend about the glorious one-night stand—in detail—she hadn't expected to see him again.

Lily cackled. "You definitely did, but you didn't tell me he was *Mason West*! How could you hold out on me like this?"

"Would you be cool? Stop shouting his name," Sawyer hissed. People were starting to stare, Lily's witchy laugh cutting through the din of the crowd and the tinny Christmas music blaring from the mall speakers. "I wasn't holding out on you. I didn't know who he was until the tree farm."

"So," Lily began with a smirk Sawyer didn't trust. "If you do get inspired and write a novel after this weird quest of y'all's, you know you have to dedicate the book to his—*and I quote*—'glorious' dick, right?"

"I did not say 'glorious,'" Sawyer insisted. She definitely had, and she wasn't wrong.

Lily continued to cackle. She was having far too much fun at Sawyer's expense. With a hefty sigh, Sawyer sulked off.

"I'm sorry," Lily said apologetically. "I'm done. But please know I'm in awe of you for boinking someone that beautiful. I knew you couldn't be so pretty for nothing."

"Dear God," Sawyer swore. "Stop trying to Mrs. Bennet me! I'm in possession of no fortune, and I'm not in want of a husband or wife or partner."

Lily bit down on her lip. "Sorry, I'm actually done this time, promise." She held out her pinkie in truce.

Sawyer wrapped her pinkie around her best friend's, ready for a subject change. She loved Lily dearly, but ever since she'd given up on their single, twentysomething heathen lifestyle and gotten married, she'd been on a mission to find Sawyer her own Beau. A beau. Ha.

"So, how is it going—y'all's mission? Are you inspired?" Lily asked as they abandoned their hunt for a table and wandered into a novelty shop.

Sawyer hummed noncommittally. "I don't think I'm *How to Lose a Guy in 10 Days*–ing him hard enough, but I'm having fun and feeling inspired to write again, so we're at least halfway doing it right."

Lily's eyes widened, and she bit her lip and wiggled her brows excitedly. "You're writing again?" For all her meddling, Lily was a great cheerleader, even for Sawyer's ideas that never made it past the idea phase.

A small smile spread across her face. "Yeah, but I'm not quite ready to talk about it yet."

Lily nodded in understanding, and didn't press her further, pausing to study the wall of coffee mugs.

Sawyer came up with a million pitches a day, but there had to be a spark, something special about the idea, something that she connected with, something that necessitated *her* being the one to write that particular story. She was close. She was mulling multiple ideas in the back of her head, but she hadn't found the thread that connected them all. It was like looking in a well-stocked fridge, knowing you had the ingredients for a feast, but not knowing what you wanted to do with them. Sure, there were lots of things she could make, but that took time, and emotional energy, and she couldn't start until she knew what she was craving.

She was close. She'd written a few thousand words of an outline and some opening scenes, but beginnings were easy. Middles were messy but doable, but endings? Endings were her kryptonite.

She'd gotten so excited about her new idea that she'd opened the writing group chat she'd muted months ago in a fit of impostor syndrome. But when she scrolled through the unread messages, impostor syndrome reared its head again. She closed out without saying anything, feeling shitty for having missed out on so many of her friends' milestones.

She'd contemplated calling her agent, Tess, multiple times over the past week to talk through her half-formed idea. But it was the holidays, and Tess was spending time with her family, and Sawyer had made that call before. An idea would take root, she'd get excited that the inspiration was finally flowing after a long drought, she'd pitch it to Tess and Emily, and she'd write five, ten, fifty thousand words and then at the crux . . . she got stuck. She'd either write herself into a corner, or she'd drop the plot threads that she'd been carefully weaving, or the characters would stop speaking to her . . . The thought of trunking yet another unfinished story ate at her, her eyes stinging.

She pushed the thought away, blinking rapidly to clear her blurred vision. She couldn't afford to think like that. Literally. She couldn't afford it. She wasn't going to fail again. Her publisher wasn't going to drop her because she *would* finish this time.

"So," Lily hedged, suddenly very interested in a reindeer mug and avoiding eye contact. "I know I said I'd drop it, and I promise I will, but can't you do the whole *How to Lose a Guy in 10 Days* thing and still get laid?"

CHAPTER TWELVE

EVERYONE CAN SEE IT BUT THEM –
No explanation necessary.

It was the day before Christmas, and the mall was packed. As usual, Luis had left Christmas shopping until the last minute, and as his best friend and brother-in-law, Mason was obligated to accompany him. Or so Luis claimed when he'd called him yesterday and told him he had to tag along.

"So, how are things with the lady?" Luis hedged, inspecting the Williams Sonoma kitchen gadget nearest them. Mason had no idea what it was for, and apparently neither did Luis, who spun it around curiously before promptly setting it down when something inside made an ominous *clunk*.

Mason choked on his coffee, partially from laughter and partially at the mention of Kara.

"We broke up, remember? Twice," Mason reminded him.

He should get an Oscar for his ability to appear unbothered. It wasn't that he still wanted Kara. He'd started the process of moving on months ago. It was that she'd broken up with him because he was "too serious, too fast," and now, she was engaged.

Luis glanced sidelong at him, smirking. "And you know I'm not talking about Kara."

Now it was Mason's turn to feign interest in the nearest kitchen gadget. "Why are we even in this store? Margot doesn't cook."

"Yeah, but I do," Luis countered. "Don't change the subject. Who's the girl?"

"What makes you think there's a girl?" he deflected. Checking the time on his phone, he prayed it was time for him to meet up with Sawyer so he could ditch Luis and avoid this conversation altogether. No such luck. He still had two hours left until they ruined IKEA, which, frankly, wouldn't be hard. Mason already hated that place, but he'd been putting off getting a second nightstand for months now.

"With you?" Luis laughed. "There's always a girl. Especially when you check your phone every five minutes." Luis flicked the corner of his phone, and Mason frowned, shoving it back into his pocket. "I know you're meeting up with someone after this and you only have, like, two friends. I'm already here, and per Alissa's Instagram, she's in Toronto with her girlfriend, so—" He gestured as if it were the only logical conclusion.

Mason hated that he was right. He wasn't sure when most of his friendships had faded, but between all the night shoots, failed relationships, and multiple transcontinental moves, his pool of friends had whittled down to only Luis and Alissa. Which, frankly, he was fine with. Mason and Luis had been best friends since middle school, and while Alissa was Mason's invaluable lifeline in the industry, there was something to be said for having at least one person who knew you and liked you before you were "someone." Luis supported Mason's career, but he couldn't care less about all the peacocking, bringing Mason back down to earth when he got too caught up in the microcosm that was the acting world. And he was going to have to leave him behind when he moved to LA. Guilt twisted his gut that he hadn't told Luis yet. He knew Luis would take it better than his family, but now that Luis *was* family, he couldn't ask him to keep that secret from Margot.

It was weird, at first. His best friend dating his older sister, but it did mean they got to spend all their holidays together, and he much preferred Luis's company to the insufferable boyfriends Margot had brought home before.

"I'm judging by your lack of refusal that I'm right, so: What's her name?"

All his warm and fuzzy thoughts about Luis and their steadfast friendship vanished. Of course Luis assumed that. Mason had a bad habit of retreating into his own head mid-conversation, so used to biting his tongue he sometimes forgot he had people he could speak freely around. But this... He didn't want to involve his family in his and Sawyer's shenanigans. He wasn't sure how to avoid the conversation without piquing Luis's interest further, so he did what his mother had taught him to do when the press asked a question he didn't like: he gave a half answer. "Her name is Sawyer, but it's not like that."

"So you're not sleeping with her?"

Mason cleared his throat. "No."

Technically, it wasn't a lie. Had they slept together? Yes. Were they currently? No. Did he still think about it constantly? Irrelevant.

Luis stared at him wide-eyed, and Mason feared his friend was going to call his bluff. What good were all those years of acting if he couldn't even lie convincingly?

"Wait... did you—*did you make another friend*?"

Mason waved away his comment, which was apparently the wrong thing to do, because Luis's eyes narrowed suspiciously. Which was how Luis managed to squeeze the entire story out of him. Mason skipped the LA detail, but he told him about getting stuck in the elevator, the run-in at the Christkindlmarket, the pact at Kuma's, the Christmas tree farm, then shouting about balls at the Millennium Park ice rink. By the end, Luis was laughing so hard that the other shoppers had begun to stare, some of their gazes lingering on Mason longer than he was comfortable with.

"C'mon," Luis managed between gasps of laughter. "Let's get out of here before someone recognizes you and I get stuck photographing you in front of the oversized marshmallows."

Mason rolled his eyes. "Next thing you know, the tabloids will be bemoaning that I'm eating my feelings."

"Mason West," Luis began dramatically. "Would you say that a marshmallow a day keeps the heartbreak away? Is it—" Luis paused for effect. "Just what the doctor ordered?"

Mason couldn't help the snort that escaped him, ducking into the novelty shop to avoid the stares he drew.

"Okay, but seriously. You and this girl—"

"Sawyer," Mason reminded him, wandering over to a wall of mugs.

"How does doing romantic shit with this girl cure you of your romanticism?"

He shook his head, reading a few of the quotes on the mugs as he tried to find the right words. He normally found the inspirational quotes endearing, but today he found them suffocating.

Maybe the mission was working.

"It's not just about me. The 'romantic shit' is supposed to break her writer's block, and I think it's helping." He smiled to himself at the thought. "As for me, it's like exposure therapy. I put way too much stock in the butterflies, but butterflies don't last—and neither do my relationships." Not when it wasn't the right person.

Not when *he* might be the problem. He'd put a lot of thought into Sawyer's suggestion to call up his exes, to figure out why his relationships kept failing. After she halted his impulsive decision to call Kara, he hadn't found the nerve to do it again, but he thought about it often, a secret item that he added to their list.

Luis stared at him like he was speaking gibberish. "I guess," he said skeptically. "You do tend to fall like—" He snapped his fingers.

He didn't know how to respond to that. He hadn't planned on telling anyone about his and Sawyer's pact, because he hadn't expected anyone to get it. If anyone could, however, it would be Luis. Luis was always his first call when he needed a night of pizza and beer, because, yeah, Mason *did* eat his feelings after a breakup. The only exception to that rule had been Kara, all thanks to Sawyer distracting him.

"So, like, what's her huge flaw? Because I saw her at the Christkindlmarket before she slipped off like fucking Cinderella at midnight and she's—" He raised his brows, brown eyes widening to imply Sawyer's attractiveness. "How are you planning on *not* falling for her?"

Luis had a point. He had a history of falling for people who weren't falling back. Normally, he'd read too far into the easy, teasing banter he had with Sawyer. It was a habit he needed to unlearn. Because with her, he knew it couldn't become anything. And even if he did spend more time thinking about her than he should, he was leaving. But he couldn't say that to Luis. He'd thought waiting until after the holidays to tell his family about LA was the right call, but right now, the prospect of lying to them for the next few days...

He shook his head to clear it, focusing on the conversation at hand and trying to steer it into less murky waters. "Knowing she has zero interest in a relationship upfront makes it pretty easy to not accidentally get the wrong idea. We're doing 'romantic shit,' yeah, but hanging out with Sawyer doesn't feel like dating. It just feels like hanging out with my friend." He'd almost called her his best friend, a term he'd bestowed on very few people in his life. People he'd known for years, not mere weeks. Yet, he couldn't shake the rightness. Best friend.

The corners of Luis's mouth turned down, considering. "Alright. Well, good luck, I guess. How many things do you have left to ruin?"

He shrugged. "We made a list, but it's kind of open-ended."

Luis frowned but, for once, said nothing.

When *did* it end? Their last "date" was his New Year's Eve party, one week from now. Was that it? Panic gripped his insides. They hadn't discussed it, but the idea that they would go their separate ways once the list was done seemed implied. The thought of never seeing Sawyer again after that didn't sit right with him. He didn't want to think too hard about why he was suddenly contemplating rom-com physics and how to get them stuck in a time loop together.

He forced himself to turn away from the wall of mugs and the person he'd subconsciously been picking one out for, only to turn around and come face-to-face with said person.

"Sawyer!" he said in surprise. Beside him, Luis perked up like a puppy who just heard the word *treat*.

"Álvarez-West," she drawled. She reached past him to grab a mug with a seventies-style mushroom pattern from the shelf. The smell of coconut drowned his senses, and he felt himself relax.

"And I'm Luis," his friend interjected, seizing the opening. "Wanted to introduce myself this time before you could bolt."

Sawyer frowned in faux concentration. "I'm sure I have no idea what you're talking about."

Luis sucked on his teeth and shook his head, smiling.

A redhead appeared at Sawyer's side. "Are we doing the introductions thing? I'm the best friend, Lily."

As Luis and Lily shook hands, Mason locked eyes with Sawyer, biting his lip to keep from grinning. They hadn't discussed whether or not to keep their mission a secret, to keep family and friends out of it, but oh well. Too late now. Luis and Lily were swapping holiday plans like old friends, not two people who'd met five seconds ago.

Can you believe them? Sawyer's dancing green eyes seemed to say.

"You should come!" Lily exclaimed.

Mason tore his gaze from Sawyer's, tuning back into the conversation. "Sorry, what?"

Lily smiled at him knowingly. How long had he and Sawyer been staring at each other? "New Year's Day! We're doing a hangover brunch. I couldn't convince this one to spend New Year's Eve with me—"

"It's you and Beau's first anniversary!" Sawyer protested. "I'm not third-wheeling that!"

Lily waved away her words like she'd heard it a million times. She probably had. "Oh? And what's your excuse for Christmas, then?"

"It's your first Christmas together," Sawyer said emphatically.

"Ohmigod," Lily moaned. "We've spent the last two Christmases together."

"Wait," Mason interjected. He got the impression that Sawyer and her parents didn't speak, so if she wasn't spending the holidays with them or Lily... "What *are* you doing for Christmas?"

Sawyer hesitated, her gaze bouncing around their little circle nervously. "Reading, relaxing, the usual."

"Nonsense," Luis declared. "You're spending it with us. No anniversaries here, so you can't say no—and you don't want to, because my Christmas dinner is better than anything you could cater."

"You can say no," Mason offered softly. Spending Christmas together was leagues deeper than their agreed-upon surface-level rule, but the idea of Sawyer alone on Christmas, eating shredded cheese straight out of the bag...Yeah, no. She was coming to dinner. "But I'd love for you to come."

"She'd *love* to come," Lily declared for her. Before Mason could decipher whether that heavy-handed innuendo was intentional or not, she plowed on. "And if Luis gets you for Christmas, then I get you for New Year's Day."

Sawyer straightened. "I'm sorry, are you two our divorced parents, divvying up the holidays?"

"Yes," Luis and Lily said at the same time.

"What are you doing two weeks after New Year's?" Luis asked Lily, like they were entering business negotiations.

Mason shot him a warning look. That was the tamale party—with the entire extended Álvarez family. The only people more hopelessly romantic than Mason were his aunties. If he brought Sawyer to that, he'd never hear the end of it. For the rest of his life, they'd ask him about the spicy blonde he brought over that one time, why he'd let her get away—and he'd never have a satisfactory answer.

"We'll just start with Christmas and New Year's," Luis amended with a clearing of his throat. "For now." As if there would be more holidays to divvy up in the future, and not like they'd be out of each other's lives in a week's time.

Sawyer shot Mason a befuddled look, clearly wondering the same thing as him: How had this happened in the span of five minutes? But Luis's question was still lingering in the back of Mason's mind. When did this thing with Sawyer end? Their last concrete plan was New Year's Eve, but Lily's brunch would buy him another day. He wasn't ready to lose her. His friend. His friend whom he liked spending friendly time with, as a friend. Who looked fucking amazing in the baggy old-man sweater she wore, sexy in a totally platonic way.

"Alright, well," Sawyer said brightly, returning the mug to the shelf with a wistful look. "I'd say it's been fun, but, frankly, I'm terrified to let you two scheme further, so Mason and I are gonna skedaddle. IKEA's calling, gotta go ruin romance and maybe friendship now, too. Just to be safe."

They said their goodbyes, Sawyer practically dragging him out of the store. They both glanced back at the last minute, Luis and Lily waving them off like proud parents on a porch stoop.

"I don't trust that," Sawyer said with a frown.

"Oh, I definitely don't trust that."

CHAPTER THIRTEEN

<u>KISS ME SO WE CAN HIDE</u> – The bad guys are
coming, and if we mash our faces together,
we'll become invisible. Probably.

"God, I hate this place," Mason mumbled under his breath.

They'd been in IKEA for only five minutes—not counting the ten minutes it took them to find each other again after parking—and it was the second time he'd said it. Sawyer stood on her tiptoes to peer around the family in front of them who had stopped to examine the room setup, effectively blocking the walkway.

She let out a frustrated sigh that sent her bangs fluttering. "Well, we're here now and there's only one way out: through."

"This is my personal horror movie."

"You're the one who needed a nightstand," she grumbled. "I don't get why you couldn't do it the easy way."

"Oh yeah? What's that?"

She scoffed. "Get wine drunk and impulse order one online. Obviously."

Spotting a gap in the crowd, Mason grabbed her hand and dragged her through with him, his tall stature making the family part for him in a way they hadn't for her. He dropped her hand once they were through, a strange tingling sensation left in its wake.

"I tried," he grumbled. "I want one to match my current one, but they all look the same online."

"Do you really have so many sex toys that you need a second nightstand?"

Mason's eyes danced as he stared down at her. "Some people use their nightstands for more than just vibrators, Sawyer."

She raised her brows pointedly. "Like what?"

"Books?"

Touché.

Mason slowed his steps, something unreadable crossing his expression.

"What?" she asked, glancing around for the source of his sudden change in demeanor.

"Do you wanna get out of here?" he asked urgently.

"I mean, yes, always, but why?"

He exhaled heavily, pushing up the brim of his gray beanie to run a hand through his absurdly shiny hair. It was longer than when they'd first met a month ago, his previously short sides now grown out and curling above his ears. He pulled the hat down, and Sawyer resisted the strange urge to push it back, to play with the barely there curls.

"I don't need it."

Sawyer's brows knit together. That was a valid reason and one she used often, but she didn't exactly have money to spare. If Mason wanted a second nightstand, he could definitely get one.

"I was only getting one because Kara always complained about not having one when she spent the night."

Ah. Sawyer puffed out her cheeks, unsure how to navigate this. "Okay," she hedged carefully. "Do *you* want one, though? We are already here."

"That's true…" He puckered his lips, considering. "No," he said decisively. "I'm not getting one, because *I* don't need it. It would only be used by a houseguest, and the whole point of this is I'm not looking for one."

"Attaboy," she cheered.

"Which means," he said, deflated. "We are suffering at IKEA for no fucking reason."

"Ugh," Sawyer groaned. "Wanna go test the beds?"

"Sawyer, there are children here," Mason chastised.

She rolled her eyes. "Not like that, you horndog." She gestured for him to follow her, the yellow arrows on the floor guiding them through the maze. When they reached the floor of living room setups, they froze. Mason's face was everywhere. A more groomed Mason in powder-blue scrubs and a lab coat was walking down a hospital hallway, having a muted conversation with his costar ex, Kara.

Sawyer's gaze slid to Mason in slow motion, as if they didn't move, no one would notice them frozen in the middle of the aisle. She'd never seen Mason so pale, his face transforming into the blandly smiling mask that she'd come to know as his PR Face, so unlike his usually expressive self.

She pressed her lips together, eyes darting across the massive floor. They had to get out of here. People were giving them dirty looks for blocking the walkway, and it was the last thing they needed—people looking at Mason while his face was on every wall. Mercifully, the episode moved on to a scene that didn't have him in it, but it was only a matter of time.

Sawyer dragged Mason off to the side, into a tiny cubby between rooms, attempting to bodily conceal him—a feat that would be easier if he weren't so much bigger than her. Arching onto her tiptoes so her face concealed his, she steadied herself against his chest by curling her fingers around his coat lapels.

She hadn't been this close to Mason—had made a point to avoid it—in a long time, and it was, well, a lot. He smelled fantastic.

"What are you doing?" he whispered.

"Hiding you," she breathed.

She had a front-row seat to the smile that spread across his face, his eyes crinkling in the corners. "A valiant effort," he commended her, tapping his forehead against hers. "But if we get caught all snuggled up, that's worse for me than being caught shopping at IKEA."

"Fuck," Sawyer breathed. "I didn't think of that." She picked up a nearby succulent, holding it up as if inspecting it, and effectively hiding their faces from view. "I was thinking more like, let's ruin the 'kiss me so we don't get made by the bad guys' trope."

"Is that a trope?" Mason said, tilting his head to the side quizzically.

She swatted his chest. "It totally is. Think, action-adventure rom-com."

One side of Mason's mouth quirked up in a cocksure grin. "If you wanna kiss me, Greene, you don't need to come up with an excuse."

What in the Wattpad?

"Cool it, Álvarez. Rule number two, remember?"

"Oh, I remember the rules. You're the one trying to kiss me," he said flippantly. "The scrubs really did it for you, huh?" He flicked his attention to the nearest TV, where his character was back, looking admittedly very attractive in his powder-blue scrubs, leaning against a lab counter, feet crossed at the ankles.

Sawyer whisper-screamed, "Oh my God, is that Mason West?"

The smile slid from Mason's face. "You wouldn't dare."

Sawyer gave him a shit-eating grin. "You do look cute in the scrubs, though. You should wear them for me sometime," she teased.

"Rule number two," he said, faux scandalized, the effect ruined by the laugh rumbling out of him, jostling her against his chest. He braced a hand at the small of her back to hold her steady. "Okay," he said seriously. "Safe to say I'm immune to IKEA-adjacent romantic notions."

"I think that was true before we got here, but—" Sawyer mimed crossing an item off the list before making eye contact with him and adding another tally mark under her name. As predicted, she'd won this one, no contest.

"Fair. We probably could've skipped this one. No one could make this place fun for me."

Sawyer snorted. "Agreed."

"Alright. Game plan."

"Right," Sawyer said gravely. "How are we getting out of here alive?"

"Well, the plant has to come with us. It now knows too much."

Sawyer bounced excitedly as an idea took hold. "It can be our Love Fern! Except, a love succulent because succulents are cooler and only—" She checked the price tag. "Eight ninety-nine."

Mason hummed thoughtfully. "You do have big Kate Hudson energy."

"Thank you," Sawyer breathed, deeply flattered.

Mason laughed. "So, do we keep the Love Succulent alive or let it die?"

Sawyer frowned. "Feels like bad karma to purposefully let a plant die, but I can't keep anything alive, so…maybe skip the Love Succulent?"

Mason ran his thumb over one of the green leaves, squeezing it gently. Sawyer had a visceral reaction to it, the memory of his thumb brushing across her lip, pressing down between her thighs.

He grinned mischievously at her. Could he tell what she was thinking? Plants. They were talking about plants.

"Let's make it our Friendship Succulent." He studied her out of the corner of his eye. "We're officially friends now, right?"

Sawyer shrugged. "I mean, we do know each other biblically and still like each other, so yeah."

Mason's answering smile made her chest ache. Not with, like, feelings or anything, but, like, a heart attack maybe. He was too pretty. She was just reacting to his nice face. That she'd sat on, once upon a time. She curb-stomped that thought.

All her not masturbating had her feeling like a frayed nerve, and the close proximity had her sweating more than a Victorian woman catching a flash of bare wrist. She really needed to get out of this alcove that was making her all too aware of everywhere they were touching.

Mason's face went back into mission mode. "Okay—" Pointing over her shoulder, he laid out their plan to get through the maze of couches and coffee tables as efficiently as possible. It was silly and possibly making a bigger hubbub than just strolling across the floor, but it was *fun*.

Escape route plotted, they waited for the TVs to cut to a non-Mason scene. Both of them were so tightly wound, anticipation was a palpable thing between them.

The episode changed to another subplot and, miraculously, a gap in the crowd appeared, the two of them slipping back into the throng of holiday shoppers.

As they wove between Ektorp couches and Knarrevik nightstands

and more things with more consonants than Sawyer could pho-
netically parse, Mason grabbed her hand to keep them from being
separated by a family with multiple crying children. The swooping
sensation in her stomach was definitely due to her almost tripping on
a stray table leg and not at the skin contact.

When they finally reached the base level, they were both flushed
and breathing heavily.

Mason dropped her hand, and they grinned at each other like
they'd just stolen the Declaration of Independence. Then they spied
the ungodly long line. Nothing killed the mood like a warehouse
packed with cranky holiday shoppers.

Not that there was a mood to kill, or anything.

"We don't have to get it," Sawyer announced. She tried to take
their laughably tiny purchase from him, but he tucked it under his
arm like a football.

"Oh, we're getting it," Mason said definitely. "And I expect you
to be so goddamn inspired by this excursion that you dedicate your
novel to our Friendship Succulent."

"For Friendshipulent," she crooned. "My steadfast companion
through the murky drafting waters."

"Are you writing again?" The way Mason's face lit up was...
something. Made her insides feel all weird and gooey.

Her usual nonanswer stuck in her throat. Talking about her books
was deeply personal, and they'd agreed to keep things superficial,
only sharing list-relevant information, but wasn't breaking her writer's
block the whole reason she agreed to this weird mission-quest thing?
She wanted him to know his efforts were working. Besides, her pitch
to Emily was due soon, so this was good practice.

Before she could think twice, she told him the story she'd been
hoarding inside her brain—and three different restarted Word

documents titled "New Idea," "New Idea_Take Two," and "New Idea for Real This Time." She told him of the guy and the girl who had fallen in love and let that love go by the wayside, of the guy's terminally ill mother and the ring she'd gifted him, of the girl not being able to give an answer to his proposal, and their journey to honor his mother's gift by trying to rekindle what they once had, one romance trope at a time.

Mason smiled softly as she spoke, the two of them shuffling closer to the checkout line all the while. "So, basically the opposite of what we're doing. I love it."

Sawyer nodded. She pulled out her phone to jot down the two new ideas she'd had while messily explaining the plot to him, the book seemingly unfolding in her mind as she spoke. He said nothing as her thumbs flew across the screen. By the time she finished, she had a wall of typo-riddled text, but it felt like a light at the end of the tunnel, tugging her forward to the next scenes she couldn't wait to write. When she looked up again, they'd reached the front of the queue, and Mason had already paid for Friendshipulent.

"What? No!" she protested.

"Just make sure I get to play the lead when your book gets picked up for an adaptation."

She raised her brows at him. "You know authors have no control over any of that."

He frowned. "Yeah. They should, though."

She shrugged. "That's why I haven't sold any of my other film rights. There have been offers, and I could definitely use the money, but you saw what they did to *Almost Lovers*. It was like the studio had an idea for a movie they wanted to make and my book was doing well, so they took scraps of my book, slapped my name and title on it, and now the thing I'm most known for is barely even mine."

That wasn't the full story, and she had the uncanny feeling that Mason could tell she was holding back the real reason that adaptation didn't sit well with her.

He frowned, but didn't push the subject, thankfully. "That's not fair. Your book is good. All your books are good, prime for an adaptation. Producers should want your input."

That was *not* how it worked, but there was an edge to his voice, a protectiveness that warmed her insides. "Thank you," she said sincerely.

"Of course. What else are friends for? And since we are officially friends," Mason announced, handing her Friendshipulent. "I will pick you up tomorrow at two o'clock for Christmas dinner."

Her heart skipped a beat. Meeting the family. She wasn't Meeting the Family, but wow. "Okay," she said tightly. Since the tree-decorating detour, she'd upheld her resolution to keep things between them about the list, but on this, she would have to break her rule. She really didn't want to be alone on Christmas.

Mason beamed, his smile softening as he met her gaze. "And I'm really happy to hear you're writing again. It's kinda cool, being a part of the process."

Sawyer hoped the smile she gave him read as genuine. She tried to let his excitement buoy her, but she couldn't help but brace for the inevitable moment when it stopped being "cool," when the veil of mystery was pulled back. The late nights and early mornings and days spent with her butt glued to her chair, and *no*, she wasn't writing words, but sitting in that chair and trying was a part of it; and no, she couldn't just pop out to the store or to a party, because writing time was sacred, and when the inspiration was flowing, she was its captive. The creative well wasn't a tap that she could turn on and off when it was convenient for her—much less for others.

Maybe one day she'd find someone who got it—got her—but first, she needed to get her shit back together. Then, maybe, she could share it with someone. For now, she would guard this fragile ember of her career with her life.

Oblivious to her mental spiral, Mason's smile faltered, his attention darting behind her briefly. "I think I had fun...at IKEA," he said, mildly disgusted.

She huffed in surprise. "Y'know, I think I did, too, somehow." Her shoulders drooped in defeat as she mimed removing the tally mark from under her name and giving it to him. "I'm sorry. I'm not doing a very good job of ruining things, am I?"

He shook his head. "No, don't change. I think this is better, actually. If you were horrendous, I'd just blame it all not being fun on that. This way..." He chewed on his bottom lip thoughtfully. "This way someone has to be more fun than you for me to be tempted."

She scoffed. "Well, good luck, because I am a barrel of fun."

He grinned cheekily, and her stomach swooped.

"You are, too, by the way," she said softly. "See you tomorrow?"

He nodded. "See you tomorrow," he echoed. He took one step back before doing a full spin and coming back to stand before her. "I forgot, uh—" He rubbed the back of his neck, glancing around the parking lot to make sure no one was paying them any attention. "My family doesn't know about LA, or the production company, or me leaving *Diagnostics*, so—"

Sawyer mimed zipping her lips. It wouldn't be a family dinner without some level of secrecy and deceit. At least Mason was hiding good news.

"Thank you," he breathed. "I want to get through the holidays before breaking the news that I'm leaving."

"I get it." She absolutely didn't. She'd never been close with her family. Coming out as bi at seventeen had squashed any chance of that changing. When she went to college in another state, they hadn't been surprised, hadn't batted an eye when she said she wasn't coming home for holidays or summer break or ever again. Mason was lucky to have a family that would miss him. She was more than a little touched that he'd confided in her at all.

"Tomorrow," he promised with a roguish grin.

"Tomorrow," she echoed.

He took a few steps back before turning, his long strides carrying him swiftly across the parking lot.

The happy feeling in her gut soured as she watched his dwindling figure. He'd probably only confided in her about LA because he didn't care about her like that. It wasn't like he was leaving her behind, not like his family. This thing between them had always had an expiration date. There was no "them."

Tearing her gaze off his back, she tamped down the twisting sensation in her gut as she mentally crossed one more thing off their rapidly dwindling list. They didn't have many items left, and she steeled her resolve. He'd helped her, and it was time to hold up her end of their bargain. And maybe Mason was right. She'd been going about this all wrong. Ruining romance wasn't the answer. She needed to raise Mason's bar for romance, to set the new standard.

She was going to become the blueprint for Mason's other half.

CHAPTER FOURTEEN

SECRETS, SECRETS – Romance statistics calculate
that if you have a secret, the odds of it coming out at
the absolute worst possible moment are 100 percent.

The knock came at *exactly* two o'clock. Which was perfect,
because she'd been ready for an hour. Or so she thought.

Swinging the door open, she saw Mason had swapped out his
usual gray peacoat for a trim black one. Her hand reached out of
its own volition, tugging open the lapels of his coat. Her stomach
dropped. He looked especially dapper in his fitted charcoal-gray
slacks and crimson button-down with the top two buttons undone.
If his sleeves were rolled up under that coat, it was over for her. She
couldn't be held responsible for her actions where exposed forearms
were involved. Her libido simply couldn't take it. Whoever made the
rule about them not sleeping together again was delusional, clearly.

"Oh no," she said, taking a step back, fisting the hem of her oversized sweater nervously.

"It's fine," Mason said immediately. "It's my fault. I should have
warned you my family is extra. This way, at least one of us is comfortable. Let's go."

She shook her head adamantly. "Give me, like, five minutes. You
can time me."

He raised one brow, tugging his phone from his coat pocket with an amused quirk of his lips. She watched as his thumb swiped up, and she bolted across her apartment before he could start the timer. She'd need every second.

She didn't have very many nice dresses. She didn't often have the occasion to wear them, and she sent a telepathic thank-you to Lily for getting married in the winter and not cursing her with a hideous maid-of-honor dress. She grumbled as she fished out her least favorite bra from the back of her lingerie drawer, the one with the poke-y underwire. It was the only one that worked with the dress, however, so she apologized to each boob personally before hooking it on.

"I will let you out as soon as I can," she promised them.

She kicked her comfortable pleather leggings into the corner of her closet before stepping into a pair of patterned black tights. Last year's maid-of-honor dress was a simple, long-sleeved wrap dress made of emerald velvet and felt like a hug. She cinched it around her waist before giving herself a quick once-over in the mirror. She darted back into the closet and nudged aside her weather-appropriate ankle boots and slipped on her Mary Jane pumps.

"Will this do?" she asked as she reemerged from her bedroom.

Mason looked up from his phone and froze like a video game glitch. The timer on his phone went off and he jumped, a myriad of expressions flashing across his face as he silenced it without looking. He cleared his throat. "That'll definitely do," he said tightly.

Silence stretched between them, every inch of her aware of the slow drag of Mason's gaze over her. When he raked his teeth over his bottom lip, she felt it in her core, the distance between them both too far and too close. She gave her head a little shake to clear it, pulling the neckline of her dress closed to hide the flush in her chest.

"Great." The word came out garbled, as if she'd experience the entirety of puberty in that one sentence. "But now I need something else to wear for New Year's Eve, because this is the full extent of my nice dress wardrobe."

"I'll buy you a dress," he said offhand.

Sawyer froze in the middle of adjusting her T-straps, teetering slightly to the side. Mason reached out, steadying her.

"You don't— I didn't mean—"

"Sawyer." He interrupted her stammering with a smile. Had he always said her name like that? Surely, he'd said her name plenty of times before, so why did it feel so...*intimate*? "If I'm dragging you to a snobby party, I should provide you with a snobby dress."

"Okay. The snobbiest," she agreed with a limp smile. She was still thinking about the way her name sounded in his deep, rumbling voice that she forgot she hated accepting help, but she sure as shit couldn't afford a dress nice enough for a Hollywood party—even Chicago Hollywood.

Mason shoved his hands in his pockets, pulling out a small package wrapped in gold paper. She froze as he extended it to her.

"I didn't get you anything," she confessed. "You didn't say we were doing presents!"

Mason waved her concern away. "It's for Friendshipulent."

She eyed him warily. God, this was embarrassing. She hadn't made a new friend in so long, she forgot that they did things like this. She bought gifts for Lily every year, but that was *Lily*. She was the closest thing Sawyer had to family. The gold wrapping paper fell away, and she slid off the square lid. It was the mushroom mug she'd been eyeing at the mall. Her gaze flitted between him and the mug. "How did you—?"

"Luis grabbed it for me after we left."

"Then it *wasn't* for Friendshipulent. We hadn't adopted him yet!" she accused with a jab of her finger to his hard chest. Nevertheless, she strode over to the succulent in its plastic pot, slipping it into the vintage mug, the orange mushroom pattern and the sage-green plant a happy combination.

"I'll have to get some soil to repot it."

Mason stared at her blankly, a smile slowly spreading across his face.

"What?"

He pressed his lips together, shaking his head.

"What?"

"Sawyer, I—" A laugh bubbled past his lips. "I don't know how to break this to you, but... Friendshipulent is a fake succulent."

She gasped, snatching the plant off the counter. Upon closer inspection, she could see where the layers notched together, the edge of the mold used to create the squishy leaves.

"You watered it, didn't you?"

"No," she lied, meeting his gaze sternly. They stared each other down for a long moment before Sawyer broke. "Fine, I did, but it's not my fault that all succulents look fake, so, whatever. I'm getting you a present," she pivoted, praying a change of subject would cause her face to stop burning.

"You in that dress and those tights is gift enough."

Well, that didn't help. The flush in her cheeks spread to her chest, her core. Gathering herself, she put on her best come-hither look, allowing one leg to slide out of the dress's slit. "Oh yeah?"

He fixed her with a stern look, his Adam's apple bobbing as he swallowed thickly. "Don't be a tease. At least, any more than you usually are, by just, y'know"—he gestured in her general direction—"existing."

Her heartbeat was akin to a gallop in her ears. She really needed him to stop talking like this. Of course, she knew he was attracted to her on some level. They'd slept together. But they weren't *into* each other. She needed to divert this conversation into calmer waters. Friendly ones. Cool-as-a-cucumber waters. Sawyer could be cool, even if her neglected vagina was anything but.

She hummed thoughtfully. "I mean," she said skeptically. "We did sleep together the night we met, so I don't know if that makes me a very good tease."

He laughed, effectively breaking the tension. "Agree to disagree."

The tension snapped right back into place. She tore her gaze away from his, her chest feeling tight.

Glancing at the time on her microwave, she crossed over to the fridge to grab the fancy cheese she'd panic bought yesterday. She'd googled "housewarming gifts for someone who probably already has everything and you're hella broke." Surprisingly, there was an article for that. Unsurprisingly, there hadn't been an article for her first search: "what to bring to your one-night stand's family's house for Christmas dinner." Given the last minute–ness, neither search had been particularly fruitful. So, after checking with Mason that his entire family wasn't tragically lactose intolerant, she went with her default: cheese. As far as Sawyer was concerned, it wasn't a party unless there was cheese.

She gestured with the wooden cheese wheel box toward the door. "Shall we?"

Silence fell between them as she locked up, the silence stretching as she followed him to his car. Something was different, but she couldn't put her finger on it. They were no strangers to flirty comments, but today it felt charged. Before, they'd laugh it off, remind each other of the rules, but now . . . it refused to be stifled.

She ran back the events at IKEA, the afternoon at the skating rink, relived all their conversations, but she couldn't pinpoint anything out of place. They'd always teased each other, maybe with a bit more innuendo than necessary, but, like, they'd fucked each other's brains out a month ago. Of course they made sex jokes. It was fine. It was chillllll. They were *friends*. Friends could make innuendos, right? She was reading too much into it. She blamed it on all the masturbating she hadn't been doing lately. It was making her tense.

She silently made a pact with her vagina to take care of business later tonight if it could just cool it for a few hours.

* * *

The forty-five-minute drive passed in a blur. Despite talking the entire time, Sawyer couldn't remember a single thing they talked about, only coming to when Mason began parallel parking along a side street with houses that cost more than all of Sawyer's advances combined.

"What does your sister do?" she crowed, gawking at the houses and trying to suss out which one was Margot's.

Mason didn't answer right away, his eyes on the rearview. Sawyer melted a few inches lower in her seat when he placed his hand on the back of her headrest, smoothly sliding into the only available parking spot by turning the wheel in expert increments with the heel of his palm. She was too horny to be in public if she was getting off on parallel parking.

"She's an econometrician," Mason answered as he shifted the car into park.

Sawyer considered any job title that had more syllables than she had fingers on one hand to mean one thing: money. "Nice job, Luis," she murmured appreciatively.

Mason grinned. "Don't count him out. I made sure to connect

him with my costars when he opened his gym, so he was doing just fine long before he and Margot got together."

"Well, shit, connect me!" she said without thinking.

Something unreadable flashed across his face for the second time that evening, and she flinched internally. People probably badgered him for connections all the time. This—them—had never been about that. Sure, her career was floundering, and in a roundabout way, he was helping, but she couldn't live with herself if she took a handout. She would save her career by herself or not at all.

Mason opened his mouth to speak, but she cut him off. "Sorry, I didn't mean anything by it."

He closed his mouth, hesitating a moment before nodding resolutely and getting out of the car.

She waited until the door shut behind him before letting out a long-suffering sigh. Why were things so weird with them tonight? She hastily composed herself before stepping out of the car.

Mason was unloading immaculately wrapped presents from the trunk—a smaller pile than she'd anticipated, given his aforementioned large family.

"Fess up," she teased. "You ate all those fudge boxes from the Christkindlmarket."

Mason laughed, patting his toned stomach affectionately. "This is the body fudge built, no doubt. But no. The extended family celebrates on Christmas Eve, so it's just immediate family and a few friends today. I gave the kiddos their gifts last night."

"Favorite uncle status secured?" she asked.

"It was never in question," he said confidently as they walked up the freshly shoveled sidewalk to a beautiful brick town house with a little Christmas tree in the yard. Glancing up and down the block, she noticed that every house had a small decorated tree in their yard.

From the porch, she could see a second tree beyond the window. This was the kind of rich people shit she could get behind. *Two trees.*

The wind picked up, sneaking under her coat, and she shivered, leaning into Mason's warmth automatically as he rang the doorbell.

"It's open!" a voice called.

Mason removed his hand from her lower back just long enough to open the door, guiding her with him across the threshold. He placed the handful of presents at the base of the tree before helping her out of her coat. As he hung it in the hall closet, a little boy came careening into the entryway.

"Uncle Mason! Uncle Mason!" he screamed.

Mason scooped the kid into his arms, making the little boy squeal as he tickled his middle. Sawyer took the moment to take in the house. The foyer was predominantly devoted to the tree, but beyond it, there was a living room best described as a study in white. Sawyer couldn't fathom owning a white couch. She'd ruin it in a day. Minutes, probably.

The sounds of laughter and cooking flowed out from a door to their left. Luis appeared in the entryway, wearing an apron and furiously whisking something in a bowl. At the sight of his dad, the little boy squirmed out of Mason's arms and made a beeline for the kitchen.

Luis yelled something after the boy in Spanish before turning back to them. "Sawyer!" He greeted her warmly as Mason tucked her shoes into the closet next to his. "You look lovely."

"Thanks, man," Mason joked.

Luis frowned. "Didn't you wear that last year?"

Mason glanced down at his clothes helplessly. "You cannot win in this family," he muttered under his breath to Sawyer.

She grinned, leaning in and air-kissing Luis on the cheek. "Thank you for inviting me."

"Of course!" Luis said, like they were old friends and not strangers who had met yesterday. But Luis was one of those people who made you feel instantly comfortable. "C'mon," he said with a jerk of his head. She fell into step beside him, bypassing the kitchen and through the living room to...a second living room?

Luis paused, face screwing up as he spotted Mason following them. "What are you doing? Suit up." He handed Mason the bowl of cream he'd been whipping and eased the fancy cheese from Sawyer's grasp, handing it to Mason as well. "Your dad just started the stuffing."

Mason's eyes darted to hers, as if asking for her permission to leave her alone, a gesture that didn't go unnoticed by Luis.

"I got this one," Luis said, all but shooing Mason out of the room. Turning back to Sawyer, he grinned, eyes crinkling in the corners. "Let's get you a drink before introductions. One outsider to another—" He lowered his voice. "This family is best with a drink or two in you."

Sawyer nodded knowingly. "Ah. My family is the same—but with a drink and also a few hundred miles."

Luis laughed knowingly, coming to a stop in front of the bar. "I get that completely. I've been spending the holidays with the Wests since I was sixteen because my family is..." He trailed off, staring at the wall.

Sawyer understood without him saying anything. Her mother and pastor father hadn't spoken to her in years. It was easier for everyone if she stayed gone. Luis blinked, turning back on his million-watt smile. "The Wests are great," he clarified. "They're—well, you're a writer, so you'll know what I mean when I say they're *characters*."

She grinned wickedly. "Don't threaten me with a good time."

Matching her grin, Luis grabbed a bottle from the back bar. "Mason said you prefer whiskey? And two ice cubes but only if they're square?" he asked, as if unsure he remembered that correctly.

She nodded in confirmation, her throat suddenly too tight to speak. She really had to stop getting emotional over ice cube shapes.

Luis broke the paper seal over the brand-new bottle before pulling the cork out. Jesus Christ. Had they really gone out and bought a bottle for her? He portioned a healthy amount into a rocks glass and popped two ice cubes into it before picking up a bottle of tequila and pouring a shot for himself. "Cheers," he said conspiratorially.

She clinked her glass against his and took a small sip as he tossed back his shot.

Luis gestured for her to follow him, talking over his shoulder as they walked toward the adjoining dining room, decked to the nines in Christmas decorations, each place setting complete with a unique ornament. This was some HGTV-level hosting shit Sawyer was wholly unaccustomed to. "—and the red salsa is gringo-safe spicy, but proceed with caution around the green one. Okay." He clapped his hands together. "I gotta get back to cooking, so I'll let Mason give you the tour later, whenever the two of you need to sneak off."

"Oh, we're not together," Sawyer insisted good-naturedly.

Luis raised his eyebrows. "I know," he said, but it sounded like *Sure, bud.*

As they rounded the corner, Sawyer nearly tripped over her feet. She didn't cook, but if she had a kitchen like this, she would learn.

The island alone was as big as her apartment's galley kitchen. A massive slab of quartz with veins of gold running through it matched the tile behind the stove and counters. Mason was chatting with an attractive older man that could only be his father, both wearing aprons that matched the one Luis wore. Luis wandered over to inspect the stove, and as the four women occupying the plush barstools fixed their attention on her, Sawyer took a large gulp of her drink.

At the lull in conversation, Mason looked up, snapping to her side like a magnet.

"Everyone, this is Sawyer. Sawyer, my mom, Moira—" He gestured to a beautiful older woman with white-blond hair and Mason's eyes—though hers were an icy blue to Mason's warm brown. Sawyer sent up a prayer that she aged half as gracefully.

"Pleasure to meet you," she said congenially, her expression sharpening as it landed on Mason. "Though we've heard nothing about you because my son prefers I learn about his love life from the tabloids."

"Mom," Mason groaned. "I told you. Sawyer's a friend. Retract the claws."

Moira pursed her lips, swirling her goblet of white wine slowly. "Very well. But you're not getting any younger, and I want grandbabies."

To Moira's left, Margot made a choking noise. "Mom, you have two already." She gestured emphatically to the tortilla chip–covered child in her lap.

"Yes, and I love my Milo," Moira said affectionately, brushing a crumb from the boy's cheek. "And my Max!" She called to the house at large, an ominous giggle resounding somewhere to Sawyer's right that she couldn't place. "But we need someone to carry on the West name."

"My name isn't West. Mom, *you* named me," Mason pointed out. From the stove, Mason's dad cackled. "And you know I don't want kids."

Moira bristled, taking a prim sip of her wine. "Yes, well, you also didn't want to take the *Diagnostics* gig—" Addressing the room at large, she continued, "But I told him to just take the meeting." Then, back to Mason: "And look how happy you are now."

Silence fell for a moment before Mason started laughing. Sawyer wondered if anyone else picked up on the slight strain to his laugh. "Anyway," he said tightly. "Margot, you've met—" His sister gave a small wave before hastily stopping the child in her lap from upending the plate in front of him. "And Milo. My mom's best friend, Lynn." The older woman next to Margot waved, her many, many bracelets twinkling. "Her daughter, Bex." By comparison, Bex was considerably less adorned, but striking all the same with her large hazel eyes and honey-brown curls. "My father, Antonio, and Luis you know," Mason finished.

Sawyer took a deep breath. "Moira, Margot, Milo, Max—" Another giggle, the boy's hiding spot still a mystery. "Lynn, Bex, Antonio, and Luis. Got it."

"And I'm Mason," he added.

She rolled her eyes, and he grinned down at her, giving her a gentle nudge toward the empty chair next to Bex. The kitchen island was laden with appetizers—most notably, a massive cheese board that had her humming the Hilary Duff classic "What Dreams Are Made Of" under her breath.

Rejoining his father at the stove, Mason rolled up the sleeves of his button-down, toned forearms on full display. Sawyer started sweating in a place that wasn't her underarms.

The arms, the snug fit of his pants, the goddamn apron…It was all really doing it for her. She was tempted to sneak a picture and send it to Lily, captioned with fire and eggplant emojis, but she knew exactly what Lily would say in response. While Sawyer was normally immune to Lily's goading and prodding, tonight it might be the straw that broke the camel's back. Or the final drop in the bucket that broke the dam she'd built to contain her (purely physical) attraction to Mason. And maybe Lily *was* right. The fact that she was here, introduced to his family like it's no big deal—because it was no big deal to him—was proof enough that he wasn't falling for her. Maybe they could sleep together and still do their mission. Maybe just once, to dispel this persistent tension between them, to get it out of their systems.

"So, Sawyer," Lynn called, leaning around her daughter. Judging by the knowing smirk she wore, she had definitely seen Sawyer ogling Mason with *fuck me* eyes. "What do you do?"

Sawyer was so grateful for the interruption to her lust-laden thoughts she almost kissed the woman, momentarily forgetting she hated this question, simply for the follow-up questions it necessitated.

She traced the pattern of the cut-crystal tumbler to avoid making eye contact, forcing lightness into her tone as she answered. "I'm a writer."

"She's a *New York Times* bestselling author," Mason supplied.

Her gaze snapped to him, where he watched her with crossed arms, wooden spoon in one hand and *those goddamn forearms*. As the women at the island beside her cooed in excitement for her, he winked before turning back to the stove.

The conversation played out exactly like it always did. "Anything I would know?" followed by "Oh, I loved that movie!" followed by Sawyer choking out a thank-you despite the fact that she felt no ownership of it. She wasn't the only author to have their work bastardized in an adaptation, but that didn't make it sting any less. Accepting praise for it felt like reopening a half-healed wound every time.

"The book's better," Mason supplied. Sawyer felt a rush of affection for him so strong that she was grateful she was already sitting down.

"Well, of course," Moira agreed. "I've always said writers don't get enough credit. We actors interpret, yes, but there's not much you can do if the source material is bad." The approving look Moira gave Sawyer made her chest feel tight. Though Mason's mother was on her eye level, Moira seemed larger than life from her perch at the other end of the island. It wasn't hard to imagine how that presence translated on-screen. It was like sitting across the table from Meryl Streep and Meryl Streep had just paid you a compliment. But she could also easily see how that presence could be stifling.

"Like your role on *In the Hills*?" Lynn nagged.

Everyone erupted into hoots and howls.

"We don't talk about that project in this house!" Moira declared, feigning upset.

Sawyer smiled behind her drink, watching as they fell into what was clearly a running joke among them. She caught Luis's attention, his eyes crinkling at the corners.

Bex turned to her, shaking her head in disbelief. "They bring it up every year without fail. After a few years, you know the whole routine."

The kitchen was an absolute cacophony as everyone talked over each other, but Sawyer couldn't help but think it was a right sight better than the oppressive silence that had been her family dinners. From the raucous laughter to the mash-up of cultures represented in the dishes on the kitchen island—this felt more like the Queermas dinners she'd spent with Sadie and their friends. She didn't realize how much she'd missed it, how lonely she'd been, until now.

"So what do you do, Bex?" Anything to keep herself from going down that mental rabbit hole.

"Oh." Bex blushed. "I'm an intimacy coordinator."

Sawyer sat up straighter. "That's awesome."

Bex allowed herself a little smile. "Thanks. That's not usually the response I get." When Sawyer raised her brows in question, Bex sighed. "Usually there's some suggestive joke, which is ironic, because that's kind of the whole reason my role is needed on set in the first place."

Before Sawyer could ask more about her job, another giggle resounded from somewhere in the room. Sawyer glanced around, this time spotting the mismatched socks peeking out from behind the window curtains. Sawyer made a mental note to give the drapes a wide berth.

"So," Lynn said loudly. Though Sawyer was beginning to suspect that was Lynn's one and only volume level. "How do you and Mason know each other?"

The din of the kitchen died down immediately, and Sawyer found Mason's eyes across the room. "We got trapped in an elevator together." She wished there were a less rom-com-y way to spin it, but that was how it happened.

"Oh, you poor thing," Lynn trilled to Mason. "After what happened on set—"

"We don't need to talk about it," Mason said with a flush.

At Sawyer's confused expression, Bex leaned in. "A few years back, they were filming a scene at this sketchy warehouse, and Mason and his costar got stuck in the service elevator for half an hour."

"In my defense, it felt *much* longer."

"I'm sure Davi Shah having a full-blown panic attack did not help."

"I've never felt more useless or helpless in my life. I didn't know phobias were contagious, but experiencing that with her … It stuck."

Lynn sighed wistfully. "I always hoped the two of you would get together. You two had such good chemistry."

"Mom," Bex chastised. "Not in front of—" She gestured meaningfully to Sawyer.

Sawyer interjected at the same time as Mason.

"Oh, we're not—"

"Just friends."

The tension in the kitchen could've been cut with a knife, the only sound Antonio chopping, blissfully ignorant to the conversation—or too used his family's antics to care.

Luis cleared his throat pointedly. "Personally, I'm glad you're not together. I like you, and maybe this way, you'll last longer than the next few months."

Everyone laughed, save for Mason, who threw a green bean at Luis. Sawyer watched it all unfold from behind her drink, which needed refilling, but she had a feeling she needed to stay sharp around this bunch.

Any buzz she might have had was immediately squashed by Bex's next words.

"Oh, that's right!" she trilled. "When are you leaving? When shooting wraps?"

Sawyer expected the entire room to freeze, to slowly turn and stare at Mason, but it didn't. Lynn was talking baby talk to Milo while Margot bounced him in her lap. Luis and Antonio were inspecting the turkey through the oven window. Mason's back visibly tensed beneath his burgundy shirt, turning slowly. His PR Face was firmly in place, but his eyes gave him away in the nervous flick toward his mother. Moira moved a cup out of Milo's reach as if on instinct alone, refilling her glass of wine with her other hand.

"Where are you going, dear?" she asked Mason offhand, clearly unaware of the gravity of what Bex had just revealed.

Bex's mouth parted slightly as she realized what she'd done. Grabbing her own glass of wine, she stared down into it like she wanted to drown in it.

"To LA, for work," Mason said with forced casualness.

Sawyer still couldn't believe that everyone was carrying on as usual, like Mason wasn't broaching a topic he'd spent months hiding from them. Maybe it was fine, maybe it wouldn't be a big deal. But looking around at everyone, the natural rhythms they had together . . . He was leaving this behind. Sawyer wished she had more than melted ice in her glass but couldn't get up to refill it, not when she was holding her breath, waiting for the other shoe to drop.

Moira blinked, tearing her attention away from Milo. "Wait, why would you go there *after* shooting wrapped?"

God, the woman knew how to commandeer a room. The slightest shift in her tone, and suddenly everyone was paying attention, the silence in the kitchen now deafening.

Wild thoughts flashed through Sawyer's brain. Maybe she could fake a violent bout of sudden-onset diarrhea and get them out of here so Mason wouldn't have to talk about this before he was ready. Maybe she could fake an ankle sprain—but she wasn't a very good actor, and she was in a room full of professionals. Her heart ached with the need to protect him. She knew how deep the hurt only family could cause went. All she could do was sit and watch, her eyes trained on Mason, as if she could telepathically send him support.

He met her gaze, taking a deep, steadying breath as he set down the spatula, put aside the bowl, and carefully wiped his hands on the dish towel thrown over his shoulder. "Because I'm moving there." His voice was quiet, but the room was quieter. The way Margot gasped, you'd think Mason had said something profane. Mason's eyes were still locked on Sawyer's, as if he couldn't look away or he'd lose his nerve. "Alissa is starting her production company, Guiding Light, and she wants me as her producer."

More silence greeted his words.

Next to her, Bex gulped down the last of her wine before primly wiping the corners of her mouth and gingerly setting the empty crystal on the marble countertop. "Firstly," she said shakily. "I'm an ass. I thought everyone knew. I'm so sorry. Secondly," she said more fiercely, earning Mason's gaze, which clearly conveyed he was a drowning man in need of a lifeline. She gave him a reassuring nod. "When Kara told me, I thought it was brilliant. With Kara leaving to do Marvel, and Nurse Lia and Dr. Santiago's storylines so integrated, it's the perfect time for both your characters to exit the show. You've been producing on episodes the past two seasons and on Alissa's productions before that—you're going to be an amazing producer."

The way she said it left little room for adverse opinions, which was no doubt her goal. This was Mason's moment. Sawyer had admittedly had to ask Mason what the hell a producer did, and he'd explained that he'd be in charge of securing funds for the films and managing all the departments and their schedules while Alissa helmed the creative side of things. It was no small job, and Bex had managed to deftly remind everyone that this was bigger than just Mason moving across the country. That this was a good thing for him, and not about them. Sawyer resisted the urge to clap.

"And you better throw some work my way," she added with levity.

Mason grinned, the tension in the air lessening a fraction. "Obviously."

"Oh, but you'll be so far from family!" Lynn crowed. "We just got you back."

Goddamn it, Lynn.

Sawyer chanced a glance at Moira, whose face was strangely neutral, in what Sawyer could only assume was her own version of PR Face. Sawyer held her breath, waiting for Moira to comment. It was less a conscious choice than it seemed all the air had been sucked out of the room, the tone for the rest of the evening to be determined by which way the pinch at the corner of Moira's mouth turned.

"He can fly home just like I do," Bex said pointedly.

"And it's Christmas," Luis reminded everyone as he refilled Bex's wineglass for her. "Time to be selfless and celebrate." If he was upset that Mason had kept this from him, he hid it well, a good enough friend to have Mason's back.

"Agreed," Moira said with a sniff. God, her posture was immaculate. She raised her glass, everyone in the room doing the same. Sawyer raised her tumbler of melted ice obediently. "To Mason robbing Hollywood of all their money."

Everyone laughed as they clinked glasses and drank deeply. It was so perfectly in sync, Sawyer wouldn't have been surprised to find someone in the corner holding cue cards.

The conversation moved on, but the tension remained, and Sawyer began to suspect there were more than two actors in this room, that their whole routine of rehashing old bits was a perfectly choreographed dance around conversational eggshells. Mason was avoiding his mother's gaze like everyone in the room was avoiding the bomb that had just dropped.

This felt much more like the family dinners Sawyer was used to.

Bex mouthed, *Sorry!* to Mason, and he gave her a smile that

Sawyer suspected was supposed to be comforting, but it came out strained.

The timer on the stove dinged softly, and Mason exhaled heavily. "Thank God."

Antonio pulled the turkey out of the oven, sprinkling herbs over top with a flourish. "Dinner's ready!"

Luis directed everyone to grab a dish, tossing them potholders and dish towels, effectively keeping everyone too busy to corner Mason. The man was a mastermind. Chairs scraped across the hardwood floors as everyone pushed back, grabbing platters to carry into the adjacent dining room. As the guest, Sawyer wasn't allowed to carry anything, which was for the best, because as she crossed in front of the bay window, Max pounced.

"Boo!"

She screamed bloody murder and dropped to the floor.

CHAPTER FIFTEEN

<u>JUST ONCE, TO GET IT OUT OF OUR SYSTEMS</u> –
The heroes are convinced their feelings are purely
physical and the only solution is to act on them.
Once. Just once. The heroes are also
probably really bad at math.

Normally, Mason found Max's shenanigans endearing, but as the kid rolled around on the ground next to a sheet-white Sawyer, he was tempted to join in on Luis's whispered admonishments, frog-marching his eldest son out of the room. Extending a hand, he guided Sawyer to her feet. His mother, sister, father, Lynn, and Bex all crowded in the archway between the kitchen and dining room, and he waved them off, uncharacteristically annoyed with them as well for hovering.

"Are you alright?" he asked once they were alone. He rubbed her shoulders comfortingly as she fussed with her bangs, pink tinging the tops of her cheeks.

"I'm fine. Just embarrassed," she said, avoiding his gaze. "I knew he was there and he still scared the shit out of me." She offered him a weak smile, and his chest felt tight. "I'm sorry for making a scene."

"Don't apologize—especially not for making a scene. Not in this dramatic-ass family."

That made her laugh, and the knot behind his rib cage loosened slightly.

"Well, at least I changed the subject," she said with a grimace. "Are *you* alright?"

His hand at her shoulder flexed of its own volition, his jaw aching as he clenched it. "Not how I would have done it, but…it's done. Thankfully, my mother is too proud to lose face, so I'm spared her making this about her—for now." He grimaced. He tried not to talk about his mom that way to anyone outside of Luis or Alissa, but he'd never been good at filtering himself around Sawyer. "Are you sure you're alright?"

Sawyer nodded, and he was grateful that he could count on her not to push the issue. He didn't want to talk about it now, not here. He wanted to forget, to enjoy this time with his family, a luxury he'd taken for granted the past few years. Yes, his mother drove him up a wall with her meddling, but he still loved her. While misguided, her efforts were because she loved him—all of them. He would miss being near his family when he left.

Sawyer adjusted her skirt, letting out a small whimper that had his heart jumping into his throat.

"My tights," she mourned.

Glancing down, he spied the rip in the knee of her patterned hose. They'd been sexy to begin with, but the run that now ran up her thigh…Mason resisted the urge to follow it with his fingers, to see where it led. He didn't need to, however, as Sawyer stuck her leg out of the slit of the dress, tugging on the material around her calves and guiding it upward. Rearranging her skirt, she effectively hid the damage to her tights, but the lid Mason had put on his attraction to Sawyer was straining under all the pressure.

She glanced up, clearly proud of her maneuvering. Mason wasn't quick enough to conceal the lust no doubt written all over his face. A smirk curved her red lips. "Cool it, Álvarez."

"Just keep that run in your tights hidden." His voice came out strangled.

"Fine," she said, keeping her voice low so it wouldn't carry into the next room. "So long as you keep those forearms covered."

He glanced down at the sleeves he'd rolled up. "Oh, these?" he asked innocently. He flexed his hand, and Sawyer pressed her lips together, a small *mm-hmm* escaping her. He pushed his sleeves up past his elbows and extended his hand to her. She placed her hand in his and allowed him to lead her into the dining room, but the look in her eyes promised war.

He had no fucking clue what he'd just gotten himself into. He always seemed to feel that way when he was with her, so even though it was par for the course with them, he couldn't help the trill of excitement coursing through him. It was a welcome distraction.

As soon as they sat down, Sawyer crossed her legs under the table, the panel of her dress slipping to the side, the hole in her tights on full display for him. It was a *very* welcome distraction.

He wasn't sure he tasted a single thing at dinner. He was vaguely aware of participating in the conversation around the table, but they rehashed the same stories every year, actors giving scripted talk show sound bites, so he was on autopilot. They were all on autopilot, pointedly avoiding talking about the bomb Bex had accidentally dropped. She and Kara were close, but that Kara would've mentioned it, the need to warn Bex to not bring up Guiding Light...It hadn't even crossed his mind. Too late now. He just had to get through dinner. He would deal with the fallout later.

Luis sent him a loaded look at one point, and guilt panged in his chest. Out of everyone, he felt worst about not telling Luis. He knew Luis would support him, not make it about himself, but he hadn't wanted to force Luis to keep a secret from Margot. His logic seemed airtight before, but now it felt so flimsy. He was going to have to make a lot of apologies tomorrow.

He startled as a hand slid on top of his thigh, squeezing gently. Sawyer leaned over slightly. "You're frowning," she murmured.

Mason realized his mask had slipped. He focused on relaxing his clenched jaw, unfurrowing his brow. Sawyer nodded once in approval, and Mason wasn't sure how he felt that she was aware he treated being around his mother like doing press. He had to be on. Placing his hand on top of hers, he squeezed appreciatively. If she weren't here, he wasn't sure what he'd do. If she weren't here, he didn't know what his mom would have done, if she would have bothered saving face in front of Lynn. Lynn was practically family, so he didn't understand why they had to keep up the charade of Perfect Family when they were already a pretty damn perfect family, but Moira's media training ran deep, and mess was not allowed. You bottled that shit right up. Tonight, however, he was grateful for the charade. He just wanted to enjoy the rest of this night, as much as he could.

Sawyer slid her hand from beneath his, and he lamented the loss of the grounding contact. Then she guided his hand into her lap, right next to the all-too-tempting rip in her tights. She effortlessly jumped into the table conversation, dropping her napkin in her lap and effectively covering his hand that was far higher on her thigh than was appropriate.

He didn't know what to do. He knew what he *wanted* to do. He wanted to get the fuck out of here and take Sawyer back to his place and slowly peel off those goddamn tights. But that would be against Rule #2: No sex. This was clearly an invitation, but was it purely to distract him? Or was she flirting? Her comment about his forearms—was she struggling with their rules as much as he was? The possibility hadn't occurred to him until now.

She was so goddamn blasé about everything all time, she was impossible for him to read, save for those rare occasions when she let him peek inside that fascinating brain of hers. Everyone had layers, like an onion, but Sawyer was like the coconuts she always smelled of. You had to be fucking determined if you wanted to get to the heart of her. He liked to think he was slowly making progress. While he was beginning to suspect this attraction wasn't just one-sided—and he would happily throw Rule #2 out the window—Rule #1: No feelings, had to stay if he wanted any hope of coming out of this in one piece.

Lifting one finger, he traced the pattern of her tights until he found the run. Following it down to the source, he curled his fingertip, tucking it inside and tugging lightly. Sawyer inhaled sharply, and he could feel her thighs pressing together beneath his grip, her hips tilting forward. He removed his hand from her thigh before he could be tempted to do more, shifting in his seat to hide the evidence of how effective her distraction had been.

It was the longest dinner of Mason's life.

After dessert, when Bex and Lynn announced they had to head out, Moira and Antonio piggybacking on their exit, Mason sighed in relief. Normally, this was his favorite part of the night. When the parents left and they could drop the act, stop reciting the same old bits, and just *be*. Normally, he would've seen them off and slipped into a food-induced coma on Luis's couch. But he'd been too on edge to eat or drink as much as he usually did on holidays, and he latched on to their departure as a way to make his own exit. He knew he needed to talk to his family, but tonight had been long enough already. He wanted to slip off into the night with Sawyer and do whatever it was her subtle looks had been implying they might do.

As Lynn hugged his parents goodbye, Bex cornered him by the coat closet. "Mason, I am *so* sorry," she said for easily the tenth time.

"It's fine," he insisted. "It had to come out eventually. You couldn't have known."

Still, she frowned regretfully. Her attention snagged over his shoulder, and he followed her gaze. Sawyer in her yellow coat, doubling back to grab the last scattered glasses from the living room, despite Margot and Luis's many insistences to "just leave it."

"Well," she sighed. "At least you have a beautiful distraction for the rest of the night."

Mason laughed. "It's not like that." Though he desperately hoped it was about to become Like That.

Bex snorted. "Okay," she said, though it sounded like *Yeah, right*. "I must have hallucinated you two eye fucking each other all night whenever you thought the other wasn't looking."

He opted not to respond, because he had definitely been doing that, but he thought he'd been subtle enough not to get caught.

Bex gave him a knowing smile before bringing him in for a hug. "I'm really, truly sorry, but I meant everything I said. This is the right move for you." She hazarded a glance at their parents, who were still saying the world's longest goodbye. "Don't let anything make you doubt that." With one last meaningful glance, she ushered her mother and his parents out the door before they could drag out leaving for another half hour.

Luis appeared at his side almost immediately, puffing out his cheeks as he exhaled slowly. "We did it." Turning toward him, Luis studied him closely. "You alright?"

Mason took his time answering as he shrugged on his coat, his attention half on Sawyer as she disappeared down the hallway, slipping into the powder room. "I'm good," he said automatically. "But I owe you an apology—"

Luis waved that away. "Tomorrow's problem. Besides, I kept dating your sister a secret for months. By my math, we're even now."

"I've been working on Guiding Light for years."

Luis shrugged. "Well, I never said I was good at math. Anyhow, you've told me about it. I was just in denial that one day it would become real and I might lose you. It's been great having you back in Chi, but you haven't been happy working on *Diagnostics* in years. I want you to love what you do again."

Gratitude for his best friend swelled in his chest, and there weren't words for how much Mason appreciated him, so he pulled him into a tight hug. "Thank you. For everything. And for dinner. Food was great, as usual."

Luis clapped him on the back before pulling away, keeping his voice low even though everyone else had already left. The boys had been put to bed hours ago, the only sound Margot pouring herself a glass of wine in the next room. "She's great," Luis hedged carefully, jerking his head in the direction Sawyer had disappeared to.

Mason shook his head adamantly. "I told you—it's not like that." He'd said it so many times tonight, the words seemed to have lost their meaning.

Luis nodded. "I know. But do you?"

"I know what I'm doing," he said under his breath.

As he spoke, Sawyer reappeared, her yellow coat like a beacon at the end of the hall.

"Your face says otherwise," Luis muttered.

Sawyer reached them at that moment, so he couldn't have responded—even if he knew how.

"Thank you so much for having me," she said warmly, embracing Luis like an old friend.

Margot reappeared with her goblet of wine, kissing Sawyer on both cheeks. "It was so lovely to meet you, and thank you for the book recommendations. I hope we see you again soon."

His sister had never said that to any of his girlfriends, and he didn't think it was simply the wine talking. Sawyer had made Margot laugh more than once during dinner, and Margot wasn't an easy one to crack. He'd even seen Sawyer and Bex swapping numbers before she left. When she pulled back from Margot and Luis and caught his eye, he couldn't ignore the slight raise in his spirits.

Fuck.

Luis was right.

He'd done it again.

He liked Sawyer Greene and he couldn't do a goddamn thing about it except let her ruin him.

They walked to his car in silence, Mason too in his head to notice that Sawyer was watching him curiously, only coming to when she placed her hand atop his when he opened the car door for her.

Narrowing her eyes, she scrutinized him. "Are you alright?"

"Yeah, I didn't even finish the glass of wine I poured hours ago."

Sawyer nodded. "I know. That wasn't what I meant."

He breathed in deeply, the cold winter air bringing his thoughts back into focus. *Get it together, West.* Tonight had been long, and he didn't want to think about his family or Guiding Light or LA, much less talk about it. "Still thinking about your tights." There. Back to their usual teasing.

Sawyer's brows rose slowly, her lips parting slightly. Composing herself, she ducked into the car, and Mason took a few more gulps of the frigid air. It helped, but when he settled into the driver's seat, glancing sidelong at Sawyer as she shrugged out of her coat, he nearly swallowed his tongue.

"Did you lose your bra between the bathroom and the car?"

She blinked up at him innocently. "I didn't lose it." She plucked it out of her coat pocket and twirled it like a party favor.

The back of Mason's head hit the headrest with a thud.

"What?" Sawyer laughed. "It's a long drive. I wanted to be comfortable." The laughter faded from her voice, dropping to a husky whisper. "That okay with you?"

He took a steadying breath before leaning across the center console, reaching for her seat belt and clicking it into place. "Of course. Let me know if there's anything else I can do to make you more—" He adjusted the strap across her chest, letting his knuckle graze over her peaked nipple, her breath hitching. "Comfortable." He swore her legs squeezed tighter together. A thrill ran through him. "If there's anything else you want to take off, be my guest."

She nodded jerkily, her voice a rasp. "I'll keep that in mind, thanks."

It was an effort to pull back from her. He counted to three before starting the car.

He was grateful to lose himself in the familiar drive, silently drinking in the beauty of Lake Shore Drive at night. He definitely wasn't overthinking how their usual taunting banter had progressed into something physical. He may have gotten a little too lost in the drive, going into autopilot as all their teasing touches replayed in his mind, realizing a beat too late he'd missed the exit to Sawyer's place. "Shit."

"It's alright. Take the next one."

He definitely wasn't overanalyzing the faraway sound of her voice. "Take a right here."

His brows knit together, trying to make out the dark street. "Sawyer, this is a parking lot."

"I know," she said tightly. "Could you pull over?"

And just like that, he was officially overthinking. She'd sensed the shift, too, was going to tell him that this wasn't a good idea, that they'd pushed too far tonight, to remember their rules. Or, worse, that they should stop this ridiculous mission altogether. His heart rammed against his rib cage at the thought. No. They still had another week—at least.

He was bracing himself to fight for her, when she undid her seat belt, kicking off her pinup girl shoes—a fantasy he didn't know he had until he saw her wearing them. She leaned over, swinging her leg across the console. He shifted automatically to make room for her to straddle his lap.

He had no idea what they were doing, but some vague sense of self-preservation told him that whatever it was, it was definitely against the rules and they probably shouldn't be doing it. He promptly ignored that ridiculous notion. Of course they should be doing this.

He exhaled shakily, meeting her gaze. Her green eyes were intent on his, asking him if this was okay. He nodded, not daring to speak lest he say the wrong thing and break the spell, because he was utterly spellbound. There was a hunger and determination in her gaze as she slowly untied her dress, the dark green velvet falling open like wrapping paper to the best Christmas present he had ever—or would ever—receive.

Tearing his eyes away from her chest, he glanced up at her for permission. She gave him a small smile, nodding once.

Leaning in, he breathed in her ever-present coconut smell, placing a small kiss between her breasts as his hands came up to gently squeeze them, his thumbs rubbing over her peaked nipples. She made a noise of approval, arching her back, egging him on impatiently. He grinned as he took one nipple into his mouth, laving it with his tongue before allowing his teeth to scrape over it. She moaned, shifting her weight on his lap and rubbing herself against his thigh.

His cock throbbed, straining against his slacks, but he didn't dare reach down, not even to readjust himself. He directed his attention to her other breast, and she ground against his leg once more, groaning in frustration.

"Mason," she panted.

He dragged one of his hands up her thigh. "Need some help?"

"Yes," she breathed. "Please."

Biting down on his lip, he slid one of his fingers into the run of her tights, the one she'd been taunting him with all night. "Can I—?"

She glanced down, her lips parting as she inhaled sharply. "Yes."

He gripped her thigh roughly, bunching the fabric under his grasp and tugging. The hose gave a satisfying rip, and he grinned victoriously. Fucking finally.

With another tug, the run reached the top, where the waistband refused to yield, but Mason wasn't easily deterred. This was undeniably the hottest thing he'd ever done. He knew without a doubt that, for as long as he lived, this would remain the hottest thing he ever did.

From the fire burning in Sawyer's eyes, they were on the same page about that.

Slipping his hand beneath what remained of her tights, he pushed her panties aside, moaning at how wet she was. He traced a fingertip along her seam, parting her folds, alternating teasing her entrance and her clit.

When he eased one finger into her, she fell back against the steering wheel. A *honk* sounded out in the dead of night, but for all the reaction Sawyer gave, he didn't think she even realized. She ground against his hand impatiently, and he pulled out of her, teasing her before sliding in two fingers. She angled her hips so his hand was flush against her, grinding on his hand and his thigh. She let out a tiny gasp of pleasure as his other hand came up to brush against her nipple.

He groaned as he felt her hand cupping him through his pants.

"Can I?"

"Yes. *Yes*," he rasped.

With his permission, she had his zipper down and his cock in her hand in a flash. She pumped him slowly, running her thumb over the tip before resuming her slow pleasuring of herself atop his hand. He shifted so the heel of his hand could press gently down upon her clit, and she whimpered, bucking slightly. Fucking hell. She was close already, but goddamn if he wasn't, too. It had been a little over a month since they'd slept together, but it felt like he'd been waiting his whole life to touch her again.

He eased his cock from her hands, and she made a tiny noise of protest. "I got this."

Her eyes fluttered shut and she nodded, slowly rocking back and forth on his hand. Mason dropped his head back against the headrest as he worked himself and her closer to the edge. They locked eyes for a moment, Sawyer's mouth falling open on a sound caught in her throat. He wanted to kiss her so badly, but she hadn't kissed him, and he wasn't sure it was allowed. He hadn't thought what they were currently doing was allowed, but here they were, doing it, in his fucking car in some random fucking parking lot.

Her eyes fluttered shut, and she bowed forward, her head coming to rest on his shoulder. He momentarily forgot about pleasuring himself as her inner walls clamped down around his fingers, her teeth biting into his shoulder as climax seized her.

Her head fell back, and the unguarded bliss on her slack mouth as he brought her back down nearly undid him. She pressed her forehead against his, lifting her hips slightly so he could ease his fingers out of her. Grabbing hold of his wrist, she brought his fingers to her lips and sucked.

Mason loosed a long sigh mingled with a moan, her other hand gently nudging his out of the way as she claimed his cock.

Tearing his gaze from hers, his attention drifted from the sight of his fingers in her red-painted mouth, to the untied dress, to her exposed breasts and ripped tights, to her hand around his shaft.

This woman really was trying to ruin him.

"Sawyer," he growled. She grinned, allowing his fingers to fall from her mouth, his hand grabbing the first thing it landed on—her hip—and squeezing roughly as his own orgasm barreled through him, his release coming out in a splash across her stomach. She stroked him slowly through the last throes before rubbing her thumb across his tip and bringing it to her mouth as she sank back into her own seat.

Mason couldn't do anything but watch her as she shimmied out of her torn tights, using them to wipe his come off her stomach before carefully folding them up and tucking them into her coat pocket—presumably the same pocket as the bra she'd taken off that had started this whole thing.

Her head lolled against the headrest, her eyes connecting with his watchful gaze as she clumsily retied her dress. "Merry Christmas."

CHAPTER SIXTEEN

THE WRITER™ – Montage scene of the creative
character producing their craft. It will only take them,
like, a few wistful gazes into the sunset to produce an
entire book that requires zero edits before
becoming an instant bestseller.

Sawyer kicked off her shoes in the entryway, too exhausted to put them in the hall closet or carry them to her bedroom. She hadn't met that many new people in so long, and while there hadn't been the explosion she'd expected following the LA announcement, the tension of *not* talking about it was almost worse. She threw her ruined tights in the trash with a barely suppressed smirk. She'd meant to make a point that it was a one-time thing, but then she'd gotten caught up in the feel of him, all the tension from the evening finally getting some release.

Trudging to the bathroom on leaden feet, Sawyer went through her face-hair-teeth routine on autopilot. She was drained, the tension at the dinner table a little too close to home, so at odds with the jelly feeling in her bones after an orgasm. By the time she crawled into bed, groaning like her body was much older than twenty-six, her mind was no longer on the Wests or the Greenes. Her characters swirled through her mind, and she wondered what their family gatherings would be like. She jotted a few ideas into her Notes app before plugging her phone in to charge. Burrowing deeper under the covers, she willed her brain to shut off.

She lasted all of five minutes. Rolling over to write down another idea, she typed until her arms began to ache with the effort of holding her phone aloft without dropping it on her face. With a sigh, she resigned herself to getting out of bed. It wasn't just her partners that her wily imagination and unpredictable bouts of inspiration drove crazy. It wasn't always fun for her either. Well, that was untrue. She loved writing with a fierceness even she couldn't put into words. But that didn't make staying up until two in the morning after an already long day any less draining.

When she'd finally managed to empty her brain, she had two new chapters drafted and a hodgepodge of scattered dialogue for upcoming scenes. She'd started writing at the kitchen table, but her body demanded cushions, so she'd wound up on the couch. It was worse for her, hunching over her laptop like that, but the blankets and throw pillows had been too tempting to resist. She saved and triple saved her progress before shoving her laptop onto the coffee table and falling sideways onto the couch, allowing it to fully consume her. She would rest her eyes for a few minutes, then move to the bed.

Sawyer woke up with the sun, a crick in her neck and more ideas demanding to be written. She forced herself to get up, brew a pot of tea, and eat something before allowing herself to be re-consumed by the words and the couch cushions.

She wasn't sure how long she sat there, typing, staring, typing, deleting, retyping, until her phone buzzed. She had no idea where it even was. Upending pillows and blankets, she found it wedged between two cushions, but the call had already gone to voicemail. Mason.

"Shit," she swore. She'd been writing for hours. Her back popped as she stretched, wincing at the ache in her muscles from her shit posture. She dragged her laptop and a blanket back to her kitchen table before unlocking her phone.

She couldn't call him back right now, not when the words were flowing so easily, flowing for the first time in years. But after what they'd done last night, she should say *something*.

Opening their text thread, she saw two texts from him that she hadn't seen, phone eaten by couch and all. Shit. The first, a tentative **Hey** and the second, **Sawyer?** Shit, shit, shit. She'd been too lost in the new world beginning to come into focus in front of her to check her phone.

sorry, writing. text you later?

Was that too brusque? Her fingers hovered over the keys, and she shook her head in frustration. She could write thousands of words in a day, but one simple text was nearly debilitating.

She should say more after what they'd done in his car last night, but to Sawyer, it felt like a million years ago, another person. She wasn't Sawyer right now. She was a conduit for this story that she needed to get out of her. She hadn't felt this kind of urgency to write in a long time, and she wasn't going to let it slip through her fingers, wasn't going to dwell on what Last Night Sawyer had initiated in Mason's car, how to explain to Mason it was a one-time thing because Horny Sawyer's leash had slipped. That was a problem for Tomorrow Sawyer. Or maybe Never Sawyer. She hoped her lame five-word text would suffice for now, that Mason would understand that in this moment, her words were reserved for the page.

Before she could hit the button to turn off her screen, three little dots appeared. She held her breath, a smile breaking across her face at his response: a GIF of Patrick from *SpongeBob* waving flags with the caption "Rooting for you."

She exhaled a laugh before putting her phone face down on the table, sinking back into the chair that was now permanently molded to the shape of her ass. It was a long time before the smile faded from her face, a warmth spreading through her, fueling her as her fingers flew across the keys. It had been so long since she had someone in her corner, rooting for her. A void in her she hadn't known she'd had, slowly filling up to the brim.

She lost track of time again, letting the words flow. The scenes were messy and imperfect, but she needed to finish this draft. It was quickly becoming her lifeline. She needed to prove to herself that she could still do this. That she could still tell stories, that she hadn't gotten her dream job and ruined it. That in all her rookie juggling, she hadn't dropped her gift. She had to believe that this skill she'd honed since she was a child—first telling herself stories during her father's sermons that she could never seem to pay attention to, then to distract herself from the muffled sounds of her parents' fighting in the next room over—that she could still use it to create joy rather than hide pain. Creating safe spaces to disappear into when the real world became too much.

She couldn't think about that right now either. Thinking about her family required many hours of therapy and staring at walls. So she shoved those thoughts down, down much deeper than her thoughts about Mason. She would think about him later. Her family—she tried to think about them never.

So she dove deeper into her world of make believe. Every time she finished a scene, she snagged more snippets from her outline, keeping them at the bottom of the page like fairy lights leading her deeper into the forest. She wasn't scared of the forest, of getting stuck, so long as she had those little guideposts to show her the way.

Until the next afternoon, on day two of her writing frenzy, when following the fairy lights led her straight into a plot hole. She stared at the wall of text for what felt like hours, trying to figure out how to dig herself back out, how to put a Band-Aid on it—or if she could ignore it and keep going, figure it out later . . .

She couldn't. Once she'd seen it, it was all she could see.

Normally, she'd hash it out with Tess or Emily, but she hadn't even gotten this pitch approved yet. So she pivoted. She cleaned up her outline, churned out a synopsis and pitch, and gave her opening chapters a perfunctory edit before sending it off to Tess. She chewed on a hangnail as she watched the message land in her outbox, and with a whoosh, move to her sent folder. She'd sent lots of pitches in the past year, only to hate the idea once she started writing it. This felt different. There were still so many nebulous details she had yet to figure out, but she knew how it ended. She would finish this one. She had to.

Apparently, she was feeling extra brave tonight, and opened her muted writer friends chat and turned the notifications back on. She sent GIFs of the Kool-Aid Man bursting through the wall and Steve Buscemi's "How do you do, fellow kids?" before pasting the pitch for her book into the chat and hitting send. She closed her laptop before anyone could reply, because, baby steps.

Her stomach growled, and she stretched, jumping when her gaze landed on the oven clock. It was nearly dinnertime. She'd promised herself to stop for lunch hours ago, her kitchen table an absolute travesty of drafting snacks. Her morning yogurt had been banished to a far corner. Granola, banana peels, and an empty family-sized bag of cheesy puffs littered her makeshift desk.

Her neck cracked loudly when she rolled it, and she sighed, staring around her apartment, really seeing it for the first time in two days. Her heels were still by the door from where she'd kicked them off after Christmas dinner with the Wests. Her sink was full of dishes—mostly because her sink was so tiny it was full after putting three whole things in it. She was wearing the same pajamas she'd put on after her shower two days ago, barely having moved from her kitchen table save to pee and catch a few hours of sleep. Drafting Sawyer was not the best at keeping a routine or being a human. It wasn't really a surprise no one wanted to be with her when she was like this.

She was too exhausted to cook—even her approximation of cooking, which was really just mixing things together. She unearthed her phone from beneath an empty bag of chocolate chips, mentally running through her favorite delivery spots. When she opened her phone, however, her text thread with Mason was still open. She smiled fondly down at it, perhaps assigning way too much significance to a GIF, but there had been a time when her need to give work her singular focus had driven away the person that was most important to her.

Mason might not be the most important person in her life—she couldn't afford that level of distraction, making herself vulnerable to imploding her life again—but he was…something. A something she enjoyed. Drafting often left her drained and seeking solitude to recharge, but Mason's presence felt like the only thing that could refill her. And so, even though she was out of words for the day, she forced herself to type a few more. She resisted the urge to apologize. She was done apologizing for working. Nonetheless, when she hit send—and even though her relationship with God had long been on the rocks—she prayed that her days-long silence hadn't ruined everything. Again.

CHAPTER SEVENTEEN

CATCHING FEELINGS – When the casual
hookup is occupying a not-so-casual
amount of your brain space.

"We hooked up again."

The confession came out of him on a grunt as he began
the last rep of his set. Luis gave him a look but said nothing, hands
at the ready to spot should he need it. The gym wasn't the logical
place to have a heart-to-heart. Talking was nearly impossible when
a hundred-plus pounds of weight were hovering over your face, but
Mason needed to exhaust himself physically, because mentally and
emotionally, he was running on fumes. And yet, he'd been unable to
sleep the past two nights.

He'd spent the last two days trying to smooth over the botched
LA move announcement. His mother had all but begged him to stay
in Chicago, to "keep the family whole," and it was almost tempting. He could stay on *Diagnostics*, be there for whatever sports or arts
events Milo and Max did, be with Sawyer.

It never took long for his thoughts to circle back to her. He wanted
to talk to her about what they'd done after dinner, about how
exhausted he was from having to console his mom when he wanted
to be excited for this next step in his career. He'd texted Sawyer the

morning after…and then spent the next two days staring at his phone like a teenage boy, waiting on a text from his crush.

While a text from Sawyer had eventually come—a single, five-word response promising to text him later—she had not, in fact, *texted him later*. But she was writing, and that knowledge made him want to jump and click his heels together. Their strange quest was working—for her, at least.

For Mason, it was a goddamn tragedy. He knew he had no business developing feelings for Sawyer. And yet, after two days of near radio silence from her, and his ensuing panic that what they'd done in his car had pushed her away, he'd at least confronted the fact that he was in over his head. He'd gone and grown attached to her. She wasn't interested in dating, and he was leaving in a few months. But *fuck*. He loved being with her, her erratic thought patterns and philosophies on life that were so unmistakably *Sawyer*.

He'd talked himself out of texting her again a thousand times. Leaving his phone in his locker while he and Luis worked out was a relief. He needed to wear himself out to the point that sleep could no longer elude him. He didn't want to know what he'd get up to after another night of no sleep.

Last night, he'd cleaned the grout in his shower at two a.m., for fuck's sake.

He was a mess, and it felt good to lose himself in the repetitious movements of the gym. Being here with his best friend was the most normal thing to happen to him in weeks. His skin thrummed with energy and heat, his muscles slick with sweat and tingling with exertion, the familiar ache of exhaustion already setting in.

Luis helped him guide the barbell back onto the rack, and once it was slotted into place, Mason sat up, feeling like he'd let go of a lot more than just weight. All his secrets were finally out. Well, almost all of them.

Luis gave him an inscrutable look before plopping down on the mat in front of him to begin cooling down. Sinking onto the mat next to him, Mason lay flat on his back, giving up all pretense of stretching even though he knew he needed to or he'd be in knots tomorrow. In more knots than he already was mentally.

Luis's brown eyes flicked to his. "What do you mean you 'hooked up again'? She— She's engaged, dude."

Mason blinked. "What?"

His friend stared out the window, frowning. "Kara's been back in town less than a day. How—"

Mason sat up with a grunt. "No. No way. Not Kara. I didn't even know she was back." He waited for the gut punch of her being in town and him none the wiser, but none came.

Luis turned to him, relief washing over his face. "Oh, thank God. But wait, if we're not talking about Kara, who—?" Luis cut himself off, eyes going wide as his jaw snapped shut with understanding. "What do you mean '*again*'?"

Mason grimaced. He forgot he hadn't told Luis about the first time he'd slept with Sawyer. At first because, well, that was private. Later, when he'd filled Luis in on their mission, he'd told the truth about getting stuck in an elevator with her and having a drink after getting re-dumped by Kara. But he'd pointedly omitted all the sex they'd had afterward to avoid the look now on Luis's face as he came clean about it. And since he was coming clean—and because Mason still felt guilty for the LA secret even though Luis had said multiple times he was excited for him—he figured he might as well come all the way clean.

He told him about his futile attempts to keep things platonic with

Sawyer and how after Christmas, that had become impossible, him accepting that he had feelings but would have to get over it, but then he'd spent the last two days with the people he loved most, only to realize the person he most wanted to be with was her. He inhaled shakily, gesturing vaguely, staring up at the ceiling from flat on his back. "So that's all," he said with mock lightness, as if he hadn't spilled his heart out on the sweaty gym floor.

Next to them, a bodybuilder with a neck the size of Mason's thighs let out a high-pitched groan that wouldn't be out of place in a porno. Mason and Luis immediately locked eyes before averting their gazes as they stifled their laughs.

Once recovered, Luis shook his head slowly. "'That's all'?" His chest shook, laughter rattling its way out. "Holy shit, dude." Running a hand over his face, Luis stared blankly off to the side as he processed. After a long beat, his brows drew together in the middle. "You guys had sex in my driveway? I've never even had sex in my driveway."

Mason punched him in the arm. "You're married to my sister, please do not ever forget that, thank you. And no, not in your driveway, down the street from her place. It's fine. Also, literally not the point."

Dramatically rubbing the spot he'd punched, Luis chewed on his cheek. "So what's the problem? You like her. She likes you. You have great sex. Sounds like something to celebrate, not have a crisis over."

"I don't know that she does...like me," he finished uncertainly. He felt like a whiny teenager, but he'd known Luis since before he was a whiny teenager, so there was little room for pride between them.

Luis barked out a laugh. "Are you kidding? I literally have to call my wife after this and tell her I owe her fifty bucks."

Mason rolled his head sideways on the mat. "What? Why?"

"Because you told me it wasn't like that between you two, and I believed you, so, after Christmas dinner, when wine-drunk Margot bet me fifty bucks that the two of you were fucking, I took her up on that bet because I didn't know *you were currently having sex in my driveway.*"

"Not in the driveway," Mason reminded him with a shit-eating grin.

"Literally not the point," Luis mocked. "The point, my friend, is that that girl was ogling you all night and everyone saw it—even me—but you said it wasn't a thing because she doesn't do the very thing you do all the time, the thing you expressly said you wouldn't do with her, which is fall hard."

"I know," Mason groaned, hiding his face behind his shirt under the pretext of wiping off his sweat with the hem. The thing was . . . he thought he'd fallen hard before, but this thing with Sawyer—this thing that wasn't even a real thing—felt more real than anything he'd ever had before.

He waited for the meathead next to them to finish his set—and weirdly sexual grunting—before continuing. It was hard to have a sincere conversation about feelings when the guy next to you sounded like he was one hip thrust away from busting. But now that Mason had started talking, he couldn't stop. Coming clean to his best friend was the emotional equivalent of hitting the panic button on the looping treadmill of his thoughts.

"I just—" He blew out a breath, sitting up and staring at the wall as he dredged up the one thing that hadn't slipped out of him when he rambled the whole story to Luis. "I feel like she might. There was this moment . . ." Her face swam before his, her grounding presence at Christmas when Bex accidentally spilled the LA secret. There had been a fierceness in her gaze that had nothing to do with their usual teasing. It was like her edges, the ones she kept sharp so no one could get too close, had softened. Like she'd let down her walls long enough to let him in, so she could safeguard him behind them.

Luis nodded, and Mason realized he'd said all of that aloud. "And you can't just ask her."

It wasn't a question, but Mason shook his head in response anyway.

"Do you want my opinion or a sounding board?" Luis asked quietly.

Mason drew one knee to his chest in a half-hearted attempt to pretend he was stretching. "Opinion," he said at long last. He was fairly certain he had the answer to the question he still had yet to articulate, but with Luis, he could hand him a word salad, and his friend would know what he meant.

"The way I see it," Luis grunted as he moved into a new stretch position. "You have three options: walk away—"

"No," Mason ground out. It was the smartest option. Walking away was the only way to protect himself. But he was already in too deep for that.

"I know," Luis said. "So, that leaves asking her—"

They exchanged a long look. Asking Sawyer if she had feelings for him after they'd expressly stated they weren't doing that and she'd practically ghosted him after they hooked up in his car . . . Yeah, that wasn't an option either.

"Or wait."

Mason hung his head, resting his forehead against his knee. "That makes me feel like a creep who can't take no for an answer."

He could feel Luis's frown without looking. "You are not that guy. Sometimes, we fall for people we don't expect to—like your best friend's older sister—" Mason cut him a wry look, and Luis smirked unapologetically. "And when that happens, all you can do is love them and wait and pray it works out, because on the off chance that it does... it's worth it."

When Mason didn't respond, Luis continued, and Mason had to admit his optimism was infectious. "Besides, aren't y'all almost done?"

Mason nodded numbly, dread squashing the small balloon of hope that had been building. The last thing on their list—at least, the ones they figured out how to do, both of them in a standoff over who would do the dramatic musical grand gesture—was New Year's Eve. There was also the New Year's brunch at Lily's after that, but that wasn't a list item—though he was sure Sawyer would find a way to make it a list item. She always did. He was really beginning to resent that list.

"Being done is a good thing," Luis rushed out. "When the list is done, y'all have no obligation to keep doing this unless you both want to. So when she stays, as I have no doubt she will..." He trailed off, allowing Mason to draw the natural conclusion.

He prayed it were that simple. He wasn't going to pressure Sawyer into anything. He never meant for this to happen, but now that it had, he wanted it. He wanted her. Badly. He wanted her in a way he'd never fathomed. Maybe their stupid list was working, because he didn't feel the need to shower her with romantic overtures the way he normally would. He wanted to wake up with her, wanted to do all the things he thought he hated—like running errands at IKEA— and finding out he didn't mind them so long as he was with her. He wanted her in the quiet, in the spaces between the big moments. His eyes fluttered shut, and he took a series of controlled breaths. He just hoped she wanted it, too.

"Oh," Luis added as an afterthought. "And stop hooking up with her."

Mason's brows rose. "Excuse you."

Luis smirked. "Trust me. Right now, she not only has the cake, but she's eating it with a large glass of milk that you gave her for free."

Mason pulled a face. "You just mixed so many metaphors."

"You know what I mean," Luis chuckled. "Besides, friends with benefits isn't really your style. Especially when that's not what it is for you." Luis widened his eyes, blinking accusatorially.

His friend was right. He couldn't keep hooking up with Sawyer when it meant something to him and nothing to her. Or maybe it did mean something to her. Who knew? Not Mason.

He sighed, feeling deflated. "What about LA? The whole point of doing this with Sawyer was to stay single. The tabloids are only just now moving on. I don't want to give them anything new to write about, much less drag her into it—" He cut himself off, running a hand through his sweat-slicked hair in frustration.

His eyes flew open as Luis clapped him on the back. Hard.

"Falling in love sucks," Luis said frankly. "You'll both figure it out. One step at a time."

His friend clambered to his feet, extending a hand to Mason, which he took automatically. As Luis pulled him up, he felt like he'd left his stomach back on the mat.

Love?

Spilling everything out to Luis had left his mind empty for the first time in days, and that single word now clanged around inside his skull like a warning bell and a symphony all in one.

CHAPTER EIGHTEEN

LOUNGERIE – The undeniable intimacy of seeing
a person in loungewear for the first time;
see also gray sweatpants.

It hadn't been snowing this hard when Mason left his apartment. Fat globs of snow clung half melted to the sidewalk, his gym shoes struggling to find purchase. The pristine white powder would be covered in city grime in a matter of hours, but for now, the world was quiet—as quiet as the city ever got. There was a stillness to a snowstorm that Mason loved. He leaned into that stillness, a blissful calm after the roller coaster of the past few days.

There were still no texts from Sawyer when he retrieved his phone from the gym locker, but he was trying to make his peace with that. As he strolled down the slushy sidewalk, he drank in the skyline that had been his home the past few years. It was finally beginning to hit him. It was all happening. A big, wide future awaited him in LA, but amid the excitement was a tinge of panic. His time in Chicago was drawing to a close, and he didn't quite feel done with it.

His hair was still wet from his gym shower, and he was freezing, but he decided to walk the long way home so he could stop at his favorite pho spot. How many more chances would he get to eat there? He hoped a stomach full of rich broth would drown out his anxiety about the city—and the woman within it—that he didn't want to leave yet.

It might have worked, too, had Sawyer not chosen that moment to text him back.

> hey, sorry, finally came up for air, buttttttt 37,000 words, baby!!

He grinned down at his phone. He had no clue how many words were in a novel, but that sounded like a lot. Either way, she was writing and that warmed him more than a shot of whiskey.

AMAZING.

Before he could compose a second response, three dots appeared, and he froze in the middle of the sidewalk, waiting.

> thanks, i'm stuck now but i'm gonna take the night off, refuel, eat?? i've heard feeding your flesh prison is necessary to function, apparently.

He laughed. He loved the way she texted. No capitalization, run-on sentences, either no punctuation or a plethora of it. He could hear her voice when he read them, the exact tone she'd say it in.

Who knew?! How do you feel about pho?

> VERY positive feelings

Excellent.

He pulled up the menu on his phone and texted it to her. She responded in a matter of seconds with her order.

> P3, B17, and split A6 with me pleaseeeee!!! you are an ANGEL i'd say you don't have to but i fucking love that place and now nothing else will do

He would drive to Australia to grab her a snack if that's what it took to see her. He'd been hoping for a text back, something to let him know they were okay after what happened on Christmas, and it seemed like they were, maybe? As the comfort of that thought sank in, a new fear unlocked inside his mind. Were they pretending it didn't happen? Just like their all-night-and-the-next-morning stand? Though they hadn't ever pretended *that* didn't happen. They both had made plenty of jokes about it. So what, exactly, the fuck was happening?

He still hadn't decided by the time their food was ready, nor had he decided on the short drive to Sawyer's, or the walk up to her apartment. So he did what he did when he forgot lines on set—improvised and prayed he didn't stray too far from the script.

He exhaled heavily as he removed his beanie, shaking off the layer of ice that had formed, the snow really coming down now. He knocked, and she answered in a flash.

Her face lit up at the sight of the large paper bag in his hands, and he was grateful she wasn't looking at him while he was looking at her.

Jesus Christ. She was wearing the tiniest shorts he'd ever seen. Not sleeping with her again would be a hell of a lot easier if his body didn't react to her so readily. The joggers he'd changed into before grabbing his car did little to conceal, well, anything.

"How much do I owe you?" she asked, stepping aside to let him in.

"Nothing. We're celebrating!" He hoped he didn't notice the slight panic in his voice as he hastily adjusted himself, pointedly keeping his attention on the top half of her body and not those goddamn shorts.

Sawyer glanced over her shoulder, eyes widening in excitement. "Oooh! What are we celebrating?"

He blinked at her back as he kicked off his shoes. "You? Writing?"

She froze in the middle of opening a drawer, something unreadable crossing her face. "Oh." She flushed, turning away from him and rifling through the drawer. "It's not a big deal. It's literally my job."

Crossing over to her, he set down the giant bag of takeout before taking her gently by the shoulders. Placing a finger under her chin, he guided her to look at him. "It is a big deal. And we're celebrating."

A smile spread across her face, but it didn't fully chase away whatever emotion clouded her normally bright eyes. "Alright. Well, if you insist— I'll even let you pick the mugs."

He placed a hand over his heart. "I'm honored."

Crossing over to the hutch, he smiled fondly at the Christmas tree in the corner. He paused, doing a double take. "Sawyer?"

"Hmm?" she answered distractedly, using her arm to scoop the contents scattered on her kitchen table into the garbage in one fell swoop.

"Why is there a dildo atop our tree?"

She stilled, her gaze darting between him and the pearlescent sex toy cresting the tree. "Well, so, the porcelain angel fell off. Her face cracked and I tried to fix it, but I'm not exactly Martha Stewart here, alright? And the tree looked so sad without a topper, and I thought the glitter gave it a festive vibe," she finished with jazz hands.

"It's a vibe, alright," he agreed with an astonished laugh. "I love it, for the record."

She beamed. "Thanks."

Abandoning her cleaning of the kitchen table, she moved a stack of books off the coffee table and spread the food out on it instead.

Perusing her extensive mug collection, he selected one with a swooning Victorian woman for himself. From the back of the hutch, he unearthed a mug with a bold western font that declared, "Damn, I'm good." Pouring a shot of whiskey for them both, he handed her the latter.

She grinned at his choices, nodding in approval. "Thank you," she said softly, tapping her mug against his and taking a sip.

He studied her over the rim of his mug as he drank. There was something to her voice, the unnamable thing still shadowing her expressions. Was it because of what they'd done the other night in his car? Before he could make sense of it, she sank down onto the couch, letting out a beleaguered sigh before pulling a steaming bowl of pho broth toward her.

"Is it okay—that I'm here?" he asked.

She glanced up at him in the middle of tearing basil leaves into her soup. "Mason. I invited you."

He nodded once, sinking onto the couch cushion next to her. He stole glances at her as he added jalapeños and bean sprouts to his own broth, trying to take solace in the routine of preparing his comfort meal.

She caught him staring again as he stirred sriracha into his broth. "What?" She managed to pack more emotion into that singular syllable than most of his costars did in a page-long monologue.

"Sorry," he mumbled. "I just—you seem different. Is it because of . . . the other night?"

Sawyer took a deep breath, her eyes fluttering shut. "No. I'm just tired. This is what I'm like when I'm drafting. It takes me a while to get my head back after spending so long in another world. I don't usually—" She gestured between the two of them. "Socialize after a writing binge. It's like I spend so much time crafting their personalities that it kinda drains mine. So, I'm sorry. I might not be very entertaining. Oh—I'll ruin romance writers for you, how about that?"

"Sawyer," he said softly. "You don't have to 'be' anything. Not everything we do has to be for the list. I just wanted to know you're okay—we're okay."

She nodded. "We're good. It's not you, it's me," she said with a half-hearted sly grin that he could tell even she didn't buy. She blew out a breath, her bangs fluttering with the force of it. "I also…" Averting her gaze to her soup, she stirred it absentmindedly, and he waited. "I haven't written like this in a while, but I also haven't had someone be excited for me that wasn't someone who got paid when I wrote."

He thought of Lily, her friend that he'd met at the mall.

She met his eyes, and as if his thoughts were written on his face, she nodded. "I met Lily while I was editing *Why We're Not Together*, so she missed this phase." She gestured around her messy apartment. She tapped her spoon against the side of the bowl, staring at the wall as if deciding whether or not to keep talking. He hoped she kept talking. Every piece of her that she chose to share felt like both a gift and a hard-won battle. "I'm sure you've realized my parents and I aren't close—not like you and yours. Even with the awkwardness, that Christmas dinner was the best family meal I think I can remember. My family and I…" She ran her thumb along her bottom lip, still staring at the wall across from them. "Well, I wasn't exactly the ideal preacher's kid, but it still stung when I sent them an advance copy of my first book and they sent it back without even cracking the spine."

Mason scrubbed his hands over his face, unsure what to say. Their experiences couldn't be more different. His mother had nearly suffocated him with support.

"It's okay," she mumbled. "You don't have to say anything."

He wanted to tell her it wasn't okay, but he could tell she already knew that, that she'd made her peace with it and nothing he said was going to assuage that hurt. What he couldn't wrap his mind around was how someone could know Sawyer, had some hand in shaping her, see the wily, wistful wonder that she was—and walk away. In the Venn diagram of "knowing Sawyer" and "loving Sawyer," for Mason, it was a circle.

A memory played out in his mind's eye—not a memory. A scene from the *Almost Lovers* movie, where the main character reconciles with her estranged family. A scene that hadn't been in the book. Mason suddenly felt hollowed out. He hadn't understood why Sawyer hated her book's adaptation so much. Until now. She'd given a delicate piece of herself to her character, and the studio had bastardized it, as if the only way to be happily ever after is to have everything tied up in a glossy bow where, for Sawyer, there would always be a severed thread.

"Anyway." Sawyer sipped her broth before continuing. "I took that copy and made a new family. I brought it to every signing I did for *Almost Lovers*, and let my readers sign it. It was so battered by the last one that I had to tape the spine."

"Could I see it?" he asked tentatively.

The soft smile on her face fell, and she stared down at her soup like she wanted to drown in it. "I don't have it anymore. Sadie and I broke up right before the launch, but I still thought we'd get back together, once everything calmed down. But when I got back from tour, Sadie sent her brother to grab the last of her things, and I left because I couldn't watch. It was weeks before I realized the book was gone."

Anger speared through him, white-hot. "They took it?"

Sawyer shrugged with false nonchalance, taking a large bite of noodles before answering. "It's possible I lost it."

"You don't believe that."

She exhaled heavily. "No. But getting it back would require talking to her." She took another bite, chewing thoughtfully. "Is it pathetic that even after all this time I'm scared to do it?"

"No," Mason said adamantly. He still hadn't mustered the nerve to call Kara or any of his other exes.

"I think what I'm most scared of," she admitted quietly, staring at her pho as if it were easier to confess this to a bowl of noodles. "Is that they did something to it. At least this way, I can pretend it's still out there, bursting at the seams with messages of love."

Sawyer Greene had the biggest heart, and she didn't even know it. He envied the person who one day got to hold it, to fill in the cracks left by those who hadn't recognized it for the gift that it was.

"I'm sure it is," he said, squeezing her knee reassuringly.

She smiled weakly, nodding once.

They ate in silence after that. Mason's conversation with Luis swam through his head, and he finally understood what Luis meant about waiting it out. Mason was no stranger to showing up unannounced and professing feelings. He believed that if you cared about someone, you should tell them. But Sawyer was opening up to him, slowly, and while she may never be ready for a relationship—the thought gutted him—the thought of having no relationship with her at all hurt worse. So Mason bit back any grand confessions that dared to surface. But he couldn't shake the need to share something personal with her, to let her know that he appreciated the full weight of her sharing things with him. He had a suspicion it wasn't a thing she did often. Truthfully, it wasn't something he did often either.

She tipped her bowl to drain the last of the broth before dropping her chopsticks and spoon back into it and pushing it away. Lying back on the couch, she wormed her feet over his lap, through the circle created by his elbows propped on his knees. "Make yourself comfortable," he laughed, adjusting his position so she could stretch out.

"I always do," she said with a smile.

The memory of them in his car two nights ago flashed before his eyes, the bra she'd taken off to get "comfortable." He shoved that down. He wasn't sure what that had been. She didn't seem keen to discuss it, and it definitely wasn't the vibe tonight, so he would take her cue.

Draining the last of his soup, he stacked their empty bowls before sinking into the couch, absentmindedly massaging her calves. "I'm really happy you're writing again," he admitted quietly.

"Me, too," she said softly, a light sparking in her eyes. She glanced away, smiling bigger, before turning back to him and nudging his ribs with her toe. "I feel like this is all working out unfairly in my favor. Put me to work." She twisted around, grabbing the remote off the coffee table. Netflix *gong*ed loudly as she queued it up. "Pick a rom-com and I'll ruin it for you."

He squeezed her knee. "Not everything we do has to be about the list."

She made a face. "Favorite rom-com: go." When he didn't immediately answer, she nudged him in the ribs impatiently.

"*10 Things*."

She stiffened. "No. Pick another one."

He laughed. "You asked for my favorite. That's my favorite."

She groaned dramatically, tossing her head back against the couch cushions. "Yeah, but it's *my* favorite. I can't ruin it. It's perfect."

He threw his hands up in defeat. "Just put something on."

"No," Sawyer insisted, propping herself up on her elbows. "I want to hold up my end of the bargain, but I don't know how. Maybe...I don't know, I don't know that I totally *get* you."

He blinked in surprise. He'd already told her more than he'd ever told anyone.

Oblivious to his shock, she continued, "Tell me: How did you become such a romantic?"

"My parents," he said automatically. Sawyer settled in deeper, listening. "They had a meet-cute for the ages."

She patted the space on the couch next to her, scooting over slightly to make room for him to lie down, too. He settled in next to her, his arm around her back to keep her from falling off the couch that was far too small for two people to lie down without being practically on top of each other. Maybe their weird mission *was* working for him, too, because he didn't immediately overthink what it meant that she was lying with him like this.

"Tell me more about this meet-cute," she said. It took Mason a moment to clock that this was exactly what he'd said to her when he was panicking in the elevator. The fact that she remembered...He hoped she couldn't feel the way his heart stuttered from where she was perched on his chest.

"They met on set of *In the Hills*."

Sawyer scrunched up her face in concentration. "Wasn't that the movie Lynn was mocking at dinner?"

Mason nodded. "Yep. The movie's god-awful," he laughed. "But it's where my parents met. My mom was just starting out. I think she was, like, twenty-one? Twenty-two? My dad was a few years older and a stuntman—" He waggled his eyebrows suggestively, and Sawyer giggled. "They'd blocked his fight scene multiple times, and everything had been perfect—until the cameras actually started rolling and the film's lead threw my dad across the room—in the wrong direction. My mom grabbed him half a second before he went through the window. Only, he was moving so fast that they toppled to the ground—"

"Stop," Sawyer breathed.

Mason laughed as he nodded.

"They landed on top of each other, didn't they?" she asked breathlessly.

"Yep," he confirmed.

Sawyer groaned as if in pain from how cute it was. "I bet the media had a field day."

Mason shook his head. "They didn't go public for a long time. She was faking a relationship with the film's lead at the time, so my dad courted her in secret. Everything for the media has always been fake with my mom. 'Give them something to talk about so you can keep the real stuff for yourself,'" he parroted.

Sawyer grinned up at him. "Puh-lease make all my romance writer dreams come true and tell me you've faked a relationship for PR."

Mason couldn't help but return her smile, bopping her on the tip of her adorably scrunched nose. "With the amount of costars I've dated, you would think, right? But, other than my first relationship where everyone knew it was fake but me, no. They've all been real."

Sawyer's jaw dropped before she promptly mimed zipping it shut. He knew it was taking all her self-control not to ask for details, but he was opting for rose-colored glasses tonight where his mother was concerned. He didn't want to get into all that.

He shrugged the shoulder her head wasn't propped on. "In any other industry, dating a coworker is taboo, but sets are such a microcosm. There's not really anyone else to date except your coworkers. The media loves it and it's great press, and it's easier to give them their photo op, the sound bite, than to sneak around and get caught unawares. I've never kept it a secret that I want what my parents have. They're so solid. I want to find that. I like going all out. I love love."

There was that word again. But using it to describe his past relationships didn't fit quite right. He'd loved some of them, but he was no longer so sure he'd been fully *in* love. Like he'd been in the shallow end of the pool all along and was only just now learning how to swim in the deep end. The depth was both thrilling and terrifying.

He didn't need to keep talking, but he found himself wanting to anyway, even if it went against all his instincts to let his internal mess unspool. He leaned into Sawyer's touch, leaned into the feeling of trusting someone with his whole self, even the parts that wouldn't make for a titillating late-night talk show bit.

"But…despite all that, no matter how hard I tried to get everything right, my relationships never lasted longer than the production schedule. So, when I got the *Diagnostics* offer, it felt like the answer to all my problems. My relationship with my mom had been strained ever since I fired her as my manager—yes, I'm *that* child actor cliché—but I wasn't a kid anymore. I knew who I was outside of just being Moira West's son. And I was lonely. I wanted to come home. But, as with all things that seem too good to be true…the *Diagnostics* showrunner makes our lives hell. It—"

As if sensing him shutting down, Sawyer threaded her fingers through his hair, scratching his scalp comfortingly. He couldn't remember the last time he'd let it all out like this, if he'd ever let it all out at once like this. Now that he'd started, he needed to see it through, from both a need for Sawyer to understand, and a need to understand himself.

"It's not that I don't want to tell you all the toxic shit we put up with, I just don't want to ruin the rest of our night," he said, laughing darkly. "When filming resumes next month, you'll be sick of me complaining about it. But, for now, let's just say it's no coincidence that I'm leaving this show to start my own production company. It doesn't have to be that way. We convince ourselves that the bad days on set are okay because they're big names, that these out-of-touch old white dudes can make or break our career, but—" He shook his head. "There's a new generation of actors and directors and producers, and we can choose not to perpetuate that." Glancing down at her, he gave her a crooked grin. "This is where you tell me that in addition to being an incurable romantic, I'm also a hopeless dreamer."

Sawyer shook her head. "I wasn't going to say that at all," she said softly. "I love your dream."

Mason wasn't sure why that made him want to cry. He squeezed his eyes shut, inhaling deeply and holding it for a moment before releasing it. He'd had this conversation with his family multiple times over the past two days, explaining the vision for Guiding Light, why he had to move to LA, but he'd been on the defensive. Now, for the first time in days, he was excited. "Sorry," he mumbled. "That was a lot."

Sawyer's hands stilled in his hair, and she shifted, curling into his side so she could look up at him, studying his expression. "Álvarez," she scolded him. "Why are you apologizing?"

She had a point. He wished he could be more like her, to not feel the need to apologize for going after what he wanted. But he'd grown up under the thumb of Moira West, where you kept the messy thoughts shoved under the rug. Mason had been pretending everything was fine, always putting his best foot forward, never letting the bad thoughts out, been masking his expressions for so long, he couldn't remember the last time he'd talked without tailoring it for his audience.

"I'm not very good at keeping things surface level with you."

Sawyer shrugged, waving away his comment. "Fuck that rule. We're friends."

Friends didn't feel like a big enough word for what she was to him. It scared him how easy it was for him to drop all of his acts around her. With her, he wasn't Dr. Santiago or Moira West's son or the media's favorite doting boyfriend. With her, he could just be Mason Álvarez. "Thank you for listening," he said sincerely.

"Of course," she breathed. "What do you need in this moment?"

He exhaled heavily. "It's been a long two days. I just want to lie here and go back to not thinking about it."

She smiled softly, nudging his chest with her nose. "I am *great* at avoiding things, but thank you for telling me," she said with a soft smile. "I know sometimes simply talking about it helps."

He nodded distractedly. He did feel better, lighter.

Sensing that he wasn't going to say anything else, she resumed her scroll through Netflix.

He sank deeper into the couch, dragging an incredibly soft blanket off the back and draping it over them.

Rolling onto his side, he kept his arm around her tight, not wanting her to move. He was so full, his head mercifully empty for the first time in days, and her couch was comfortable. *She* was comfortable—and not just her body, her back now pressed into his front—but her presence was like a weighted blanket, soothing him and dragging him under. Seeing her again after two days of worrying felt like an immense weight had been lifted off his shoulders, a contented warmth taking its place.

He felt rather than saw her twist her head, momentarily pausing her perusal of movie options. He had a vague inclination that she'd asked him something. "What?" he mumbled.

"Are you about to fall asleep on me?"

The last thing he remembered was uttering an adamant "No" before sleep dragged him under.

*   *   *

"Mason."

He blinked awake, the dull light from the street barely illuminating Sawyer's apartment. A few inches of snow had accumulated on the narrow window ledge, and more poured steadily down. He was still on Sawyer's couch, a thin blanket thrown haphazardly over him. He laughed to himself. Of course she hadn't woken him up and offered to share her bed. She'd probably say she was ruining "only one bed" for him. Though maybe she had tried to wake him up. He was so goddamn tired after not sleeping for two days that he had no sense of how long he'd been out. It could have been minutes or days.

"Mason."

He tensed, eyes straining in the darkness. Sawyer's door was slightly ajar, the sound of rustling bedsheets coming from the other room. Had she heard him wake up? Maybe she would share her bed after all. The couch was far too small for him to stretch out comfortably, and his muscles ached from the gym and the cramped position he'd passed out in. His feet had barely hit the cold hardwood when he heard Sawyer moan.

The realization hit him like a brick wall. Sawyer was touching herself, and it was his name on her lips while she did it.

He brought his fist to his mouth, clamping down. This woman was going to be his undoing. Every muscle in his body went stiff as he willed himself not to move.

A vibrating noise joined the soft moans coming from the next room, and Mason was so turned on he was seeing spots. Listening seemed wrong. Interrupting seemed worse. Joining her sounded best, but Luis's cake-milk metaphor rang in his head. He'd already broken Rule #1: No feelings. Rule #2 had to stay in place.

He tried not to eavesdrop, but there was no mistaking the little gasp Sawyer made when she came. He gripped the edge of the couch so hard, he wouldn't have been surprised if stuffing oozed out the seams.

It was an effort to control his ragged breathing, almost missing Sawyer's quiet murmur.

"Thank you, Mason."

A drawer opened and closed, and he heard her sheets rustle as she settled in for the night.

He shook with silent laughter.

Was her vibrator named Mason?

Half-delirious with lust, he felt hope bloom in his chest. Maybe he wasn't the only one who was too far gone.

CHAPTER NINETEEN

<u>SHOPPING MONTAGE</u> – In the wise words of
Donna Meagle and Tom Haverford, "treat yo self."

Sawyer was fairly certain she'd hailed the only taxi driver in the city who drove the speed limit. She drummed her fingers along the back of her phone case anxiously, willing him to go faster. He braked for the yellow light rather than running it, and she fought back an aggravated scream. It wasn't his fault. She was going to be late all on her own. She'd finally found her writing flow an hour before she was due to leave, and she cursed herself for not getting ready earlier.

Being late was only half of her frustration. She'd finally hit the midpoint of her incredibly messy draft, and her characters were starting to fall for each other again. She'd written them a steamy sex scene that was so long she'd definitely have to cut it back later, but she was so goddamn horny herself that she wanted *someone* to get some release. Before she could finish the scene, she realized she was running late. For the second time in as many days, she was left hanging.

After Mason crashed on her couch, she'd planned on suggesting they take Rule #2 off the table. Things were good with them. If they could remain friends after a one-night stand and car sex, it seemed silly for them not to keep the benefits—and orgasms—coming. But when she came out of her bedroom to state her case for morning sex, Mason already had his shoes on. He kissed her on the forehead briefly before leaving her to write, which was, well, annoyingly considerate.

She wasn't easily deterred, however. She was so tightly wound after writing smut all morning that if his hair was doing that cute floppy-ends thing, she may throw herself at him. God forbid he gave her a hug and their hips touched and— Sawyer gripped the taxi seat as her vision swam, squeezing her legs together to provide a modicum of relief. She may have named all her vibrators Mason, but they paled in comparison to the real thing. And she wanted the real thing. Soon. Today, preferably.

Her phone buzzed in her hand, and she was so grateful for the distraction that she'd already swiped to accept before realizing it wasn't Mason calling to see where she was.

"Hi, Tess," she said in surprise.

"Sawyer!" her agent exclaimed. "*Sawyer.*"

She laughed nervously. "Is this a good call or a bad call?"

On the other end of the line, Tess snorted. "Please. You know I save bad calls for after the holidays." Sawyer filed that away under Things to Be Anxious About Later. "I just finished your proposal and had to call you. I *love* it. Emily's going to love it, too. It's so fresh and so you, and I'm dying to read the rest."

Sawyer's eyes stung, and she blinked rapidly, swallowing thickly to dislodge the unexpected swell of emotion stuck there. Her writing group chat had exploded with praise for her pitch, their support picking right back up as if she'd never disappeared. It had buoyed her, silenced her impostor syndrome, but she hadn't realized how much she'd been dreading Tess's verdict until now.

"Wow, um, well, I guess I should finish writing it?" She still needed her publisher to accept the proposal, but Tess's enthusiasm was like a balm. She had more people in her corner than she thought.

"Yes," Tess said emphatically. "I'm going to put a polish on your pitch and send it over to Emily this afternoon. Sound good?"

Sawyer nodded before remembering that Tess couldn't see her. "Yes, I—yes. Thank you." Even if they accepted this pitch, she still had to finish the draft and a round of edits to get paid. Only then would her bank account's steady dwindling stop haunting her.

The taxi pulled over outside Mason's building, and Sawyer slid the driver cash and told him to keep the change. No matter how broke she was, she wouldn't not tip. She bade the driver a good day before stepping out onto the curb.

"Sawyer," Tess said again, softly. Sawyer had the distinct impression Tess had been speaking that whole time and she'd completely zoned out, too happy and hopeful to process anything else. "I know this is an early draft, but it's already really, really good. Whatever you're doing, don't stop."

Mason appeared, wearing his usual gray coat and navy beanie, her smile widening as she met his gaze. "I don't plan on it," she promised.

"Good," Tess said sternly. "Now get back to work."

"Will do," Sawyer said around a laugh before hanging up.

Mason smiled down at her, excited for her even though he had no idea why she was smiling. Yet another person in her corner. It had been so long, she didn't know what to do with the feelings threatening to bubble over. Stretching up on her tiptoes, she flung her arms around his neck, making a point of keeping her hips away from his as she rocked from side to side happily.

If Mason found her exuberant greeting odd, he didn't show it. He wrapped his arms around her, squeezing her back in a rib-crushing hug.

"Sorry I'm late," she mumbled, pulling back.

He shook his head. "It's fine. I called ahead and let them know. Who was that?" He jerked his head toward her phone.

The grin worked its way across her face again, and when Mason's hand took up residence at the small of her back as they walked, she was fairly certain the grin was there to stay. "My agent. I sent her my proposal a few days ago, and she really liked it."

Mason beamed down at her. "Of course she did. She has taste."

Sawyer wrapped an arm around Mason, too happy to reply. It was a completely impractical way to walk, but neither of them stopped. If he stopped touching her, she may float away.

Mason's steps slowed as they neared a boutique with faceless mannequins in the windows. He opened the door for her, and she simpered at the gesture before entering the store. It *smelled* expensive. She barely had a moment to feel guilty about the snow sludge she'd tracked onto the gleaming tiled entryway before her attention was sucked in by the racks of gowns. Silky dresses, embroidered lace, dresses that sparkled like diamonds, dresses in every color of the rainbow. It was a riot of color and texture and somehow felt elevated in a way her explosion-of-color apartment never could.

"Dress-shopping montage is another cliché," she muttered out of the side of her mouth as Mason came to stand beside her. "Add it to the list so we can cross it off." Outside of Christmas dinner, they'd done a good job of sticking to the list. Well, that and when he brought her pho. Okay, they were doing a terrible job, but if she wanted to bend the rules—aka obliterate the cursed Rule #2—then she needed to stick to her other resolutions.

She couldn't read the expression on Mason's face before his PR Face slid into place at the sound of heels approaching. She hated that he felt like he always had to filter himself around other people, but she was grateful he never did it with her, at least.

"Mason!" A middle-aged woman in a fitted amethyst pantsuit approached them, arms extended toward him. She kissed him on both cheeks warmly.

"Celia," he greeted. "Thank you for seeing us last minute."

The older woman tittered. "Of course. Anything for Moira. Now, Mason, introduce me to your lovely lady."

Sawyer started, too busy taking in Celia's many rings and eyeshadow the same color as her suit. "I'm Sawyer," she said after a beat. Extending her hand, she fumbled her way through an air-kiss when Celia leaned in instead.

"Beautiful," Celia said, her eyes sweeping over Sawyer from head to toe.

That was generous. She'd gotten ready in the cab, finger-combing her hair and using her phone camera to apply lipstick and mascara between potholes.

They followed her to the back of the store, Celia taking their coats before settling Mason on a leather couch with a glass of champagne. When Celia's back was turned, he pointed to the glass with boyish glee.

Sawyer repressed a smile, trying to channel Mason's enthusiasm. She had never been big on shopping. She'd never really had the money to spare, her closet curated over many years of thrifting. Life as an author wasn't exactly luxurious. The royalty payments were unpredictable and spent almost immediately on her one-bedroom apartment's exorbitant rent.

Celia pressed a flute of champagne into her hand and instructed her to look around while she hung up their coats. Sawyer wandered along the racks, fingers trailing over the lush fabrics, occasionally pulling one out before slotting it carefully back into place. There were no price tags. The champagne did little to ease the dryness in her mouth.

"Mason," she hissed, crossing over to him. "This is too much."

He grinned up at her. "It's one dress, Sawyer."

She glanced around to ensure Celia wasn't lurking nearby. "And how much does one dress here cost?"

Mason shrugged. "The price of my sanity at not having to go to this party alone. Now." He shooed her away with a hand. "Put on something sexy for me." He draped his arms along the back of the couch, champagne dangling casually from one hand as he sank deeper into the cushions, legs falling slightly open.

Sawyer straightened like she'd been struck by lightning, lust pooling in her gut. He was so— Fuck. Cocky Mason was something. She wanted to crawl on top of him, to straddle him until that smirk slid from his face. Before she could do any of that, Celia reappeared.

"Anything catch your eye?" she asked brightly.

"Oh, um—" Sawyer dragged her attention from Mason as he took a sip of champagne, licking his lips afterward. Slowly, like he knew the deep dive into Horny Town her thoughts had taken. "I'm not sure. What are you wearing?" she asked Mason.

The corners of Mason's mouth turned down as he considered. "Black? But I also have navy, gray, maroon. Whichever."

"Men have it so easy," Celia whispered conspiratorially, and Sawyer couldn't help but warm to her. Celia stepped back, assessing gaze bouncing between the two of them, her attention landing on Sawyer's red lipstick. "Mason, you'll wear the maroon suit, it will complement her best. We'll work backward from there."

Mason nodded curtly at the order, biting down on his lip to keep from laughing. Yeah, Sawyer liked this lady. She followed Celia back over to the rack, forcing the words out before her nerves could swallow them. "What do you think would look best with—" She gestured to her full chest and hips.

Celia studied her for a moment, but when she met Sawyer's gaze, her eyes were fierce. "Oh, honey—everything."

Sawyer was too surprised to respond. As much as Sawyer loved her body—she was kinda stuck with it her whole life, so she figured "might as well"—the self-loathing always kicked in when she had to dress it, and things never fit quite right. She knew from shopping with Lily that it wasn't any easier on the tall and willowy end of the spectrum, but that knowledge didn't make it any less of a buzzkill to try something on and have it distort your mental image of yourself like a fun house mirror.

Celia seemed to sense that Sawyer was out of her depth, snapping into action and marching over to a rack across the room and grabbing a flowy navy number, a ruby sheath, a millennial-pink cloud of tulle, and a few other dresses. Sawyer had no idea how she kept track, but she knew the woman had very specific things in mind by the way she approached the rack and had a dress in her hands with minimal perusal. Celia doubled back to grab one last dress before gesturing for Sawyer to follow.

She knew the navy was a no before Celia even finished clipping her into it, but Sawyer allowed Celia to lead her out onto the pedestal in front of the three mirrors. It was worth it simply for Mason's reaction. He ran a hand over his face to compose himself as Celia situated the skirt and slight train. Sawyer simply smirked at him as his gaze met hers in the mirror. The sheer fabric crisscrossed over her chest, leaving asymmetrical gaps beneath her breasts, along her rib cage, her lower back. It was beautiful, but far more skin than Sawyer was used to showing, especially to a roomful of strangers.

Correctly gauging her expression, Celia nodded curtly. "We can do better."

Sawyer was going to leave this woman the most glowing review online.

The pink tulle explosion was next, and while Sawyer was surprised at how much fun the skirt was, it was simply too much dress. Mason was a fan of that one as well, but she had a feeling it was simply for the fact that the corset top made her tits look amazing. She gave him a little shimmy when Celia's back was turned, and he feigned passing out on the couch. The ruby dress was a masterpiece of lace and leather accents with a slit so high she thought Mason was going to cry when she said it wasn't the dress.

When she passed on the next two, she expected Celia to grow frustrated with her, but the woman simply smiled and asked her what she had liked and disliked about each dress. She told her clumsily, trying to remember what little she knew about dress styles, and Celia nodded along.

"Sexy is fine, but—conservative sexy, I guess. Is that a thing?"

Celia tittered out a laugh. "Yes. I love an old-fashioned gal."

Sawyer waited until Celia disappeared out of the changing room to laugh. The only thing old-fashioned about Sawyer was that she liked to drink an old-fashioned. She was ready to be done with this outing so she could drag Mason back to her apartment and put on an entirely different type of fashion show, where the silk and lace garments were much, much smaller. Sawyer bit back a moan at the idea of flouncing around in lingerie while Mason manspread all over her couch. She hoped the lust wasn't apparent on her face when Celia reappeared a moment later.

Sawyer's eyes widened at the flimsy thing in her arms and wondered if the woman had been listening to her at all, but agreed to try it on. As Celia zipped her up, she sighed.

"You're a magician," Sawyer breathed.

Celia smiled from over her shoulder. "I don't think we should show him, do you? Keep it a surprise."

Sawyer nodded in agreement, and Celia helped her out of the dress before taking down her measurements and her address, promising to courier over the dress once they had made a few alterations.

Mason's eyes widened in surprise when she stepped back out in her jeans and baggy sweater. "Nothing?" he asked, looking crestfallen—not with her, but like he'd failed her.

Sawyer shook her head. "No, we found it. You'll see it on New Year's."

A smirk spread slowly across his face. He pushed up off the couch, standing so close she had to tilt her head all the way back to look at him. His hand cupped the back of her neck, thumb stroking up and down over her wildly thrumming pulse point. "Tease," he breathed.

"You like it," she shot back.

"I do."

His breath coasted across her brow, and she shivered at the low timbre of his voice, the promise it held. She was infinitely grateful that her Christmas gift hadn't ruined anything between them. She was going to take Rule #2 off the table so smoothly, it would be like a waiter yanking off the tablecloth but the place settings remained undisturbed.

Mason's gaze lingered on her mouth and she smirked. Rule #2's days were numbered. He placed a quick kiss against her brow before following Celia, who watched them fondly, and Sawyer felt strangely guilty, like they were lying to her.

Sawyer hovered awkwardly behind him while he paid, still feeling a little uneasy about it, but it was his event, and normal people didn't have gowns sitting around for *work parties*. She tried to push the discomfort aside. Clearly, he had no qualms about it, and if she got her way, soon, clothes would be an unnecessary thing between them.

That thought buoyed her instantly, grinning eagerly when Mason turned, gesturing for her to follow him out.

"Champagne always goes straight to my head," he mumbled once they were on the sidewalk, his cheeks slightly pink from the cold and the bubbles. "Wanna grab something to eat? Do you have time?"

She leaned against his front, propping her chin on his chest. "I need to get back to writing, but I have some time. Buuuut," she drawled with a sly smile up at him.

His gaze met hers, mirroring her smile hesitantly. "But?"

"But I don't want to eat." She arched on her tiptoes to bring their faces closer together. She wrapped her arms behind his neck as his came around her waist. She nudged the tip of her nose against his, brushing her lips across his in the barest hint of a kiss. "I spent the whole morning writing about orgasms and could really fucking use one."

Mason pulled back slightly, not meeting her gaze.

She guided him to look at her, her smile faltering. His eyes were flat and tight where before they'd been soft and molten. "I thought we needed the rules so it didn't get complicated, but we've slept together twice and nothing's changed, right?" she asked with a forced lightness.

He took a step back, out of the circle of her arms, shoving his hands into his coat pockets.

It wasn't that cold today, mild by Chicago winter standards, but suddenly Sawyer felt like her very bones were shaking, the expression on his face speaking volumes before he even opened his mouth.

"I can't do it," he said quietly.

"Okay." It was a wonder how her voice cracked so many times in the span of two syllables. "We don't have to sleep together. Let's just—let's get some food," she suggested clumsily, embarrassment stinging her cheeks. Had she really misread things so badly?

He pressed his lips together, taking a controlled inhale. "No, I—I need to say this."

Sawyer's bones were shaking so violently, she wasn't sure how she was still standing. "Okay. I—should we go somewhere to talk?"

His eyes fluttered shut, and he shook his head jerkily. "No. Because we'll go, and you'll say something witty and make me laugh, and I'll forget why this is important."

She nodded for him to continue, absently wondering if this was what it felt like to die by quicksand—slowly, knowing it's futile to struggle, accepting the end.

"I hate shopping." He glanced behind them to Celia's boutique. "I hate IKEA. I hate crowded public places like the Millennium Park ice skating rink. But doing them all with you—I don't hate."

"I don't hate doing them with you either," she admitted, her voice barely audible above the wind coming off the nearby lake. "I'm sorry. I know I'm doing a terrible job at upholding my side of the list."

"Forget the list."

Her brows shot upward at the edge in his voice.

"This——" He gestured between the two of them. "Isn't about some list for me. It hasn't been for a long time. Rules or no rules, this is already complicated, Sawyer. *Everything* has changed." He stared at her imploringly. "What happens when we're done with the list? What are we then?"

She knew what he wanted her to say, that the reason she kept adding items to their list was to buy more time with him, to write off the way they couldn't stop finding excuses to spend time together.

"We're friends," she said weakly.

Mason's gaze softened. "Of course we are. But we're not *just* friends. Friends don't name their vibrators after each other."

Sawyer's cheeks burned. She knew it had been risky to do that with Mason in the next room, but if she was being honest with herself, she'd been half hoping he would catch her. And he had, but she'd underestimated his self-control.

Before she could come up with a response, Mason took half a step closer. He was so close, a hairbreadth away, purposefully not touching her. "Don't be embarrassed. I think about you, too. All the time. Trust me—I want nothing more than to go back to your apartment right now, but if I do, I'm not going as your 'friend.' I'm not going to fuck you like we're friends or a one-night stand or whatever that was on Christmas. If we have sex again, we have to be on the same page about what it means, and right now . . ." He shook his head, taking a controlled inhale.

Her heart was pounding in her throat, as if when she opened her mouth, it was going to jump ship.

They were in a standoff. They had only two rules left, and they each wanted to take a different one off the table. But it didn't really matter, did it? Sex or no sex, feelings or no feelings, this was always the way it was going to go with Mason. He was leaving. LA was always there, looming on the horizon. Better now than later, when she'd grown even more accustomed to his presence in her life.

"So, we're done," she said flatly. "With the list." She wasn't sure why she felt the need to clarify, other than it was easier to focus on that than the fact that she was losing yet another friend.

Mason turned away, taking a jolting step backward. When he met her gaze, his normally expressive face was unreadable, PR Face firmly in place. She'd seen him do it plenty of times, but never for her. It was like a kick in the gut.

"I . . . Yeah. I think I'm done. I mean, it's clearly not working. I'm still hopeless, but the tabloids are moving on at least, and you're writing again, so—" His voice was detached, like they were business partners concluding a deal. He ran his hand over his face, though it only seemed to further wipe all emotion from his features.

The quicksand was up to her chest now, pressing in on all sides, making it hard to breathe. She wanted to bolt, but she was stuck.

He studied her for a long moment before inhaling shakily. "Okay, well—"

"I should get back to work," she said at the same time, relieved her voice had mostly returned to normal.

She could almost visibly see him latch on to her excuse like a lifeline. He nodded. "Let me call you a Lyft," he offered, pulling his phone from his pocket.

"I got it," she said hastily. She tapped through her phone on autopilot, summoning a car. "I'll see you later?"

They both knew "later" was a conveniently vague way of promising something while promising nothing.

He nodded, not fully meeting her eye. "Bye, Sawyer."

His gaze raked over her, as if desperately trying to memorize her, one last look before never seeing her again.

As soon as his back was turned, the quaking in her bones turned into a full-body shudder, and she practically fell sideways into her rideshare when it arrived. She'd ended plenty of friends-with-benefits situations before, so why did her whole body feel simultaneously flushed and chilled? Her head felt light, and she was barely able to remember her own name when the driver asked for it. She'd never felt like this before. Perhaps she was coming down with something.

CHAPTER TWENTY

THE "EX" FACTOR – "It's not you, it's me."
But what if it *is* you?

It wasn't Mason's first time tagging along for dress shopping, but it was definitely the first time it was fun. And not just because there was champagne.

Watching Sawyer strut in and out in the ones she felt best in, the shimmies and shakes she'd do for him from when Celia wasn't looking, the way he wanted to hide her in his coat when he could tell she was self-conscious in one.

He hated that she'd turned their shopping trip into a list item, like it was all there was between them.

He'd spent half an hour being frustrated with Sawyer and then the past few days being mad at himself. He'd picked up his phone to call her a million times, shoving it between the couch cushions before he could hit dial. He wanted to apologize, ask to rewind, go back to how things were before, but there was no going back for him. He thought he could do it. Wait for her. But feeling about her the way he did and having her want nothing but sex had gutted him.

They'd gone to IKEA to ruin *500 Days of Summer*, but this fight, this feeling, was truly ruining that movie for him. He, too, had fallen for the girl who told him she didn't want anything serious. But the way he felt about Sawyer—it wasn't like anything he'd felt before.

He didn't care about fancy yacht dates or tree farms or ice skating under twinkly lights, he just wanted her. Maybe their list was working. Maybe he was changing. But maybe...he just didn't get to be different with her. The thought didn't sit right with him. Maybe their list *wasn't* working, because he couldn't quite let go of the idea that all of this had to mean something. But he didn't know what else he could do about it either.

Mason hadn't meant to fall for her—but now that he had, he couldn't pretend things were casual for him. It felt like lying. It made him feel cheap. He wanted someone to care back, to want him as much as he wanted them. Was that too much to ask? What was it about him that made him so easy to stay detached from?

He knew he'd done the right thing, but that didn't mean he felt good about it. He felt like he'd broken her trust by doing the one thing he said he wouldn't, but he couldn't keep pretending they were just friends. The thing was...the more he thought about it— and he thought about it *a lot*, no matter how he tried to distract himself—he didn't think she thought of them as friends either.

Or...was he just seeing what he wanted to see? Whether she had feelings for him or not, if she didn't want more, he could accept that. He respected her boundaries, but if they were going to stay friends— *just friends*—he needed to set a few of his own.

With a sigh, he pulled the script on his coffee table into his lap. Twirling the blue pen in his hand, he tried to pick back up where he left off, but he'd lost the thread of the scene. He'd given his agent the go-ahead to notify *Diagnostics* that season six would be his final season—after the New Year, of course. He didn't want to spend the entirety of the New Year's Eve party explaining where he was going and why. But ever since he'd done it, and even though he knew it was the right call, he felt exposed. Even more exposed than when the tabloids had been writing lies about him. He felt raw, like he'd shed a skin and this new one hadn't quite toughened yet. Reading the script for the season six premiere made him feel like a fraud, and reading about Dr. Santiago and Nurse Lia's breakup over a simple miscommunication made him want to throw the script at the wall. He knew they had to write Kara out somehow, but this was just bad writing, and the showrunner's not-so-secret dislike for Kara was practically jumping off the page.

Tossing the script back onto the coffee table, Mason let his head fall back against the couch. This was the whole point, wasn't it? Things would be different at Guiding Light. They could be the change the industry so desperately needed. Granted, they were a small company, and they couldn't change everything, but it felt good, it felt *right* that they were doing something, trying.

Mason felt like he'd been trying for years. Trying to be a better son, better actor, better boyfriend. Sure, his life wasn't terrible by any means, but he thought he'd be happy by now. He kept thinking if he got this role, or made his partner happy, or even got some rare Moira West praise, that he'd finally feel content, and yet...he was still searching. What the fuck was he doing wrong? Was it him?

And how did he fix things with Sawyer? Somehow, his thoughts always spiraled downward back to her.

He had no fucking idea what to do. He knew what he wanted to do. He wanted to race across town and explain himself better. That, yes, he *was* done with their list because he didn't think he could stop being a romantic any more than she could stop being a romance writer. And he hoped Luis was right, that once the list—their obligations to each other—was off the table, she'd want to be with him anyway. He didn't care if it was irrational or that he was leaving in a few months: this thing with Sawyer felt different in a way he couldn't explain, and it was killing him not to know if she felt it, too. If she'd let herself feel it.

He had to get out of his own head.

Pulling his phone out from between the couch cushions, he pulled up Alissa's contact and hit dial.

"Guiding Light Productions, Alissa Moreno speaking," she said crisply.

A smile spread over his face, the muscles in his face aching. He hadn't smiled in days. "Um, yes, hi," he simpered. "I was hoping you might be hiring."

Alissa laughed on the other end of the line. "I am *so* excited for the announcement to go live."

He loosed a long sigh. "I'm excited for it to all be in the open." He'd already filled her in on the disaster reveal at Christmas and the ensuing conversation with his mother that had somehow been more about her than him. "And I promise no more tabloids for the next few days."

Alissa scoffed. "Fuck 'em. It never wavered my belief in you or my desire to have you on board. I am glad they seem to be leaving you alone, though. I want you to be able to enjoy this moment."

They'd been working toward this for years, but he couldn't help feeling like it was happening all at once. The Guiding Light announcement would go live a week into the New Year. He hoped he was up for the job of managing it all. It was easily the most responsibility he'd ever had on a production, and he spent more time than he'd admit daydreaming about call sheets and schedules and whom he'd hit up first for investor calls.

Oblivious to his inner turmoil, Alissa plowed on. "I just signed off on the social media graphics for the announcement. You have impeccable timing. I also—" The line went silent for a moment, the whoosh of an email sending the only sound. "Just sent you a pitch deck. Potential first project."

Mason switched his phone to speaker so he could open the email that had just *ding*ed into his inbox. "I thought we already had that lined up."

Alissa hummed noncommittally. "Me, too. But now I'm thinking it feels more like a second project, and we should go a little more mainstream for the first one before going down Artsy Fartsy Lane."

"Trust your gut, Alissa. The first script was perfect," he reassured her. And he meant it. He'd read it one sitting, staying up well into the night to finish it.

She sighed. "You may be right, but it's *your* fault I'm questioning this."

Mason blinked. "My fault?"

"Yes," she groaned. "I tried to get the rights for that book you sent me, and their agent auto-rejected me."

"What?" Mason asked hollowly, a ringing starting in his ears.

"Yeah, apparently the author won't sell her rights, so thanks for the tip, but it might be a no-go. I sent her agent another email requesting an audience with the author. It would be the perfect first project for Guiding Light. As soon as I read it, it felt like everything was falling into place. It's everything we stand for. Written by a woman, queer rep from a queer author, would have mass appeal as a rom-com, but also there's so much depth and weight and realness that I could see it sweeping at Sundance—which I know we're not supposed to talk about, but…I just felt like I could see the future of Guiding Light and that was our jumping-off point to doing everything we wanna do."

Mason felt like an ice bucket had been dumped over his head. "You requested the rights for *Why We're Not Together*?"

Alissa was silent for a moment, her confusion palpable on the other end of the line. "Yeah? Isn't that why you sent it to me?"

Mason ran a hand over his face. It *was* why he'd sent it to her. It would be a perfect debut project, but that was before everything, before he really knew Sawyer. He hadn't thought about it in so long, hadn't realized Alissa had been thinking about it for the past month—not just thinking, *working* on it. "Yeah, I did. I just...I know her—the author."

"What?" Alissa screeched. "Put me in touch with her! I know I can convince her if I could only—"

"I can't," Mason said numbly. The following silence on the line was heavy. "We're...not really speaking right now."

"I see," Alissa said slowly. He could practically feel her words welling up behind a dam, threatening to burst free. "Mason, I swear to God. If your dick is what's ruining this for me—"

A laugh burst out of him, flat and humorless. "My dick wasn't the problem. My emotions were."

"Ah. I'm sorry, that—that really sucks, actually."

"It's fine," he sighed heavily, not feeling fine in the slightest. "It's just fresh. And honestly, I'm sorry. First the tabloids delaying the announcement and now this—"

"Mason—" She cut him off. "I love you, but this one's not about you."

He nodded. "She had a bad experience with her first book's adaptation." He could feel Alissa's attention sharpen on the other end of the line.

"How so?"

He did his best to relay what little Sawyer shared, and he knew what Alissa was thinking—all the ways Guiding Light would be different from that big studio. He could already visualize the Power-Point Alissa would put together at four in the morning when her hunger for this project kept her awake. When he finished, however, instead of spitting out all the reasons Sawyer was wrong, Alissa was quiet.

"Now tell me about her."

And just like that, the whole story came tumbling out of him. After their fight outside Celia's, he'd contemplated calling Luis and telling him what happened, but he hadn't been ready for anyone else's opinions. But between work and Sawyer and now this unexpected overlap between work *and* Sawyer, he needed to let it all out. By the time he finished, he felt wrung out but lighter. "I don't know how I keep ending up here. Even while trying to unlearn this pattern, I repeated it."

Alissa went silent for a beat. "Have you considered *Why We're Not Together*–ing yourself?"

"Did you really just make that a verb?"

"I did. It was pretty good, wasn't it?"

He heard the sound of a door slamming on her end of the line, Alissa's girlfriend screaming something lewd in the background that he pretended not to hear. He coughed to cover his laugh. "I'll let you go. Sounds like you've got a date night to get to."

Alissa giggled on the other end of the line. "I do. I love you. Thank you for calling."

Before he could warn her not to make any further moves on Sawyer's film rights, she'd already hung up. He didn't want to interrupt her evening, so he hit the side of his phone to make it go black, making a mental note to mention it the next time they spoke.

He exhaled heavily, his head drooping back onto the couch cushions. He was happy for Alissa, but he couldn't help the ugly twinge of jealousy. He wanted someone to celebrate the wins with.

He dragged the script back onto his lap, clicking his pen purposefully. Only, he couldn't stop thinking about Alissa's last question. Sawyer had asked him nearly the same thing after the tree farm. Was John Cusack on to something? Did his exes have the answer to why his relationships never lasted?

He scrolled through his phone, summoning up the same name he'd pulled up that day in Sawyer's apartment. Only, this time, there was no Sawyer to stop him from hitting dial. The phone rang twice before connecting. He clutched a pillow to his chest for moral support.

"Hello?"

What he was doing finally sank in, and he blinked down at the phone in horror, mouth open but no words coming out. In hindsight, he was grateful he hadn't done this in front of Sawyer. He envisioned her smirking at him from the other side of the couch, mouthing, *Smooth*. He waved the visual away.

"Mason?"

The sound of his own name jerked him out of his stupor. "Hi!" he said a little too brightly. "Kara, how are you?"

"I'm good," she replied, still clearly confused. "How are you?"

Clearing his throat, Mason leaned forward, bracing his elbows on his knees. "I'm great," he lied. "How are you?" His eyes fluttered shut as he realized he'd already asked that.

On the other end of the line, Kara laughed softly. "Good to know I'm not the only one nervous about the party tomorrow. I wanted to call you, but I wasn't sure you'd want to hear from me." She took a steadying breath. "That wasn't how I wanted people—*you*—to find out about the engagement."

"Congrats, by the way." He meant it. They'd been friends for years before dating. As lost as he felt right now, he wasn't so lost that someone else's happiness made him bitter.

"Thank you. And you should know, I'm bringing Peter to the party. If I have to spend my New Year's with our shit boss, I'm not going solo."

He knew exactly why she was telling him.

His mother's advice rang in his ears.

You should be seen out with someone new, dear.

It pained him to admit he'd unwittingly planned to follow his mother's advice. But damn it, she was right. Facing Kara again— with her man in tow—would be easier for everyone if he had a date of his own. It was why he'd initially invited Sawyer, but he'd been so hung up on missing Sawyer that he'd completely forgotten about seeing Kara. Every eye in the room would be on them to see how they behaved, a litmus test for how they'd be around each other when filming resumed.

"I'm bringing someone, too." Well, he hoped that was still true. "But that wasn't why I called."

The quiet hum on Kara's end of the line seemed to ask, *So why are you calling?*

"Well, I guess, it kinda is why I'm calling. I think I'm bringing someone. I hope, at least," he laughed humorlessly. "I've been doing a lot of thinking lately, trying to figure out what I keep getting wrong. And I figured if anyone could tell me, it'd be you."

He resisted the urge to hide his face in embarrassment. He had grossly underestimated how uncomfortable this would be. Neither *High Fidelity* nor *Why We're Not Together* had prepared him for this.

"Oh," Kara said awkwardly. "Mason, you were a great boyfriend."

"Sorry," he sighed. "I know this is weird. I'm not calling to win you back, or make you feel bad, I just—I try so hard to do everything right, but clearly I'm missing something. I want to know what I'm doing wrong so I can stop fucking it up." He laughed hollowly, hoping the manic tinge to it didn't translate.

Kara exhaled heavily on the other end of the line. "Okay," she said, as if hyping herself up.

Mason sat up straighter.

"It's that you *do* try so hard. Before we dated, I thought, '*God*, if I could just find a man like that. One who wasn't playing games, wanted to commit, wasn't scared to talk about a future.' And then, when we did date—"

She took a steadying breath on the other end of the line. "You were so goddamn perfect," she laughed. "Our first date was a fairy tale, except you were the idyllic Disney prince and I was the slightly terrifying Hans Christian Andersen version. You were doing everything I thought I wanted, but it's like, as soon as we started dating, you stopped being my best friend who I decompressed with in the makeup trailer, and started playing the role of the perfect boyfriend. I just wanted Mason. I thought, maybe it's a growing pain of our relationship changing, but then you told me you loved me and wanted to come to LA with me, and I felt like I knew you less than ever, and—I panicked. It was so much so fast. I thought taking a break while I was in LA would shake us out of it, but...then I met Peter, and from the jump he was so open. Everything that was missing with us was just *there*, effortlessly. I don't know how to explain it."

Mason nodded. He knew exactly what she meant. It had been the same for him with Sawyer. Effortless. And he'd still fucked it up.

His brain whirred with everything she said, unsure what to do with the information.

Kara let out one of the high-pitched laughs she only did when she was nervous. "I feel like a dick. It's—you didn't do anything wrong, but that was kinda it. I didn't want media-darling, hopeless-romantic Mason West. I just wanted my friend."

He nodded numbly. "I'm sorry."

She laughed. "Mason, I'm not mad. You're the only ex I still consider a friend. We were just better as friends. You're gonna find someone you can be your whole self with, and she's going to be so fucking lucky to be with someone who has such a big heart and wants to go above and beyond. But…don't rush it. Give her time before dropping the L-word," she laughed. "Happily ever after is a journey, not a destination."

He laughed with her, but it was forced. He was fairly certain he'd already found that person.

They chatted a bit more, but as they talked, Mason could feel how he was holding back. And yes, maybe it was because this was the first time they'd really talked since breaking up (again), so he had no business diving deep right now. But now that she'd pointed it out, he realized it was true. He'd grown up under the thumb of Moira West, who coached him how to navigate the public eye, how to be genuine while also maintaining a level of privacy. Had he let that infiltrate his private life? He always blamed his transient lifestyle for the end of most of his relationships, but maybe there was more to it than that. Maybe he was so easy to leave because he'd never let them in in the first place.

He thought he'd been doing all the right things, anything to make them happy. He hadn't wanted to burden anyone with his problems. He didn't realize that in doing so, he was hurting not only himself, but their relationship. But the more he thought about it, his thoughts inevitably drifted back to Sawyer.

Sawyer, whom he'd let in more than anyone else, because they were never supposed to be anything more than friends. And yet, he'd fallen for her in a way he'd never expected, felt more than he had with anyone before, because he'd let her all the way in. And the irony was, she might actually—finally—hold up her end of their bargain, and ruin him.

CHAPTER TWENTY-ONE

<u>RACE ACROSS TOWN</u> – Wherein the hero has
to catch their love interest before they get on a train or
plane or walk down the aisle to someone
decidedly Not Them.

S awyer awoke to the sound of knocking on her door.
Loud, insistent knocking.

"Miss Greene?"

She blinked awake blearily, staring up at the ceiling. Her neck
protested at the odd angle she'd slept in. On the couch. Again.
Because she'd stayed up too late trying and failing to write, not
because she *wanted* to sleep on her couch because it smelled like
Mason and she hadn't heard from him since their fight and she was
up in arms about it. Because she wasn't. She was fine.

"Miss Greene?"

More knocking.

Sawyer jolted up, moving her laptop out of her lap and onto the
coffee table before heading for the door. She avoided looking in any
reflective surfaces, only bothering to wipe the crust of sleep from her
eyes because her right one was half sealed shut.

Opening the door, she jumped back at the stranger awaiting her.

She wasn't sure whom she expected—certainly no one who knew her had any misconceptions about her being a "miss."

To his credit, the teenager on her doorstep barely reacted to her very high level of disheveled, keeping his attention respectfully locked on her face after a quick assessment. "Your dress, ma'am."

He extended a massive garment bag to her, and she took it automatically, her tongue in knots. She recognized the soft cursive logo of Celia's boutique on the upper right corner of the bag. Fuck. Was today New Year's Eve?

She couldn't accept this dress, not now. Mason was done with her. Done with their list, done putting up with her shit—as she knew he inevitably would be.

"Ms. Celia also sent you this."

She blinked up at the young boy, taking the small black bag with black-and-white-striped tissue paper.

"Have a good day, Miss Greene."

He was three steps away before her tongue unstuck.

"I can't accept this," she blurted.

He turned, seeming to curl in on himself. "I just get paid to deliver things, ma'am. I don't handle returns."

His posture alone told her that he'd had to deal with more than his fair share of awful customers, so she simply nodded and thanked him before closing the door. She'd figure out what to do with the dress later, hanging it carefully in her front closet. The tiny gift bag hung from her finger, and she made to loop it over the hanger, when curiosity got the best of her.

As she tugged the tissue paper free, a small card fell out. Retrieving it from the floor, she slid her finger under the seal to open it, her hands shaking, though she wasn't sure why. She *had* felt mildly sick the past two days.

Dear Sawyer,

This came into the store yesterday, and I couldn't think of a more perfect match for it than your dress.

Give Mason my love,
xx Celia

Gently, she pulled the elaborate gold chains from the bag, flipping them over to study the diagram on the back. Hair jewelry. Rich people could adorn anything. Only, unlike vajazzling, she was kinda into this. She could picture the delicate gold interwoven with the updo Celia had taught her how to do in the dressing room. It was a shame she couldn't wear it.

Her chest felt tight, much like it had the past two days. Her whole body ached like she'd jumped out of a moving vehicle and rolled for miles. She'd taken her temperature, but nothing. She didn't have a cough or a fever, just unending nausea and lack of energy.

Her phone buzzed on the coffee table, and she rushed over, disappointment clogging her throat that it wasn't Mason.

Not that she was waiting to hear from him or anything.

"Hi, Lily," she sighed, sinking back into her couch. A waft of eau de Mason floated up from the cushions, enveloping her in its musky, spicy scent. It was truly a wonder how ingrained it was, though at this point it might be a side effect of whatever illness she had. Delusional scents or something. She'd looked it up online, but that only led her down a rabbit hole of obscure diseases that all meant she was dying.

"Wow," Lily said brusquely. "You don't answer my texts and then you answer my call like the Grim Reaper himself is phoning you."

"Sorry," Sawyer groaned, lying sideways so she could nuzzle her face into a Mason-scented pillow. Not that that was *why* she was doing it. "I've felt like shit the past two days."

"Oh no," Lily said sympathetically. "Are you okay? Anything I can do?"

Sawyer shrugged at the ceiling. "No. Don't worry, I'll rally by tomorrow."

"Good." She could feel Lily's beaming smile on the other end of the line. "We're so excited to host you and Mason tomorrow."

Sawyer's stomach bottomed out like she was about to have a violent bout of diarrhea. She'd been so focused on beating her writer's block, she'd forgotten Lily had wrangled Mason into attending hangover brunch. "Oh, uh, about that. Mason and I, uh, I dunno, we're, like, done?"

The noise Lily made could only be described as the human version of a record scratch. "Say what now?"

"I don't really want to talk about it," Sawyer sighed, before launching into the whole story anyway.

Lily listened in such complete silence that Sawyer had to check more than once that the call hadn't dropped. The longer she spoke, her words became more rambling, less a clinical retelling of what happened and more a downward spiral. She thought she'd finally found her rhythm. But when Mason threw her that curveball, she hadn't known what to do. It was easier to stick to what she knew, what was working. It would be less painful, she'd thought, to just let that one ball drop than to try to juggle it all and risk dropping everything. But dropping Mason…she still wasn't sure whether he was glass or plastic.

"Everything was going great, and then Horny Sawyer took over and ruined everything. I really care about him, Lils. I want him to be happy so badly it's painful. Is that normal? I—"

Lily snorted, and it was so unexpected that Sawyer's rambling cut off immediately.

"What?"

"Yeah, Sawyer, it's normal. I think there's a word for it, hold on. Hey, hon." She raised her voice, calling across their apartment. She heard the answering grunt from Beau. "What's the word for when you really care about someone and their happiness and also want to fuck them on a consistent basis?"

She didn't hear Beau's response.

"No, I can't say that," Lily replied. "That'll give Sawyer heart palpitations."

Another muffled reply from Beau.

"No, she's not actually having heart palpitations, she's just having *feelings*."

"I hate you," Sawyer mumbled.

"No, you don't," Lily said matter-of-factly. "Sawyer, you know what this is, right?"

She wasn't sure she wanted to hear the answer, so she said nothing, but Lily wasn't easily deterred.

"You're acting just like you did when Sadie left."

"I didn't know you then," she protested feebly.

"No," Lily agreed. "But you told me all about it that night we each had a bottle of wine. How you thought you had the flu for two months, but really you were heartbroken. Though I'm sure this is only a cold, because you couldn't possibly be heartbroken now. The two of you were just friends, right?"

"Right," Sawyer agreed, not trusting the innocent affect Lily was putting on. It was like Lily had heard all the thoughts Sawyer had left unsaid and was calling her out on it.

"So," Lily continued. "Stop moping. You haven't lost Mason. He just doesn't want to sleep with you if things are purely platonic, which is fair of him. But also, yeah, I understand your need to mourn your vagina's loss because the man is—" She let out a low whistle.

Somewhere in the background, Beau said, "*Hey*."

"Sorry, babe, I mean it in a purely clinical way," she called back. "I told you Sawyer banged the guy from *Diagnostics*, right?"

As Lily and Beau went back and forth on which character Mason was—"No, Dr. Santiago. Remember, he was dating the ER nurse and then the actors started dating and everyone lost their minds?"—their conversation grew muffled, Lily presumably pressing the speaker to her chest. Sawyer stared up at the ceiling, blinking slowly as her fragmented thoughts aligned.

Kara. Mason. The cast party. Mason was going to have to see Kara for the first time since their breakup, since finding out she was engaged to the guy she'd started seeing while they were "on a break." Not only would he have to see her, but he'd have to smile and congratulate her on her engagement, most likely shake the hand of her fiancé. That was why he hadn't wanted to go alone. And now he was, because of her.

Sawyer sat up straight, staring at her reflection in the window. She was vaguely aware Lily was talking to her again, but she pulled the phone from her ear, checking the time. Five o'clock. The plan had been for her and Mason to get dinner before the party. She desperately needed to shower, so there was no way she'd make it to the restaurant in time for their six o'clock reservation, but maybe she could catch him before he left for the party.

She wasn't sure if he'd want her to go with him, after everything, but she was going to *try*. She wasn't going to hide out and pout because he'd set his own boundaries, same as her. She didn't have time to be anyone's girlfriend. He didn't know how to be casual. Despite it all, before they'd given in to their libidos, they'd been good at being friends. Sawyer didn't take that lightly. She didn't have many people in her life she could count on. What they had was special—and worth fighting for. Even if there was a small part of her—a small part that was growing steadily less small—that wanted more, she was going to be there for her friend.

"Sawyer? Did you hear me? We've got plenty of champagne and charcuterie and would love for you to come over."

She inhaled sharply. "Sorry—wait, that's right. It's your anniversary. What are you doing calling me? Go celebrate!"

"Oh, we have. We celebrated this morning when we woke up. And again after breakfast. Probably gonna celebrate some more—"

"Okay," Sawyer cut her off. "I got it."

Lily let out one of her trademark cackles. "My point is, come over. Spend the night and we'll have hangover brunch tomorrow morning once we're all functional enough to cook without burning down the place."

Sawyer shook her head. "Maybe. But first, I got a party to crash."

Lily gasped. "You're gonna crash his party?"

"Er, no, it just sounded cool. I'm gonna try to talk to Mason—before the party, try to smooth things over and save our friendship. And maybe go to the party with him, if he wants me to. If not, I'm going to be *very* overdressed for a night of Netflix and cheese."

Lily squealed. "This is just like the end of a rom-com."

Closing her eyes for patience, Sawyer took a deep breath. "This is not that. Just a friend going to support a friend, okay?"

"Sure," Lily said dubiously. "But it's also okay if you want to be more than friends. Y'know, just floating the thought."

"I don't have time for a relationship right now," Sawyer reminded her.

Lily snorted. "Clearly, you do. You're basically already in one."

Sawyer's mouth clamped shut, unsure how to respond. Sinking back into the pillows, she sighed. "Even if I had time for a relationship right now—which I don't—it doesn't matter. He's moving to LA soon, remember?"

Lily made a noise of intrigue. "Oh, I'm sorry," she laughed breathlessly. I thought I was talking to Sawyer Greene, Little Miss Short-Term Low-Commitment Only. The sex must be fantastic if he's got you daydreaming about a future."

"I'm not—"

"Be happy, Sawyer," Lily interrupted, firmly but not without softness. "He makes you happy, I know he does. Date him, don't date him, whatever, but for the love of God just *let* yourself be happy, babe."

"And when it blows up in my face?" she countered.

Lily groaned. "What if it doesn't?" When Sawyer didn't reply, Lily plowed on, voice softer. "I know you're worried about it all imploding like last time. But answer me this: How much have you written in the past month?"

Sawyer rattled off her latest word count without having to think, the number tied to her mental well-being in a way that she was well aware was unhealthy.

"And how much have you written since your lovers' quarrel with Mason?"

"Barely anything," Sawyer admitted on a heavy exhale.

"I rest my case," Lily said triumphantly. "He's good for you. I haven't seen you *live* this much in a long time, babe. So go get 'em."

Sawyer's lips puckered in frustration, Lily calling her on

her shit the way only Lily could. "Okay, well, I gotta get ready. I'llseeyoutomorrowbye!"

*   *   *

Sawyer washed her hair and shaved her legs faster than she ever had in her life, alternating between yelling at her blow-dryer to "do better!" and murmuring sweet encouragements as it feebly blew barely warm air. She applied foundation all over her face, creating a blank canvas that always made her look like Leatherface until she painted and contoured her features back on.

She was racing against the clock, turning her phone over and refusing to look at it after her hand started shaking so badly she had to redo her dark red lipstick twice.

She allowed herself to peep at the time once her makeup was done, her heart dropping when she saw it was a quarter past six. She hadn't realized she'd been hoping Mason would call, asking why she was late to dinner, until the time came and went with no word from him. She wanted to sink to the floor, wrap her arms around herself, and cry. Instead, she tightened the knot around her robe, as if it could hold her together as she finished getting ready.

She hurried to grab the dress from the front hall, spinning a roll of boob tape around her finger as she went. A knock sounded at the door and she jumped in surprise, boob tape flying across the entryway. She watched it roll away under her end table, before diverting her attention back to the door, heart in her throat.

It wasn't Mason. It was a neighbor or something. She tried to quell the frantic jump of her pulse, but it was no use. She wanted it to be Mason with an intensity she couldn't ignore. But she knew it wasn't going to be him. People didn't just show up at other people's doors as much as *One Tree Hill* wanted you to believe. Never mind she was planning on doing exactly that with Mason—but they had a predetermined meetup, so this was *different*. Definitely not a rom-com-worthy grand gesture, no matter what Lily purported.

Stretching up on her tiptoes, Sawyer peered out the peephole. A strangled noise escaped her, one hand already on the lock, the other on the doorknob, practically ripping the door off its hinges in her enthusiasm.

Mason was wearing the same black coat he'd worn on Christmas, with burgundy slacks underneath. The fact that he'd worn the suit Celia told him to because it would complement her best made her heart constrict. He'd styled his hair, and while she missed the unruly curls that flipped out around his ears, she had to admit he looked handsome. If she were wearing panties, she would have dropped them.

Mason smirked at the sight of her robe, the one he'd worn for his "modesty" while she washed his muddy lumberjack clothes. "I know I'm supposed to be staying out of the tabloids, but I really do think we need *People* to decide: Who wore it better?"

"You, obviously," she said automatically.

He grinned, eyes dancing with amusement. With how they left things last time, bantering with him felt like a breath of fresh air. Maybe they were okay. Returning his smile, she leaned more heavily against the door. Fuck, she'd missed him. Never mind that it had only been two days.

"Can I, uh, come in?"

She started. Right. That was the customary thing to do, not mooning in the doorway.

Not that she was mooning.

Stepping aside, she gestured for him to come inside. Mason was here! He'd come to see her, and while she'd been planning to hunt him down so they could talk, she was suddenly incapable of making words.

When she didn't say anything, didn't move from where she propped herself up against the door, he hovered awkwardly in the entryway.

"Hi," he hedged tentatively. "I just, um, wanted to stop by."

She sank an inch lower down the door. He was only stopping by, not here to pick her up. She nodded numbly, her elation at his presence evaporating as quickly as it arrived.

His gaze ran over her briefly, his attention snagging on her arms wrapped around herself. "I'm sorry about the other day."

The sincerity of his tone thawed out her frozen tongue. "Mason, you don't need to—"

"I do," he insisted. "I'm not sorry for what I said, but I am sorry for how I said it. You've been nothing but honest with me from the beginning about what this was. I thought I was okay with it, but when you asked me to come back to your place…I knew it meant something different for me than it did for you, and that didn't feel right. But when I said I couldn't do this, I didn't mean us. I don't want to lose you, Sawyer, and I couldn't close out the year without talking to you."

Sawyer made a noise that was half sob, half sigh of relief. He wanted to stay friends. That was what she wanted, too, wasn't it? So why, now that he'd shown up at her door like fucking John Cusack, giving her the platonic grand gesture she was planning to do herself, did she feel lonelier than ever?

Mason's eyes traveled slowly over her face. "You look beautiful, by the way."

She rarely found it worth the time to do more than mascara and lipstick, but tonight she'd gone all out. Brows: plucked. Cheekbones: contoured. Lashes: fake as hell.

She laughed shakily. "Well, good, because it was all for you."

"What?" His brows drew together, and he tilted his head to the side suspiciously. "For our list? Because I don't want to ruin midnight kisses—or whatever else we had left on the list."

Sawyer didn't either. She didn't want to ruin any of it anymore. She didn't want to pretend to hate it all. And goddamn Lily for being right, but she missed being happy, and Mason—Mason made her happier than she'd been in a really long time. If only she could just...tell him.

The words lodged in her throat, and she cleared it brusquely. "No, not the list. I was thinking about you going to that party alone and having to face Kara and her hideously big diamond, and I couldn't let you go without backup."

"You were coming to find me?" he asked in disbelief.

She nodded again. "I'm sorry, too. I know this started as a somewhat silly mission, but when you said you were done, I thought you meant with me and—" She inhaled sharply, her heart twisting. "I know I'm not the easiest person to get close to—I go dark for hours or days at a time, and that's not going to magically change, but whether there's half a city or half a country between us, I don't want to not know you."

A cautious smile spread across his face, and her heart threw itself against her rib cage with blinding force.

"I don't want to not know you either," he said tenderly. "And I hope you know your crazy schedule doesn't bother me. When filming resumes, *I'm* going to be the one who's working insane hours and disappearing for long periods of time. And then——" He stared off to the side, a look of bewilderment on his face. "And then I'm starting a business, which probably won't be time-consuming at all."

She grinned, shrugging one shoulder. "Probably not."

He grinned softly, opening his arms.

She pushed off the door, using him to hold her up instead, suddenly very weak in the knees over *that smile*. They stood like that for a while, swaying gently on the spot, her hands on his chest and his arms encircling her, his face pressed into her hair.

This was the moment. If she wanted to come clean, now was the time. She wanted so desperately to be able to give him everything, to tell him that she wanted more, too, but even saying what little she had left her feeling wrung out. Though she was no longer sure if the effort of keeping it repressed was more exhausting than opening up. She wished she could be the grand-gesture type, to get up on a platform and make a soul-baring speech, but she wasn't, and what was the point, anyway? He was moving. They'd crossed a lot of lines, but if they crossed *that* line, there would be no going back. So she would take what she could, give what she could, be his friend, and spare them both the inevitable heartache. She'd rather have him halfway than not at all. If she tried to have him all the way, how long until she couldn't give him the storybook romance he craved, and she lost him all over again? Where would that leave her——crushed, alone, stuck? It was better this way.

Inhaling the scent of his spicy cologne, she tried to make peace with her choice, Mason's presence soothing the ache in her chest that had been there since they last spoke.

Mason eased out of their embrace, his attention on the stuffed garment bag taking up the majority of her hall closet. "There's not a body in there, is there?" he whispered conspiratorially.

"Open it and find out," she challenged.

He grinned, giving the bag an assessing squeeze. Apparently satisfied that it was tulle and not limbs, he eased the bag off the rack before dropping down to one knee. "Sawyer Greene," he began, his face screwing up in concentration. "What is your middle name?" he whispered as an aside.

She groaned. "Jo."

His whole face lit up. "Of course it is. Sawyer Jo Greene, will you go to the ball with me?"

She pressed her lips together to hold back a snort, settling on a single nod instead.

"Go ahead and say whatever filthy thing you're trying not to say," he said with a twist of his mouth.

She pressed her lips together and shook her head, not wanting to ruin the moment with a balls joke that she should have stopped finding funny a decade ago.

Mason hid his face behind the garment bag as he laughed, despite her not telling her joke.

Pushing the bag aside so she could see him, she grinned, feeling a sense of victory that she was the one who got to make him laugh like this, to make him light up, to see behind Mason West's PR Face.

Wrapping his arm around her knees, he pulled her closer until she stood between his legs, her knees to his chest. "I think you might be my favorite person."

"Of course I am, I'm fantastic," she said instead of what she really meant, which was *I think you might be my favorite, too*. It was better this way.

So why didn't she feel better?

CHAPTER TWENTY-TWO

<u>THE MAIN EVENT</u> – Everything's been leading
up to this, and it will go either very right…
or very wrong.

Mason was on cloud nine. He watched Sawyer finish getting ready in a near reverent silence, the simple act of watching her putz around her bathroom as intimate as anything they'd already done. She kicked him out before she put on her dress, murmuring something about not knowing how sausage was made.

Sawyer was quieter than usual, but he supposed so was he. He liked this quieter version of them equally as much. He wanted to spend all his lazy mornings with her in companionable silence. To come home from a long shoot and do nothing with her. He kept those thoughts to himself, however. Sawyer hadn't exactly said they were just friends. For maybe the first time ever, she hadn't pushed that point, and it didn't go unnoticed by him. Whatever she felt comfortable giving was enough. He wasn't going to rush this time.

He hadn't told her about calling Kara. She'd always claimed to want no part of that secret list item. Telling Sawyer all the ways he'd screwed up in the past and how he was trying not to repeat those mistakes with her felt like the opposite of not rushing her.

"Get ready, Álvarez," Sawyer called through the door.

He grinned. He liked that she called him that, as if a reminder of who he was, that he could be himself with her.

"So ready," he called back. He was ready, but was she? Would she let herself be ready? He was fairly certain he wasn't the only one not saying everything they'd been thinking the past two days, but he had to take Luis and Kara's advice and wait, to not rush.

That resolution was a hard one to keep when she came out of the bathroom.

"Zip me up?" she asked, spinning around and watching him over her shoulder.

She looked like a glass of champagne, and he wanted to drink every last drop. Her dress was pale gold, with an overlay of crystals that caught the light when she spun around to give him access to the zipper. Besides the corset waist, the fit was loose, her arms covered by billowy sheer sleeves. It would be borderline conservative, if not for the low V in the front and back that had his mouth watering. It took everything in him not to throw his own rules out the window and make them late on purpose.

"Ready, Greene?" he asked.

"So ready," she echoed.

He tried not to read more into that than he should, repeating Kara's words in his head like a mantra. *Don't rush, don't rush, don't rush.*

*   *   *

"What's your producer's name again?" Sawyer asked as their driver pulled into the circular driveway in front of the absurdly large house.

"Richard Smalls," he reminded her.

She turned away from the window to peer back at him, green eyes alight. "Does he ever go by Dick?"

Mason fixed her with a look, already knowing where this was going.

She was still laughing at her unsaid joke when they stepped into the opulently festive foyer, Richard bounding over to greet them before they were even fully out of their coats.

In the dictionary under "smarmy rich white dude," there was a photo of Richard: watery eyes, ruddy cheeks, and a shellacked comb-over.

"Mason," Richard said warmly, embracing him and clapping him on the back. Richard wasn't normally the physically affectionate type, but then Mason spotted the studio execs hovering stiffly beyond him at the bar. Of course.

The cast got together sometimes during the offseason, but this party was a first, and the "attendance is mandatory" was heavily implied. Mason had no doubt that the core cast's upcoming contract renewals was a major factor in Richard's sudden change in demeanor. Funny how they suddenly weren't so "replaceable."

Mason didn't have to fake a smile, opting to imagine Richard's face when he heard Mason was turning down the contract for renewal.

A few members of the production crew arrived, and Mason took the chance to slip away. Slipping an arm around Sawyer's waist, he guided her over to the bar, promising to catch up with Richard later, though he had no intention of doing so. There was an expected script at work events, and Mason knew very well what role he was supposed to play. Ever since his call with Kara, he couldn't stop noticing how often he slipped into the role of Mason West. It was exhausting.

He wished he were bringing Sawyer to a wrap party for one of Alissa's productions instead. He allowed himself to briefly fantasize about a future where Sawyer had sold *Why We're Not Together*'s rights to Guiding Light. At that wrap party, they'd be in jeans and drinking craft beers, Alissa insistent they drink local while on location. He craved that vision of the future with a ferocity that nearly bowled him sideways. They had a snowball's chance in hell of Sawyer selling her rights—but now was not the time for him to broach that with her. All that mattered right now was she was here with him, and Richard *was* a dick, so Mason ordered two of the most expensive whiskeys on the back bar.

The little noise of approval Sawyer made when she took her first sip was worth it. Her eyes darted up to his in surprise, as if she hadn't meant to moan.

He smiled down at her, tucking an errant piece of hair back into her updo. She'd twisted her bangs off to the side, her face on full display. He knew she was wearing more makeup than she usually did, and he couldn't help but be floored. She'd put in a lot of effort but still looked effortless, letting the dress shine—literally. Her dark red lips pursed in a smirk as he took her in for the millionth time.

"Keep it in your pants, Álvarez."

He let out a strangled laugh. Beyond drinking her in when he'd zipped her up, he hadn't let his mind wander that far. He'd laid it all out, as best he could, and now . . . he had to wait. He would wait forever for her to be ready. Well, he'd wait until LA, and then he'd have to get realistic, but for now, for tonight, he could pretend the only countdown that mattered was the one counting down to midnight.

"I take it you're not upset I didn't pick the formfitting one you liked?"

He grinned, leaning in to whisper in her ear. "That one didn't leave much to the imagination, and I'm honored to be the only one here who knows what you look like under that dress, Sawyer Jo."

Sawyer blushed violently, her green eyes bright. "Álvarez," she chastised. Pulling back, she studied him. "Wait, what's *your* middle name?"

"Alexander."

Sawyer groaned. "Mason Alexander. Are you kidding? Why is your name so hot?"

He smiled down at her. "'Twas my destiny, I suppose."

She laughed up at him, and he cupped her face with his hand, needing to touch her, to feel her joy as it rippled out of her.

He wanted nothing more than to start the New Year with a kiss from Sawyer. Not for their list, not to ruin it, but to show her why it was a cliché in the first place. He was trying not to rush her, but he wasn't above reminding her just how fucking good they could be together. He brushed the pad of his thumb across her bottom lip, but her lipstick remained immaculate. "Is this kiss-proof?"

The sparkle in her eyes turned molten. "All kinds of smudge-proof," she confirmed in a low voice that settled somewhere deep inside of him.

Before he could overthink the implication in her voice, he heard his name from across the room. He already knew whom that voice belonged to, and following the sound, he held out his hand to Sawyer. She slid her hand into his, and a thrill shot through him. Given everything they'd done together, how was it that the simple act of holding her hand in a crowded room felt like the height of intimacy? They were doing everything backward. He was barely conscious of the myriad of people who greeted him as they crossed the room toward Bex, his focus solely on the feel of Sawyer's hand in his.

"Sawyer, what a surprise!" Bex exclaimed, the two of them exchanging air-kisses. "Love your dress."

"Thanks! It has pockets!" Sawyer did a little hop of excitement, the human equivalent of an exclamation point.

"Mine, too!" Bex said, matching her enthusiasm and shoving one hand in the pocket of her sapphire gown and twirling.

As they devolved into a conversation about a box of books Sawyer had apparently mailed Bex at some point between Christmas and now, Mason leaned in close, whispering in her ear. "I'm going to do the obligatory rounds. You good?"

Sawyer barely missed a beat, glancing up at him and nodding. Unable to stop himself, he pressed a kiss into her hair before breaking away, but not before he saw Bex's eyes widen. He supposed he deserved that, after all their insistence at Christmas that they weren't dating. He hoped she didn't give Sawyer too hard a time about it. Nevertheless, he was grateful Sawyer had a friendly face here besides his.

As he made his way around the room, smiling for the studio execs and genuinely laughing with his costars, he kept his head on a swivel. Partially checking in on Sawyer, who was still deep in conversation with Bex and now his costar Davi, and partially keeping an eye out for Kara's arrival. After their call, he wasn't nervous about seeing her again, but he would be happy to have it over with. Every eye in the room would be watching them for clues. Having number three and number five on your call sheet break up could alter the entire tone on set—and their production was already tense enough thanks to Richard.

Excusing himself to go to the bathroom, he took a few practiced breaths, wiggling his jaw back and forth to ease the ache in his cheeks from smiling so much. When he returned, he scanned the room, eyes tripping over Bex and Davi whispering conspiratorially in a corner, sans Sawyer. He did another sweep of the room, cursing that she was so short, his attention finally catching on the sparkle of her dress by the bar.

Sawyer, gold chains in her silvery blond hair, smiling over at… Kara.

CHAPTER TWENTY-THREE

THE DREADED EX – Tired: they're the epitome
of evil and you wonder how anyone ever dated them.
Wired: you would've dated them, too.

Another Blanton's?" the bartender asked, gesturing to Sawyer's empty glass.

"Yes, please," she said, hoping the desperation didn't show in her voice. She was infinitely grateful that Bex was here to keep her company, but it still didn't totally eliminate the fish-out-of-water feeling. Bex had introduced her to Davi Shah, who was equally as hilarious as she was beautiful, the two of them bonding over both having been stuck in an elevator with Mason. The conversation had eventually turned to set gossip, and Sawyer smiled and nodded and drank and pretended she had any idea what happened on sets. Her drink was empty all too soon.

This house was bigger than her entire apartment building, and the holiday decorations had definitely not come from the sale section at Party City. There was a tuxedoed pianist playing tasteful covers of pop songs, for fuck's sake. At this point, if the queen herself showed up and declared someone the diamond of the season, she wouldn't be surprised. Or worse, Usher would show up, and she would have to dance battle it out for Mason's heart, a la *She's All That*.

"Make that two, please," a husky voice called from her right.

Sawyer did a double take. She recognized her from the night at the bar—and the photos of her and Mason, photoshopped to appear torn down the middle.

The bartender placed their drinks in front of them, and Kara grabbed hers immediately, turning to face Sawyer, crystal glass extended. "Cheers."

Sawyer took a beat too long to jump into action, too busy staring at her. Flawless amber skin, silky black hair that Sawyer swore was a mile long, enchanting dark eyes, a cute as hell little mole on her cheekbone. "Cheers," she mumbled.

Her eyes widened as Kara threw back the entirety of the drink, and Sawyer tried not to do the mental math on how many dollars she'd just swallowed without tasting it.

"Another one, please," she said to the bartender. "And we'll pretend it's my first."

The bartender smiled. "I'm not here to judge," he said with a flirty grin before spotting the ring on her hand, still wrapped around the glass.

And God, what a ring. Sawyer was wearing a gown covered in crystals, but the rock on Kara's hand outshone her by far.

"Beautiful dress," Kara commented, giving her an approving sweep from head to toe.

"Thanks, it has pockets," Sawyer said automatically. She was fairly certain she was contractually obligated to reveal that fun fact.

Kara groaned. "Jealous," she said, taking a small sip of her new drink. She ran a hand over her fitted teal sheath as if hoping pockets would materialize. "One of these days, I'm going to throw one of these, and either everyone has to wear Spanx and heels or no one does."

Sawyer snorted into her drink, and Kara smiled. Goddamn

it. Sawyer didn't want to like her. She didn't want to hate her either—she didn't believe in that kind of petty woman-on-woman competition—but it didn't change the fact that Kara had hurt Mason. But she also wanted to thank her, because without their second breakup, Sawyer never would've met Mason.

Kara groaned, glancing across the room as she took another sip of her drink. "That one's my pockets."

Following her gaze, Sawyer spotted Peter Levine. "Oh my," Sawyer said with a barely suppressed giggle. Sawyer wasn't incredibly savvy on the Who's Who of Hollywood, but everyone knew Peter Levine, the son of a former Bond girl and a notorious party boy. There was a rosy flush to his cheeks, and if that weren't enough to signal that he was already half in the bag, his over-the-top hand gestures would have given it away.

"Would you believe that this is our third party of the night?" Kara murmured under her breath. She held up her hand. "Actually, don't answer that."

Sawyer smiled weakly.

By comparison, despite tossing back her first drink, Kara seemed entirely sober. Seeming to read her train of thought, Kara nodded. "I don't normally drink, but my ex is here somewhere, and we're cool, but I know everyone else is going to make it weird, so—" She raised her glass by way of explanation.

Sawyer cleared her throat nervously, because now it felt like lying to pretend she didn't know who she was. "Kara," she began, not entirely sure how to broach this topic. Before she could find the words, a hand appeared at the small of her back. She knew it was Mason without looking, but even if she didn't, the way Kara's eyes went wide, gaze bouncing between the two of them, reading their body language like a book, would have given it away.

Sawyer swore the volume of conversation in the massive room quieted to watch as the on-screen couple, off-screen exes greeted each other.

"Kara." Mason's PR Face was firmly in place, his tone the epitome of pleasant.

Kara composed herself in a blink, smiling warmly and leaning in to air-kiss his cheek. "Mason."

"I see you already met my—" Mason broke off, the hand at her back flexing slightly as he struggled to figure out how to introduce her. She hoped Kara hadn't seen the bolt of terror and excitement that shot through her when she thought Mason was about to call her his girlfriend.

"Sawyer," she finished for him, extending her hand.

If Kara noticed anything, she gave away nothing, and Sawyer suspected her PR mask was as fine-tuned as Mason's. Kara shook her hand briefly, glancing over her shoulder to where Peter was holding court. "Well, I'd introduce you, but—" She took a prim sip of her drink, sharing a knowing look with Mason that Sawyer didn't like. "I'll spare you." Peter gestured grandly, stumbling sideways half a step. Kara sighed heavily. "Actually, I should probably..." She gestured vaguely in Peter's direction. "It was nice to meet you, Sawyer," she said warmly. "Mason."

"Kara."

As she made her exit, Sawyer loosed a breath. Mason's hand at her back began rubbing slow circles. She leaned into his side instinctively.

"What did you two talk about?" Mason asked.

"Your bedroom prowess."

Mason concealed his too-loud laugh with a cough. "What did you actually talk about?"

His expression was still PR Face neutral, and she hated that she had no context clues to know how he was feeling about seeing Kara for the first time. And frankly, she was trying to pretend she wasn't still reeling from the strange pang of jealousy at Kara and Mason's unspoken interaction. Jealousy and...longing. She used to have that with Sadie. She missed having it. A voice that sounded a lot like Lily's rang through her head, reminding her she could have it, if she wanted it. He was standing right next to her, wanting it. The only thing stopping them was, well, her.

Whatever was written on her face cracked his neutral expression, a slight crease forming between his brows. "You alright?" he asked quietly.

Sliding her hand into his, she led him across the room, down the enormous hallway, trying the first door she saw, relieved to find it unlocked. The sounds of the party fell away as the door shut behind them. She gave the lavish office a cursory glance before refocusing on Mason, who leaned against a curio case, pulling her by their still-joined hands to stand between his legs.

Setting down her drink, she placed her hands on either side of his face. His eyes fluttered shut, and exhaling slowly, his PR Face melted away. When he reopened his eyes, he smiled. "Hi."

"Hi," she echoed. "Are *you* alright?"

He nodded. "Glad that's over. Better, now that it's us."

The word *us* made her stomach swoop far more than two letters had any right to. She nodded, leaning into him.

"I'm sorry I fumbled your introduction," he said with a wince.

She smiled, nudging her nose against his and earning a smile. "It doesn't matter. I know what we are."

Mason stared down at her, his expression unreadable.

She knew he was resisting the urge to press her for clarification. She traced one of the buttons on his black shirt with her fingertip, trying to figure out a way to tell him what she was feeling without slamming the emotional equivalent of the panic button. She was tired of pretending, too. Tired of pretending she didn't feel anything at all. She stifled her instinct to make a joke, trying to find a way to meet in the middle of what he wanted and what she could give.

For someone who wrote thousands of words for a living, she was not very good at them in real life. With books, she had multiple chances to get it right, to reword it, to express it all wrong, and then edit it until what was left accurately conveyed what was in her head and in her heart. It didn't work like that with people. You weren't guaranteed a do-over, and they were already on their second chance.

She envied Mason's ease with his feelings, the way he'd conveyed so much when all he'd said was *I think you might be my favorite person.* Simple words that spoke volumes.

She traced the lines of his face with her fingertips, hoping he could feel the way she felt through her touch, could read it in her expression. But just in case, she would try to tell him with her words, too.

"I envy you, you know," she managed.

Mason's eyes widened, brows shooting upward.

"This may come as a surprise," she began with heavy sarcasm. "But losing Sadie the way I did—it fucked me up. I envy the way you've never stopped chasing love and joy." She swallowed the lump in her throat, pressing her lips together to fight back the prickle in her eyes. "I'm so scared of ending back up in that place that I stop myself from getting too attached, because it can't hurt me if I never let it in." Sawyer laughed humorlessly. "I'm doing a shit job of selling myself, aren't I?"

The corner of Mason's mouth twitched up, his dark eyes scanning her face with so much barely restrained hope. "Sawyer." Her name came out in a deep rumble, as if it lived in the depths of his chest. "You don't need to sell me. I've been sold. Since the very first accidental innuendo."

The sincerity in his voice made all of Sawyer's self-preservation instincts light up, to backtrack before she could disappoint him. Taking a deep breath, she pushed past the fear.

"Me, too, probably," she admitted with a laugh. "I just wouldn't let myself feel it. And I haven't magically changed. I'm still scared. My life is still a mess I'm trying to clean up. I just know it's better with you in it." The way Mason's face lit up was both a balm and a blaring alarm. She didn't want to get hurt again, but more than that, she didn't want to hurt *him*. She took a deep breath for courage. "I'm telling you all this because I wouldn't have minded if you called me your girlfriend, but I also don't care if you don't, so long as we know what we are to each other."

Mason made a confused jerk of his head, half nodding, half shaking it. "And what…are we?" He was the living incarnation of half agony, half hope. If he was Wentworth, then she was Knightley. If she cared about him less, she might be able to talk about it more. Was this what happened when you let yourself fall for someone? Suddenly, every interaction became narrated by Jane Austen?

She brushed her lips against his. "We're each other's person." He sagged against her, bringing their foreheads together as he exhaled shakily. "I'm yours." His hands on her waist tightened, as if checking that she was really there. "And you're mine?"

His gaze flicked up to hers, watching her through his lashes. "Of course I am, Sawyer. I've been yours."

She shuddered, his words washing over her like the shock of ice water and a warm blanket all in one. And then they were both moving.

She'd almost forgotten what kissing Mason was like, how all-consuming, but her mouth had not, the memory of him imprinted on her lips.

Their mouths met in a clash of teeth and tongues, as if to make up for lost time. He moaned into her mouth when she took his bottom lip between her teeth, claiming it. His hands at her hips roved south, cupping her ass and squeezing roughly, pulling her into him all the while. Their hips met, and they both groaned, Sawyer instinctively grinding into him. Her hands tangled in his hair, undoing his careful styling, needing him closer. She had the strangest sensation that she wanted to devour him, or to crawl inside him, to consume and be consumed.

The door to their right opened, and they both went as still as statues.

Someone muttered a soft "*oops!*" before closing the door behind them.

Sawyer's eyes traveled back to Mason's. His hands were still full of her, her hands frozen in his hair, their chests heaving in tandem with their labored breathing. They remembered themselves in fragments, Mason loosening his grip on her, her dress that he'd been gradually working up falling back to the ground in a whisper of fabric. She smoothed back his hair, but once freed, the curls didn't want to lie back in quite the same way.

"Oops," Sawyer breathed innocently.

Mason grinned, cupping her face between his hands and bringing her back to him in a crushing closed-mouth kiss. "You wanna get out of here?" he murmured against her lips.

"Is that an option?" She rolled her hips against him, eliciting a hiss of pleasure from him.

He pressed a kiss to the corner of her mouth, her brow, the crown of her head, as if needing to gradually pull away, like doing it all at once would be too much. She could relate. "Yes."

A loud grumbling cut through the quiet, and Sawyer realized it was her stomach. A laugh burst out of them both.

"We did skip dinner," Mason said reasonably.

Sawyer snorted. "Speak for yourself. I made that charcuterie table my bitch while you were off brownnosing."

"Charcuterie is dinner foreplay," Mason said dismissively. Intertwining their fingers, he brought her hand to his lips. "May I take you to dinner, Sawyer Jo?"

She didn't have the heart to tell him that she hated her middle name, especially not when it sounded so sweet when he said it, the exact opposite of the way she was used to hearing it.

"If this relationship is going to work, you should know that I consider anything after nine p.m. too late for dinner. Late nights belong to the breakfast gods."

Mason nodded seriously, and Sawyer wondered if she'd ever be able to date a nonactor after this. The way Mason committed to her bits so readily, not only keeping pace with her nonsense, but reveling in it—she was growing accustomed to it all too fast.

Easing his phone from inside his coat pocket, Mason flashed her the time. Ten fifteen. He grinned broadly. "Waffles," Mason moaned.

"And here I thought only I could get you to make those noises."

He grinned, kissing her hand once more. Fingers intertwined, they slipped out of the room, trying very hard not to look like two kids who'd been caught making out beneath the bleachers. Between Mason's mussed hair and the grin Sawyer couldn't seem to wipe from her face, she didn't think they were very convincing.

Mason never dropped her hand, keeping her close to him as they skirted the room, promising to catch up with people later. Judging by everyone's level of inebriation, they wouldn't remember that they never came back.

When Mason got snagged by a sweet older woman he couldn't say no to, he guided her behind him, pressing something into her hand. Glancing down, she saw their coat check ticket and a folded bill. She slipped away before the darling woman could notice her, tucking herself into the alcove beside the coat check and praying neither Bex, Kara, nor Davi would spot her while she tried to facilitate their escape.

Mason found her a few minutes later, but there was something off about his posture. She handed him his coat with a quizzical look, and he nodded down. Following his gaze, she grinned at the bottle of champagne he'd nicked from *somewhere*, concealing it beneath his suit jacket. They slipped out the front door, giggling like loons.

As they sank into the back of a black car, Sawyer curled into Mason's side while he gave the driver the address for his favorite dive-y diner. His arms came around her, making quick work of the champagne bottle's foil, cage, and cork before the driver reached the front. If the driver noticed them hastily guzzling the foam that poured out—Sawyer licking it off the bottle as Mason licked it off *her*—he said nothing.

Sawyer was lightheaded, and it had nothing to do with the bottle of bubbles they passed back and forth. Okay, maybe it was a little bit the champagne's fault. But she knew it was mostly the guy beside her, who made her feel bubbly all on his own.

She traced the contours of his jaw with her eyes, watched his Adam's apple bob as he took a swig from the bottle.

"I think you might be my favorite person, Mason Alexander."

CHAPTER TWENTY-FOUR

<u>THE NEW YEAR'S EVE KISS</u> – The tradition
comes from the Romans, who believed not kissing
someone at midnight would beget a year of loneliness.
So no pressure.

It was nearly midnight by the time they reached Fred's roadside
diner, and Mason couldn't think of a better way to ring in the New
Year than with Sawyer, a stack of waffles, a plate of greasy bacon,
and a stomach full of stolen champagne.

Maybe it was the champagne, but he wasn't as worried as he
should be about being recognized. They had the place largely to
themselves, most people still out at parties. In a few hours, Fred's
would be full of drunk partygoers in need of grease and carbs to
soak up the alcohol in their systems. He was having too much fun
to worry about that right now. All he could think about was how he
wanted to preserve this moment—this feeling—forever.

"What are you doing?" Sawyer said around a giggle.

He slid off the stool, shrugging on his coat. "Stay here," he
instructed, placing a quick kiss against her lips. God, what a luxury
it was to casually kiss Sawyer Greene.

"Okay," she said, giggling again—she had barely stopped since
they finished the bottle of champagne.

Slipping out the front door, he took a few steps back, sliding his phone from his pocket and lining up his shot.

Fred's wasn't a fancy place. Glass windows wrapped around the front, providing a clear view of the bar, the line of swiveling stools, the massive greasy flattop beyond it. Sawyer smirked at him over her shoulder. He snapped his photo.

It was slightly fuzzy, but it was the perfect encapsulation of the moment. Sawyer's half smile, her sparkly gold gown spilling over the cracked green leather barstool, looking like...Mason frowned, trying to find the right words in his drunken haze. Like a guiding light. He shook his head. No, that was the production company. But the longer he watched Sawyer, the dull lighting of Fred's catching and refracting off her with the barest of her movements, the phrase settled deep into his gut, like the answers to all his unanswered questions were right in front of him. *Diagnostics*. Guiding Light. Sawyer Greene.

He was still standing there, dumbfounded, when Fred himself dropped off their food.

Sawyer glanced back, raising a brow at him before grabbing a fork and digging in.

God, he loved her so much.

When Luis first suggested it—that he was falling in love with her—it caught him off guard. It was like a puzzle piece he'd been trying to slot into place for years, in all the wrong places, and he'd finally—*finally*—gotten it right, sliding it into place without even trying. Watching her face light up as she dug into a chocolate chip waffle, knowing he got to be the one sharing that waffle...

As soon as he took his spot next to her, she held out her fork, bite of waffle ready for him. With her other hand, she polished off a strip of bacon in two bites.

He moaned as he chewed, satisfaction that only chocolate and carbs could provide coursing through him.

One of the other groups in the diner got up, turning on the volume of the muted TV at the other end of the bar. One minute until midnight. As the ball began to drop, the other diners began to chant, counting down. Sawyer simply smiled, alternating bites of waffle and bacon, like nothing of consequence was happening. Like Mason wasn't falling in love with her in a crappy diner. It felt both like a monumental moment and the most normal thing in the world.

When the countdown reached the final seconds, Sawyer wiped her mouth on her napkin, leaning in to kiss him as the clock struck midnight. Cheers erupted around the room, and Mason pulled her in closer, coaxing her mouth open with his tongue. She smiled, her lips parting for him. She tasted sweet like champagne and chocolate waffles, smoky like whiskey and bacon, the best of both worlds.

"Happy New Year." She gave him a quick kiss, leaning back before he could pull her in for another kiss.

"Y'know," he said thoughtfully, spearing a square of waffle with his fork. "I never got all the hype before, but I think New Year's might be my new favorite holiday."

Sawyer eyed him over the rim of her water glass, raising her brows slowly. "Even more than Christmas?"

A smile spread slowly across his face, warmth pooling at the base of his spine as he remembered how his Christmas had ended. It paled in comparison to having Sawyer with him now, trying to build something together. "Even more than Christmas," he confirmed. Dropping her off at her apartment that night had been nearly impossible. He'd wanted to follow her up, to spend the night, but he couldn't do that back then. "Could I ask you something?"

She watched him warily out of the corner of her eye, and he

couldn't wait to fully earn her trust, to soothe the jagged edges left behind by those who had come before him. She nodded jerkily, her attention back on her food as she dragged a waffle square through syrup.

"I know spending the night is a thing for you, so you can say no, but—" He brought her free hand to his mouth, his lips brushing her wrist. "I want to wake up to you." His teeth scraped over her pulse point, making it jump. "To start my days with you." He placed one last kiss to the inside of her wrist. "When you're ready."

"Okay," she said simply, like it was settled. She stroked his cheek affectionately before turning her attention back to their syrup-soaked waffles.

He didn't have the slightest idea if she meant "okay" she'd let him know when she was ready, or "okay" she'd spend the night. He was trying not to rush her—he'd already gotten more than he'd dared hope for—but he trusted Sawyer wouldn't do anything she didn't want to do. He would let her set the pace.

So, after paying their tab and leaving a generous tip for Fred, Mason ordered a rideshare. He handed his phone to her to put in their destination. Her green eyes glowed in the yellow light from Fred's, smiling softly as she tapped Mason's home preset.

The drive back to his apartment was painfully slow. The view from his Mag Mile apartment was beautiful, but *getting there* on holidays was a nightmare. Drunk partygoers jaywalked everywhere, Mason and Sawyer's car inching along. When they were only a few blocks away, Mason looked over at Sawyer, and she nodded sleepily in agreement.

"We'll walk from here," he told their driver. He left them a generous tip, too, for their trouble.

Sawyer picked up her dress as they walked so it wouldn't drag through whatever miscellaneous liquids were making the sidewalks wet today. They made it one block before Mason paused.

"Climb on," he said, jerking his head behind him.

She looked at him like he was ridiculous before grinning giddily. Wrapping her arms around his neck, she hopped up. He hooked his arms under her legs—with difficulty, there was a lot of dress to finagle—and hoisted her higher, which made her cry out in alarm.

"I got you," he said softly.

She kissed the side of his head before nuzzling her face into the crook of his neck. "I know."

If Luther, the building's doorman, thought they were a weird sight—Mason in his suit with a sparkly Sawyer on his back, rolling in at one in the morning—he didn't show it. He simply nodded in greeting, opening the door for them before calling the elevator.

Once inside, Sawyer made to hop down, but he leaned back, pressing her against the back wall, letting it hold her weight while they ascended. She squealed, swatting at his shoulders, her laughter devolving into snorts as they reached his floor.

"My keys are inside my coat pocket," he told her as he carried her down the hall.

"Okay," she said around a hiccuping laugh. "Which pocket?" she asked, shoving her hands inside his coat. Her palms brushed across his chest, roaming down, her nails scraping across his abs.

"Not a pocket," he groaned as her hand brushed along his waistband.

She giggled, pinching his nipples instead.

He couldn't help but laugh. She was simultaneously the most filthy and silly person he'd ever met. She took his earlobe between her teeth and tugged as her hand slid inside his coat pocket, tickling his ribs through the silk lining.

When they reached his door, he still didn't let her down, bending at the waist so she could unlock the door. They were both laughing so hard, it was a feat he managed not to topple over. He wasn't sure what was so funny, except now that he'd started, he couldn't stop, all the happiness from the past few hours pouring out of him in a rumble of laughter.

After much fumbling of his keys, they finally made it inside. Mason let go of her legs, and she slid from his back in a hiss of fabric. Gently, she spun him around, pulling him up against her. He pressed a kiss to her still-laughing mouth, walking her backward so he could press her up against the wall. She sighed against his lips, sagging against him.

"Mason," she breathed.

He hummed against her neck, leaving a trail of kisses along the column of her throat.

"I can't believe I'm saying this, but I don't think I can have sex."

He leaned back slightly. "I'm so full," he admitted.

"Me, too," she laughed.

He kissed her forehead, letting his hand drop from her hair to tangle his fingers with hers, pulling her behind him to his bedroom. He took his time helping her out of her dress, placing kisses everywhere, so in love with the way she watched him, the emotions she couldn't say aloud so clear in her eyes. He eased nearly a hundred bobby pins from her hair, gently untangling the gold chains Celia had gifted her, before he massaged her scalp. Sawyer went completely limp against him.

"Okay," she breathed. "I'm gonna fall asleep if you keep doing that."

"Bed's right there," he said with a nod toward it.

Sawyer straightened. "Not yet, I gotta—" She gestured to her face full of makeup.

While she showered, he grabbed water and aspirin for them both, knowing the champagne that had made them feel so light was going to bring them right back down tomorrow. He grabbed a shirt for her, placing it next to the water and aspirin on the bathroom counter for her. He was fairly certain she didn't like to sleep naked. That, and he selfishly wanted to see her in one of his shirts.

She did not disappoint. Coming around to his side of the bed, wearing only his shirt, she straddled his lap, taking a long sip of water.

"Should've talked you into that second nightstand," she said with a smirk. Leaning forward, she placed her glass on his nightstand, smothering his face with her chest.

"I see no flaws with this system," he said, his voice muffled as he nuzzled his face deeper.

She laughed, threading her fingers through his hair and tilting his face back so she could plant a kiss on his smiling mouth. "But fuck IKEA. We're ordering one online," she promised with a quick kiss before crawling off him and sliding under the covers. He sidled up behind her, burying his face in her neck, relishing the way his shampoo and body wash smelled on her, the way "we" sounded coming from her lips.

"Good night, Sawyer Jo," he murmured into her neck before settling onto the pillow behind her.

She pulled his arm tighter around her waist. "Goodnight, Álvarez."

Spending the night or getting a second nightstand might not seem like a big deal, but Mason knew, for Sawyer, it might be the grandest gesture of all. With the right person, the most ordinary moments became grand.

If he weren't already lying down, he'd swoon.

Pressing a kiss into her hair, he'd never felt so content. It took all of his self-control not to tell her how much he loved her.

CHAPTER TWENTY-FIVE

<u>MULTIPLE ORGASMS</u> – Well, it wouldn't be a
fantasy if the sex were bad, would it?

S awyer awoke to the sounds of Mason's slow, steady breathing.

She never spent the night—not since Sadie, not even the chef she'd had a brief thing with, who'd come over at the end of his shifts, well after midnight, and leave at three in the morning, when she kicked him out after they were done.

But she hadn't wanted last night to end. Though, judging by the darkness outside Mason's bedroom window, it was still night—or early morning. God, she'd spent the night and hadn't even had sex. Who was she?

She still felt full, but in a different way, like she could barely breathe there was so much emotion clogging her throat. It was a little disconcerting, how quickly it had rushed in. Like it had been waiting in the wings, and as soon as she'd opened the door to the possibility that this thing with Mason could be more, there was no way of doing it halfway. Even if he was leaving soon. She shoved that thought aside, sinking back against Mason's chest. He stirred, his arm around her coming up, his hand sliding beneath her shirt, trailing a slow path between her breasts, across her stomach, over her hips, and down her thighs.

She'd only slept for a few hours at most, and it was the best sleep she'd had in a long time. Rolling over to face him, she trapped his roaming hand between her thighs. "Yes, Mason?"

Mason grinned, bashfully nuzzling his face deeper into the pillow, one eye cracking open. "Sawyer."

Her eyes fluttered shut as he brought his forehead to rest against hers. She loved the way he said her name. There was an intimacy to it, as if it were more than just a name, and in those two syllables he'd managed to express a novel's worth of emotion.

She slipped her hand around his waist, guiding him on top of her, sighing as he put some of his weight on her, pressing her into the mattress. She licked her lips, her tongue wetting both hers and his. She sucked in a breath. "Sorry," she mumbled automatically, her lips brushing against his as they formed the words.

"I'm not."

A whimper got stuck in her throat, and his attention darted down at the small sound that managed to escape. He grazed his mouth over hers, testing. "Is this what you woke me up for?"

"Yes," she breathed, not even bothering to argue that she was fairly certain he'd woken her up. It didn't matter. Her hand at his jaw traveled up, twirling the hair that curled above his ears before burying her fingers in his hair, her nails scraping across his scalp.

"You want this?"

Her hand stilled, meeting his gaze. They'd done this before. They'd done all of it before, but he was still asking for her permission as she was dragging him on top of her. She also knew he wasn't just talking about sex. She meant to say yes but what came out was "Do you?" He'd rebuffed her before, and he wouldn't be the first person to decide she wasn't worth the effort.

Mason cupped her face, gently pushing her bangs back out of her eyes. "Yes," he all but growled. "I think about this—*you*—all the time."

"Me, too." She expected him to pounce at that, but he stayed just out of reach, his eyes boring into hers, like he was waiting for something. What else did he need? A goddamn formal invitation?

Dear Mr. Álvarez-West,

You are cordially invited to fuck me into the next century, starting now.
    Please RSVP at my convenience, which is also now.

                                                    xoxo,
                                                    Sawyer

"Mason," she warned. "If you don't kiss me soon, I'm going to develop a complex."

He grinned against her mouth, nibbling affectionately on her bottom lip. Her fingers in his hair tightened their grip, and he groaned. Leaning in, she longed to capture the sound in her mouth, their lips meeting in a bruising kiss. He kissed her like he was starved. As if they hadn't spent all of last night kissing, as if last night were a half-remembered dream and that if they didn't break this kiss, then they could stay in it forever.

The first time they had sex, she'd been bossy, impatient, telling him where to touch her and how. Now, however, she was content to move at the pace Mason set. His hands wandered slowly, gently squeezing and teasing as his teeth scraped over her bottom lip, along her jawline, her earlobe, gently sucking on her pulse point. He moved with a concentrated intensity that she had no desire to interrupt, letting him consume her. Her hands roamed the broad planes of his back, her nails scraping slightly and leaving trails of goose bumps in their wake.

Guiding him fully on top of her, he settled between her legs like a warm, weighted blanket. Outside the window, snow swirled lazily in the early dawn light, and the world was quiet save for the sound of rustling bedsheets.

His fingers danced along her side, tickling her rib cage. She arched up, trying to guide his hand where she wanted it, but their chests were pressed flush against each other, and she couldn't bring herself to pull back from him even a fraction. She squirmed beneath him, equal parts impatient and never wanting this to stop.

His hand slid up, gently cupping her breast through her shirt, his thumb brushing across her nipple, eliciting a whimper of relief from her. "Is this what you want?" he whispered against the shell of her ear.

"Yes," she breathed.

His mouth grazed along her neck, her collarbones, his hands pushing up her shirt to expose her chest. Her hands left his back long enough to guide her shirt over her head. She buried her hands in his dark curls as his teeth and tongue took turns nipping and soothing, working in tandem with his fingertips that circled and teased.

"What about this?" he asked, his mouth moving lower.

She tensed, her hand in his hair tightening. "No," she rasped, surprising herself. Who was she? She never turned down oral, but right now, she wanted him on top of her, inside of her, surrounding her, filling her. Her body was practically buzzing with the need of it. "I want—" She gestured with a limp hand toward the bedside table, and she swore his gaze darkened.

He didn't say anything, climbing back up her body and pressing her into the mattress with a kiss. He shifted his weight, pulling the drawer open. She caught the glint of foil as he palmed it, sliding the drawer shut and settling back atop her. His expression softened as he rested his forehead against hers. "You really are going to ruin me."

Her eyes fluttered shut, letting the words wash over her. She wasn't sure that she could, even if she wanted to. She wanted to burrow deep into his cinnamon roll soul, where it was warm and gooey and the exact opposite of her own. She wasn't the one who would get to keep him and love him, but it felt nice for a moment to picture that there was no LA.

She knew what she should do. She should stop this now, before she fell even harder. She should play the role of the vixen, whisper something scandalous in his ear so that he fucked her hard and fast, like he wasn't redefining everything she thought she wanted from a partner. But she didn't do either of those things. She wanted to pretend for a little bit longer that she was that girl, the one who woke up with a doting partner in her bed and had lazy morning sex with them before starting her day.

"I can practically feel your beautiful brain whirring," he murmured against her temple, placing a kiss there. "Talk to me."

She smiled softly, angling her head to look him in the face, their noses bumping against each other. She traced the angles of his face with her fingertip, the broad planes of his cheekbones, his strong brow, the soft curve of his lips.

She wanted him, but not in the way she usually wanted things. However he wanted her, she wanted it. She wanted to feel wanted by him. The words tumbled out of her before they even registered mentally. "I want you to lead."

At her words, his focus seemed to sharpen, like he hadn't been fully awake until that moment. Her heartbeat seemed to slow and pick up all at once. He moaned her name into her ear before pulling back, rocking onto his heels. Cool air rushed in with the lack of his body heat, but the way he stared down at her had her flushing with a new warmth all her own.

His palms ran up and down her thighs slowly before coming to rest atop her knees, spreading them and wrapping them around his waist. As he drank her in, she took the moment to take in the sight of him, the strain of his erection against his boxers.

The full intensity of his attention, the raw *want* on his face, was making it hard to breathe. They'd been in a fight not twenty-four hours ago, and now he was looking at her like—

They weren't talking, but his expression was saying *plenty*. Her preservation instinct kicked in, and she couldn't help but lighten the mood. "Draw me like one of your French girls, Jack."

He huffed a laugh, like she knew he would, biting down on his bottom lip, also like she knew he would. "First of all," he growled, running a hand roughly along her inner thigh. "My name is Mason."

A laugh burst out of her, too loud but just right, dislodging the emotion stuck in her throat and allowing her to rasp in a breath. "Second of all?" she asked.

He bent to place a kiss at the inside of her knee. "Second of all," he said slowly, and she knew there hadn't been a "second of all." "I hope you'd share your door with me."

She grinned cheekily at him as he kissed the inside of her other thigh. "I'd totally share my door with you."

She could feel his lips curve against her skin and then part, his tongue darting out briefly before his teeth scraped along the sensitive flesh.

"And third of all—" He glanced up at her from between her thighs, her breath hitching at the intensity in his gaze, his pupils so blown out, his eyes were nearly all black. "If you throw Friendshipulent into the ocean at the end, I'm going to be so fucking pissed."

Her laugh dissolved into a moan as he lowered himself on top of her, the feel of his bare chest against hers too fucking good. She guided him closer, higher, all the while trying to work herself lower, to notch their hips against each other.

"Patience," he grumbled. That one word, the gruff, low timbre of it, made her still. The ache between her legs grew, seeming to spread throughout her body, thrumming beneath her skin like a second pulse.

He ran his thumb over her bottom lip before kissing her deeply once more. She'd been so impatient for him to kiss her before, and she still felt just as needy. Each swipe of his tongue and nip of his teeth, the way her body reacted to it felt like the thrill of a first time. She had a feeling he was having a similar revelation, his hands slowly roaming, fingers gently splaying in her hair, curling around the hinge of her jaw, the shell of her ear, kissing her all the while, as if determined to make up for all the time they'd wasted not kissing.

She broke the kiss, needing to catch her breath, panting like they'd run a marathon and he'd barely even touched her. She full-body shuddered as she filled her lungs, dizzy with the high of him. His mouth traveled south slowly, so fucking slowly. Of course he was going to take his time. It shouldn't surprise her in the slightest that this was his style, the exact opposite of hers, though she didn't mind it. Her back arched as his teeth scraped across the underside of her breast, the promise of his mouth on her sending a flash of heat through her core as if he had actually touched her. How was he doing that?

"Mason," she mumbled. She wasn't sure when she'd started

shaking, but if he didn't stop teasing her and start following through on the promises his tongue and teeth and fingers were making, she was going to lose her mind.

He hummed against her rib cage, seemingly oblivious to her unraveling. "Yes?" he asked innocently.

Before she could answer, one of his hands slid between her legs, one fingertip teasing her. Her hips bucked up, begging for more.

A sound akin to a sob worked its way past her lips, along with his name and *please* and *fuck* and other nonsense.

She could feel him grinning as he brushed his lips over her navel, his finger still teasing around where she wanted it. His hand disappeared as he settled between her legs, wrapping his arms around them, palms flat on her thighs to push them open wider. She was only too happy to comply, her head falling back against the pillows at the first flick of his tongue.

He moaned like he was the one getting oral, his lips vibrating against her clit as he sucked. His hands pressed down on her thighs, keeping her spread wide for him even as she fought to squeeze them shut against the rising tide of pleasure inside her. She didn't want it to ever stop, couldn't believe she was about to hurtle over the edge from the barest suction, the teasing flick of his tongue so at odds with the bruising grip of his hands. He'd gone down on her before, but he'd never done *this*.

"Mason, I'm—" she rasped on a sharp inhale.

He groaned against her, pulling her impossibly closer, and her hands twisted in his hair, holding him there, her body curling in on itself, no longer able to differentiate each touch, her body one giant explosion of sensation. She screamed. She actually fucking screamed. She fell back onto the bed as his tongue laved over her, working her down as tremors continued to shake her. She usually felt limp after an orgasm, but whatever he'd just done to her left every nerve in her body feeling like a live wire.

She grasped at his hair, guiding him up, needing him back on top of her. He obliged, but slowly, ignorant to her desperate tugs. Giving up, accepting that he was only going to go at the pace he wanted and make her fucking wait for it, she let her hands fall limp at her sides. Something stuck to her palm, and in her haze of bliss and seemingly unending need for him, she recognized it as the condom he'd grabbed earlier. She all but threw it at him in her impatience.

His laugh coasted across her peaked nipple, and she arched her back, needing more.

"I don't think I've ever had a woman literally *throw* a condom at me before."

"Please," she begged, grabbing the foil with her numb fingers and pressing it into his chest. She'd put it on him herself, but that required more focus than she had right now.

Taking the square foil from her, he placed it between his lips as he eased his boxers down and off.

Her mouth watered as his erection sprang free, and she slid lower on the bed, aligning her hips with his. She watched Mason greedily, his eyes fluttering shut as she rubbed herself along the length of him. She could practically see Mason fraying at the edges, his patience and careful control coming undone. His eyes were blown out as he grabbed her hip, pressing her back into the mattress.

"Please," she said again.

He deftly ripped the foil open. "I think begging Sawyer might be my favorite," he said gruffly as he rolled the condom on.

She grinned at the ceiling. "I think Mason in charge might be my new favorite."

"What was your old favorite?" he asked with the sexy quirk of a singular eyebrow.

She couldn't think straight. She wanted him too badly to focus on making words when he was sitting between her legs looking like a fucking Adonis.

He dragged his tip up the core of her, parting her. "Sawyer?"

She nearly choked. "I don't know," she answered distractedly. "All of them."

The cocky expression on his face softened as he came to hover over her, taking her face in his hand. With his other hand, he reached between them, teasing her, the tip of his finger dipping in slightly before starting over. Running her hands over his chest and back, she could feel his muscles cording with restraint, a thrill shooting through her that he was as keyed up as she was. As if they hadn't done this before. But that time, it hadn't meant anything, and this time—if she thought too hard about what was written so clearly on Mason's face, the panic would set in, so she shoved it away.

Her hands traveled south, grabbing a handful of his wonderful ass, guiding his hips forward. His eyes fluttered shut, a crease forming between his brows as she guided him inside of her. A choked noise escaped him, his breath coasting across her collarbones as he dropped his face into the crook of her shoulder. She stilled beneath him, giving him a moment even though she longed to bury him inside her.

His mouth found hers, and she smiled. When he pushed fully into her, she broke the kiss, her jaw falling open as he filled and stretched her. Ugh, he was going to make her enjoy missionary, wasn't he?

She rolled her hips against his, moaning at the press of his skin against the most sensitive parts of her. His hand at her hip kept her in place as they found their rhythm, and she was so lost in him, so full of him, that she could already feel her live-wire nerves sparking. She shuddered beneath him, bucking against the hand gripping her. With a grunt, he pulled her with him as he sank onto the balls of his feet, before sliding back into her with a renewed sense of urgency. Her hands fisted the sheets, her back arching as he held her at the exact right angle, their hips coming together and apart at a pace that was both too fast and too slow.

Mason in charge was absolutely her new favorite thing.

He grinned, and she realized she'd said that aloud. His arm slipped around her waist, guiding her up so she was sitting on his lap. She wrapped her arms around his neck automatically, Mason never breaking his perfect rhythm.

"I lied earlier," he grunted.

She watched him as he watched them coming together and apart, over and over. "Oh yeah?" she prompted.

"Watching you come is my favorite." He brought one hand between them, his thumb pressing down on her clit.

Oh.

Fuck.

A tremor raced down her spine, and Mason buried a hand in her hair as her head started to fall back, holding her gaze. Her mouth fell open on a silent gasp as her orgasm seized her. Her insides simultaneously felt like molten lava and smoke, a tidal wave of pleasure crashing through her, coursing through her limbs to the rhythm of Mason's hips. Pressing their foreheads together, he ground more forcefully into her, their hips picking up a blinding speed as he raced to follow her over the edge. Burying himself inside her, his teeth scraped over her shoulder as he came with a grunt.

"Fuck," she breathed into his hair. Scraping her nails across his scalp, she waited for him to move first, not wanting to ruin the moment.

Every orgasm she'd had before felt like the discount store brand and she'd just experienced the real thing for the first time. It wasn't that she hadn't had good orgasms before. Hell, she'd had them with him before, but this was different. The voice at the back of her mind that she'd silenced before was back now. It felt different this time because they weren't just fucking. That was ... *making love*.

The realization raced through her with a physical shudder, and suddenly she didn't care about ruining the moment, because somehow, in their weird, twisted mission, *he* was ruining *her*. Easing off him, she flopped gracelessly against the mattress, too stunned to do anything else. She couldn't think about this while he was still inside her.

Oblivious to her mental spiral, he sank into the mattress next to her, also staring up at the ceiling.

This wasn't supposed to happen. Rule #1: No feelings. She'd put that into place for *him*, not her. And yes, she knew she had feelings, but she hadn't realized how big they were until now, until the thought of him leaving for LA made her chest ache. She squeezed her eyes shut, a tear leaking out unbidden. She buried her face into the pillow to hide it.

Mason placed a kiss to her shoulder. "What are you thinking about right now?"

"The Killers," she mumbled into pillow.

A surprised laugh bubbled out of Mason. "What?"

"It started out with a one-night stand, how did it end up like this?" she half sang, in her best impersonation of "Mr. Brightside."

The bed shook with Mason's laughter, and she was grateful he'd interpreted that as a joke and not the existential crisis that it was.

"I love your mind," he murmured, placing a kiss to her temple before easing out of bed to dispose of the condom.

The only thing that scared Sawyer more than catching feelings was getting a UTI, so she forced herself out of bed and followed Mason into the bathroom. He ran a washcloth under warm water for her and planted an all-too-sweet kiss to her forehead before leaving her alone to pee. Meeting her own hollow gaze in the mirror, she took a deep, shaky breath.

It was going to be fine. She was going to be fine. She always knew she'd have to let him go eventually. For now, she wanted to be self-ish. She hadn't felt this way in a long time, and she wanted to snuggle down deeper into it. She wanted to spend their remaining time together fogging up car windows and dragging their hands through the condensation, pointedly ignoring that they were heading straight for the ship-sinking iceberg that was her doing something as dumb as catching big feelings for someone moving halfway across the country.

CHAPTER TWENTY-SIX

GRAY SWEATPANTS – You know the ones.

Mason woke her up with lazy kisses. "Good morning," he breathed into her hair.

"Good morning," she murmured sleepily back.

She'd slept naked. She never slept naked, hating the way her skin stuck to itself. However, she didn't hate the feeling of Mason behind her, wrapped around her. She stretched like a cat in sunshine, relishing the tightness of her muscles after what they'd done in the middle of the night. The sun was fully risen now, a peek of it visible around the edges of Mason's blackout curtains.

"What time is it?"

Mason reached blindly for his phone, nearly knocking it off the bedside table and catching it at the last minute.

"Ten," he said. She could see the moment he reached the same conclusion she did.

"Brunch," they said in unison.

Mason jumped out of bed before turning back and scooping her up, carrying them both into the shower. At the first spray of cold water, they both screamed. Passing soap and shampoo back and forth, they washed the evidence of last night from their bodies, an easy rhythm like they'd done this a million times.

It wasn't until she got out of the shower that she realized her dilemma. She had no clothes. She loved last night's dress, but there was no way she was putting it back on. It was too early to mess with that much dress. The boning of the corset meant she hadn't worn a bra, so all she had was last night's underwear, and she wasn't putting those back on either.

Sensing her mental dilemma, Mason rifled through his dresser, tossing her a T-shirt and sweatpants. She tugged them on, tightening the drawstring of the pants and fantasizing about a bed-headed Mason wearing them slung low over his hips.

"What're you thinking about over there?" he said with a crooked grin, waiting until she made eye contact to slowly zip up his jeans.

"How good you would look in these sweatpants." Crossing over to him, she slid her hands into his back pockets.

He grinned down at her, resting his forehead against hers. "We're already late," he reminded her, brushing his lips across hers. "Should we be later?"

With a groan, she pulled back. "No. We can make up for it later." She didn't miss the way his eyes lit up at the word *later*.

The one thing she couldn't borrow from Mason was shoes, so she resigned herself to strapping her heels on, because there was no way she was going barefoot down the streets of Chicago. She rolled the legs of the sweatpants up so they wouldn't drag on the ground, and struck a pose.

Gold heels. Gray sweatpants. Black T-shirt.

Mason's dark eyes swept over her from head to toe, once, twice. "You are the sexiest woman I've ever seen," he said around a laugh.

They made it back to her place in record time, the roads mercifully empty as most of Chicago had yet to poke their heads out.

we're gonna be late, she texted Lily on the way, to which Lily replied, WE?! Sawyer ignored that, running up to her apartment and changing as quickly as her throbbing head would allow. Hurrying and hangovers did not go well together. Mason, by comparison, seemed completely fine.

"I was too busy schmoozing to raid the open bar," he explained when she pointed out how not hungover he was for hangover brunch.

Sawyer groaned good-naturedly as they hopped off the L train and walked the remaining distance to Lily and Beau's. On the whole, she didn't feel terrible, beyond a slightly pulsing headache that she hoped would abate after a carb-loaded breakfast and some hair of the dog.

Lily and Beau's apartment was only a quick train ride from her apartment, in an up-and-coming artsy neighborhood that Sawyer would love to live in, but she wasn't willing to take on a roommate to afford the rent. Thankfully, Lily and Beau were always happy to host her, and she was well-acquainted with being their third wheel to bar openings and Shakespeare in the Parks.

Sawyer froze with her hand over the door, turning to Mason. "I know you've met Lily, but I feel like I should warn you that her and Beau are, like...*a lot*. In a good way, like being cuddled to death by a litter of very hyper puppies."

Mason grinned. "You said Beau is in tech, right?"

Sawyer laughed at herself. "Er, like he manages the tech crew at Steppenwolf."

Mason's brows rose slightly, impressed, before leaning down to whisper in her ear. "Are you really forewarning me about meeting your actor friends?"

Sawyer blinked at him. "Right. I forgot."

He stared down at her, bemused, before rapping on the door with his fist.

If she hadn't already warned him, the answering cheers from the other side of the door would have sufficed.

"And don't eat the red jam in the fridge," she cautioned. "It's not jam."

Mason fixed her with a quizzical look. "What is it?"

"Stage blood."

Mason choked on a laugh. "Do you know this from personal experience, or—?"

Thankfully, Beau opened the door, sparing her from having to come clean about the toast incident. Lily bounded out, dragging Sawyer into a hug. For such a string bean of a person, she gave fierce hugs. There was an attempt to temper her excitement for Mason's benefit, holding her hand out for a handshake—then enveloping him in a hug anyway. Beau hugged Sawyer before appropriately greeting Mason, who was still wearing a slightly baffled expression.

Lily and Beau ushered them inside, and Sawyer watched Mason take in the space. Their walls were decorated with Lily's watercolor art and stage props Beau called "mementos" that were actually "pilfered." None of it went together, but it provided Sawyer some solace that someone's apartment was even more eclectic than hers. On top of the mishmash of styles, they had black and gold New Year's decorations and what appeared to be wedding decor to celebrate their anniversary.

If Mason found any of this odd, he didn't show it. But it wasn't his PR Face. He seemed genuinely enraptured by it all. Sawyer slid her hand into his and squeezed. The gesture didn't go unnoticed by Lily, who gratefully didn't comment on it beyond a widening of her eyes as she led them over to the makeshift bar.

"Mimosas?"

Sawyer groaned. "Please. No more bubbles. I can't."

Beau lit up. "Bloody Marys!"

Beau pulled a bottle of booze from beneath the bar and began constructing their drinks with obvious enthusiasm—though Beau rarely did anything in any other way.

As Beau twirled their pint glasses in seasoned salt, Mason listened attentively to Beau as he described the extensive research he'd done to perfect his Bloody Mary recipe.

"So," Lily said from behind her half-empty mimosa, dragging Sawyer into the kitchen under the pretext of checking on the breakfast potatoes. "What happened between yesterday and now? Not that I thought your grand gesture wouldn't be successful— obviously, the two of you are meant to be together. But I'd be lying if I didn't expect not to hear about it for weeks, in true Sawyer fashion."

Sawyer ignored the gibe. She told Lily everything. Maybe not immediately, but once she knew how she felt, she always told her. "It wasn't a grand gesture," she mumbled defensively.

Lily waved this away. "Listen, the faster you tell me, the faster we can save Mason from my wonderful husband's Bloody Mary monologue."

Sawyer smirked. Under her breath, she relayed an abbreviated version of events. Mason came over while she was getting ready—"Oh my God, it's like you were both metaphorically running across the field into each other's arms, only the field was a very dirty city!"— they both apologized, went to the party, ran into Kara, went out for waffles, had sex, and came to brunch.

"You spent the night?" Lily whispered. Her eyes were so wide with anticipation, Sawyer was growing concerned they might fall out and roll across the floor.

"It was late, and Ubers on New Year's are ungodly expensive," she said nonchalantly, hoping Lily would take the hint to not make it a big deal.

She did not. She barely stifled a squeal.

Beau poked his head into the kitchen, handing Sawyer her drink. It was at least 50 percent garnishes, as any self-respecting Bloody Mary should be.

They drifted over to the small living room while the potatoes finished cooking, Sawyer silently housing half a basket of pigs in a blanket while Lily and Beau downloaded them on their most recent projects. She hadn't thought much of it before, but of course there was a lot of overlap between theater and film, and Beau was clearly thrilled to have a fresh audience. Mason listened intently and actually seemed to understand the technical stuff Beau did, and asked questions that Sawyer could only assume were insightful, judging by how Beau couldn't stop nodding like a bobblehead. Their easy rapport gave Sawyer a weird doughy feeling in her stomach, and she didn't think it was just from the pigs in a blanket.

She slid her hand into Mason's once more, placing a quick kiss to his shoulder. She hadn't realized how nervous she'd been about him meeting what were essentially her only friends.

Lily seemed to be feeling some type of way about her and Mason's reconciliation. Sawyer caught her staring at their conjoined hands more than once, smiling like Mrs. Bennet about to marry off another daughter.

Sawyer wished she would stop. It made her feel like an animal in a zoo. She'd brought partners around before, though perhaps *partner* was too strong a word for what those relationships had been, given they had all been physical and temporary.

Was that what Mason was—her partner? It wasn't just physical, and it didn't feel temporary, but Mason's future was in LA. Sawyer had fought too hard to get her life back on track to uproot it all for someone she hadn't even been in a relationship with for twenty-four hours. Thinking about it made her palms sweat. Was there any version of this where the ending wasn't a goddamn tragedy?

Sliding her hand from Mason's, she wiped her hands off on her jeans. Without missing a beat, Mason pulled her legs across his lap, resting his hand on her knee. Lily jumped up as if to cheer like a baseball fan watching a home run, instead announcing she was going to check on the potatoes and dragging Beau with her to help set the table.

Mason squeezed her knee. "You alright?" he whispered, keeping his voice low enough so they couldn't be overheard in the cozy apartment.

She nodded. "I think Lily's going to give herself a hernia with all her barely restrained excitement about us reconciling."

Mason grinned, ducking down to kiss her temple. "That makes two of us, but I wouldn't call it a hernia, per se..."

Sawyer snorted. "Oh yeah?"

Shamelessly, his gaze roved over her, and she regretted not taking him up on his offer to be even later to brunch. She pressed her legs together to fight the growing ache there. The movement did not go unnoticed by Mason, one corner of his mouth quirking up in a crooked grin.

"We should rejoin them before we scandalize their couch." She nuzzled his cheek before standing, pulling Mason up after her.

"So, how did you two meet?" Mason asked as they migrated over to the dining room table.

Lily lit up. "Well, we didn't get stuck in an elevator together or anything adorable like that—" she began with a saccharine smile.

Sawyer took a pull from her Bloody Mary. This was going to be a long brunch. She could only pray that after this initial meeting, the novelty of Sawyer Dating Someone would wear off.

"Anyway," Lily said, catching her breath after giving Mason an unabridged version of her and Beau's relationship timeline. "We got married last New Year's Eve, rented out a bunch of cabins an hour north. Kept it small and partied for three days straight. Highly recommend."

Sawyer tensed. Lily had *not* just implied they were getting married not even twenty-four hours after they'd decided to try this whole . . . whatever they were doing.

"Sounds fun," Mason said diplomatically.

She simultaneously wanted to kiss him and slither down her chair to the floor. She made a mental note to not leave Lily and Mason alone together. Between Lily's big Mrs. Bennet energy and Mason's romanticism, Sawyer and Mason's entire life would be planned out less than a day after Sawyer finally managed to wrap her head around being in a relationship that was about more than just sex for the first time in years. She stabbed a potato morosely.

"It was fun," Beau agreed with a pointed cough. "Sawyer, how's the book coming along?"

Despite her mental turmoil, she smiled. "Not to jinx it, but pretty good." Mason squeezed her knee under the table, and she grinned more broadly. Normally, she'd leave it at that, but she couldn't help but gush, rambling about the subplots and character arcs and some of the Easter eggs she'd snuck in from her prior books, especially one from *Why We're Not Together* that she hoped would survive edits.

"That one's my favorite," Beau said sweetly, and Sawyer felt a rush of affection for him. It was her favorite, too, even if finishing it had been the hardest thing she'd ever done, dragging herself through the edits after losing Sadie, the title of the book like a slap in the face every time. "I always thought it'd make a good movie."

Sawyer focused on scooping eggs onto her fork, praying the conversation would move on effortlessly. Alas, today was not her day.

"Oooh, yes," Lily cooed supportively. "What do you think, Mason? You know movies better than us."

Sawyer's head snapped to the side to gauge his reaction.

Mason tugged at the collar of his shirt, his gaze darting to her furtively. "Er, yeah, it would. But that's kind of up to Sawyer."

She couldn't make sense of his tone, his PR Face suddenly in place. She didn't miss the subtle fidgeting. Mason didn't fidget.

"Would you?" Beau asked, genuinely curious.

She shoved down the vehement refusal that was a knee-jerk reaction at this point. It wasn't Beau's fault that Hollywood believed the only way to be happily ever after was for every aspect of your life to magically work out in the end, that the "small tweak" they'd made to the ending of her book was the vulnerable fragment of herself she'd given to her character, and that character now had closure, where Sawyer would always have an open wound. It was bullshit. Wounded characters deserved happily ever afters, too.

Once she was certain she wouldn't unjustly bite Beau's head off for his innocent question, she shook her head. But she didn't look at Beau as she answered, opting instead to study Mason, to riddle out his sudden shift. "No. Not after *Almost Lovers*."

"You don't know it would be the same—"

"It's her choice, Lily," Beau reminded his wife gently as Sawyer glared down at her potatoes.

She loved Lily, truly, but she was supportive to a fault. The world's best cheerleader when you needed one, and sometimes even when you didn't want one. Like now.

"Anyone need another drink?" Beau said brightly, already pushing back from the table.

The conversation moved on, but Sawyer couldn't stop analyzing the way Mason had clammed up. In all their chats about her film rights, he'd never given his opinion, but of course he had one, given his future job. If his reaction today said anything, they were on very different pages. No matter. It wasn't an argument worth having, especially not in the middle of brunch. Chancing a glance at him out of the corner of her eye, she was relieved to see the PR Face was gone, he and Lily arguing amicably over the best types of potatoes.

Sawyer took a deep breath, pushing down the well of panic at Lily's near suffocating joy for her, the inevitable disappointment her friend would feel when Mason moved to LA and this thing between them had to come to an end. She shoved it all down. One thing at a time. First, get through this brunch. Fall apart later. She could feel it coming like a storm, like someone had turned up the speed of the music, forcing her to dance along faster, like she'd been thrown seventeen new balls to juggle, faster, faster, don't drop them or they'll shatter, faster, faster.

"French fries," she blurted out, her voice a little too loud, needing to drown out the flurry inside her head. "French fries are the best form of potato, hands down."

"Agreed, but which type?" Mason countered.

"Skinny."

The table erupted with cries of outrage ("Jojo!" "Waffle!" "Curly!"), and the remainder of brunch devolved into a battle for potato supremacy. At some point, Beau produced a piece of paper and made a bracket, and they made a pact to meet up every two weeks, a style of potato advancing each week until only the Chosen Spud remained.

Sawyer had so much fun brainstorming types of potatoes and which restaurants made them best that she almost forgot the way her legs were beginning to quake under the weight of keeping it all spinning. Almost didn't notice that the bracket would take six months to finish, long after Mason was gone.

CHAPTER TWENTY-SEVEN

<u>THE L-WORD</u> – Once it's been said, it can't be
unsaid. Better hope it was said at the right time, and
not, say, in the middle of an argument.
That would be tragic.

The two weeks after New Year's passed in a blur. Sawyer's editor had accepted her book proposal, and Sawyer was glued to her laptop, unable to shake the fear that if she slowed down or took a day off, the creative well would get up and walk out.

Her protagonists had fallen back in love and everything was going well for them, but the journey wasn't over yet. Sawyer could feel her fingers typing slower by the day, wanting to live in this moment of bliss with them forever. She didn't want to write the big finale fight. She knew if she could get past it, they'd be happy, but the fight she had planned for them was going to hurt, and right now, Sawyer didn't want to hurt, because she was happy—mostly.

Ever since brunch at Lily's, she'd done her best to squash the anxiety that at any moment, the other shoe was going to drop. They'd gone out with Lily and Beau a few times. First, to kick off their potato bracket—Tater Tots had beaten hash browns, much to Beau's dismay—and again last weekend, putting Lily and Beau's endless energy to use at the Álvarez family tamale party. Sawyer's tiny freezer was now positively packed with tamales and menudo.

Things were going well, but when things got quiet, Sawyer couldn't keep the doubt from creeping in.

Mason was gearing up for *Diagnostics* to resume shooting, and was spending an exorbitant amount of time at the gym with Luis to "erase the sins of Christmas past." When he wasn't doing that, he was in meeting after meeting with Alissa discussing Guiding Light. The announcement that Mason was joining the production company had created a lot of buzz, due in part to the simultaneous announcement that he was leaving *Diagnostics*. Thankfully, the press seemed to have come around to Team Mason, no doubt in the hopes that they'd be the ones to get the scoop on Guiding Light's first project.

Mason was even keeping tight-lipped about their first project with Sawyer, only teasing her with the hint that they might be switching the lineup, if Alissa got her way—which, according to Mason, she usually did.

Their schedules had become increasingly difficult to align, but Mason never complained. Not even when she'd paused on her way out the door to go see him to jot down a plot point and ended up skipping their date to write late into the night. She'd made it up to him with phone sex later, both of them too tired to travel half an hour across town to the other's apartment. At least, she told herself it was just exhaustion in his voice, and not that he was growing to resent her unpredictable writing bouts. Mason wasn't Sadie, and she *was* trying, but it didn't negate the fact that she needed to finish this book, needed to get paid, needed to get her life back in the black for the first time in years. She was juggling more than she had in years, and she couldn't shake the feeling that it was only a matter of time before she dropped something.

She hadn't seen him in three days—which was nothing, really, and she felt ridiculous griping about it, even inside her own head. It would be nothing—if she had been busy. After that late-night writing sprint, she'd hit a wall. With her deadline fast approaching, she couldn't afford to be stuck, and she'd been stuck for two days.

She wasted an hour whining about writer's block to her writer friends, but when she reopened her manuscript, it had the audacity to have not written itself while she was on social media. She spent the next hour alternating between staring at the blinking cursor and writing nothing—or writing something and immediately deleting it. Accepting that today would be another wash, she caved and called Mason. If her creative well was empty, she had to refill it.

"Hello, muse," she purred.

He laughed. "I don't think I've ever been a muse before. I'm honored."

"Get me out of my apartment, please. I don't care where, or what, I just don't want to decide."

Mason hummed thoughtfully, the line going quiet as he typed something into his phone. "Okay. I just got back from the gym, so I need to shower first. Meet me at Michigan and Illinois?"

Resisting the urge to ask him what they were doing, she agreed and was on the train in a flash. Mason had the day off today, but he hadn't pressured her to make plans with him, knowing she would reach out once she hit her word count for the day. Maybe this thing with Mason could work after all.

Her optimism was quickly dampened when she stepped off the train and into a puddle, snow sludge and wet garbage soaking through her left boot and sock. Swearing, she tugged her phone from her pocket as she felt it buzz.

"Tess!" she answered in surprise. What day was it? Did she have a call scheduled with her and forget?

"Hi, hi!" her agent said cheerily. "Sorry to call out of the blue, but I have good news. Got a minute?"

"For good news?" Sawyer laughed. "I always have time for good news. Especially right now." She shook a piece of wet garbage off her boot.

"Okay." Tess took a deep breath, and despite her claim that it was good news, Sawyer couldn't help but feel like Tess was bracing for impact. "So, we have an offer—"

Sawyer screamed, dancing in a small circle on the train platform, not caring how many people were now staring at her. "They want another book?!"

"Er—no. Someone wants to buy your film rights—"

"No," Sawyer said flatly. She took a soggy step over to the platform railing. She'd fought the studio when they'd changed the ending to *Almost Lovers*, when they had her main character reconcile with her homophobic parents. She'd lost the fight. It wasn't personal, they said, but it sure as shit felt personal. As if her character couldn't have a happily ever after without it. She hated the message it sent to her readers, to *her*.

If the only thing she could control was her books, her words, then she would cling to them with everything she had. She wouldn't make the mistake of letting someone else have control again.

The line went silent, and Sawyer knew Tess was pinching her brow the way she did when praying for patience. "I told them that already, but she requested to speak to you directly, and I know what you're going to say," Tess cut her off. "But this wouldn't be like *Almost Lovers*, Sawyer. Alissa really seems to love the book and wants to adapt it, true to the source."

Every muscle in Sawyer's body locked up. "I'm sorry. What studio did you say?"

"I didn't. It's a small company called Guiding Light," Tess hedged hopefully. "They're new—brand new, actually, but they've got Alissa Moreno at the helm, and she's got plenty of films under her belt."

The train screeched away from the platform, and Sawyer stared blankly off into space. "Alissa Moreno, huh?"

A navy beanie came into view over the steps to the train platform, Mason's tall frame following.

Sawyer's jaw clenched. "Thanks, Tess. I'll think about it."

"Really?" Tess said in surprise. Then, apparently thinking better of it: "Of course. Take all the time you need. Have a good weekend, Sawyer."

"You, too," she said numbly before disconnecting the call.

Mason walked over to her slowly, brows knitting together as he saw the tight set of her features. "Everything okay?"

Sawyer laughed, though there was no humor in it. "That was Tess. Some new production company wants the rights to *Why We're Not Together*."

He came to a halt half a step in front of her. She was fairly certain a flicker of panic crossed his face. "Oh?"

"Yeah. Guiding Light." Definite flicker of panic. "Ever heard of it?"

Mason sighed, eyes fluttering shut as he tugged off his beanie, running a hand through his too-long hair roughly. "Sawyer," he said apologetically.

"You knew, didn't you?" She already had the answer to her question, but she wanted him to admit it. Production companies were still a bit confusing to her, but Mason was too integral to the project to not know.

Meeting her gaze, he nodded slowly, twisting his beanie between his hands. "May I explain?"

Sawyer forced herself to look away, glaring off to the side. "How did Alissa come across my book?"

"I sent it to her—on an impulse," Mason rushed out. "After we first met and I read all your books. I stayed up until one in the morning to finish it because I couldn't put it down. I could see it all so clearly in my head. It was like reading a movie. As soon as I finished, I bought a second copy, shipping it to Alissa. I didn't know you yet. I didn't know how you felt about protecting your film rights."

"And once you did...did you know she was going to offer?"

Once again, he nodded, grimacing.

"And you still didn't tell me?"

"Sawyer—" His voice broke. "I wanted you to hear her out, and I wanted her to have that chance."

"And you think I wouldn't if you'd asked? You thought it was best to go behind my back, surprise me, get my agent involved, give her one more thing to be disappointed in me for?" She took a steadying breath. She hadn't meant to raise her voice, but the hysteria was kicking in. All the panic and all the fears that she'd been repressing were bubbling to the surface like a physical force, like vomit. She swallowed thickly. She was not going to panic-vomit-comet on this train platform.

"Sawyer, that's not it at all—"

"It *is*, though, Mason. This is my career! You don't get to meddle with it! How would you feel if I went behind your back to push you to make the career choice that I thought was best? That's what your mom did to you for years, right?"

Mason blinked as if she'd slapped him. Maybe pulling the Mom Card was a bit of a low blow, but she'd read between the lines of all the things he hadn't said about the early years of his career, the indie films he'd done to put distance between him and Moira's helicopter mom—ing. He glanced around warily, their mostly hushed argument having drawn the attention of more than a few people at this point.

"Could we go back to my place and talk about this?" he asked in an undertone.

Sawyer scoffed, nearly choking on the panic clawing its way up her throat. "How long?"

"What?"

Sawyer tried to swallow the lump in her throat, but it had taken up residence there, started paying rent. "How long have you known Alissa was pursuing my book's rights?"

Mason swallowed thickly. "After Celia's."

A memory bubbled to the surface. Hangover brunch, when Beau asked about a *Why We're Not Together* movie and Mason had been so uncharacteristically fidgety. Suddenly, it all made sense. She could understand not telling her at brunch, but after? It had been weeks. He'd known for weeks and not told her, actively chosen not to tell her every time she asked him how things were going with Guiding Light.

"Mason? Mason West?"

They both flinched, remembering they were in public. A petite brunette woman in a very expensive-looking cream coat stood a few feet away, a hesitantly hopeful look on her face. Her friend hovered a few steps behind her, pretending not to be watching as she scrolled through her phone with a manicured finger.

Mason's face changed in an instant, PR Face slamming into place. "Hi."

The woman let out a girlish squeal before bounding over. Sawyer turned and stormed off. She didn't care if it was petty. She wasn't going to stand there and take pictures of them with Mason's stupidly beautiful, smiling face when she wanted to scream at him.

She hoped walking would calm her down, but the pounding of her boots against the pavement—well, half pounding, half squelching—only incensed her further. She could excuse sending Alissa the book—they hadn't known each other then, but since? He *knew* how she felt about selling her film rights. He'd known and decided not to tell her. Over and over again, he'd chosen to say nothing. All this time, she thought he'd been so gracious about her chaotic schedule, but what if it was all just to butter her up, to woo her into giving him the rights?

Sawyer hadn't realized where she'd been walking until she pulled up short outside of Mason's apartment building. The sweet doorman smiled warmly at her.

"Good day, Miss Sawyer. I'm afraid Mr. West just left."

"I know." She exhaled heavily. "Thanks, Luther. I'm not—"

"Ah! Never mind, here he comes now."

Sawyer whipped around as Mason jogged across the street, eyes locked on her. She was fairly certain he was attempting to smile pleasantly, but it looked more like a grimace. Apparently, she wasn't the only one whose mood hadn't improved with a walk.

"Seriously, Sawyer? You just *left*?"

"Oh, I'm sorry," she simpered. "Did you need me to play photographer for you and your hot moms fan club?"

Luther cleared his throat awkwardly, opening the lobby door for them.

Mason placed a hand at her elbow to guide her inside. She childishly wrenched it from his grasp, storming inside without waiting for him.

"Sawyer," he sighed. "This argument is stupid."

"Oh? My feelings about how you went behind my back and meddled in my career are stupid?"

He ran a hand over his face roughly. "No, I—I said that wrong. Of course it's not. I went about it wrong, but this wouldn't be like last time—"

"That's just it, Mason," she fumed. "You think you know, but you don't. It's not that they just changed a few things about my book and my ego was too big to handle it, they—" Sawyer's eyes stung and she blinked furiously, even angrier with herself that she was seriously going to cry right now.

"I know, Sawyer," he pleaded. "I know what they did, which is why I wanted to make sure we could give you everything you needed to feel comfortable doing this before telling you. Alissa wants to cowrite the script with you. We'd make you an executive producer. You'd have veto power over any changes you don't like. You could stay with me in LA—"

Her heart was in her throat, suffocating her. It would be foolish not to take this offer. But this wasn't part of her plan. Hell, she didn't *have* a plan beyond her deadline, her entire future hinging on whether or not she could salvage her career. The mere thought of one more thing to juggle made her want to sink to the floor and dissolve into a puddle. She felt backed into a corner, backed into a future she hadn't signed up for.

"You make it sound so simple," she said hollowly. "Sell my rights, pack up my life, follow you to La-La Land. What if this doesn't have the happily ever after you hoped? Then what? I've sold my rights to my ex?"

"Why do you assume it's not going to work out?"

"Because in my experience, it doesn't! Can you honestly say your track record is any better than mine? This whole mission, the list, was about both of us getting our careers back on track, and we've done that. Mixing them—" Her hands were somehow shaking and going numb at the same time. "I'm so grateful that our non-sense mission worked, but the last time I said yes to everything, I lost everything. You're asking me to juggle too much, I—" She sucked in a deep breath, unsure of the last time she'd breathed.

Mason, on the other hand, was completely calm. Of course he was. He'd had weeks to think this through. "You wouldn't have to juggle it all on your own, babe. I would be with you, every step of the way. Let me help. It's a lot—I know it's a lot—but we can work this out."

He made it sound so simple, so easy. If she hadn't already done this before, she'd probably believe him. But she'd been here before, everything she'd ever wanted at her fingertips, only to end up more alone than she'd ever been—and that was when she'd kept it all separate. Involving Mason directly was inviting disaster, another two-year slump where she could feel the color leaching out of her soul with every day spent unable to do the one that thing that she'd ever felt *good* at. She was just starting to feel like herself again. She was so proud of how far she'd come. She thought she'd found something in Mason, in how understanding he was of her schedule and deadlines, that he wasn't like Sadie, and yet . . . here she was again.

Misreading her silence, Mason continued in a soft voice, like he was talking to a wounded animal. "We don't have to figure this out right now."

"What's to figure out?" she laughed. "Mason, this is nonsensi-cal. You want me to move in—move across the country—and tie my career to some guy I've known two months, been seeing for a few weeks? You don't need to *High Fidelity* yourself, because I can tell you right now why your relationships don't last. It's too fucking much, Mason. It's been weeks and you're already asking me to give you my whole fucking life."

Mason winced, but pressed on calmly, undeterred. "I know it's a lot, that this wasn't the plan. I didn't plan on falling in love with you, but I did. And other than right now, I've been happier with you than anyone."

The edges of her vision blurred, her attention wholly on Mason and his mouth that was still moving, making words that she couldn't comprehend. "You don't," she forced out.

"What?" he asked, turning back to her from where he'd been pacing while he monologued.

"You don't love me," she said numbly.

He laughed, but there was no humor in it. "I don't think you get to decide that."

She shook her head. "You're...confused. And it's my fault, I guess. We were doing all these romantic things for the list and you fell for it, like you said you always do."

"Bullshit."

Sawyer laughed, half-hysterical. "Is now really the time for a *How to Lose a Guy* reference?"

"No, I'm calling bullshit. I didn't fall for you because of the list. I fell for you in the moments in between. I fell for you at the tree farm when you made sure that little girl got the tree you had picked out—"

"Tree farm was on the list—"

"I fell for you again when you were prancing around at Celia's—"

"Shopping montage—"

"The night we had pho at your apartment and we stayed up talking for hours—"

Before she could poke a hole in that, he continued.

"New Year's Eve, at Fred's—"

"Midnight kiss was on the list—"

"Christmas," he practically growled. "My car, parking lot. That wasn't on the list, and it sure as shit didn't mean fucking nothing."

"Just sex." The silence that followed her blatant lie was deafening, both of them staring at each other, breathing heavily, and she almost wished he would call bullshit again, in their own fucked-up version of the game. "I'll take the blame, okay?" she continued shakily. "I broke the rules, of course things got confusing."

Mason raised his hand and poked the air like he was punctuating an unspoken expletive before retracting his finger and making a fist, pressing his knuckles to his mouth. "I cannot believe you're doing this ... and maybe that makes me the most hopeless romantic in the world, because I should have known you'd do exactly this. Well, congratulations, Sawyer Greene, you've finally upheld your end of the deal and ruined romance for me. Happy?"

Not particularly.

"You'll be fine, Mason. Once this is all in the rearview, you'll realize you just got swept up again. It wasn't me you wanted. I was just there."

A muscle in Mason's jaw jumped, he was clenching it so hard. "This cannot actually be your impression of me."

"Prove me wrong," she said, flinging her arms wide. She didn't even know what that *meant*, but it was the most cutting thing she could think to say right now. She wanted to run, to puke into the umbrella stand, to scream. She wanted out of this conversation, by any means necessary.

"How?" he asked softly, his voice catching.

She took a shaky breath, barely able to get any air in around the lump in her throat. "Let me go. Respect that I don't want this. I never did. I tried, okay? But this—" She gestured between them. "This has always had an end date, so let's stop prolonging the inevitable. You're moving to LA. My life is here. The list is done. The tabloids have moved on. My writer's block is gone. I need to focus on finishing my book, and you need to focus on Guiding Light. So, let's just call it. We both got what we needed."

Hurt flashed across Mason's face. "What about what we want?"

Ignoring the pang in her chest, she forced her next words out. "I don't want this."

"Of course," he said blandly, his PR Face sliding into place.

Somehow, that hurt even more than seeing him in pain.

She met his gaze, and they watched each other with bated breath. There was a moment, a fraction of a second, where she thought he was going to cave, to beg her to stay and talk it out. The scariest part was she hoped he would. Before he could, she turned on her soggy heel and left.

She made it half a block before she puked into a trash can.

CHAPTER TWENTY-EIGHT

<u>MISCOMMUNICATION</u> – The least popular of
all rom-com tropes, perhaps because it's the most true
to life, and it sucks—in fiction and in reality.

The weeks following the fight with Sawyer were some of the longest Mason had ever experienced. He was equal parts looking forward to *Diagnostics* resuming—if only for the distraction—and dreading it. It was bittersweet. The set and crew had been his home for nearly six years, but he was ready for something new, even with the uncertainty of what "new" would look like.

The writers had sent over a few script amendments earlier that day, a new B plot for him worked into the first few episodes that would inevitably lead up to his character's departure from the show. When he arrived at the studio offices for the season six table read, the entire room quieted as he entered. He froze for a moment before heading over to craft services and grabbing a muffin he had no intention of eating.

A hand at his elbow had him turning.

"Proud of you," Kara murmured.

Meeting her gaze, he knew she meant it. Because she was his on-screen girlfriend, the last-minute changes they'd made to the script had primarily included his scenes with her. "Thanks," he said genuinely.

"It feels right that we're going out together," she said quietly. "I don't know why I'm whispering." She laughed, pouring herself a cup of coffee. "But I like the new direction."

He nodded. He did, too. It was ironic that all it took was them leaving for their characters to get the most screen time they'd had since getting together two seasons ago. The original version of this season's script had their characters headed for yet another breakup. The new version had Nurse Lia being courted by another hospital, and while they didn't have all the episodes yet, Mason was willing to bet Dr. Santiago was going to follow Nurse Lia off into the happily ever after sunset.

"Maybe I'm a sap—okay, I know I'm a sap," he laughed under his breath. "But I'm genuinely happy our characters are going to stay together."

"Me, too," she said, stirring a splash of milk into her coffee. "So, how's Sawyer? Are we there yet? Asking about the new loves?"

His chest constricted. He cleared his throat uncomfortably. "We broke up. Or, rather, we were never really together. I don't know. I'm not actually sure."

Kara furrowed her brow. "That doesn't sound like you."

He sighed. "I know. I tried doing the casual thing, but I'm not very good at it."

Kara shifted her weight from one foot to the other. "That's not what I meant. I mean—yes, you? Casual?" She laughed softly. "Not your style. But you're just giving up? I mean, I literally had to break up with you twice."

He smiled. "Sawyer…" He didn't really want to talk about this. He'd already spilled his guts to Luis and Alissa—the latter feeling responsible for their breakup. Alissa's offer might have been the spark, but Mason was convinced Sawyer's fuse had been waiting to be lit. "She—" He wasn't sure how to summarize how it imploded so quickly. "I rushed, and I don't know how I can fix it—if I can fix it. Showing up at her door might do more harm than good, but doing nothing…" He shook his head. Weeks, and he still had no idea what to do.

Kara frowned, brushing her long hair over her shoulder. It was only then that Mason noticed the lack of ring on her left hand. Catching the way his eyes followed her empty ring finger, she nodded. "I don't want to talk about it—not here, anyway—but trust me when I say I wish someone would show up at my door."

He frowned, staring at the wall without really seeing it.

Their director called for them to take their seats, and Mason fell into step behind Kara, their characters always seated next to each other. As everyone settled in, Richard remained standing, clasping his hands in front of him as he eyed Mason and Kara with paternal fondness. As if he weren't the blueprint for everything Mason was going to do differently at Guiding Light.

As Richard spoke, announcing the departure of both Mason and Kara from the show, Kara placed her hand atop his and squeezed. He was barely paying attention to what Richard said, noting the bags under Kara's eyes that she'd covered with makeup, the way her shoulders were slightly curved inward, so unlike her normally immaculate posture.

If Mason showed up at Sawyer's door, would she look similar? Was she hurting as much as he was? Worse, if he showed up, and she looked perfect as ever… he'd have to accept it was really over, and he wasn't sure he was ready to do that.

Mason wished someone would show up at his door for once. That he wouldn't always be the one crawling on his knees behind them as they walked away. But what if Kara was right? What if all the while

Mason was waiting for Sawyer to knock on his door, Sawyer was waiting for him? Where was the line between respecting her wishes and being too late?

He was so distracted, thinking himself in circles, that he missed his cue for his lines more than once. Thankfully, it was only a table read, and no one said anything when they congregated in the hall afterward, everyone "so upset" he was leaving. He noticed no one seemed equally as distraught that Kara was leaving. He couldn't help but think it was because they bought the narrative Richard touted that she was "difficult to work with," when all she'd wanted was for him to stop maligning her character. He suddenly felt less inclined to humor everyone in the room with anecdotes of what he planned on doing after, or whatever the fuck it was they were mindlessly chatting about, and excused himself.

He drove home on autopilot. He wanted to believe Kara was right so badly, that all he had to do was show up at Sawyer's door and they'd talk things out. He knew he had things to apologize for, but he wasn't sure how to do that without disrespecting her request to let her go.

He'd tried. He'd tried being mad at her, hating her, but he couldn't. She was right. He'd rushed into things again, even when he hadn't meant to. But he'd learned a long time ago, you don't get to choose how you make other people feel. He hated that she thought he'd fallen for her simply because she was *there*. He wasn't okay with that, but he wasn't sure how to fix it either.

He was so lost in his head that he didn't hear the doorman calling his name.

"Sorry, Luther," he said.

"No worries, Mr. West. I just wanted to return your lady's book," he said, hurrying around his desk and producing a small paperback. When had Sawyer loaned him a book?

Mason furrowed his brow, taking it from him and thanking him. It was an author he didn't recognize, but the swooning heroine on the front cover made his heart pang uncomfortably. The memory of Sawyer doing that exact pose at the tree farm flashed before his eyes. It felt like yesterday and years ago all at once.

"Have you read it?" Luther asked.

"No," Mason answered, flipping the book over to read the back.

Luther put his hand over the back cover, blocking the summary. "Don't spoil it for yourself," he said conspiratorially. "I prefer to go in blind. But I will say, that letter at the end..." He shook his head, staring off into the distance. "People don't talk like that anymore, but they should."

Mason grinned. "You write a lot of love letters back in the day, Luther?"

Luther's ruddy skin flushed. "Of course I did. I had to let my Rose know how I felt, to wait for me."

Standing up straighter, Mason tilted his head to the side curiously. "And what if you're the one waiting?"

Luther smacked his lips thoughtfully. "It's the same, really. Let them know how you feel. Keep the faith that if it's meant to be, they will find a way back to you. And stay busy—be someone worth coming back for." Luther smiled softly, his gaze far off. "My Rose was... well, I may not seem it now, but I was once a looker, like you. I had other options, but once I met Rose, she was the only option."

Mason knew the feeling. He thought he'd been heartbroken before, but he now knew it was the sting of loneliness. He was lonely now, yes, but it was different. Sawyer had wormed her way into his life like no one else. It wasn't only her presence that he missed—their schedules had made time together harder and harder to come by, but that hadn't bothered him. He missed talking to her, even if it was brief, hearing how her day had been or being able to tell her about his, unfiltered. It was something he hadn't known he'd needed until he had it. She'd become his best friend, and it was a loss like he'd never known before.

"Thank you, Luther," Mason said suddenly, shaking himself from his thoughts. "I'd love to hear more about Rose sometime, but right now, I—" He grinned, clearheaded for the first time in weeks. "I've got a letter to write."

Turning on his heel, he headed for the elevator, his mind made up. If this wasn't a sign, he wasn't sure what was. It didn't matter if Sawyer didn't believe in signs or grand gestures or happily ever afters. He *did*, and he believed with every corner of his hopelessly romantic heart that his and Sawyer's story wasn't over yet.

He barely even registered the elevator ride or the bumpy way it came to a stop on his floor, his mind spinning a million miles an hour. He wasn't a writer, so he wasn't sure how he was going to put everything he felt into a letter.

Thumbing through the back half of the book Sawyer had loaned Luther, he found the letter Luther mentioned. Even without the context of the rest of the book, it tugged at Mason's heartstrings, because he knew that desperate feeling.

How? How could he manage to convey to Sawyer that from now on, to him, every romance he ever watched or read would be about her? And at the same time, every single one of them would pale in comparison to his favorite love story: theirs.

CHAPTER TWENTY-NINE

<u>ROCK, MEET BOTTOM</u> – When you hit rock bottom, the only way to go is—oh, wait, she has a shovel. We're going further down.

With a beleaguered sigh, Sawyer hoisted the bag of books higher on her shoulder, promising herself yet again that *next time*, she'd find a better way to transport them. It was the first time she'd left her apartment in a week, having spent the past few days bingeing *Diagnostics*. She'd forced herself to pause season three, episode two and get off the couch. All the tension between Dr. Santiago and Nurse Lia was making *her* tense. If they didn't get together soon, she was going to have a coronary. She hadn't wanted to root for Mason's and Kara's characters, but she was eating up everything the writers hand-fed to her.

She missed Mason so much. She wanted to apologize, but she wasn't sure how, wasn't sure the words would come out right. Even if she found the perfect words, she was convinced it wouldn't be enough. It wouldn't change things. Mason was still leaving.

So, in the weeks since their fight, she'd filled the Mason-shaped void in her life with *Diagnostics*. Anything to avoid thinking about her looming deadline or how bad her writer's block was. She warred with herself. Refill the creative well by pouring *Diagnostics* down her gullet. Stop bingeing TV dramas and *write the damn book*.

She was already regretting leaving the sanctity of her pile of blankets and pillows, desperate for the thrill she felt every time Dr. Santiago graced her screen. Even if, despite what Mason said, Dr. Santiago did not, in fact, do his surgeries shirtless, much to her disappointment.

Her heart twisted as she stepped into the elevator. It wasn't the same one she'd gotten stuck in with Mason. She hadn't even realized she'd memorized which elevator it was, but apparently she had. Propping the sack of books against the wall, she rolled her muscles.

"Hold the door!"

She glanced up, her arm shooting out automatically. Her pulse quickened, déjà vu distorting her sense of reality. She was only two blocks from Mason's apartment, could it be—?

The doors shuddered back open, revealing a well-dressed man in his midfifties. He offered her a congenial smile, and she tried not to let her disappointment show on her face.

In her haste to hold the door for him, she'd stretched herself across the elevator like a one-woman game of Twister. The bag of books wobbled precariously, and before she could react, the handle ripped, the contents spilling onto the floor.

She took this as a sign that she was simply not meant to leave the house today.

With a sigh, she bent over, rushing to scoop the books back into the now handleless bag before the elevator doors opened on her floor.

By some miracle, she made it from the elevator to the bar without the whole thing toppling over again.

"Sawyer!" Alex crooned. He easily hefted the bag from the bar top to the back counter. "I was just thinking about you. We got this new whiskey in—" Reaching up, he grabbed a bottle from the top shelf. "Local. You have to try it." He plopped the bottle in front of her before disappearing to grab a tumbler.

As Sawyer picked up the bottle, her insides went cold. Leaving her apartment had definitely been a mistake. Blind Faith Distillery. She traced the distiller's signature at the bottom of the label. She would never forget the crooked way Sadie wrote her s's. She wanted to shatter the bottle against the ground, or to steal it like Sadie had done to Sawyer's reader-signed copy of *Almost Lovers*. But that would only hurt Alex, not Sadie, and leave Sawyer feeling worse.

"Have you had it before?" Alex asked, grinning, completely oblivious that he'd presented her with her ex's pride and joy.

Shaking her head, she flipped the bottle over to read the back.

"I've got time for a tasting before the lunch rush," Alex offered, grin faltering at her uncharacteristic silence.

"No, thank you," she said distractedly, her attention snagging on an address at the bottom of the label. "I have to go," she said suddenly. Tugging her phone from her pocket, she typed the address into her Maps app before handing the bottle back to a befuddled Alex. "Thank you!"

"I didn't do anything," he called after her, already halfway to the elevator.

Sawyer didn't normally believe in signs, but she was in a weird place right now. The elevator dinged to announce its arrival—the same one she'd met Mason in. Mason, who wasn't afraid of his past, to learn and grow and heal.

She knew what she had to do.

* * *

The hour and a half drive to Indiana went by in a blink. Sawyer hadn't crossed this state line in years. This place knew too much. Too many memories better left in the past. She'd thought that was where Sadie belonged, too, but Sawyer was beginning to realize she'd never really left Sadie there. She'd been dragging around that hurt for years, never letting it heal. Just like the hurt she felt over the *Almost Lovers* adaptation.

As she pulled into the gravel parking lot of the distillery, she began to shiver with nerves. Was this a dumb idea? She probably should have thought this through *before* driving all the way here. With shaking hands, she opened the door, stepped out into the frigid air, and forced her feet to carry her inside.

The minimalist warehouse exterior gave way to a warm, industrial interior. Scarred wooden beams adorned the ceilings, and rustic Edison bulbs hung from them, illuminating the space in a golden glow.

"For one?" the tattooed hostess asked over the heavy metal blaring from the speakers.

"Um." Sawyer cleared her throat. "I'm looking for Sadie. Is she in?"

The hostess raised a heavily penciled brow. "May I ask who's inquiring?"

Sawyer bit the inside of her cheek. "Oh, uh, we go way back. She has something of mine."

"And she's expecting you?"

"Not exactly," Sawyer confessed with a self-deprecating smile.

The hostess gave her an assessing once-over. "Your name?"

"Sawyer Greene," a voice to her left said.

Sawyer stiffened as if struck by lightning. Turning slowly, she inhaled sharply as her gaze landed on Sadie.

If this were one of Sawyer's books, she'd write something

dramatic like *She looked exactly as she remembered*. But that wasn't true. Sadie was impossibly better looking. Sadie wiped her hands off on a bar towel, wringing it between her tattooed hands like she probably wanted to do Sawyer's neck right now. Her pale blue eyes were bright against her tanned skin—how was she so tan in February? Her brown hair was shaved along one side, and Sawyer remembered exactly why she'd allowed this beautiful creature to break her heart in the first place.

"Hi," she managed.

Tossing the towel onto the bar top, Sadie unhooked a carabiner of keys from her belt loop. "I'm headed out," she said to the hostess. To Sawyer, she jerked her head toward the door. Grabbing her coat from the hook, Sadie shrugged on a camel-colored Carhartt.

"What are you doing here, Sawyer?"

Sawyer swallowed the lump in her throat. "Asking myself the same thing, actually." She'd come here to put her foot down, to demand Sadie give her book back, but somewhere along the drive, her anger had given way to something softer, something deeper and infinitely more sad. "I want my book back," she forced herself to say.

Sadie's brows pinched together. "What book?"

Aaaand the anger was back. "You know what book," Sawyer hissed.

"I don't, actually," Sadie said dismissively.

"Seriously?" Sawyer growled. "Just give it back. It might not mean anything to you, but to me—" She cut herself off as she felt her volume rising.

Sadie sighed, placing a hand at her elbow and guiding her outside, where the music fell away to a less mind-numbing volume. "I seriously don't know what you're talking about."

"*Almost Lovers*! You took my advance copy, the one my readers signed on my first tour." She hadn't expected to cry, and she hastily wiped away the traitorous tears that managed to escape.

Sadie stared at her helplessly. "Sawyer, I don't have it. I own, like, five whole books. I'd notice."

"Please, Sadie. I know your brother took it. I just want it back," she pleaded. Leaving the house today had been a bad idea. She was not in any state to be out in public, much less *High Fidelity*–ing her way across state lines to track down her ex.

Sadie's lips parted slightly. With a steadying breath, she tucked her hair behind her ear, nodding slowly. "Ah. I, uh, may have it." Spinning her keys around her finger, she jerked her head toward a nearby truck. "You can follow me, but we have to make this quick. I—" Sadie sighed. "Why today?"

Sawyer raised her brows. "What do you mean?"

Sadie stared at her in disbelief. "You have no idea what day it is, do you?"

Sawyer pressed her lips together. She did not. She only knew it was Sunday because that was the day Alex worked, when she did her book drops.

"Happy Valentine's Day, Sawyer," Sadie said with as much warmth as was in the air. Which was to say, zero. With that, she turned, gravel crunching under her boots as she headed toward her truck without a backward glance.

Sawyer slipped back into her car, following Sadie through the tiny town. Now that she was paying attention, she noticed the shop windows were all decked out in pink and red for the holiday.

When Sadie pulled into a town house driveway, Sawyer parked along the street before hurrying up the walkway. She couldn't believe she was doing this. She was really running the emotional gamut today, the thrill of excitement numbing her anger. She was doing this. Getting her book back.

"We have to be quick," Sadie said again as she unlocked the front door.

"Trust me, Sadie, I'm not expecting you to roll out the red carpet for me."

Sadie scoffed, swinging the door wide for her to enter. "It's not that. I just didn't factor a third wheel into my plans for tonight."

As she said it, Sawyer took in the touches around the space that were distinctly Not Sadie. The pink slippers by the door, the fluffy cardigan on the coatrack, the rainbow bowl Sadie dropped her keys into. Of course. Sadie had a new girlfriend, and they had plans for Valentine's Day. Sawyer cringed. The first and only Valentine's Days Sawyer ever celebrated had been with Sadie.

"I'm sorry," she blurted. "I know this is out of the blue. I was handed a bottle of your whiskey today, and I don't know what came over me. I just…I wanted my book back and I was done making excuses to avoid you, I guess."

Sadie nodded slowly, her gaze flickering from head to toe. "If I have it, it's back here." Kicking off her boots, she disappeared down the hall, and Sawyer followed, feeling like an intruder in Sadie's new life. As uncomfortable as it was, it was a relief, almost, to see that Sadie was fine. That she wasn't as much of a mess as Sawyer was. That there was life after love. Someone should tell Cher.

From the hall closet, Sadie pulled out a few boxes labeled "Hanuk-kah stuff," before producing an unmarked brown box covered in dust. They both stared down at it and not at each other, this physical representation of the baggage between them.

"I never opened it," Sadie confessed. "It was petty, sending him to grab my things instead of doing it myself. I didn't even need any of the stuff I sent him to get. Anyway—" She gestured to the box, rubbing the back of her neck uncomfortably. "Go for it."

Sadie disappeared down the hallway, much like Sawyer wanted to disappear altogether. Sinking onto the carpet, she tugged the flaps open, a cloud of dust making her sneeze. Gingerly, she removed a faded university T-shirt that had originally been hers, the mystery of where it had gone finally solved. She set it aside, each memento of their relationship like pouring lemon juice onto an open wound. Or maybe less like lemon juice, more like lancing something that had festered inside her because she'd closed it up without cleaning it first.

She choked on a sob when her fingers brushed paper. She inhaled shakily as she tugged her book from the miscellaneous items still in the box, her fingers reverently tracing her name on the cover. The spine was bound with clear packing tape, the glue visible beneath from where it had been opened and closed so many times. The cover was bent and fraying at the edges, but she'd never seen a more perfect copy of her first book, with the original cover, before it had been rebranded with the movie poster. Flipping it open, she couldn't even read the messages from her readers—her *first* readers—because her eyes were welling with tears faster than she could blink them away.

She closed up the box, not needing anything else from it, and placed it back by the closet. She tucked her book inside of her coat, next to her heart, following the sounds from down the hall.

"Did you find it?" Sadie asked, glancing up from where she was arranging a charcuterie board.

Sawyer nodded, flashing the book from inside her coat.

A pained expression flashed across Sadie's face. "I'm sorry. I really didn't know. I would've never—you sacrificed so much for that book…"

Sawyer rolled her eyes.

"What?" Sadie asked defensively.

"You couldn't resist one more jab, could you?"

The innocent look on Sadie's face was almost too convincing.

"You always resented me for how hard I was working. Even now, you can't not rib me for it."

Sadie's jaw went slack. "That's what you think? That I was mad because you *worked hard*?"

Sawyer raised her brows like, *Didn't you?*

Sadie laughed humorlessly. "Sawyer, your passion was what I loved about you. Writing was your whole life, and I wanted to be a part of that life, but you wouldn't let me. I understood hiding your writing from your family, but from me? Do you know how many times I found out things about your career from your fucking Twitter?" Sadie took a deep breath. "Sorry, did not expect that to still get me heated after all this time." She brought her hand to her chest in a fist. "It's not that you worked hard. It's like you got your dream and forgot how to live."

Sawyer stared at her like she was seeing her for the first time, suddenly seeing all of their arguments, the stony silences every time Sawyer hit a new milestone or canceled plans, through a new lens. And hadn't Lily said something similar? She was so worried that if she juggled too much, she'd drop the ball again. She'd made her whole life about this one thing, but that's not really living. It wasn't just her writing that had been stuck. *She* had been stuck. When she first made the deal with Mason, she thought his knight in shining armor romanticism would free her from her tower of unending writer's block. Now, she realized the dragon trapping her there was...herself.

"I—" She cleared her throat. "I'm sorry, Sadie. I guess—I don't know. Just, I'm sorry."

Sadie shook her head, her gaze landing on the book-shaped lump under Sawyer's coat. "I never understood how you could write shit so fucking beautiful that it moved me to tears, and yet you couldn't tell me how you felt."

Sawyer sucked in a breath like she'd been punched. She squeezed her eyes shut, but the tears leaked out anyway. "I'm sorry. I really am. If it makes you feel better, I'm still shit at it. And now I can't even write the beautiful shit."

"That doesn't make me feel better at all, actually," Sadie said sadly.

"Would it have changed anything," she asked the ceiling, "if, even after things imploded, I showed back up? Wanted to try?" She pressed her lips together to keep her chin from wobbling.

Sadie studied her through narrowed eyes. "I'm not the one you really want to be asking that question to, am I?"

Sawyer gave her a watery smile. "No."

Leaning forward, Sadie braced her forearms against the kitchen counter. "Then go rewrite your ending."

CHAPTER THIRTY

(UN)ROMANCE – Trying to ruin romantic clichés
only to become them. (And that's okay, actually.)

There was a large envelope waiting for her when she returned home.

Her heart leapt into her throat when she saw Mason's messy scrawl on the envelope. Then it bottomed out. Was this it? Was he returning her things?

She placed her rescued copy of *Almost Lovers* gingerly on the kitchen table, like it may shatter. Which, considering it was held together with tape and a prayer, it might. With shaking hands, she undid the seal on the envelope, turning it upside down. A dozen or so postcards fell out. Tucking one leg beneath her, she sank into the nearest chair, pulling the closest card toward her.

It was a screenshot from *When Harry Met Sally*, only the caption read "Sawyer, I came here tonight because when you realize you want to spend the rest of your life with somebody, you want the rest of your life to start as soon as possible."

Another one, from *10 Things I Hate About You*, with Heath Ledger running across the bleachers. At the bottom was her name and the opening lines to Frankie Valli's "Can't Take My Eyes Off You."

The next one, from *Pride & Prejudice* (2005). "If your feelings are still what they were last we spoke, tell me so at once. My affections and wishes have not changed, but one word from you will silence me forever. If, however, your feelings have changed, I will have to tell you: you have bewitched me, body and soul, and I love—I love—I love you. I never wish to be parted from you from this day on."

On and on it went, snapshots of some of the most iconic grand gestures, all with her name on them. When she got to the end, she was sad it was over, peering inside the envelope for more. To her delight, she found a card.

Sawyer,

I know I have a lot to apologize for, but you deserve better than for me to do it via letter. Please don't mistake my silence as anything other than my wish to give you the space you asked for. I think about you constantly, and if you ever doubt my feelings for you, know that you have ruined romance for me in the best way, in that you have become the very definition of it for me. I don't have the words to describe it, so I hope you don't mind that I borrowed some of my favorites. Whenever you're ready, I'm ready. I don't want to leave things like this. Say the word, and I'll race across town at midnight, or make a fool of myself singing Frankie Valli with a high school brass band and get arrested by campus police, or hell, I'll even go to IKEA with you to get you your nightstand. Whichever you prefer—choose your own grand gesture adventure. I want to spend the rest of my life proving to you that happily ever after is real, and worth fighting for.

Yours,
Mason

She traced the word *yours*, recalling the way it had sounded falling from his lips on New Year's Eve. They hadn't ruined the New Year's Eve kiss, and she was glad for it. They hadn't ruined anything at all, but rereading his letter, she thought she understood what he meant. She was ruined for anyone else but him. No one else would do.

She wanted to race out of her apartment to his, but it was late, and it couldn't be that easy, could it? She knew the answer to that. No. It wouldn't be easy. She was going to have to let him in, all the way in, and it was going to require work. A lot of work, long-distance work, but it *wouldn't* be work if it was Mason. Her sweet hopeless romantic of a man deserved a grand gesture for the books.

She sank to the ground in front of her bookshelf. Tugging free her dictionary, she flipped through the e's until she found "elevator." There, pressed between the pages, was a scrap of restaurant printer paper. "Rule #1: No feelings. Rule #2: No sex." The bottom of the paper was torn where Sawyer had written her phone number and given it to Mason. There was a second piece of paper, one she'd torn from a notebook.

Mission: (un)Romance

She smiled down at the list, the original version on the back where she'd crossed out multiple ideas, rewriting the approved items on the front. There, at the bottom, where she'd hastily added "end date???"

As she reread the list, her attention snagged on the final two items. She wasn't going to ruin them for Mason. She was going to spoil him with them.

*   *   *

Sawyer's grand gesture was off to a dismal start.

Blasting eighties music outside someone's window doesn't hit the same when they're on the eighteenth floor and you're on the sidewalk.

She eyed the apartment's doorman warily. The sweet old man who manned the door when she'd been here before was gone. Which was a shame, because she'd been counting on Luther recognizing her. And even if he hadn't, she knew she could outrun him. The elevators weren't that far from the front door. This new guy, however. Whew. He was built like a truck. That salt-and-pepper hair was a misdirect. He'd already thwarted her once, but she wasn't going to give up that easy.

Sawyer mustered all her acting prowess, tucking her giant note cards under her arm and strolling up to the front door like she owned the place.

"Ma'am," the doorman called as she approached. "Ma'am," he said more sternly when she ignored him and kept walking. He stepped in front of the door, wholly blocking it with his broad frame.

She looked up in feigned bewilderment, surveying the building like she'd never seen it before. "Oh, sorry," she simpered in her best airhead voice. "Wrong building!"

Not buying her shit one bit, he watched her suspiciously as she retreated half a block to replan her attack.

A businessman exited the apartment building, waving cheerily to the doorman she was now certain would become a crucial player in her villain origin story.

As luck would have it, however, the businessman paused right in front of her, patting his pockets in concern before turning on his heel and heading back the way he came. Sawyer followed half a step behind him, euphoric that being short was finally going to come in handy as she slipped into the building behind him. She only had one foot through the door when a hand grabbed her coat, jerking her back outside into the cold Chicago winter air.

"Ma'am," the doorman said again, a shiny gold name tag on his breast declaring his name to be Stan.

God, what a quintessential doorman name. It was so perfect, she nearly missed the scowl he gave her. "This is the third time," he sighed. "At least try to be inconspicuous."

She leaned closer. "Okay, I'm listening. How do I do that?"

He rolled his dark eyes. "For starters, don't carry giant poster boards and a boom box."

The man had a point. But she—she had a mission.

"For the last time," Stan said wearily. "If you're not a resident, you cannot enter the building without a resident's explicit permission."

"What if," she whispered conspiratorially, her stomach swooping when he leaned in automatically. "I told you I knew someone in the building, and I'm trying to surprise them?" She gestured to the aforementioned posters and boom box.

"I can call up and confirm that they want to be surprised," he offered.

"I don't know if we have the same definition of 'surprise,'" she countered. "Mason will be okay with it, *I promise.*"

The doorman's eyebrows shot up. "You're here to see Mr. West?"

Hope ballooned in her chest for the briefest of moments before wheezing out like a whoopee cushion. That had not been the right thing to say. Stan definitely thought she was an overzealous fan, and this level of security was probably why Mason picked this apartment in the first place. How inconvenient for her.

"I know him," she pleaded. "I promise. And maybe you're saving me a lifetime of embarrassment, but I am here to get the shit kicked out of me by love, and I really need you to let me."

Stan stared at her for a long moment, his eyes darting from hers, welling with tears, to the posters and boom box, and back again. "What in the world are you up to?"

She took a step back, setting the boom box down on the sidewalk and hitting play. Propping the posters against her chest, she waited for his eyes to scan the words before flipping to the next poster. Once finished, he frowned, screwing up his face. The cautious optimism that had been growing steadily inside her with each card guttered out.

"What in the Hallmark hell?" he muttered.

"Exactly," Sawyer said emphatically, as if that clarified everything. Though, judging by his expression, it clarified exactly nothing. "Mason and I have this list—maybe I should start at the beginning?"

He studied her for a long moment before stooping over and pausing "In Your Eyes" by Peter Gabriel. "Alright, but we're doing this inside, and I need my popcorn."

"Whatever you say," she agreed heartily. She'd run down to the corner store and buy him whatever snack he wanted if he'd consider letting her through. Though she was inside the building now. *Progress.* She contemplated making a run for the elevator—

Following her gaze, Stan clicked his tongue. "Don't even think about it. I will shut it down with you in it and let you think about your choices for half an hour *at least*," Stan threatened, gesturing to a control board atop his desk.

"I wouldn't do that." Sawyer forced a laugh that sounded more like a wheeze. "Actually," she said brightly. If there was one thing she was good at, it was telling stories. This was about to become her magnum opus. "The whole reason Mason and I know each other is because of an elevator. Only, he was the one trying to sneak on."

Stan settled back into his desk chair, swiveling back and forth before opening his bag of Garrett popcorn. "Continue."

* * *

"Wait," Stan said as he settled back into his chair. "Valentine's Day was two weeks ago."

Sawyer grimaced, readjusting the stack of cards at her feet that kept sliding across the slick tile floor. She almost felt guilty for monopolizing Stan's time. Numerous tenants had come and gone, Stan jumping up with surprising quickness for an older gentleman, hurrying back every time so she could resume her story.

"Yes, it was, but do you know how hard it is to find a working boom box these days? And a cassette? I had to get this shipped from Portland! And—" She smiled guiltily. "I may or may not have been busy with another thing…"

Stan grinned, rolling a piece of caramel corn between his fingers. "You finished your book, didn't you?"

She nodded. While she waited for her grand gesture items to be delivered, she'd resumed her *Diagnostics* binge because it was all she could think to do. When Dr. Santiago and Nurse Lia broke up at the end of season four, Sawyer screamed at Kara's character for letting him go, but Nurse Lia didn't know Dr. Santiago was on the other side of town, looking for her like she was looking for him. Sawyer had unearthed herself from the mountain of blankets and pillows on her couch to make a bowl of popcorn before starting season five, but while she stood there, watching the kernels burst in the pan, she realized how to fix her book. Dragging her laptop off the couch, she moved it to her dining room table before moving back to the couch and wrapping herself in blankets. If she was going to do this, she needed to be coddled. She sobbed her way through the final chapters, partially for her characters, giving them the happy ending she wanted, and partially for herself, because she was doing it. For the first time in years, she had finished a book.

She sent the draft off to her agent and editor, praying Emily's earlier enthusiasm wouldn't wane once she read the final product. She wasn't sure if anyone would want to read a book about two people who did everything wrong the first time finding their way back to each other, but she hoped that her readers would find their way back to her, just like her characters had.

Stan set down his bag of popcorn, wagging a finger at her. "And you're not here just to finish the list?"

Sawyer shook her head. "It's not about the list or even the grand gesture. I get it now, why our mission was always doomed to fail. All those big movie moments, they would all fall flat if the person didn't mean it. If they hadn't fought to get there. It's not about racing across town to find each other on New Year's, or interrupting a wedding, it's the vulnerability—not the act itself. It's about showing up and risking it all with no guarantee you'll get what you want. It's about trying. That's why I'm here. To try. And maybe make a complete fool of myself—" She shrugged. "But I don't care. Because I'm in love. And I want to fight for it. But first, I gotta get past this doorman who's a little too good at his job."

Stan grinned, leaning forward once more, bracing his elbows on his desk before reaching over and pushing a button. A moment later, the elevator dinged, the doors opening.

CHAPTER THIRTY-ONE

THE GRAND GESTURE – Go big or
go home, baby!

Mason ran a hand through his hair. He still wasn't used to having it Dr. Santiago short, filming due to start on Monday. Scrolling through his phone, he tried to decide what to order for dinner. He scratched absently at his stomach under the hem of his shirt. He wasn't hungry, but he knew he should eat, and he was too drained to cook.

He'd spent the afternoon cleaning his apartment, banishing everything of Sawyer's into a small drawer. She hadn't left much behind, save for the gold dress, the jewelry, and a few dozen bobby pins he was still somehow finding everywhere. He knew he should throw it all in one of the many moving boxes now scattered around his apartment and send it back to her, but he couldn't bring himself to do it just yet. It didn't seem right that he could feel so much for a person and have it all amount to nothing. He'd overnighted his letter to her two weeks ago, but even with her radio silence, he wasn't quite ready to let go.

He froze mid-scroll as the sound of drums reached him. The walls here were fairly well insulated, so he rarely heard his neighbors. Someone must be really rocking out. Though it was more like a slow jam. Was that…*was that Peter Gabriel*? Mason's attention drifted slowly toward the door.

The corner of his mouth twitched, and he tossed his phone onto the counter, all thoughts of dinner forgotten as he crossed over to the door in a few long strides, cautious hope blooming in his chest. Without bothering to check to see who it was—he knew who it was—he opened the door.

Sawyer stood across the hall, hastily shooing one of his neighbors back inside. Catching sight of him, she froze, breath visibly hitching. She straightened, and Mason leaned his shoulder against the doorjamb, taking her in.

She wore a tattered green army jacket with a plaid flannel and black T-shirt underneath. Her faded jeans were loose and ripped, combat boots peeking out beneath the frayed hem. He could only assume this was her approximation of Eighties Rom-Com Male Love Interest Chic. A massive boom box sat at her feet. Where had she found a vintage boom box—and how long had she been planning this?

He was too shocked to do or say anything. She picked up a stack of cards, and his lips twitched upward as he realized what was about to happen. Sawyer Greene was making a grand gesture. Hell must be freezing over.

As she propped the stack of white posters against her chest, he tore his attention away from her wide green eyes to her slightly trembling hands to the first card, undulating with her shaky breaths.

HI.

"Hello, Sawyer," he said quietly.

She smiled slightly, removing the first card and propping it against her shin.

He dragged his attention back to the cards.

I'M SORRY.

Next card.

I WAS SCARED.

Next card.

I'M STILL SCARED.

Next card.

BUT I WANT TO TRY WITH YOU.

Next card.

SO HERE I AM, UNROMANCING YOU.

Next card.

ONLY, UNLIKE ANDREW LINCOLN, I'M HERE WITH HOPE <u>AND</u> AN AGENDA.

Next card.

THOUGH, I'M NOT VERY GOOD AT EXPRESSING MYSELF.

Next card.

I HOPED THIS WOULD ENSURE THE WORDS CAME OUT RIGHT.

Next card.

SO:

Next card.

MASON ALEXANDER

Next card.

ÁLVAREZ-WEST*

Next card.

***ACTUALLY REAL NAME**

Mason laughed through his nose, watching as Sawyer's nervous smile faltered as she revealed the last card.

I LOVE YOU.

He could tell she'd spent extra time on this one. On the others, her messy scrawl was off-center and lopsided. But this one was perfect. The placement of the letters intentional, knowing the weight of the words they would come together to form. He stared at it for a long time, trying to keep a lid on the hope welling in his chest.

"This isn't—" he said hoarsely, clearing his throat. He needed to be sure. "This isn't for the list, right?"

She shook her head. "No, this is for me. For us, hopefully."

"Because...you love me."

She nodded. "Because I love you," she said softly.

He pushed off the doorway to scoop her into his arms, but she held up her hands. He froze.

"Wait, I—I'm not done, and if you kiss me now, I'm going to forget, because those sweatpants and that haircut are really doing it for me."

He smiled, resuming his lean against the doorframe. "By all means, gesture away, but I thought you said the note card scene was creepy."

"Well, yeah," she said hesitantly, propping the last card against her knees so it was still facing him, like a reminder. That she loved him. That was real. "That was his best friend's wife—wait, you don't have a wife in there, do you? Am I too late?!"

"No," he said around a grin. "You're right on time."

"Thank God." Her shoulders sagged visibly with relief. "Mason, I'm so sorry. I've spent so long trying to keep people at arm's length so I couldn't get hurt again, but somehow you snuck in there, and I cared about you a scary amount. I was so terrified that I would let you in and then you'd move and I'd be left a mess and everything was happening so fast and you told me you loved me in the middle of an argument and—" She took a shaky breath. "I wasn't ready to hear it then, but I get it now. We don't get to choose who we fall for or when. Sometimes it's a random girl in an elevator or a guy you were supposed to have a one-night stand with, but you do get to choose who you stay with."

He waited only half a beat to make sure she was done talking before crossing the hallway in a single stride. Pausing Peter Gabriel, he pulled her into the circle of his arms, pressing his forehead against hers. "I'm sorry, too. I shouldn't have pushed you so much. I cannot believe I Moira-ed you. You don't know how much I've kicked myself for that. Or for rushing this thing between us. I knew you needed to go slow, but it was like once we started I got completely swept up and not that that's an excuse—"

She placed a finger over his lips. "I know. I felt the same way, and it scared me. I told myself I had to focus on salvaging my career, then I'd worry about—" She gestured vaguely. "Everything else. But I was so focused, I cut myself off from living at all. You taught me how to fall in love with life again. Sharing this with you has been the best thing to happen to me in years. I haven't had someone in my corner—haven't *let* someone be in my corner," she corrected herself. "But I want you there. I want to be with someone who's going to push me. I want to be with someone who loves me not only for who I am now, but also for who they know I want to be. But—" she said with a small smile. "If we're going to make it work, I need you to talk to me, even if we don't have the perfect words yet, and I promise to do the same, because—" She took a deep breath, and Mason held his. "I love you."

His hand was in her hair in an instant, tilting her face back so he could capture her mouth with his, her lips that had just uttered the most perfect words, ones he never dared to imagine hearing. He wanted to drown in the sound and feel of it. He knew they had more to talk about, but right now all he could think about was how they'd have time to do it later. They had a *later*. That thought alone was making him lightheaded. Well, that and the fact that he'd barely breathed, so intent on pouring everything they hadn't said into his kisses, their lips conveying the breadth of feeling that words couldn't encompass.

Sawyer pulled back first, inhaling shakily. "Well, I never want to fight like that again, but, um, making up isn't exactly awful."

"For the record," he said, brushing his lips across hers. "When we inevitably do fight again, all of this was a nice touch, but not necessary. All I wanted was for you to come back."

She smiled. "I know. But I wanted you to know how serious I was, that I was all in. I couldn't expect my characters to make a grand gesture, and then cower on my couch because I was scared."

Mason straightened, a smile tugging at the corners of his mouth. "You finished your book?"

Sawyer nodded, smiling bashfully, and he pulled her in for a hug so fierce her feet left the ground. He spun her in a circle before letting her back down. "I am so fucking proud of you."

"Well, I have you to thank."

He raised his brows in question.

"I was so mad about Liatiago breaking up that I needed a happy ending, so I wrote one."

Mason's lips parted in surprise. "You watched my show?"

She shrugged like it was nothing. "I missed you, okay? I was in a bad way."

His shoulders shook with laughter, and she held up her finger, fixing him with a death glare. "I'm still behind a season, so if you spoil it for me, I swear we're fighting again."

He mimed zipping his lips.

"So, anyway," she began with a sigh. He didn't need to hear any more explanations, any more apologies, but he was also dead curious how she'd ended up here, on his doorstep with a boom box and giant poster boards. "You'd already shown up at my door once and written me my first love letter, so it was my turn to make a grand gesture. And while I still don't know if I believe in happily ever after, I've never been as happy as I was with you, and I'm not ready to let that go—not now and maybe not for a long while, if that's okay with you."

"It's more than okay with me." He grinned down at her, thumb stroking across her cheek. He still couldn't believe she was here. "Maybe we should go inside?"

Biting her lip, she nodded.

Scooping up the cards and the boom box, he dropped the latter on the kitchen counter. He carried the cards over to a safe spot in the corner. He was going to frame the last one, without a doubt. He straightened as "In Your Eyes" began again. Turning around, he watched as Sawyer mimed playing air drums.

"Y'know, I always thought this song was kinda lame, but—" She began a slow shimmy of her shoulders. "I gotta admit, once it gets going, it goes pretty hard."

The tempo picked up, and Mason extended his hand to her.

She eyed it warily before slipping her hand into his. "Are we really dancing in the kitchen?" she asked when he twirled her into him.

"Shh, embrace the cliché, Sawyer." Leaning down, his lips brushed against the shell of her ear as he whispered, "I think you secretly like it."

She laughed loudly. "I know you said it's not necessary, but I think grand gestures may suit my natural dramatic flair."

"I love your dramatic flair. You've ruined romance for me in the best possible way." He tucked her hair behind her ear, frowning. "Have I not told you I love you yet?"

She shook her head slowly.

"Allow me to correct that immediately." He squeezed her closer. "I love you, Sawyer Greene."

She sank against him, resting her chin on his chest. "And I love you."

He swayed them in time to the beat, and she burrowed deeper into his chest as they danced in the kitchen to Peter Gabriel. It was cliché, and it suited them just fine.

CHAPTER THIRTY-TWO

<u>ONE-NIGHT STAND TO STRANGERS TO</u>
<u>FRIENDS TO LOVERS TO IDIOTS TO LOVERS –</u>
Invented by Mason Álvarez-West and
Sawyer Greene, probably.

One year later...

So, Sawyer," Claire said, her smile lighting up Sawyer's laptop screen. "The Coffee and Composition community imploded when I announced this interview. It felt like we didn't hear from you for a while, and then, *bam*, film deal; *bam*, new book announcement. You have some very loyal readers, and they're hungry for news. You've clearly been very busy since *Why We're Not Together*. Could you tell us what you've been up to the past few years?"

Sawyer nodded, licking her lips as she took a deep breath. Staring straight into the tiny laptop camera, she spoke directly to her readers.

"Thank you, Claire. I can't tell you how much it means to me that I still have readers after all this time. Because yes, I've been busy, but most of the past few years have been me trying and failing to write. I started a handful of projects that didn't make it anywhere. We talk a lot about how writing is such a lonely craft, and I thought that meant I had to do it *alone*, and my writing suffered for it. But, recently, I've learned that asking for help isn't a sign of weakness, and I wouldn't be able to do all of this without the people I love supporting me and pushing me to do the things that scare me. It wasn't until I started letting people in again that I realized how much joy it brings me to share my stories, and I'm so excited for readers to discover *Otherwise, Engaged*. I hope it was worth the wait."

Claire held up her advance copy, dancing in her chair with it. "Oh my God. I will happily die of anticipation for two years if all your books are this good. *Otherwise, Engaged* ripped my heart out, shredded it, and then put it back in place." She held the cover closer to the camera to read off the back cover. "When Dom's mother loses her yearslong battle with cancer, the last thing on his mind is romance—it hasn't been on his mind in a while, actually. But when his mother's will leaves him her ring, the message is loud and clear. He proposes to his longtime girlfriend, Harlow, and receives a loaded silence in answer. The past few years have been hard on them both, and their relationship took a back seat. Harlow promises to give him an answer before their seven-year anniversary, and Dom vows to win her back by doing every rom-com cliché he can think of. Only, when the flash of the grand gesture fades, Dom realizes that unless they can rekindle the spark they once had, instead of a happily ever after, they're headed for an in memoriam montage of the love they lost." Claire hugged the book to her chest. "This is a romance so it's not a spoiler to say that watching these two fall back in love was one of the sweetest things I've ever read."

Sawyer flushed. "Thank you."

"And rumor has it, there's some real-life inspiration behind it?"

She flushed deeper, shaking her head at the wall. Ever since the dedication of the book had leaked, the rumor mill had gone rampant.

For Mason, if I had to (briefly) get stuck in an elevator with anyone, I'm glad it was you

"Dom and Harlow's story is the antithesis of ours, actually." Sawyer laughed. "The last thing Mason and I wanted when we met was a meet-cute. We did our best to fight our feelings, while *Otherwise, Engaged* is about two people fighting to find them again."

Claire nodded, pivoting. "And in other big news, your previous book *Why We're Not Together* is being adapted, and I know *I'm* anxiously awaiting casting news, which you've teased on Instagram could be announced soon?"

Sawyer smiled, crossing her fingers to the camera. "At the end of this week, I think."

"Any chance we'll be seeing a certain Dr. Santiago on the list?"

No matter how many times they denied it, this rumor wouldn't die. They'd managed to keep their relationship a secret for a few blissful months, but once Mason was in LA, where paparazzi were much more common, it had been less a question of if they'd catch them canoodling in public but *when*. And when Guiding Light announced it had bought the rights for *Why We're Not Together*, it didn't take long before everyone knew who the "mysterious blonde" on his arm was.

Sawyer would never admit it out loud, but she missed being Mysterious Blonde. If the investors had any lingering hesitations about Mason's love life jeopardizing production, they kept it to themselves, especially since Kara and other A-list exes of Mason's had expressed interest in working with Guiding Light. It was unconventional, but hey, nothing about their relationship had been normal thus far. Why start now?

She mimed zipping her lips and throwing away the key. She'd learned to simply embrace the rumor mill at this point and let it run its course. Claire took the hint and dropped the Mason topic. Sawyer had initially resisted allowing interviews to ask about him, not wanting people to think she was riding his coattails, but there was no denying that without him sending her book to Alissa, there wouldn't be a movie deal. And while she'd initially come on board with the idea kicking and screaming, she was excited for it. Mason was her biggest cheerleader, and she was proud of that.

Claire asked a few more questions about the movie, and Sawyer gave her usual answers—there wasn't much she could tell at this point. It was still in preproduction. The movie industry moved about as slow as publishing. They played a this-or-that game with Sawyer's characters from her four books before wrapping up with some general writing craft talk.

After the interview, she chatted with Claire for a bit before their time was up.

Sawyer flicked off the ring light, sinking back into her chair and smiling up at the ceiling. She'd done it. She'd specifically chosen Claire's bookstagram for her first interview. She'd worked with her before, and she'd never faltered in hyping up Sawyer's backlist, even when it looked like she'd never release another book.

A soft knock sounded, the door opening slightly. Mason poked his head into the spare bedroom of their LA apartment. *You done?* he mouthed.

She nodded, opening her arms. "All done."

He crossed the small space, scooping her up out of the chair. She wrapped her arms around his neck as he dropped her onto the bed, smothering her beneath him. "You did it," he breathed into her hair.

"I did." She smiled against his neck, running her fingers through his curls, which she hadn't let him cut since wrapping on *Diagnostics*, and was now quite long. He would say he was growing it out for a role, but she claimed sole credit for inspiring that artistic direction.

He peered down at her, a fondness in his expression that had her melting further into the plush bedding of their second bedroom that doubled as her LA office. He glanced back over his shoulder. "You turned off your camera, right?"

She smirked. "Yeah, why?"

He grinned down at her, tickling her sides. "Good."

"Mason!" She squirmed under his touch. "We don't have time, we have to go——" she protested half-heartedly, already taking off his shirt.

"We've got time," he insisted.

They did not have time, but they were late for most things these days. Thankfully, it was LA, so they could always blame it on traffic. Her apartment back in Chicago was far enough from everything that the excuse usually worked there, too.

Long distance hadn't made things easy, but they made the most of their time together. And when they were apart, Mason wrote her love letters with instructions on the outside of when to read them. "For when you miss me" or "for when you (eggplant emoji) miss me" or "for when you forget how ridiculously talented you are." She'd given him a special ringtone in her phone, so even with their chaotic schedules, a two-hour time difference, and her unpredictable writing spells, she never missed his calls, and they started and ended each day with an *I love you*.

Miraculously, they made it to the space Guiding Light had rented out only ten minutes late. Everyone was still milling about, and they tried to slip in inconspicuously. It might have worked, too, had Alissa not cried out the moment they stepped through the door, pulling them into hugs and simultaneously ushering them over to their seats on the far wall.

Sawyer exchanged a guilty look with Mason as Alissa called everyone to order. "They were totally waiting on us," she murmured.

"Worth it," Mason said, cracking open the water bottle at his place setting and taking a sip.

Sawyer straightened the pen in front of her, her attention landing on the name card before her. SAWYER GREENE, WRITER, EXECUTIVE PRODUCER. Her eyes drifted to Mason's placard next to hers. MASON WEST, EXECUTIVE PRODUCER. She smiled to herself, hoping the rumor mill wouldn't be too disappointed that Mason wouldn't be acting in a Guiding Light production until the next film on Alissa's rapidly filling docket.

Mason squeezed her hand under the table. "You ready?"

Glancing up at him, at the pride and hope in his eyes, she felt her shoulders relax, and flipped her hand over to squeeze back.

She still didn't know whether she believed in soulmates or happily ever afters, but she believed in him, and she believed in them. And for now, she was happy. Incandescently so. When she thought back on the series of events that had led them here, she didn't think of a piece of restaurant printer paper they scribbled their first list on—no feelings and no sex—the rules that they'd wasted no time in breaking. She thought of the piece of paper that was framed next to it in her Chicago apartment. "Mission: (un)Romance" where, at the bottom, she'd scribbled "end date???"

She hoped the answer to that question was never.

But for now, she smiled, staring into the eyes of the man who'd taught her to love again and seeing that same love reflected back at her, and nodded. "I'm ready."

ACKNOWLEDGMENTS

Cue the sappy music and don your best Eighties Rom-Com Love Interest Chic because I'm about to grand gesture a whole lot of people:

To my agent, Hannah Schofield – I feel like I won the agent lottery with you. Thank you for believing in me and this book, for understanding Sawyer and Mason so completely, and for loving exclamation marks and em dashes as much as I do. I'm so grateful to have you on this journey with me.

To my editors, Junessa Viloria, Katie Seaman, and Clare Gordon, this book would literally not exist without you. Thank you for taking a chance on Sawyer, Mason, and me. I could not ask for a more brilliant team of romance enthusiasts to champion my rom-com about rom-coms. You are this book's meet-cute and Happily Ever After. Many thanks to the amazing teams at Forever and HQ, to every single one of you who lent your time and talents to making this book-shaped, especially Sabrina Flemming, Dana Cuadrado, Anjuli Johnson, Angelina Krahn, Taylor Navis, Emily Baker, Kate Byrne, Isabel Williams, and Claire Brett. Thank you to Mars Valubi for your invaluable insights as Mason's authenticity reader. Any errors in Mason's rep are entirely my own. An extra special thanks to Stephanie Heathcote for the art direction and Ksenia Spizhevaya for the elevator meet-cute cover of my dreams.

To my therapist: Phew, girl. Bless you.

Shoutout to the cheese section at my grocery store, family size bags of cheesy puffs, and all the PB&Js eaten over the sink that got me through my deadlines.

My friends and family, who have long since accepted that I'll always be the weird kid who's half-lost in a daydream—thank you for loving me. (And look—I made it into a career. Who would've thought? Not me!) Y'all make my life so full. I snuck pieces of my love for you into these pages, and I hope you know they're for you when you see them.

The writing community is such a truly special place, and I've been blessed to meet so many talented people, but I'd especially like to thank the following: Courtney Kae, for championing this book back when it was a one-line pitch; Alicia Thompson, who saw the potential from the very first draft; Hailey Harlow, for always listening to me ramble about made-up people; Ande Pliego, my agent sibling whom I'm privileged to have alongside me on this journey; the 2024ever debut group, for celebrating and commiserating, for always reaching a hand back to help other writers up the publishing ladder, and for allowing me to be the 2025 caboose. Endless gratitude to Anita Kelly, Lana Ferguson, Jessica Joyce, Chip Pons, Ava Wilder, Andie Burke, Mae Bennett, Jen Comfort, Solange Bello, Kristine Lopez, and Claire Laminen. To all the bookstagrammers who lend their time and immense talent to hype up others, you deserve all the flowers.

To my biffles: Abby, Alisa, Ashley, and Lizz: The greatest love story I'll ever experience is our friendship. I write not for the swoony love interests (okay, *partially* for the swoony love interests), but because women like you deserve to be seen as the heroes of their own story. You amaze and inspire me. I'm so grateful to be in the era of my life where the number of years I've known you outnumber the ones where I hadn't met you yet. I love you 5ever.

The Karrie Kwong. My first beta reader and still the first person to read anything I write. I don't know that I'd still be writing, let alone have had the courage to chase this dream, if not for your belief in me. Thank you for keysmashing with me since (checks notes) 2005. I'm rooting for us always, and I love you endlessly. See you in the Google Doc margins.

To my parents (and my brother, I guess), thank you for letting me be me. We aren't a family of grand gestures or big speeches, but our home was always a loving, safe space—for us and for others. I do not take for granted how special that is. I hope to honor that by infusing my books with the same feeling of safety, inclusivity, and escapism. I also sincerely hope this is the only part of this book that you read. Love ya, mean it.

My wonderful pets: Basil, Paprika, Freya, and Odin—thank you for cuddling me while I lay on the floor, staring up at the ceiling, trying to remember how to write a book.

Thank you to my husband, who is both my rom and my com. I couldn't have written characters who enjoy each being around each other so immensely, whose love language is laughter, if you hadn't first shown me what it was to have a love like that.

To you, for picking up this book. Reading has always been my escape, and my writing being that for others was a wish I didn't dare speak aloud for a very long time. Thank you for gifting me your time, and helping make this dream a reality.

ONE PLACE. MANY STORIES

Bold, innovative and
empowering publishing.

FOLLOW US ON:

@HQStories